Praise for *The Words In My Hand*

'Guinevere Glasfurd's writing is fresh and elegant. I loved the subject and the way she brings Amsterdam in the 1600s into vivid, believable life. A lovely book'
Dinah Jefferies, bestselling author of *The Tea Planter's Wife*

'17th-century Amsterdam sparkles into life in this delightful, playful and beautifully written debut. I loved it!'
Rachel Hore, bestselling author of *A Week In Paris*

'A quietly powerful novel of love, ambition and betrayal. Glasfurd's depiction of the eternal tension between domestic realities and intellectual ambition is precisely nuanced, and suffused with all the cool charm of its Dutch Golden Age setting'
Kate Worsley, author of *She Rises*

'*The Words in My Hand*, Guinevere Glasfurd's captivating debut novel of a Dutch maid's affair with Descartes, is compelling, lush, impressive'
Kate Mayfield, author of *The Undertaker's Daughter*

'*The Words In My Hand* tells a moving story with quiet confidence and masterful restraint. Glasfurd's evocation of 17th-century Holland through the voice of young Helena – servant girl and mistress of Descartes – is vivid, plausible, and hugely engrossing. An astonishingly accomplished and mature first novel'
Shelley Weiner, author of *The Last Honeymoon*

the words in my hand

GUINEVERE GLASFURD

TWO
ROADS

www.tworoadsbooks.com

First published in Great Britain in 2016 by Two Roads
An imprint of John Murray Press
An Hachette UK company

1

A CIP catalogue record for this title is available from the British Library

Hardback ISBN 9781473617858
Trade Paperback ISBN 9781473617865
Ebook ISBN 9781473617841

Typeset by Palimpsest Book Production Ltd, Falkirk, Stirlingshire
Printed and bound by Clays Ltd, St Ives plc

Hodder & Stoughton policy is to use papers that are natural,
renewable and recyclable products and made from wood grown in
sustainable forests. The logging and manufacturing processes are expected
to conform to the environmental regulations of the country of origin.

Hodder & Stoughton Ltd
Carmelite House
50 Victoria Embankment
London EC4Y 0DZ

www.hodder.co.uk

for
Saskia

Contents

Acknowledgements xi

AMSTERDAM, 1635

Ice 3

AMSTERDAM, 1634

Books 9
Flowers 15

AMSTERDAM, 1632–3

Glass 31
Bruises 44
Feathers 50
Slate 59
Quay 67
Map 79

AMSTERDAM, 1634

Wax 91
Invitations 107
Crows 119
Words 130
Snowflakes 143

Swifts   157

Lines   167

DEVENTER, 1635

Sketch   175

List   186

Beeswax   193

Library   199

Alphabet   203

Air   207

Water   215

Dream   224

LEIDEN, 1636–7

Wool   233

Peat   241

Questions   248

Hearth   264

SANTPOORT, 1637–9

Seeds   275

Blood   286

Tulips   290

Eels   305

Linen   321

Echo   331

Sand   339

Ditch   345

Soot   356

AMERSFOORT, 1640

Clock   359

France   368

Paper   373

Shadow   377

Fever   382

Ash   394

Truth   398

EPILOGUE
EGMOND AAN DEN HOEF

Raindrop   403

Historical Note   409

Suggestions for Further Reading   413

About the Author   415

Acknowledgements

Special thanks to Siobhan Costello and Anni Domingo – writers and friends, who provided feedback and encouragement throughout. Thank you to Louise Doughty for her unstinting support, and to Dr Erik-Jan Bos, for answering my questions on Descartes and reading an early draft.

Thanks to Thiemo Wind, Enny de Bruijn, Robin Buning, Maartje Sheltens, the staff of the Deventer Archive, and Jos Hof, guide and local historian in Egmond aan den Hoef, for generously sharing their research and expertise. Thanks also to Elaine Bishop, Katharine McMahon, Judith Murray, Sarah Savitt, Rebecca Swift and all the lovely folk at Writers' Centre Norwich. The WCN Escalator mentoring programme gave me the opportunity to develop this book from an initial sketchy outline and supported me through the early writing stages.

Thanks to Cressida Downing for providing gin when needed, and good humour, long walks and bookish advice in between.

Thank you to my husband for his love and support. Thank you to my darling daughter, Saskia, to whom this book is dedicated, for reminding me that life exists beyond writing.

To my marvellous agent, Veronique Baxter and Alice Howe at David Higham Associates: thank you, thank you! Thank you to my copyeditor, Celia Levett. Thanks also to my UK editor and publisher, Lisa Highton, and all who make Two Roads such a fine imprint – and for publishing my book with such care and attention.

This novel was written with the support of a grant from Arts Council England, Grants for the Arts, and my sincere thanks go to them.

All these good people helped realise the book in your hands.

To live well you must live unseen.

René Descartes, letter to Mersenne, April 1634

DUTCH REPUBLIC
1635
Eendracht maakt macht

N

GRONINGEN · *Eems*
Delfzijl
Leeuwarden · Groningen
FRIESLAND · Assen
Heerenveen · DRENTHE
Emmen

Alkmaar · Hoorn
Egmond aan den Hoef
Zuyder Zee · Zwolle
Zaanstad
Santpoort · OVERIJSSEL · Almelo
Haarlem · Deventer
Amsterdam · Enschede
Leiden · Apeldoorn
GELDERLAND
Den Haag · Amersfoort
HOLLAND · UTRECHT
Delft · Utrecht · Arnhem · IJssel
Rotterdam · Nederrijn
Lek · Nijmegen
Merwede · Waal
Dordrecht · *Rijn*
Maas
's-Hertogenbosch
NOORD BRABANT
Breda · Tilburg
Vlissingen · Middelburg
Eindhoven
Westerschelde · Venlo
ZEELAND
Antwerpen
Schelde · *Maas*

Heerlen
Maastricht

✦ Provinciale hoofdsteden
● Grote stad

AMSTERDAM, 1635

Ice

I TURNED ABOUT the room, toe to toe, making the smallest circle. What I wanted was not there. His clock, his papers, his quill glass: cleared away, gone. I had seen this room empty before and had not minded; now it only magnified my loss. I did not want a coin, or token, or keepsake. I wanted words, some note – but there was none. He'd gone without taking his leave. He'd taken what was his with him.

I lifted the sheets he'd kicked down the bed, the mattress cold under my hand. *Even nothing has a shape,* I thought. *It is what was, what could have been.*

'Helena?' Mr Sergeant called from downstairs, with a sharpness I'd not heard before. 'Helena?'

I curled my fingers into my palm.

'Helena!' Louder, this time, something brittle in him, something about to break.

I grasped the banister, steadied myself, and went downstairs. I blinked back tears and wiped my eyes with the side of my hand. Below, the front door stood open; all the heat had gone from the house. I walked across the tiles I had cleaned yesterday. I did what I always did – went on tiptoe so I would not leave a mark. Then I stopped. I could see the Limousin outside with Mr Sergeant, waiting. I pressed my feet flat to the floor, raised my head, carried on walking and did not look down. When they saw me approach, they parted and stepped to one side. Neither said a word. There was no need – I knew what they were thinking.

The driver adjusted the bridle, then pitched my bundle onto the carriage roof. 'Only feathers in there?' he joked, still looking, not blinking.

The horses shuffled and champed on their bits. I bowed my head and climbed in, closing the door behind me with a click. On either seat lay a folded blanket and on the floor a wicker basket with food: apples, two large loaves of bread, a cheese, some cured meats – enough for two or three days, perhaps more. Too much food. The sight of it made me feel sick.

The driver addressed the Limousin. 'We will make Amersfoort first, then Apeldoorn. Deventer is no more than a day further on, if the route is clear. The IJssel is all ice. With this winter . . .' He shook his head. 'You would do better to wait.'

The Limousin snorted. 'Some things won't wait.'

I glanced up as the Limousin climbed into the carriage and settled himself opposite. He smelled of tobacco and wine; a sour, unwashed smell from the night before.

'Deventer?' I tried to keep the panic out of my voice.

He took a blanket and laid it across his knees, and motioned at me to do the same. I took the other blanket, unfolding cold over my lap; it sank through my skirts into my legs. I turned to look for Mr Sergeant as the carriage lurched forwards, but he had gone. And then I saw it was ended. There was no going back. The loss stopped my breath.

The Limousin crossed his arms and turned his face to

one side, the grey light flat on his cheek. He must have felt my look because his gaze flicked back.

'What?'

'Aren't we going to Leiden?'

'Leiden?' His laugh was knowing, his mouth pulled into a smile almost.

'I don't have anyone in Deventer. The Monsieur knows that.'

He inspected his fingernails, or his knuckles maybe, and shook his head at some private thought.

'Limousin, *please,* you're mistaken.'

'No mistake. The Monsieur made no mention of Leiden. We're going to Deventer.'

He looked at me and his look said, *I know what there is to know.* This carriage made him keeper, lord, master. His gaze hardened and slid to my stomach.

His legs lolled apart. I tucked my legs up against the seat but his knees knocked against mine as the carriage threaded its way out of the city.

Deventer. I tried to place it in my mind, but the map I pictured dissolved at the edges, the roads and canals faded into a blank. Sickness welled up in me and burned my throat. I lunged forwards and grabbed at the door.

'Let me out!'

The Limousin pulled my fingers away from the handle. 'Sit back. *Sit back.*'

He pushed my shoulder with the flat of his hand. He was stronger than he looked. The skin around his mouth had whitened; red spots pricked his cheeks.

'All you have to do is sit there and be still.'

I rubbed my shoulder where he had pushed me. Prinsengracht passed by, the view squeezed into a small square of window. A thin light fell on the shuttered-up houses; window after window, blank and cold, blind to me. The carriage began to gather speed. Each house we passed took us further from Westermarkt. To see the city slip away like this was more than I could bear. Deventer, Deventer, Deventer, Deventer: the word beat into my head with the clatter of hooves.

'What will I tell my mother!' The words were out before I could stop them. I covered my face with my hands and the tears I had held back all morning tipped from my eyes. My breath came in sobs.

The Limousin stared out of the window, unblinking, as if pained by my tears and crying. 'We will pray for your forgiveness, Helena.'

I squeezed my eyes tight shut and clasped my hands together as he began to pray. But I did not know this prayer of his. I moved my mouth, trying to form words I did not know, shaping sounds I had never heard.

'O Vierge des vierges, ma mère, à toi ce que je viens; devant toi je suis le pécheur repentant . . . Ne méprises pas mes prières, mais ta miséricorde entends et réponds-moi . . .'

God forgive me, God forgive me, God forgive me . . .

When I looked up again, we were out of the city. I clutched my stomach.

Oh God, Monsieur, what will become of us?

AMSTERDAM, 1634

Books

I NOTICED HIM in glances – the heavy ribbons on his shoes; the curve of his shoulder; his black, black eyelashes. I noticed his hands, delicate and smooth, fingers stained with ink. A writer's hands, smaller than mine. Pale hands that made me want to hide my rough hands away.

He had a way of touching his mouth, resting a finger against his lips as he thought, in no hurry to speak. I had to be careful not to stare, not to catch his attention. I knew better than to disturb him. I'd heard him shout at his valet, the Limousin, when he went in unannounced. I did not want to be shouted at. But how to be quiet and make it all still when the water pump squeaked and the windows rattled? Even a clean sheet, when I shook it across the bed, made a horrible *crack*. It made me wince. The more I winced, the noisier it seemed, this terrible hurdy-gurdying at the heart of Mr Sergeant's house. I went everywhere on tiptoe, afraid I'd trip on my shadow.

Betje wanted to know all about him, the Monsieur. He's French, I told her. Her eyes widened, then narrowed, and when she couldn't get anything more from me, she nipped me hard. *Monsieur*, she said, in a way that made us tip forwards and laugh.

* * *

In the two years I had been with Mr Sergeant, I had not known a lodger like him. He was different, even before he arrived. Lodgers always stayed in one of the rooms at the back. Those rooms faced north. Even on the brightest day, the light felt pinched in. Being in there was like peeping out at the day from under a blanket.

Some weeks before he arrived, and to be sure the Monsieur would be 'properly accommodated', Mr Sergeant had come with me to look at the rooms – something he never involved himself with. It was the first inkling I'd had that the Monsieur deserved more, better, than previous lodgers; that something of Mr Sergeant's reputation was tied up with this man.

He humphed up the stairs, not used to so many at once. 'Our French guest is a thinking man, Helena. He needs quiet, somewhere to work. He was quite specific on that, *une chambre tranquille,* or *tranquette* or *trompette* or something. Then there is his manservant – *the valet* – he will need a room too.'

A valet? Who'd heard of such a thing? I didn't know if it was the effort of the stairs, or all those French words, but Mr Sergeant had to stop to catch his breath. There'd be a lot more huffing and puffing before the day was done.

He swung open the door and went in. 'Oh dear,' he said, when he saw what was there. 'Oh dear, oh dear, oh dear.'

I drew my shawl around my shoulders. The room had been shut for months. He looked as though he had bitten into a lemon, having expected peach.

I didn't know what he hoped for: that the room be miracu-lously swagged with velvet and satin, and the bed piled high with a half dozen duck-down pillows, pillows he did not have? I could not imagine anyone being able to think other than dark thoughts in here. The gloominess drew in like fog. I was sure it was foggy in France too, but that was no reason to make our new lodger relive the experience daily.

Father had travelled. He'd told me what France was like. He went for weeks at a time, on a trading ship to Bordeaux. He brought my mother a yellow shawl – said he'd had it spun from sunshine he'd found in a French field. It was her favourite and she wore it until the day he did not return. Then she folded it away, and the sun seemed to slip away with it too.

Mr Sergeant turned on one heel and led the way out to the larger room at the front of the house where he kept his books. He had so many – too many for me to count. There were books in trunks and baskets, books tied in bundles, books spilling from boxes – some even on shelves, but there were not shelves for them all.

I squinted against the brightness. Mr Sergeant blew out his cheeks; he rocked back on his heels, then centred his weight. His frown lifted as a thought revealed itself and he tapped my forehead with his knuckles.

'Gloom is not conducive to good thinking, Helena. Monsieur Descartes shall have this room; valet and books at the back.'

I nodded, too surprised to say anything. When I had suggested moving the books before, he had always said no, these books *deserved* this room.

'All we need now is for them to finish that church and be done with that racket.'

Bang, bang, crack went hammers on stone outside as if to underline his point. A roar went up as a plank fell from a scaffold.

He tutted. 'Who would have thought God's work could be so noisy? I'd not have this on Herengracht.'

Mr Sergeant wishing for a house on Herengracht would be like me wishing for a tulip on my birthday. Merchants lived on Herengracht. Booksellers lived where they could. But I liked Mr Sergeant's house; it was tucked away down a side street and faced an open square. There had been a market here until it was announced a church would be built. Westerkerk. It was the finest church in Holland. Work still continued on its outside and around the square.

I still couldn't decide whether Mr Sergeant's house leaned to the left, or the windows leaned to the right. Not long after I arrived, I had stood on the pavement and tilted my head one way then the other, as if that would help set it right. Mr Sergeant had laughed when he saw me. He had gout and walked with a limp. What a funny pair they made – this tall, lopsided Dutch house and this round, limping English man – neither with a straight line between them.

Once the front room had been cleared of books and the arrival date confirmed, Mr Sergeant wasted no time in sharing his news. When Mr Veldman came by, he was hardly through the door before Mr Sergeant was on him. They were rivals in the book-selling trade, not that I heard either admit it.

Mr Veldman specialised in travel books and maps, books of the world, he called them, and Mr Sergeant in poetry and moral tracts of an 'edifying nature'. But when Mr Veldman called a latest acquisition a 'tittle-tattle tale of dubious literary merit', Mr Sergeant refused to entertain him again until a quantity of brandy had been provided to ease the hurt and erase the insult. *We'll see whose tail has been tattled,* he said, taking a long, slow sip. In the end, the jug was emptied and Mr Sergeant sound asleep in his chair, snoring.

Mr Veldman shrugged off his cape as he took in Mr Sergeant's news. 'Descartes, *the* Descartes? Are you mad?'

Mr Sergeant ignored him. 'I am flattered, I admit.'

'You heard about his previous lodgings? The time not spent at the abattoir was time spent cutting up creatures – in his room. Some not even dead.'

Mr Sergeant swallowed. 'Helena, a drink for Mr Veldman.' He looked as though he needed one himself.

I folded Mr Veldman's cape over my arm and went to fetch the tray from the dresser.

'Yes, well,' Mr Veldman continued, clearly enjoying himself, 'you can imagine . . .'

I steadied the glasses on the tray. Mr Sergeant had paled.

'And,' he added, shaking his head as if telling a cautionary tale, 'he throws animals out of the window – live animals, that is. All in the name of his *method.*'

'Well,' said Mr Sergeant, 'Lord Huygens thinks he is brilliant. That is enough for me.'

Mr Veldman covered his eyes, as though shading them, then let his hand fall. 'Dazzling. Perhaps we could arrange a soirée with the brilliant Descartes?'

'A soirée?' Mr Sergeant shifted from one foot to the other. 'I expect Monsieur Descartes will be preoccupied. Almost certainly. Very busy.'

Mr Veldman arched his eyebrows at the refusal. He took a glass from the tray. 'He's an avowed Catholic, you know.'

Mr Sergeant waved the remark away. 'Tolerance is all. We two should know that. What he does in his own time is his affair.'

'I'd like to know what he thinks of Galileo, but no matter. I doubt he will publish, not now.'

'Patience, Veldman, patience. There is more to the man, I believe.'

Mr Veldman laughed. '*Impatience*, more like, and arrogance, and ambition. A temper too, I've heard.'

Mr Sergeant took a sip from his glass, then cleared his throat. 'It will be an honour to have him here. With me.'

'I defer to your judgement on these matters – as always.' He made a small bow.

'I think you are jealous, Veldman,' Mr Sergeant teased.

Mr Veldman laughed once more. 'You must allow an ageing man his small jealousies now and then.' He held the glass up to the light. 'Very pretty,' he said, looking through it at me.

'Come, Mr Veldman, if jealousies are what please you, let me show you what I have brought from Utrecht.'

Mr Sergeant steered Mr Veldman towards his study. When the door had closed, I took the glasses away to wash them. Mr Veldman's glass I washed twice.

Flowers

THE MINISTER AT Noorderkerk said terrible things about the French – their frills and ruffles, silks and satins, ribbons and lace. It was hard to imagine a man wearing such things. Would our French guest have a collection of wigs? And drink wine before breakfast and brandy with it?

On the morning he was due, Mr Sergeant sent me to the flower market to buy flowers for the house.

'Mind you buy *French* flowers,' he said and shut himself in his study without another word.

At the market, I looked at what was for sale – peonies, daisies, honeysuckle and roses in bright bunches. But what, of any of it, was French? If Betje were here, she'd know, even if she didn't.

Peonies, perhaps? There didn't seem to be a house along the length of Herengracht without peonies in the window. *Look at us*, they seemed to say. I did not like flowers like that. They could be rotten right at the heart and you would not know. Some shed their petals at the gentlest touch, as if made only of wilting and sadness.

'Excuse me.' I raised my hand to catch the attention of the stall keeper. 'Do you have anything French?'

The stall keeper wiped her hands on her apron and studied me. 'This is what I have.'

She pointed to a basket of honeysuckle, but wasn't that as English as a rose? She raised her eyes. If it wasn't for the fact that I patted my purse to remind her I was buying, then I think she would have sent me on my way. She went to the back of her stall and returned with a smaller basket, filled with lavender.

'It's for drying, for keeping down flies. I suppose you could try it in water first if it's *French* flowers you are after.'

I chose a bunch and breathed in the scent. I closed my eyes and saw a lilac hill, a high blue sky, and the sun, pink and rosy as a peach.

The flower seller wrinkled her nose. 'I don't care for it, makes me sneeze.'

When I sniffed it again, she looked at me as if I'd taken the last of its scent. 'Buying?' she said and folded her arms.

I nodded. Yes, I was buying. Hadn't I *bouquets des fleurs* to make?

'*Boeket?*' I'd asked, when Mr Sergeant had said what he wanted.

He'd looked at me, and I'd looked at him, and blinked for us both.

'Boo-*kay*, Helena. *Boo-kay.*'

So, I put a *bookay* of roses in Mr Sergeant's study, then I traipsed upstairs again with a *bookay* of honeysuckle and lavender, wiping up drips as I went.

I set the flowers on the table and swung open the shutters to let in the sun. I dragged the desk away from the wall, and shuffled the chair to the right then to the left. Westerkerk. Westerkerk. That was the view. But I knew a way to see more. I stood by the window, with my cheek to the frame, closed one eye and squinted. A silver square of light danced into view: Prinsengracht. Not water any more, but a jewel.

I turned and looked at the table, the flowers, the empty chair. So, he'd sit here and think. Thinking was his work, Mr Sergeant had said. Not like any work I'd heard of.

I went to the bed and folded back the sheet to air it. I fetched the broom and I swept. And then I was done.

I glanced at the chair, then at the door, then at the chair. I'd only sit for as long as it took to go downstairs and back. As soon as I was seated, I closed my eyes and waited for a strange or fantastical thought to appear. Something French. Anything. But all that came to me was what I knew about already: two weeks' worth of Mr Sergeant's stockings, steeping in a bucket in the kitchen, waiting to be washed. And now that I thought about it, I realised I'd soon have the stockings of two more men to wash! The bucket became full to overflowing.

I pushed myself up from the chair. I'd much rather think standing up.

By late morning the house smelled of lavender and roses, and the spiced lamb I'd set cooking before breakfast.

Mr Sergeant peered into the pot, tapped his hands together and beamed. 'Marvellous, Helena. Exactly as it should be. All we have to do now is wait.'

I unhooked a pail of water from the fire and carried it across to the kitchen table. Mr Sergeant stepped neatly aside to let me pass. I needed no mirror to tell me how red I'd become; my feet would be redder still if I slopped this water on them.

Mr Sergeant eyed the line of pots on the table. To one side, onions, butter, lemon and tarragon, and, to the other, a pair of skinny chickens, yet to be plucked. He twisted his beard, pulling it to a point.

'Potted chicken,' I explained.

'Ah!' His expression cheered as the jumble of ingredients assembled into a meal he recognised – and this, a favourite of his.

I slid the butter into a pan with my thumb. If I could get this done, I could be out of the house first thing in the morning to meet Betje.

I plunged a chicken into the water to scald it, dunking it under with a stick. The water greyed and frothed to a scummy rime. The shitty smell of the coop still clung to the chicken, but I couldn't let that bother me. I dunked it again, swooshing it around so the water would get into the feathers. Then I counted. When I got to thirty, I started again. Four times thirty was the time needed for a chicken this size; longer than that and it would cook.

As the smell reached him, Mr Sergeant took two quick steps backwards. 'Well, I'll leave you to it,' he said, turning away so quickly the steam drew after him.

Seventeen, eighteen, nineteen, twenty, I counted, *twenty-nine, thirty.* I hoicked the chicken out, and screwed up my face in disgust.

* * *

The sun was past the church tower by the time the knock came. A quiet knock. I opened the door and there was a slim, pale man, no taller than me, dressed in a plain, black cape with a collar turned over the top. No silk or satin, no lace cuffs. No silver-tipped cane. No wig.

His hair fell to his shoulders in curls. It was black, flecked with grey, like his neat beard. A high fringe framed his face, focusing attention on his eyes. They were as dark as his hair, wide-set and heavy-lidded, and gave him a just-awake look. He blinked slowly, as if the light was too bright.

'*Bonjour*,' he said, then, in Dutch, 'hallo.'

He bowed. A small smile lifted the corner of his mouth. This was the man who threw animals out of windows? I swallowed and glanced down, then opened the door as wide as I could, hiding behind it. It was the only reply I could manage.

I heard Mr Sergeant come through from his study. 'Monsieur Descartes! Come in, come in.' He held out his hand to greet him then turned to me. 'His things, Helena, quickly.'

I peeped out from behind the door.

'No, no. My valet, my Limousin, will see to that.'

The Monsieur beckoned to a man cleaning a pipe, standing a little way behind him on the pavement. He was too tall for his clothes – all ankles, wrists and neck. At the sound of his name, he looked up, tapped the tobacco into the palm of his hand and let it fall through his fingers to the ground. Tucking the pipe into a top pocket, he bowed, first to the Monsieur and then to Mr Sergeant.

Next to him were two small cases, a small number of

books tied with a leather strap, a rolled-up rug and a wooden box, no bigger than a foot-warmer. Such a beautiful box, with a brass plate on top.

When I went to pick it up, the Limousin pushed past me. '*Pas ça!*'

'My clock,' explained the Monsieur. 'I think Limousin thinks it is his.'

'*C'est précieux.*' He drew the box to him. 'It needs careful handling.'

I flushed. Did he think I couldn't carry a box?

Mr Sergeant led the Monsieur inside. 'Let's get you settled and then we can have a glass or two of something. Later, I will show you what is to be found in the Square. There's Westerkerk. It requires a certain eye. Nothing like the cathedrals of Paris, of course! But I'm sure I could persuade you of its magnificence. Ah, Paris – now there's a city.'

The Monsieur followed Mr Sergeant into the *voorhuis*, and I went in after the Limousin. He glanced around without interest. He was older than the Monsieur, I could see that now. His cheeks hollowed below his cheekbones. Either he did not like to eat, or did not eat enough of what he liked.

'I'm Helena. Mr Sergeant's maid.' I held out my hand, in the hope he would understand.

He picked a piece of fluff from his sleeve and tugged at his rather too short cuffs, levelling his gaze on me.

I let my hand fall back to my side. 'Please, your name?'

'Li-mou-sin.'

It was as though he'd presented me with three *poffertjes*, held high above his head on a plate, each to be savoured in turn.

20

'Lee-mo-sa?'

His face fell further with each sound I made. The name seemed to disappear like a rabbit down a hole and, by the time I reached it, I had lost hold of its tail.

He looked up with a deep weariness at needing to explain. 'Limousin. It is a region of France, where I originate. A basic grasp of French geography is all that is necessary.'

'Limousin's your name?'

'It is my *préférence*.'

I frowned.

'*Voorkeur*,' he explained.

He knew more Dutch than I thought. What a strange *préférence*. Did I call myself Leiden? Or Amsterdam? Amsterdam! I did my best not to smile.

I took the Limousin upstairs so that he could inspect the rooms. He nodded his approval when he saw the Monsieur's, but seemed less pleased when I showed him his. He went to the window and peered down into the courtyard. Whatever he was thinking he kept to himself. We were not so different after all.

'I'll leave you to arrange your things,' I said and turned to go.

'One moment. If you have a question that concerns Monsieur Descartes, it is to me you must first come – understand? I am his *conduit*. I manage his affairs.'

'Yes. Yes, of course.'

'Good.'

His shoulders relaxed and he managed a weak smile. I waited a moment, in case he had anything more to say, but he turned back to the bed and prodded the mattress with

21

grim resignation. *Limousin indeed,* I thought as I went out. *Monsieur Sour Lemon more like.*

Whilst Mr Sergeant and the Monsieur ate together, the Limousin joined me in the kitchen. He took a little of the stew I had made. It was almost as good as his mother's ragoût, he said, and helped himself to a second spoonful.

'My Monsieur won't touch it of course. He avoids meat.'

I looked in dismay at my plate and then at the potted chicken I had made. It would not do. I would have to make something else. I'd not be able to get away early in the morning after all.

He kicked his boots off under the table and sliced into an apple with his pocket knife, eating from the tip of the blade. When he was done with that, he blew out his cheeks and began a tuneless whistle, tap-tapping his fingers on the table.

Mr Sergeant had said they'd be here for the summer, *at least.* I looked at his fingers, tap-tap-tapping; the whistle seemed made of one long breath after another. I curled my toes.

'Is this your first time in Amsterdam?'

He shook his head. If he seemed surprised, it was not because I'd asked, but because I didn't know. 'Goodness, no, not at all!'

How was I to know their every move? 'I hope it suits you here.'

'*Merveilleux.* Our previous rooms were not the slightest accommodating.'

'Mr Sergeant's lodgers always leave with good word.'

At this, he gave me such a pained expression. *What delight was in the man,* I thought. *No matter how much sugar he ate, he'd never find things too sweet.*

'Are you here for the summer? All of it?' I smiled, not wanting him to think I wished them gone.

He shrugged. '*Sais pas.* The Monsieur has a certain . . . a certain way of life, a *habitude.* First Dordrecht and then Franeker.' He moved his hands to the left and then to the right as he explained. 'Then Amsterdam, then Deventer. And before that . . .' He waved his hand in the air as if trying to catch the memory from it. 'Before that, Italy, Poland, Germany . . . We keep moving. Many times. I lose count.'

Poland, Italy, Germany? The names flashed bright as mirrors. I tried to think if I'd seen them on one of Mr Veldman's maps. 'I'd lose count too!'

He considered me with a cold regard and I knew at once I had stepped over the line that separated us. These lines were everywhere, doing their best to trip me up. I glanced at my hands. How else were we supposed to talk, if we didn't *talk?* He was a valet, not a bookseller, not my employer. But I was only a maid, a Dutch maid at that, not even French. I was most definitely not a *conduit.*

The lines that were there, lines he had drawn, set me as far away from him as possible. Well, he was a *knecht.* I would teach him that word one day, if he did not know it.

'It is not about counting, I can assure you. The Monsieur needs peace. No surprises. No visitors. We go, we move, wherever, until we find it. Quiet – it is a rare thing.' He turned to me as he said this, as if daring me to make a sound.

Amsterdam certainly wasn't quiet, nor without surprise.

Didn't he know of the crowds Westerkerk brought? – and not only on Sundays. Perhaps it was best not to mention that.

I poured a glass of wine for him. He held it up to the light, swirled it slowly and closed one eye as he studied it. He looked at me and nodded, then cocked his head, angling his nose as he took a sniff. His eyes widened with surprise. 'C'est bon!'

I smiled. Mr Sergeant had gone to some trouble to find it. Two glasses for the valet, I'd been told. Not a drop more.

He took a sip, holding it in his mouth for a moment, then took a larger mouthful. 'Very good. And to find it here . . . in such a place.' He stared into the glass as if he'd found France reflected in the bottom and circled the rim with one finger as he thought. 'The cold in this country is a nightmare . . . un cauchemar.'

Cauchemar? I had never heard a less nightmarish word. It sounded soft as wool.

Had he family? I wondered how often he saw them, or if he saw them at all. I saw how his life must be: following the Monsieur from place to place, without question or complaint – or at least complaints that would not reach the Monsieur's ears.

I offered him the second glass of wine. He nodded, motioning to me to fill it a little more when I stopped halfway. Putting the Monsieur in the front room had been the right decision after all. But now I worried about the Limousin in that chilly, dark room at the back of the house. I would make sure he had another blanket.

Once he had finished his wine, he folded his arms across

his chest and closed his eyes. I didn't think he was asleep, but I kept quiet just the same. I did not want to disturb him; he might want more wine and I had no more to give.

After lunch, Mr Sergeant went out with the Monsieur. I watched them cross the square. When they reached the church, Mr Sergeant pointed to one of the windows, his hand shaping an arc in a broad sweep. He was a great talker. More than once, I'd seen his customers shuffling and fidgeting, as the Monsieur was now, trying to find a reason to leave without appearing rude.

I continued my chores and closed the shutters against the dimming light. The window in the Monsieur's room had been left open and several papers had scattered across the floor. As I put them back on the table, I saw what he had done: the flowers I had so carefully arranged were dumped in a soggy heap – only a single stem of lavender remained and this he'd dunked in his drinking glass! Next to the glass, anchored by an inkwell, a simple sketch and some notes. What a strange picture it was. He had not drawn the flower head, only the stem. But the stem was not straight. Where it touched the water, it broke, and continued a little to one side into the water below.

I frowned. I crouched down so that my nose was on a level with the glass and squinted. Where the stem met the water, it looked as if it had been sliced in half. I lifted the stem out of the water, then dipped it back in again.

'Ha!' I said, my hand at my mouth.

I thought of the times I had placed flowers in water and never noticed. I would bring him a flower with a stronger stem to draw, just one. One of Mr Sergeant's roses would do.

Although I saw little of him, the Monsieur was everywhere I looked – as if he was a few steps ahead, just out of sight. Within a week, we were short of candles, then salt. Glasses went missing from the cupboard. I found them neatly arranged on the sill in his room, filled with grey water. He took an old pewter plate from the kitchen and piled it with candle stubs. On a separate plate, he dripped wax into pools. I could just make out his thumbprint in each. I left it all as I found it. I knew better than to touch.

He did not leave his room before midday, then went out, sending the Limousin on errands in the opposite direction. If Mr Sergeant had been looking forward to the Monsieur's company at mealtimes, he was disappointed, as the Monsieur preferred to eat in his room. He frequently did not return until after dinner and I'd hear him pace up and down until late into the night. I put a little food for him under a dish and left it on a tray by his door. That way, I learned what he liked and what he didn't. I found out he had a sweet tooth. I made apple cake with cinnamon; I strained buttermilk through muslin and flavoured it with vanilla to make *hangop*. Those dishes always came back empty.

There were days when the Monsieur did not go out and

I had to clean his room with him in it. I would wait until after lunch, to be sure he was awake and dressed. When I went in, I'd take off my slippers so as not to disturb him. Often he was resting with his eyes closed, sitting in a chair he had drawn up to the window. He reminded me of a cat sunning itself, neither awake nor asleep. He never noticed me.

Every day, I turned back the sheets to air his bed, smoothed them flat with the palm of my hand, to cool the still-warm mattress. Once a fortnight, I washed the bedlinen and his clothes too.

A month went by and I had not had his nightshirt. It was raining, which meant he would be in his room. I slipped in, knelt down and peered under the bed, in case the shirt had been kicked there by mistake.

'Are you looking for something?'

I startled, and brushed my apron as I straightened up. 'I—'

'Well?'

'Are there clothes for me to wash, Monsieur?'

'Certainly, but Limousin has brought you everything I have.'

I twisted my apron between my fingers.

'Is something wrong?'

'I've not had your nightshirt, Monsieur.'

'Nightshirt?'

My cheeks burned.

He clapped his hands together, threw his head back and laughed. 'What nightshirt?'

My heart raced as though I had run up ten flights of stairs.

I fled from the room, his laughter tumbling at my heels. In my haste, I realised I had left my slippers behind. I did not dare go back for them, and went barefoot for the rest of the day. When I finally summoned up the courage to retrieve them, I found them placed neatly side by side outside his door. Under one slipper was a note. I unfolded the paper and read what was there: *Your slippers – your feet will be cold without them.* Underneath, a small drawing.

I blinked. Nothing was straight. Not even a rose stem in water.

AMSTERDAM, 1632–3

Glass

WESTERKERK WAS NOT for people like me. My church was Noorderkerk. I had to walk the length of the Jordaan to reach it. I did not mind. I belonged there.

I rose an hour earlier than usual on Sundays. Fires that had been laid the night before still needed to be lit, and breakfast prepared before I left. I needed to make time for the walk from Westermarkt to the Jordaan if I was to arrive early, before six. I liked to stand in the same place in church, towards the back and to one side, where the light fell in from a high window, straight and cool. I stood there before God and tried not to stare as the congregation arrived. Some I recognised – traders from the Jordaan – and maids, like me, full of chatter until they stepped across the threshold. They gathered in groups, and fluttered like pigeons, before they settled and were still.

There were lesser merchants too, their collars pleated into ruffs so full their heads seemed cut off from their shoulders. The larger the ruff, the greater the nodding, I noticed, when the minister gave his sermon; the larger the ruff, the greater the attention of the minister after the sermon was done.

I did not want a ruff and was glad the minister never noticed me. I covered my head with a muslin square, drawing it across my brow so that my hair was tucked away. Mother had given it to me. It was all that was left from a drawerful of linen she had collected for the day I married. After Father was lost, she sold one piece, then another, and I remembered thinking: *Am I not to marry?* But I could not ask it; we had to eat. In the end, all that was left of the husband she'd saved for was tatters and threads.

'There's none but God can help us,' she said and ripped a cloth into smaller pieces to make handkerchiefs to sell.

She took in wool to spin, as she had before she married, and she taught me too. Together, what we earned made less than half a man, less than a man with one hand. Linen and wool could not feed us. Thomas, my brother, went to sea. Mother heard there was great need of maids in Amsterdam. I sat quietly as she told me this, no need even to look up.

The day I left, she set my shoulders straight. Her thin fingers nipped me as she pinned my shawl with her brooch. She hugged me to her, her warmth circled me, soft and fierce, and I felt strength in her I'd not known. A hope lifted in me that we might stay together after all. I nudged my cheek against her, but something in her seemed to tighten and stiffen as I burrowed closer, as though the thought of parting, my leaving, had wriggled cold fingers between us.

She set me gently away from her at arm's length. 'Look at you growing. You'll be working soon enough and when you're paid . . .'

I knew she was trying to cheer me, but I'd heard maids only got paid once a year; who could say what I'd get or when I'd see her again?

I swallowed. 'And you, Ma? What about you?'

'Now, now.' She lifted my chin with her hand. 'I'll manage. I'll go to the minister, if needs be.' She patted the brooch in place, but this time when I reached for her she set me away and shook her head. 'The world is in Amsterdam – *imagine*. Work hard. God will be with you – I know it, Helena.'

All I knew was what I felt, and that was the weight of everything I had against this proposal, which seemed to have gathered at my ankles and held me fast to the floor. She passed me my bundle and my Bible and I had no choice but to take them.

We walked to where the coach waited. As she watched me go, she wrapped her arms tightly around her. There were all kinds of goodbye in the world, I was learning; I'd be one less worry for her once I'd gone.

I looked back over my shoulder and waved, but only her fingers lifted in reply.

I had papers with me that would introduce me to Mr Slootmaekers, an agent who placed girls with merchant families. I could read and write. I knew my prayers. I could cook, draw water and lay a fire. In time, I would learn everything I needed to. Someone would have need of a girl like me.

But no one had need of a maid who could write. They did not even have to say so – I saw it in their faces. A shake of the head, a downturned mouth, a shrug, the long, cold gaze down the bridge of a nose, the narrowing of eyes – I saw it all as Mr Slootmaekers traipsed me the length of the Singel, then on to the Amstel, before hawking me along the Jordaan and back.

It was a dismal day, and we were at the end of it. In the murk, the houses stood shoulder to shoulder like men bundled in grey coats. Then doors opened to Mr Slootmaekers' knock, and revealed all kinds of wonder, moments of scarlet and orange and gold that were gone almost as soon as I glimpsed them. At one house, the lady came out and stood on the top step, and listened to Mr Slootmaekers make his appeal from the pavement. She was like a queen, on a throne, hands clasped together. She wore a blue-stoned ring, loose on one knuckle, as startling as the eye of God. But it did not do to stare at jewellery like that, and Mr Slootmaekers said so, and so we walked on.

By the time we arrived on Westermarkt, it was dark. Mr Slootmaekers had heard that a bookseller he knew was looking for a maid. A bookseller? What meagre fee could be had from him, he muttered, as he knocked at the door.

'Stand back, girl,' he said and tucked me behind him into the shadows, as if my being seen would curse the matter. We waited. A dim light flickered in one window, but nothing came from within. Mr Slootmaekers knocked again, a sharp rap with the end of his walking stick.

'Wait, wait.'

There was a rattle of keys, the sound of them being dropped, then of a bolt being drawn back. An elderly man, with a whiskery beard and white tufts of hair either side of his shiny head, peered at us from the doorway.

'Yes? What? Ah, Slootmaekers. I was expecting you. I waited so long, I fell asleep.' He brushed crumbs from his waistcoat and cleared his throat. He spoke with a strange accent, as if he had a fruit stone in his mouth.

'Mr Sergeant,' Mr Slootmaekers bowed, 'forgive this late intrusion.'

'Do you have someone?' Mr Sergeant said. 'I have been left dreadfully short since the last girl you brought, Gerarda, had to go.'

Mr Slootmaekers pulled me from behind him and pushed me forwards into the light. He dug in his pocket and brought out my crumpled papers. I could not bring myself to look up. 'Stand up straight!' he barked.

I lifted my head. It was all I could do to stand up at all.

Mr Sergeant took the papers and tucked them into his waistcoat pocket. 'Can you cook?'

I nodded.

He rubbed his hands together. 'Well, come in!'

'Don't you want to see her references?'

'In this light? Let's see what kind of pancake the girl makes. That's the best reference of all.'

Mr Sergeant led us through one dark room and another, and down a number of steps. The house had a smell like no other – not dirty, not clean – an animal smell, I thought, but neither cat nor dog nor any animal I might have expected in a house like this. When we reached the kitchen, he threw a handful of sticks on the fire – a fire so small and feeble, I could have cupped it in my hands.

'It'll soon get going.' He sounded more hopeful than he looked.

He picked up a pile of books from the table, then, not knowing what to do with them, or where else to put them, put them back down. I built up the fire and set a pan over it and, when all was hot, I made pancakes. And when I was done, I cut sugar from a loaf, ground it and sprinkled it over. He watched me as I did it, with a spoon in his hand all the while, and then ate the lot standing up, right there in the kitchen. From the sound he made, it seemed he had not eaten for a week. I discovered later that Gerarda had left with three days' notice and Mr Sergeant had survived on apples and plums, and a cheese he'd taken back to the rind. It was a poor to-do. There was no Mrs Sergeant, it seemed.

'Slootmaekers tells me you can write,' he said, between mouthfuls. 'My eyes are not what they were.'

I searched his face for a frown, but he raised his hands into the air as if thanking God. For one awful moment I thought he was going to hug me, but he handed me the empty plate instead.

'Wonderful!'

Mr Slootmaekers said his goodbyes and a short time after I heard Mr Sergeant go upstairs. The house fell quiet. The only light I had was that around my candle; I could find no more candles to light, only stubs that had burned down. Every pot I peered in was empty, bar one that held an onion. I lifted lid after lid and found great yawning mouths of shadow. I had not dared ask, but was I the only maid? No one to show me how, or help? My stomach tightened at the thought I had it all to do myself.

Amsterdam. The world is here. What a thing, to know it was

36

there, outside and waiting for me. I was too tired to think more on it. I slept where I sat, my head on the table, my hands still dusty with flour.

In the morning, I found my bed, tucked away in an alcove next to the kitchen chimney. Above the bed, a shelf. I untied my bundle and set out what I had: the square of muslin from my mother, my brooch and my shawl. I opened my Bible, and checked for the scrap of paper I knew was inside. I unfolded it and stared at the one word written there – *Aemilia*: the name of Thomas's ship. He'd been gone a year already, and I had another year to wait.

I closed the Bible on the note, and put it on the shelf. Beneath the bed, a drawer with bedding. I'd heard some maids slept in cellars; some had no more than a hollow, filled with straw. I patted the mattress, relieved to find it not damp; it gave gently under my hand.

Later, Mr Sergeant came through to show me around the house. First we went out into the courtyard at the back.

'The water pump, Helena,' he said and took a step back, as though introducing me to a distant relative. A ginger cat eyed me from a high wall. I was half inclined to bow. I raised the handle and lifted a length of groaning, gurgling water.

At the far end of the yard stood the peat store, with a chopping block for kindling. The courtyard led onto a shared area, threaded with washing lines where sheets billowed and sagged. Crows bickered in the trees, then flew up in an angry burst of cawing. I saw two maids come out from one of the houses opposite and draw near. One barely reached the shoulder of the other, no more than twelve, I guessed. They stopped when they saw me.

'Hello,' I said.

The younger turned to the other, whispered and giggled.

'Silly nonsense,' Mr Sergeant said and went to go back indoors.

I glanced over my shoulder as I followed him in. The younger girl spun in circles until the older girl shouted at her to stop. I used to spin in circles like that; now I had to walk in straight lines instead.

When we were inside again, Mr Sergeant took me to his study, at the front of the house. Underneath the dust, the floor shone like glass. I saw my reflection, pooled at my feet, as though I'd stepped into a puddle, as though the floor had me held fast by my ankles. I took a step back, to be certain my feet were still mine.

'Marvellous, isn't it?' Mr Sergeant said. 'A little wax will keep it tip-top.'

A *little* wax? I could imagine whole hives emptied out and there still not being enough. I saw my days ahead, on my knees, polishing, polishing. A dead ache snailed up my arms at the thought.

By the far wall stood a tall bookcase filled with leather-bound books. I knew now the source of the smell from the night before: *books*, or rather the hides that bound them. Next to the bookcase, two glass-topped cabinets had been set on display in the window. Each held a single sheet of paper, printed with a title and name. One had pictures of insects, birds and trees. I knew the letters, but not the words they made.

'Frontispieces,' Mr Sergeant explained. 'When there is interest, the book is printed. These are Latin. More and more is printed in Dutch these days, and English and French too – all of Amsterdam will be buying books soon enough – and if every Amsterdamer bought one book . . . Well, when that day comes, I shall have my house on Herengracht.' He ran his hand along a shelf, but was not checking for dust. 'One book is not enough. Never enough. What one needs is a *library*. A library is an investment in the future, Helena.'

Next, he took me up upstairs to his rooms – a sunny bedroom and a small dressing room, the contents of which appeared to have been emptied out into the other. Both rooms faced the front, directly above his study. The bedroom was simply furnished, with an oak dresser and a pair of high-backed chairs. The doors to the dresser stood open; both chairs heaped with clothes – work that waited for me. There wasn't a way to know what was clean and what was dirty. It would all have to be washed.

Between the chairs on a small table stood a pair of miniatures. One showed the portrait of a woman, her face framed with hollyhocks and roses. Alongside that, a portrait of a much younger, pink-cheeked Mr Sergeant.

'Painted,' he said, when he saw me looking, 'in my garden in Oxford. *That* was a lovely garden.'

A garden seemed like a remarkable thing, like having a flower market to yourself on the step. We had a small yard at home, but it never got the sun; not much grew there.

Above his room, and up a shorter flight of stairs, was a room with a lower ceiling, containing papers, ledgers and a large number of books. His study looked tidy by comparison. Next, he showed me through to a pair of smaller rooms at the back, set aside for lodgers.

'Lodgers,' he explained, 'keep me in tea.'

Tea? I was about to ask, but he had started to make his way downstairs again. Halfway down, he turned to me.

'This is my home. Not what I once had, but what I now have.'

'Yes, Mr Sergeant.'

'The house has not functioned well recently. It hasn't been *as it should be*.'

I nodded, though I didn't understand. It was a large house for one person. There was so much *emptiness*, room for nothing; such a distance between things. Chairs set apart for no other reason, it seemed, than to be looked at and admired. It had never occurred to me that a chair might not be just for sitting on, that you could stand and look at it instead. I thought of the papers kept behind glass in his study. How could *paper*, the words and writing on them, make for a house such as this, and everything in it, when the sacks and sacks of wool at home made so little?

'Your reference mentions your father is lost. We are both refugees in a way, Helena,' he said, his voice softening. 'Circumstances carry us where we least expect. Interesting times. Lots of circumstances. But Amsterdam is a good place for a bookseller. We have our hopes and prayers. There is consolation in that. And in a good book, of course!'

'Yes,' I whispered. I felt a long way from home.

'Good!' he said, brightening. 'Now, as I have reason to celebrate, I'll take tea – have you prepared it before?'

I shook my head. I had never heard of it.

'Then, a demonstration. Just this once.'

Mr Sergeant stood next to me as he talked me through his demonstration. It involved a series of steps, to be remembered strictly in the order he showed me. Afterwards, I realised, it was only a matter of adding water to some shrivelled leaves. First, the water had to be brought to a strong boil so the bubbles rose in the pan, but not boiled for too long else it would spoil. That water could be spoiled in this way was new to me.

'If the water is not properly hot, the tea will not infuse, and the result is insipid – terrible, and needs to be tipped away. Waste like that is too ghastly to contemplate.'

Infuse? Insipid? Ghastly? I liked these words. They made my hand tickle.

He fetched the tea, which he kept in his study, locked in a small silver caddy. He sprinkled half a teaspoon of dried leaves into a curiously shaped pot.

'No more than this, Helena, else I shall be bankrupted. Now the water, quick.'

I poured the water from a pan into the pot.

'That's it! Enough!'

I peered into the pot. In a twist of steam, the water changed to a bright earthen colour, the scent as fresh as grass after rain.

'Perfect.' He took out his pocket watch. 'Now, to time it.'

I stared at the watch, then at the tea – it had darkened

to the colour of an old shoe. I was glad I did not have to drink it.

I thought Mr Sergeant's house was like a palace, but it was a thin finger of a house when compared with the new ones being built on Herengracht. These went up with ever larger windows, as if they were competing for the sky or for God's attention. Some were built with so few bricks that from a distance they looked as though they were made from air. Others had been built so they leaned forwards into the street, as if balanced on their toes. They seemed to peer down at me, perhaps expecting me to curtsy when I went by, but I did not.

At night, before the shutters were closed and all the candles within had been lit, whole rooms shone like golden lanterns. In the blue light of morning, before the sun tipped over the rooftops, I couldn't tell where glass stopped and sky began. It was like standing in an enormous church, open to the sky and God's embrace.

One day, on my way back from Botermarkt, I stopped to watch workmen fitting new shutters to a window that reached up to twice my height or more. I felt sorry for the girl who had them to clean. I had not seen anything like them before – carved all over with cherubs and roses and cherries, and wide, wooden ribbons tied into bows. Sunlight slanted across the pane. I saw birds swoop down, my own reflection too, and clouds shift behind me. Had I fallen into the sky? Had the sky tumbled into the street? I screwed up my eyes and blinked them wide open again.

I heard a crack above me as a window was winched up. A woman leaned out and pointed at me. 'You there.'

'Me?'

'Yes, you.' She flicked a towel at me. 'Are you touching my glass?'

I stepped back, startled.

'Off the step! Shoo! How dare you touch my glass!'

I took another step, standing in the street now. 'No, I—'

'Horrid girl! You touched my glass!'

'I did not touch your glass!'

'Liar. God take your tongue and knot it.'

'I did not touch it!' I protested. 'God gave you eyes, so that you can see!'

'Well!' she spluttered.

I did not wait to hear more. I ran and ran until I was over two bridges and halfway along Prinsengracht. My heart seemed to grow bigger with every beat until there was no room left inside me to breathe. When I hadn't another step in me and could run no further, I stopped and rested against a tree, feeling around it with my fingers until I faced the canal. I curled my toes over the stone ledge and although I was laughing, I was crying too.

Bruises

MR SERGEANT RECEIVED visitors most days. Some travelled from across the provinces and needed to stay in the house for a week or more. I learned that visitors from the west liked to speak first and those from the north did not require me to speak at all. I should not ask about journeys taken, nor enquire after well-being, and never offer my hand in greeting. I should take capes, help with boots, bring drinks on a tray when instructed. I rarely saw the maids from the house opposite, but one day the older of the two girls came up to me as I took in sheets from the line.

'Where you from?' she asked, not offering to help. She crossed her arms in front of her and jutted out a hip.

'Leiden,' I said.

Wasn't it polite to say hello first? She looked older than I thought, twenty perhaps, older than me. She stepped back and considered me.

'Better here than a plague pit, I suppose.' She scuffed her toe on the ground. Before I could say anything, she went on, 'They sent her away, you know.'

'Who?'

'Gerarda. The maid before you.'

'Sent away?'

'Glad it's not me in that house – such *fancy* book folk. *Poor* Gerarda.'

'What do you mean? What happened?'

'Look at you.' She circled me, pulling my clothes and squeezing my arms. 'A bit skinny. A bit *young*. But quite a pretty little miss from Leiden. Who do you think you are, taking her place?'

I wriggled free of her grip. 'Let go!'

'Have you been asked for it yet?' She pushed her hips forwards and waggled her thumb in her mouth. When I frowned, she laughed and stepped closer. 'Don't you know?'

I set my shoulders straight. I wasn't going to tell her what I did or didn't know.

She held my gaze, not fooled for a moment. 'I'm going to have to keep an eye on you.'

There was that look again. I could not be sure if she was sorry for me or about to laugh. I bundled the sheet in my arms and turned away.

She hooked her hand under my elbow and steered me around to face her, her smile gone. 'It's not the old man you need to watch out for—'

'Mr Sergeant?'

'None of us matter, not to the likes of them. Sooner you realise that, the better.'

She let go of me, but this time she looked away.

I wondered what had happened, what she knew. It was peculiar not having a mistress in the house – but there wasn't a Mrs Sergeant and hadn't been for years. I didn't have to live by the rules other maids had to, scurrying back from market to their houses at their mistresses' beck and call. Mr Sergeant paid little attention to me. As long as the food I made was fresh and tasty and on time, and all was *as it should be* – his only rule for how a house should be kept – I was allowed to order my day as I pleased.

'Do you know your way yet? Been past the Jordaan?'

I shrugged. What was it to her? 'I've been along Herengracht. Both sides.'

Her smile flashed back, sudden as tinder. '*Both sides?* Seen it all then – I don't think.' She pushed me on the shoulder, but less hard than when she'd nipped me.

Freckles patterned her cheeks; her eyes were the palest blue. I had never seen the like of them before – like the colour of the day before it got going, of morning just tipped out of bed.

She took hold of my hand and shook it. 'I'm Betje. Meet me here tomorrow. I'll show you Amsterdam – *both sides*.'

'I don't—'

'After breakfast. I know you can. You'll be going to market anyway, won't you?'

I opened my mouth to reply, but she had already turned neatly on one heel, in no need of hearing what I had to say, and was crossing the courtyard to the house where she worked. Then she was gone, lost between the lines of washing – only a patch of scuffed ground to mark where she had been, to show she'd been there at all. She'd not even asked me my name. Was she always as bossy?

No good will come of it – of someone who makes up your mind for you like that. I let the thought surface, like a fish rising, belly flashing silver to the sun. Then I pushed it down again as far as it would go, chased it into the deep. I could go if I wanted.

I gathered in the rest of the washing from the line and hurried back inside.

But the next morning, when I went to find her, she was not there. I'd gone as soon as I could, like she'd said. I'd cleared the breakfast dishes from the table, leaving Mr Sergeant, knife mid-air, still chewing a last mouthful of herring.

'I hadn't quite—' he said, half turning, as I whisked the plate away.

I near skipped from the room, hoping he'd think I'd not heard, hoping he'd not call me back. Once out, I stopped, listened at the door, and counted to three – still nothing. I dashed to the kitchen, dunked his plate into a bucket, then grabbed my cap and ran.

I found the circle of scuffed ground where we'd been the day before and waited. No Betje. Perhaps I was early. I counted trees. I counted the nests in the trees. She did not come.

I walked around to the front of Mr Sergeant's in case she was there, but she wasn't there either. In the end, I made my way across the courtyard to the house where I knew she worked, threading myself between the washing: flat sheets, lank petticoats and so many stockings, dangling like empty legs, lengthening as they dripped. Would she have gone without me? Changed her mind after all? My heart sank as I realised the answer to both was *yes*.

The house was much larger than Mr Sergeant's and larger still the closer I got. I couldn't just wander in, so I waited by the wall. I did not want to go to market on my own. I wanted to go with Betje. I tried to push away the doubts I had. She'd come – wouldn't she?

The gate had been left open and beyond that the kitchen door stood ajar. Then, there was Betje, but not dressed for going out; that much I could see; she still had on her work apron. She was gone as soon as I saw her, plates stacked up under her chin. The younger maid followed behind her, carrying as many plates as Betje, it seemed. She buckled under their weight, bent like a sapling branch. A much older woman, the housekeeper, lumbered into the doorway and shouldered the door wider. I shrank back so she'd not see me. She looked up at the sky and held out her hand to feel the day – warm already, the first good drying day in weeks. She slapped her side and scowled.

'Betje!' she called, going back into the house. 'Get over here.'

There was a sudden crash, crockery splintering on tiles, followed by such a tumult of shouting and words that were not fit for saying, not even for thinking.

'You midden-handed slabbard! God give you maggots for fingers?'

There came a sound of something being dropped, like dough thumped down on a table. Then a cry. Bread didn't cry. Then another thump, another cry. And a whimper that pulled into a wail. I heard pottery being swept up and rattling into a bin.

'Shut up, the pair of you! I'll see that you pay, Betje.'

I shot a look around the corner of the gate and saw Betje, in the doorway, rubbing away tears. The housekeeper loomed across the gap in the door and yanked her by the arm, so that she faced her.

'Think I'll stand for any more of it? Do you? Ten stuivers! Ten stuivers! Ten more than you're worth! Shift your arse out of my way! Out!' She shoved Betje between the shoulders, pushing her twice more until she was out of the house.

'Betje!' I said, as she stormed past. She wrenched at the strings of her apron, hair flying loose from her cap; her eyes red-rimmed and shining.

'Come on,' she said, not looking at me, not stopping. I followed behind her, the path too narrow to walk by her side. 'Wasn't me broke the plate. Arse? Arse herself! Lard arse. Face like bad fat too.'

'Why'd you . . . why'd she blame you?' I struggled to get the words out as she strode ahead.

'I said it was me. So Antje wouldn't get clouted.'

Antje? The younger maid?

Betje screwed up her apron into her fist, not seeming to care that the ties trailed on the ground. I looked at her arms, slapped red and covered in grey smudges too, like soot from the grate. Not smudges, but bruises, I realised, as I took it all in. One, two, three, four lines . . . fingers? A handprint. The mark of the housekeeper's hand on Betje's arm.

'Betje! Who did that? Did she do it? Did she?' Mr Sergeant would never do such a thing to me.

She tugged at her sleeves, which were still rolled up. 'It's nothing.' She tugged again, yanking the sleeves into place, then buttoned the cuffs.

We walked the length of Prinsengracht and the only words I heard were the words of others passing by. I tried to talk, but Betje wouldn't. She set her mouth shut as though she'd decided never to speak again.

49

Feathers

I HAD BEEN in service for four months and it was autumn. Grey mornings crept in from the IJ. The canals filled with mist.

One afternoon, Mr Sergeant called me to his study. On his desk he'd set out a sheet of paper and an inkwell. He took out a pocket knife and cut a nib into a quill. He blew on it, squinted, and then held the quill out to me.

'Show me how well you can write.'

Write? *With a quill?* My heart leapt. I took it from him and gripped it tight.

'Goodness! Not like that! You'll break it.'

When I went to reach across the desk for the ink, he batted my hand away.

'No! No! Here.' He stood up and beckoned to me to come and sit in his chair behind his desk.

I settled in his seat, which was still warm from him sitting in it. I hadn't noticed the shape of me before; the chair had never seemed that large. How thin my arms looked on the armrests. When I leaned back, my spine arched awkwardly, more room behind me than I had body to fill. I shuffled forwards, dipped the quill in the ink, dipped it again to be sure and waited for his instructions.

He waved one hand, as if what he wanted was obvious. 'Your name. Write your name.'

Helena Jans van der Strom.

I looked at what I had written. I supposed it was my name, but I might as well have written it with my eyes closed. It hadn't helped that my hand shook so. I lifted the sheet for him to see. He peered at it, then at me, as if not seeing what joined us, and tutted. I knew the words were not right, cobbled together as they were from letters that slanted left and right, some larger than others, but I felt the sting of his disappointment nonetheless.

'Again,' he said. 'Do it again.'

He walked over to the window and looked out for a while, thinking. He rocked backwards onto his heels, his hands clasped behind his back.

'Let's try some poetry, perhaps that will inspire:

Siet alderhande jongen
Die pijpen even soo gelijck de moeders songen . . .'

I bent my head to the page, as if being closer might help anchor the words, but I couldn't keep up with those that tumbled out of his mouth. The nib caught on the paper as I wrote. By the time I had finished, the page was dotted with ink blots; half the words seemed to have skeddadled before I had a chance to write them, and the others to have splashed through puddles of ink.

'No, stop! Slow down. Rest the quill lightly between your fingers; the words will write themselves. *Again.*'

I tried and I tried, but couldn't stop the ink blotting as I touched the nib to the page. *How was a word ever written?* It wasn't possible.

I looked at the ledger on Mr Sergeant's desk, listing book titles and their prices. No blots there; the ink had been applied evenly and smoothly, and without any hint of the temper now rising in me.

I stared at my page, covered in blots. Mr Sergeant seemed lost in his recitation. One blot looked a bit like an apple, I thought. I added a stalk and a small leaf. I chose another blot, and another, and then I drew an apple from scratch. Scratch! Ha! Now I understood. *Aple*, I wrote alongside.

'What's this?' Mr Sergeant said, when he saw what I had done.

'Apples.' It was clear to me what they were.

'I see that. Ink apples, pleasing to the eye though they may be, are of no use to a bookseller. I need words, Helena, not *fruit*.' His shoulders sagged. 'It is time to close the shutters, I think.'

And with that he dismissed me.

Once I was outside his room, I rubbed my hands together. I hated them. 'Stupid hands,' I said. 'Stupid, stupid hands.'

I should have told him I hadn't used a quill before. Now he would think I couldn't write.

Later, in bed, I sat with my knees drawn up to my chest. Why hadn't the words worked? Had they gone? I traced my name with my finger on the palm of my hand. This time, the letters flowed through and over each other without any hitch. I huddled under the sheet as I had the first night when Thomas had refused to show me the letters he'd been taught at school. I'd begged him to; I'd hung on to his arm, then his leg, then the end of his shirt until it ripped and he'd swung round at me with his fist. But he didn't stop me. I started with 'I', tracing the letter on the palm of my hand in the dark. That's how I began – with one letter, with a word: *I* – with me. *Me.* Over and over, until the letters fixed there, first one, then another, and another. Then the words of a prayer. *Oh, Heavenly Father,* I wrote, and by the end of that summer, my tenth year, I could write the whole prayer on my hand.

I wrote the prayer now across my palm, to be sure it was still in me. The words were there. They were in my head and in my hand, part of me. All I needed was practice.

The next morning, as soon as I heard Mr Sergeant in his study, I knocked at the door. 'Mr Sergeant?'

'Yes, Helena?'

I peeped around the edge of the door. 'Can I write for you?'

He looked up from the papers on his desk and shook his head. 'No, I don't think so. Later, perhaps.'

But there was no call from him later, not that day, nor the day after that. After the third day, I stopped asking. I did not mention it again.

All that week, disappointment trailed after me like my shadow. Every book I dusted, and paper I tidied, felt three times heavier, as if weighted by my own stupidity. Every tidy word on each neat page seemed to look at me and laugh.

I was to prepare quills instead. If that's what I was good for, then I was determined to be good at it. I stripped back the feather, the way I'd been shown, cleaning it so there was no stubble. Mr Sergeant rubbed his thumb and fore-finger together.

It must be smooth, he said, *so a thought has nowhere to snag . . . no excuse at all, no reason to tarry, trip, or stop.*

The first quills I prepared would have hooked whole paragraphs of words. I threw them straight on the fire.

A quill has to have grace. A quill without grace is a duck, Mr Sergeant said, and laughed at his own joke. He made a great show of resting the quills I'd prepared in his hand, arm stretched out in front, as though balancing a knife. Neither ink nor paper were needed for him to know if it was wrong.

'Duck!' he said and tossed it over his shoulder. 'Another! This time, bring me a swan!'

That's how I knew, how I learned what a quill should be. And all of it had to be right before the nib was cut – sharp or blunt, a decision that changed everything too. It seemed one in twenty quills was good enough; the rest ended up on the fire or at his feet. Sometimes, the floor round his chair looked as though he'd been preening; some days as though he'd been plucked.

I swept up the quills that weren't wanted. It was a shame to waste them, I thought.

I wondered which would suit my hand.

I had quills, but no ink nor paper, nor money for either. I ground up charcoal on the back step with a stone, then spent the rest of the afternoon scrubbing off the mess. Charcoal did not make good ink. Neither did soot. Blood clotted and clagged the nib; cocoa wouldn't dissolve in cold water. Beetroot made lovely pink ink, but I had to boil the liquor almost to nothing and Mr Sergeant complained of the stink. I did not dare take his tea, but dipped my quill in the dregs in his cup. Those words shone like amber, then faded as they dried until all that was left were their ghosts.

Of everything I tried, beetroot was best. I had quills, and now I had ink, but no paper. Mr Sergeant had paper, but if I was caught with any of that I would be dismissed. I could not take it without asking. And if I asked, he'd want to know why, what I wanted it for. What would I say?

I want to write, Mr Sergeant – I know you decided I couldn't, but I've decided I can.

What would he say to that? I had to find something else to write on instead. But finding something other than paper made learning how to cut quills seem simple, and the making of pink ink an undertaking of the most ordinary kind.

I tried everything to hand that wouldn't be missed or found. I wrote on old sheeting, on the table, on a plate. The sheeting, even when pegged flat like a canvas, soaked up the ink and the words bled into each other and fused into blobs. They looked like a line of piglets, but I refused to let the thought please me. I wrote on the table, but had to wipe the words off before they became stuck. A plate made the best page of all – but those words refused to dry and I lost patience and swilled the lot into a bucket. I baked a thin pastry crust, hard as a board, and would have written on that, had Mr Sergeant not tried to eat it first.

Then, late at night, after Mr Sergeant had gone to bed,

and with nothing else to write on, I rolled up my sleeve. Those first words – the words that ran from the inside of my elbow to my wrist – were the most ticklish. When there was no more room, I lifted my skirt and wrote above my knee, then on my thigh.

I wrote and I wrote and I wrote.

Betje could be rough, I was learning – both with her words and with her hands. I didn't think she meant it. Those bruises had to find a way out somehow.

We were pegging out washing one day, the winter sunshine weak and milky.

'What's that?' she said, catching hold of my arm and bending it back, snaking closer.

I hadn't noticed that the button had come off my cuff and the sleeve was loose at my wrist. Betje stared open-mouthed. Although the words had faded and weren't the neatest I'd written, they were, without doubt, *words*.

'Ow!' I tried to twist away.

'What's that on your arm?'

'Nothing,' I said.

'Not nothing!' She pushed up my sleeve. 'Writing? You've got words on you. *All over you!*'

She shook her head as though trying to make sense of a peculiar rash, then rubbed at a word with her thumb.

'How'd they get there?'

'I wrote them.' It was no good telling her otherwise; she'd only have kept on at me until she knew.

'Wrote them?' She tilted her head to get a better look. '*You* wrote *this*?'

'Y—'

'What d'they say?'

I knew the words by heart. '*Nordakirk. Godt. Beteeye* . . .'

'*Godt!* You wrote God's name?' Then, 'Betje! That's me. Let's look.' When I showed her the word, she prodded it, as if expecting it to move, or bite. 'Go on then. Read the rest.'

I didn't want to. She tightened her grip and pointed to another word. 'What's this then?'

'*Sly gubbins* . . .'

'*Sly gubbins?* That's what I say! I never said you could write it! You never told me you could write.'

'I only write words . . . words I like.'

She stepped back, astonished. 'My name?'

'Yes.'

She pointed to a tree. 'You could write about that?'

I nodded.

She pointed at one thing, then another. 'And that stone? And the wall? And that house there? And the sky? Amsterdam?' She swept her arms wide. '*Holland?*'

I rubbed at the words on my arm. I didn't want her to think me proud, or above her. She looked at me, trying to work out what it all meant.

'You writing one of Mr Sergeant's books?'

'No!'

'You're a strange one, you are.' She traced a finger over her name. 'How do you do it? Can I learn it too?'

I hadn't expected that! 'I'm still learning, Betje.'

'You've written my name. That's more than I can do.' She

jabbed at the ground with her heel. 'They're not just yours, you know.'

I thought of the quills I'd snapped in frustration, the beetroot I'd had to tip away with the night soil so as to hide the smell. I thought for a moment. 'Can you read?'

She shook her head.

'You have to read, Betje. I'll show you that first.'

Show her? *First?* What was I saying? I had no idea how I could show her anything at all. But the thought, now I'd thought it, went higher and higher and would not come down.

Betje's eyes widened as she took it all in. 'Will you? Promise me?'

I thought of Thomas as I held out my hand. Perhaps this promise would be easier to keep, but I doubted it. 'Promise.'

Then she did something she never did again. She pulled me to her and gave me a hug.

Slate

AUTUMN GAVE WAY to winter and the year wheeled round into spring. I'd been Mr Sergeant's maid a year and, when he paid me, he gave me a slate and some chalk.

'This is for you. I've had the most marvellous idea, Helena. It's for record keeping. In the kitchen. I can write down anything I need, if you are out.'

The kitchen had never been so far from my mind. I clasped the slate to me as if it were made of silver. Without realising it, he'd given me the means to teach Betje. 'Thank you!' I said.

Betje and I saw each other most days. We went to market together and, as the days lengthened into summer, we spent more and more time outside. There was no less work to be done indoors, but summer errands spilled into the evenings that winter cut so short. I liked Betje's company, even though she would talk for me, taking words from my mouth before I'd had a chance to speak. Her words swept mine away. She did her best to think for me too. But my thoughts and hers did not often agree.

'No,' she said, stepping between me and the butcher who held out a slab of belly pork that she'd decided was no good. She pulled a face and pushed his hand away. 'She's not having any of that.'

The meat was not the best I'd ever seen, but better than anything else on offer that day.

Betje steered me to one side and whispered in my ear, 'We'll come back later; he'll want rid of it then.'

But when we went back, he'd packed up and gone, and I had to settle for pork with a grey rind. I folded my arms, not happy. That first pork, the pork I'd wanted, had been pink.

I showed Betje the slate and then how she should hold the chalk. 'A,' I said and wrote the letter down. 'Your turn.'

She took the chalk and angled the slate away so I could not see. When she was done, she turned the slate back – revealing a letter the size of a bread roll.

'Good,' I said, but I could see the sulk in the set of her shoulders. I think she expected just to be able to write.

I liked writing with chalk. It was easier to hold than a quill. It didn't blot, it didn't stain, and if I made a mistake I could wipe the slate clean and start again. I made a good deal of dust doing that and had to be careful not to get it on anything black. Then I thought of Mr Sergeant's papers. Chalk was better than nothing, but it was not the stuff of ledgers and books.

It was difficult to find time when we would not be missed or caught. We could not use the drying area; other maids used that too. If I wasn't careful, I'd be running a school for all Westermarkt maids out in the open.

'I could come to the kitchen, when Mr Sergeant is out.'

I did not like that idea. Mr Sergeant did not keep a strict routine and treated the kitchen as his second study – leaving papers and books lying around as he wandered in and out in search of 'some tasty morsel' to keep him going between meals.

'How would I get word to you that he is out?' I could not simply walk into Betje's house and ask for her. I remembered her housekeeper's ways. We most certainly could not meet there.

No. We had to find somewhere else, somewhere where two maids would go unnoticed; where it would not be unusual to spend small pockets of time at any part of the day.

'Noorderkerk!' I said, saying the thought out loud as it came to me.

I might as well have asked Betje to dance in church from the look she gave me.

'We can't do that!'

'We'll still pray,' I said. 'I'll write the words on the slate before we go and then you'll read them.'

And so we began, one prayer at a time. We tucked ourselves away, hiding the slate that passed between us. Her prayers might have stuttered, her finger smudging the words as she followed them, but God would hear her just the same. And as Betje prayed, so did I. I prayed for Mother and I prayed for Thomas. I prayed for Father. I prayed for Mr Sergeant and Betje too. I prayed the words would find her, and her them.

At night, I read my Bible and tried to remember spellings, repeating words, letter by letter, over and over under my breath. I was learning as much as Betje. It took weeks. It took months.

But at this rate, it would take years. I wondered why Betje wanted to learn. When I asked her, she accused me again of wanting to keep it all to myself.

'It's the boys who keep it for themselves, Betje,' I protested. I remembered Thomas refusing to teach me; writing the name of his ship, thinking I'd not be able to myself.

'All Mrs Hoek ever does is shout and arrange flowers,' said Betje. 'Do you think she could have had ships like Mr Hoek if she'd been schooled the same?'

The question stunned us. We looked at each other and at our hands. Betje, I thought, concentrated hardest that day.

We could not write on the slate in church. For that, we needed somewhere noisy, where the scratching of chalk would not be heard. We settled on some steps on Lindengracht – no one paid attention to two maids stopping to rest there. It was not the wisest place, I soon learned. Betje threw more than one piece of chalk away in a temper, aiming for the canal. She only stopped when I told her I'd not teach her if she did it again.

She kicked her heels against the step. 'What's the use of it anyway? What can you do with any of it? Write lists?'

'Once it's learned, it sticks, Betje. You'll not forget.'

'Lists!'

I took hold of her hand and turned it over to the palm, and traced her name with my finger.

Betje snatched her hand away. 'That tickles!'

'It's not a tickle. It's not a list. It's your name, see?' I closed her fingers over her palm.

'If God wanted us to write he'd keep us in school. It's wrong, it is.'

'Perhaps we're the first, Betje. Perhaps he's changing his mind.'

Betje went quiet.

What have I said? I thought as we walked back. *These words change everything, even what I think.*

The next time I saw Betje, she did not want to write. She delved to the bottom of her basket and brought out a letter. The wax seal was cracked and broken, the paper yellowed and spotted. Her hand shook as she held it out.

'Here,' she said, not looking at me.

As I took it from her, her face folded with grief. When I went to comfort her, she raised a hand to stop me.

I opened the letter, glancing from it to her. It took a while to make sense of it. It did not begin *Dear Betje*, or *Dear Mr Hoek*, or *Dear Anyone*. There were a few lines of writing and a note, pinned to one side.

'What does it say? I've tried to read it, but I can't get it. I know it's about me. Saw my name on the front. Is it about my mother? It is, isn't it? Tell me, Helena, tell me!'

'It . . .'

I struggled to take in what I had read. The sun on the

paper, even though it was faded, hurt my eyes; the pain of the words becoming a pain in my eyes.

'Oh, Betje.' I let my hand fall to my side. She'd never told me about herself and now I knew too much.

'Read it!'

So I told her what was there, what it said. I showed her the title – Amsterdam Orphanage and Children's Home – and the date: 16 February 1605. All the while, she stared at a point beyond me, as if into the past.

'It's from the day you were taken to the orphanage. You were two.'

'Two?' Tears filled her eyes again.

'Yes. See, here, your mother's name, right here.' I stopped reading and looked up. My finger paused under the line I was about to read.

'Tell me!'

This child brought to our care by Elizabet Andringa – mother. The name was difficult to make out, the paper worn through.

'By my mother?'

'Yes. She brought you from Alkmaar.'

'Alkmaar?' She snatched the letter from me. 'Alkmaar! Where does it say that?'

I pointed to the word, so she would know it.

'There's no father, is there? I understood that much.'

'No. No father.'

She passed the letter back, pointing to a short note that had been fastened on with a small pin. 'What's this?'

The note was not signed. There was a crooked X – the mark of Elizabet Andringa, Betje's mother. I read the note aloud.

'Dearest Betje, I would never have let you go. You could not be hidden, you cannot be mine. Forgive me.'

I folded the letter again.

'She gave me up.' Betje buried her head in her arm. I felt pinched in too.

'Where did you find it, Betje?'

'They kept it, the Hoeks. They kept it from me.' Betje paced as she talked, dangerously close to the canal edge, but she seemed not to notice nor care. 'It wasn't *theirs* to keep, it's mine!' She slapped one hand to her chest. 'Alkmaar? Why bring me here? *Here?*'

I did not know. None of it mattered, not now.

'Betje, Betje. You need to take this letter back. Put it back where you found it. They'll throw you out if they think you've been taking from them.'

'They should not have kept it from me. Told me I was an orphan, same as Antje. I never was an orphan! My own mother brought me here – by herself!'

'Betje, listen!' I took hold of her shoulders to get her to stop. 'It's years ago now. Take the letter back. The Hoeks don't care, Betje. But they're your employment. Without it, what are you? Where would you go?' I hated myself for saying this – Betje needed kinder words – but it was true. 'Where did you find it?'

'In Mr Hoek's writing desk.'

I gasped. I looked at the letter as though it would burn me. 'What were you doing at his desk?'

'I wanted paper to write on.'

I thrust the letter at her. 'You're to take it back, Betje. Now! What's past is past.'

She snatched the letter away. 'I wish you never taught me!'

Anger flashed up in me, sudden and hot. 'And I wish you'd never asked!'

We stared at each other, miserable to our hearts, the shock of our words silencing us.

'Oh Betje, I'm sorry.'

She wiped her eyes on her sleeve; her breath shuddered through her, then became a small laugh. 'Alkmaar. I never knew. I'd never have known if I couldn't – if *you* couldn't read.'

Quay

BETJE DID NOT mention the letter again. When I asked, all she said was, *It's done with.*

One day, we'd started back from the fish market, alone with our thoughts. Betje stripped seeds from a clump of grasses by the verge, and blew them from her palm into the canal.

'You've got family. I can tell.' It was almost an accusation, the way she said it.

'A brother – Thomas.'

'Just one?'

I nodded. 'He's older. A sailor.'

'A sailor? You never told me you had a sailor brother!'

'Might as well not. He's in the East Indies.'

'The East Indies!' She twisted left and right, her hands on her hips.

'I've not seen him since he sailed. It's a year there, a year back. He left months before I came here. I don't think he'll ever come home.'

'You don't know that!' Betje said with a keen brightness. She'd had her own losses to think on.

'I went to the quay.'

'You went to the quay?'

I saw her surprise. I'd done something she thought I'd never do, not on my own.

'Who'd you ask?'

I picked at a scratch on my hand, making it bleed. I didn't want to talk about it any more.

'You can't just go asking, expecting folk to know.'

'No one had word of him.'

'You know the quay, do you?'

'Yes . . .' I already sounded less certain.

'You know that the ships that come in have to declare at the Custom House?'

When I said nothing, she clapped her hands. 'Ha! I knew it!'

Before I could say anything, or object, Betje had me turned in the opposite direction to Westermarkt. 'Come on!'

'Where?'

'The quay! We're halfway there. Unless you'd rather go on your own? We'll find the Custom House. They can tell us if his ship's been in. Come *on*, minnow – he may already have been and gone!'

She stopped and held out her hand. But what if he was still not there? What if the only news was news that he was lost? The worry sank its weight deep in me. Of the two of us, I was the one dragging my feet.

'*Come on.* More boats come back than not. Would I be working for Mr Hoek if they didn't? He'd not have me, *or* Mrs Hoek, *or* his fine house and all that is in it, if his boats kept showing their sterns to the sky.' She patted her bottom, to be sure I understood.

We had time. Mr Sergeant wouldn't miss me, only his plate if it was not on the table at suppertime. So I let Betje take my hand, and as we walked, she sang – a song I didn't know about a woman waiting for her lover. It was a long, sad song and she knew all the words. All I could do was hum as we went, a little out of tune.

I didn't know whether it was because of Betje's song, or the fact I missed Thomas so, but I decided there and then I'd never marry a sailor. I remembered how Mother and Father were when he left for the sea, how still they became as they held each other. I hadn't thought of it then. But how Mother had lived with not knowing if that goodbye would be their last, I did not know.

The day seemed made of couples. Some went by, arm in arm, hand in hand, smiling. Their happiness made me wonder. Others, I noticed, stone-set, as though they'd used up the words they had for each other and had none left. I supposed I would marry one day. The thought of a husband was a strange thing, as strange as wearing britches.

I looked for Thomas on the way, half hoping I'd see him, half knowing I'd not.

The day he said he'd signed to a trading ship headed for the East Indies, I felt I'd been pitched out to sea too.

'You can't go!' I said.

I looked at Mother, to see if she could keep him home. But how could she stop Thomas from doing what he said he was born to?

'Make Father proud, won't I?' he said and wrapped

an arm around her shoulders, squeezing a small smile from her.

'When you leaving?'

'Soon as I've registered. Means I'll be in Amsterdam before you!' He picked up the salt cellar and an apple from a dish. 'See here – this is Holland.' He placed the salt cellar in the centre of the table, then set the apple not far from it. 'And here's France.' He took a coin out of his pocket and slid it to the far corner of the table. 'And the East Indies – *that's* where the money is.' He tapped the coin with his finger. 'There.'

How small the world seemed, set out on the tabletop like that. But Father had been gone weeks at a time and then only as far as France. If the salt was Holland and the coin was the East Indies, then the line Thomas traced between the two would take months to cross.

'Don't fret! I'll be back!' He pinched my cheek, wearing his confidence in a wide smile. 'Look out for me in Amsterdam when you get there. Promise? I'm on the *Aemilia.*'

He wrote the name in charcoal on a scrap of paper and gave it to me. When I touched it, it smudged. That night, I copied it over and over again onto the palm of my hand, to be sure I had it, to be sure I never forgot.

Dear, rapscallion brother. How his eyes had glittered, something of the sea reflected there already. But when I took hold of his hand, I knew. I knew because I felt it. There was something about his grip, the way his gaze slipped from mine, that told me he might not be back. I should have hung on, hung on tight, but the moment passed and I let go. He slid the coin to the edge of the table, knocked it into the air and grinned as he caught it.

Promises, like coins, are brightest when new. A year there, a year back, he'd said – in two springtimes, then, he'd return.

I had gone to the quay, but there was no word. Some looked at me as though I was mad for asking.

'Two years? And the rest!' one sailor had said, when I'd explained where Thomas had sailed.

Then I realised, the promise he'd made was no more than a straggling hope; a talisman against the tempest; a length of string, floating on the water, left there so that he might one day feel along it and find his way home.

Betje had stopped singing. We'd reached Niewe Brugh and turned left towards the quay.

I could smell the place, hear it, before I could see it. A thick smoke hung in the air, from barrels of tar being boiled for caulking. The warm day had brought bucket after bucket out on deck; I watched men in amazement as they swabbed and mopped. It was busier again than the last time I was here, if that was possible; even the mast tops bristled with birds, squabbling over the best lookouts. I'd never seen so many ships, ships of all sizes, from all over the world, rafted together.

In the tussle and scrum, I felt myself squeezed thinner and thinner, as though being folded in on myself. My dress had no pockets in it to pick, but that did not stop such a nipping and riffling of hands as they tried to find whatever meagre item I might have hidden away.

'You know the kind of woman that comes here,' Betje said.

It didn't take me long to find out.

Pretty, pretty, one man said, bumping into me, grinning a line of black teeth. *Lovely piece of cod I have for you here,* said another, hands jiggling between his legs. *Do excuse me!* said another, catching hold and spinning me about. He doffed his hat with one apologetic hand and grabbed at me with the other.

'There, that's it,' Betje said, as we came out into a clearing, and pointed to a square red-brick building, set apart from the others. She must have caught the question in my eye, the question I was about to ask, because she added, 'Mr Hoek says all boats must declare at the Custom House. He thinks I can't hear when I'm serving dinner. But I can.' She crossed her eyes and stuck out her tongue.

Mr Hoek was a shipbuilder and had a small fleet of his own. Mr Sergeant was after his attention, a few guilders from his purse and filling his house with books. And I knew that because Mr Sergeant sometimes spoke as if my ears weren't for hearing with either.

Betje pointed to a forest of masts. 'There. East India ships, right there.'

I followed the line of her finger. There were so many ships. How did she know which were which? Betje tucked me to her side, took tight hold of my hand, and we set off again. She slipped through the crowd, pulling me along behind her. When a man tried to kiss her, she elbowed him away. She was like an eel sliding through water, nothing hindered her. I kept my head down and clung on – better to be the eel's tail than an elver.

After much pushing and shoving and angling of

elbows, we made it along the quay to the red-brick building. Betje went to go up the steps.

'No, wait.'

She twisted around. 'Come on.'

I looked at the coat of arms above the door, wrought with anchors and ropes. Beneath, chiselled into a stone plinth, the building's name.

'This isn't the Custom House, Betje.' I pointed to the sign and read it out. '*Masterful Guild of Shipwrights and Shipbuilders, Amsterdam.*'

'I don't know those words.' It was not an apology – just a simple truth. She shrugged. 'Well, what about there? Is that it?'

I looked over to where she pointed – *The Rope Makers' Guild.* Betje would have us in and out of every guild in Amsterdam at this rate.

We continued our way past a number of company houses. I read the names out to Betje as we went, but the Custom House was not among them. We followed the row around, away from the quay, to a square.

'Look, Betje! West India Company house!'

My heart skipped. It must be here, somewhere. Just then, a man in a red wool coat came out of West India Company house and made his way towards us. His coat fitted neatly across his shoulders – shoulder and hip linked by a swag of gold brocade. The coat nipped in at his waist, at the point where his sword rested. Brass buttons, polished bright, flashed in the sunshine. As he approached, he came alive with the clink of brass and buckles.

'Please, sir!' I called, but as he swung round, his gaze passed straight over my head. Then his eye dropped and found mine.

Betje tugged my sleeve. 'Come away!' she hissed.

If he heard, he paid no heed. He smiled. 'Hello. Are you lost?'

'No,' said Betje.

'Yes,' I said. 'A little.'

He looked from Betje to me, his smile more a look of amusement it seemed to me now. His thumb circled the hilt of his sword. Still he looked. Betje kneaded a knuckle in my back.

'Are you young ladies on your way somewhere?'

'Yes . . .' I said, 'almost.'

'Almost!' Such a laugh came out of him then; I'd never seen a mouth open wider.

'We're all right, thank you,' said Betje.

I glared at her. 'We're looking for the East India Company. Do you know it?'

'Aha! Spies! I knew it as soon as I saw you.'

His eyes were full of sparkle. I felt the sun, hot on my face. I couldn't stop myself. 'Yes. A man spy would be obvious, don't you think?'

My heart hammered so fast – these words, though I'd said them, had nothing to do with me. Betje tugged sharply at my dress. She was the only one not smiling.

'Indeed,' he said and laughed some more. He licked a finger and smoothed his moustache. 'Well, well, *ladies* . . .'

'We're going now,' said Betje, sounding more like me than I did.

He considered her as he might a child who had been told to keep quiet, then turned back to me. 'You are not quite almost in the right place. Vereenigde Oost-Indische Compagnie is on Kloveniersburgwal.'

Kloveniersburgwal, of course! I pictured it immediately. Although I did not need directions, I listened as he told me and repeated them back to him, stumbling a little, nodding and smiling when corrected.

'We know where it is,' Betje said. She had given up pulling my dress and now had hold of my arm.

'Any time, *ladies* . . . Look for the VOC! Can't miss it! But let me come with you. It is a pleasant walk. We could get to know one another. I—'

I didn't get to hear more. Betje had marched me away – we were already crossing the street. *Maybe I'd marry a sailor after all.* No man had smiled at me like that.

'Stop it,' said Betje, snapping the thought clean in half. 'You're headed for trouble, you are.' She clasped her hands together, eyes fluttering, showing me a truth I did not like. '*A man spy would be so plain* . . . Plain to me what he was after!'

I flushed. It hadn't been like that. As the sounds of the quay dropped away and the polite chatter of Herengracht took its place, my feet fell flatter with every step. The red wool coat, the bright brass buckles, became a garish fancy, blown high into the sky by the wind.

There was no mistaking the Vereenigde Oost-Indische Compagnie. Betje pointed to the letters above the door.

'VOC!' she said, reading them without difficulty.

Inside, a man in a black overcoat peered down at us from

behind a high desk. His waistcoat was pulled tight across his stomach, as round and hard as a turnip. I could not imagine him in a fine red wool coat.

When we asked for news of the *Aemilia*, he scowled. 'That information is not for the likes of you.' He coughed and spat the production into a dish on his desk, then took out a handkerchief and wiped his nose, covering his face.

Betje drew me to one side. 'Which way?'

I looked about. We were in a large entrance room with several corridors leading out from it. A recruitment stall was set out in the middle, and around this such a knot of men had gathered, pushing and shoving, vying for the recruiting officer's attention. Was this where Thomas had signed up to join the *Aemilia*? I hadn't time to think about that. I looked at the signs, all richly carved and gilded: *Chart Room, Library, Board Room, Registry.*

'Registry?' I pointed out the sign to Betje.

The man behind the desk sneezed, knocking his wig sideways, but if he fell off his chair, we did not see it; we were along the corridor and gone.

The Registry was smaller than I expected, with a table and room around it for only four chairs. One wall was lined with shelves and these held the registers – bound in the same pale pigskin as Mr Sergeant's books.

'See, Betje, how they're listed: A–E, F–H, I–M, N–R, S–Z.' They were listed by year too; the older the book, the grubbier the binding.

'It'll be quicker with us both.'

She pulled down a register from the shelf and flicked

through it, flipping pages backwards and forwards, then shut it with a thump.

The book she'd chosen was from 1622, years before Thomas had gone to sea. Hadn't she numbers either?

'Let me,' I said. 'You go see if anyone is coming.'

She pulled a face as she pushed herself up from the table. When I next looked, she was back in the room, peering at a map on the wall.

'See this, Helena?'

I glanced at the map, recognising it – Mr Sergeant had the same. It was bordered with pictures of men in baggy trousers, swagged in long robes, and women with veils and pointed hats that made them half as tall again. I could see why Betje was drawn to it.

Betje tilted her head as she read. 'EV-RO-PA. Europe? Is that what it says?'

'Yes.'

I opened a register for 1632. It listed the ships, their voyages, with dates of *Departure* and *Return*. I traced my finger down the page: cargo carried, the number of sailors and their rank. *Cargo – outward*: bricks, glass, wool, linens – *Cargo – return*: sandalwood, rosewood, teak, pepper, black cardamom and cloves. The poor souls who perished were listed last of all as *The Deceased*.

I leafed through, page after page, but could find no mention of the *Aemilia*.

I pulled down the register for 1633, the binding brightest of all from so little handling. I flicked through to the end, to the most recent entries, turning the pages quickly. There it was – *Aemilia* – Thomas's ship!

'I've found it!'

Betje went to the door and peeked out. Her eyes widened in alarm. 'Hurry up!'

I ran my finger down the list, my eyes trying to keep up. If only my finger could read instead.

'*Quickly*, Helena.'

Down, down, down the list I went, and then I had it: 7 August 1633, his ship had berthed in Amsterdam. *But that was last month!*

Then my eyes snagged on a note at the bottom. I'd not seen the like before. It was the shortest list I'd come across and had only three names. Any joy I felt vanished in an instant.

~ ABSCONDED ~

Henk Klaum

Isaak de Vriet

Thomas van der Strom

Thomas? Absconded? The words tumbled in a panic, but then Betje hauled me to my feet.

'Come on!' she hissed.

She snapped the register shut and then we were out of the room, walking, half running, ignoring the puzzled look of a clerk heading towards us.

He turned as we passed.

'I say, you two—' he called after us, but we did not stop.

By the time we'd made it to the end of the corridor, and turned the corner, we had our feet flat to the floor and were running.

Map

MR SERGEANT CALLED me to his study as soon as I returned.

'I wonder if you can explain this?'

In one hand, he held a bunch of old quills.

'And this?'

In the other, a cup, so badly chipped it looked as if the rim had been nibbled right round.

'I found them whilst looking for bread. In the bread pot. I go looking for a simple crust and find evidence of nefarious activity instead. As I did not place these items in the bread pot, I shall assume, unless you provide evidence to the contrary, it was you.'

I recognised them immediately: the quills with the pink-stained tips, the cup that held the – now dried-up – ink. I had been so busy learning spellings, I'd not used them for weeks. I stared at them now, almost as surprised as he. I kept bread wrapped in a cloth, not in a pot, but he wouldn't know that. I saw the pots he had been through, onions on the floor, parsnips and carrots heaped in a pile. He'd looked in most, it seemed, and come away hungry.

'Oh.'

'Have you been writing, without' – he searched for the words he needed – 'without my *say-so?*'

'I—'

'Hold out your hands. Hold them out. Let me see.'

I held out my hands in front of me. He narrowed his eyes and humphed.

'Other side.'

Both sides were clean.

'I gave you a slate. And chalk. For kitchen notes and such like.'

'Yes, Mr Sergeant.'

'I shall take them back if you have no use of them.'

'No, Mr Sergeant!'

'Yes, Mr Sergeant, no, Mr Sergeant,' he muttered. 'I'm not entirely pleased, Helena, you realise. Not pleased at all.'

'I'm sorry, Mr Sergeant.'

'I should think you are. It is your *function* to cook and clean. You do these well, I am happy to say. I do not pay you to be distracted,' – he peered into the cup – 'with ink.'

He began a lecture about the importance of not being distracted. He, for example, needed to weed out works of an inferior, even salacious, nature. And as tempting as they might be, whole days might be lost reading them, and with there being only limited time in the day and mental capacity to absorb, process and reflect . . .

He waved his hands in the air as he talked. He still had hold of the quills. They looked like they belonged to a bird on one of Mr Veldman's maps. A faraway bird, from a faraway place. *A bird of paradise.*

'I shall have to confiscate them, Helena. You have your slate and chalk. Quills and ink: they're for—'

It took me a moment to realise he was waiting for me to finish his sentence.

'Proper writing, Mr Sergeant,' I said. *Proper writing men do.*

'Indeed they are. Proper writing, yes.' He pulled his shoulders back. 'Exactly so.'

He held up the cup with the dry ink, sniffed it and pulled a face. 'What *is* it?'

'Beetroot.'

'I have to admire your inventiveness.'

He poured a little water into the cup, then, not having a spoon, stirred it with his finger. He wiped his finger clean on his trousers, dipped a quill in the ink and, taking a new sheet of paper, started to write. When he was done, he seemed pleased.

'Rather a striking effect . . .'

I looked at the page and Mr Sergeant's upside-down words. The colour seemed to have died in the cup as it dried up, the brightness lost.

'It is very pink when fresh.'

'I do not doubt it. However, for the purposes of illustrating our little *experiment*, I think it quite pink enough.'

I could not be in worse trouble. 'Mr Sergeant?'

'Yes, Helena?'

'What does *absconded* mean?'

'Run away, in fear of arrest. Why? Is it something you are considering?'

'No, Mr Sergeant.'

'Good. I shouldn't want that. Beetroot or not.' He held out the cup to me. 'Take it away, wash it.'

As I went to go, he called me back. 'I'd be pleased if you used your slate and chalk. In your own time, of course.'

'Yes, Mr Sergeant.'

I could not tell him my chalk was gone – half of it thrown into the Lindengracht by Betje. Now I had no chalk, no ink, no quills.

But writing had never been furthermost from my mind. Thomas hadn't just run away. He had *absconded*. He was in terrible trouble.

Betje walked with me to the Veldmans'. Thursday was Veldman day. Laundry day. Bite my tongue and not say a word day.

'What's with you? Is it Thomas you're worried for?'

I nodded. 'I don't know what to do. Where could he be?'

She blew out her cheeks. 'Nowhere near the quay, that's certain.'

I thought of where he might go. He wouldn't go home, I knew that. I could not imagine what Mother would say. The disgrace of it, only made worse now that Father had been lost. I did not know what difficulties Thomas had lived with, but Father must have endured them too. He hadn't absconded.

Abscond. For the first time in my life, I hated a word. I wanted it out of my head; I wished I'd never seen it.

'What did he say about the ink?'

I'd been over the story again and again with Betje, but for some reason she found Mr Sergeant's comments extraordinarily funny.

'He said it had "a rather striking effect".' I put on my Mr Sergeant voice as I said it, but was only half-hearted about it today.

It still made Betje laugh; the story no less worn from having been told before.

'As we neared the Veldmans', my step slowed.

'It'll be over soon enough.' Betje smiled gently. She knew my feelings towards this place.

I pulled a face. A day of washing and wringing and hanging and folding lay ahead. I liked errands, that's what I liked, Mr Sergeant's errands. Errands that took me all over Amsterdam. Laundry, I liked least. It hadn't taken me long to learn how to fold a sheet flat on my own – but once I'd mastered that, there was no way of folding it flatter. But Amsterdam, *Amsterdam*. There seemed no edge to it, to what waited to be found.

I'd been coming to the Veldmans' house every week for months now to help with the laundry. The arrangement rewarded Mr Sergeant with a half-jug of brandy. I had to carry it home with me at the end of the day – had to concentrate on not spilling a drop when I was fit to drop myself. If the level was a little low, Mr Sergeant would eye me sternly, the implication being I had either spilled it or had slacked in some way, making Mr Veldman mean with his measure.

I dreaded Thursdays. I still had all of Mr Sergeant's work to do, to squeeze in, so that the day felt as though two had been rolled up in one.

I said my goodbyes to Betje and traipsed up the steps to the Veldmans' house. I tapped at the door, hoping their maid, Jette, would hear. Sometimes I had to tap, tap, tap to get her attention. Tap, tap, tap! I sounded like a sparrow on the gutter, cleaning its beak. But I couldn't knock, not at this hour, with the shutters still closed and the Veldmans tucked up in their beds.

They presented grim company at the best of times. Company? There was nothing companionable about them: Mr Veldman; his wife; his son, Bartels; and his two daughters, Sofia and Cokkie, as brittle as sticks, whose moods, underneath the white linen, seemed made of fingernails and teeth. *Capricious* was how Mr Sergeant described them and, once I knew what the word meant, I thought him too kind.

Mr Veldman dealt in maps. He had maps of Paris, London, Edinburgh, Berlin. Maps of places and countries I'd never heard of – places that seemed made of dreaming, more imagined than real. On one wall he had a map of the world with fish big as boats, and trees topped with feathers, and cats the size of sheep curled up asleep. I thought of the fish that could swallow a boat whole, and I thought of the people who lived in those places, standing on hard ground like me. The map had lines drawn on it, showing the routes to the East. I imagined pulling the lines in tight, drawing the world into a ball in my hand.

Jette opened the door to let me in. She yawned and knotted her hair into a bun. She hadn't put her apron on yet. Neither had I. What the Veldmans didn't see wouldn't worry them. We nodded our greetings. Jette had three or four words in her at most. I soon worked out it was her way. Maybe the girl who first arrived here had once been full of chatter. And then, day by day, word by word, all of it had been lost.

Jette had lit the fire under the copper, to boil water for

the wash. I smiled my thanks to her and she smiled her thanks back.

Sofia and Cokkie never went out. Never on Thursdays, at least. Whenever I saw them, they were a picture of boredom: embroidery stabbed at; books kicked under chairs; their Bible, on its stand, left open at the same page. A virginal was bought and tinkled with tunelessly for a week or two. After that, it became a kind of desk. They arranged flowers in glum silence, breaking stems, snapping flower heads, foliage foresting the floor. Afternoons brought the sudden sounds of squabbling, and Jette and I would stop, look up, realise what was happening, then carry on what we had been doing.

Betje once said we were lucky and I hadn't understood. It was only by going to the Veldmans' that I learned I had a freedom his daughters didn't. They reminded me of the chickens I'd seen stuffed in baskets at market, eyes wide open in panic. Who would want to live like Mr Veldman's daughters? Cooped up? Confined? *Captive?*

Not me.

Whilst the washing boiled, I had to sweep Mr Veldman's study. He kept the room shuttered. I'd been scolded on my first day for throwing the shutters open.

'You stupid girl!' Mrs Veldman had shrieked and cuffed me over the head. 'The inks! The inks!'

The inks that she meant were the ones used to colour the maps he had on display. Light could fade some colours – red in particular. It seemed odd, to make a map that could only be squinted at in the dark.

Most times, he had something new hanging on the wall. This time, when I went in, I could not believe what was there. Even in the dingy half-light, I could make it out. A street map of Amsterdam! Oh, if only I'd had a map like this when I'd first arrived. Then, I could find my way only by following the main canals: journeys that took me in long straight lines, with letters and invitations to come and see Mr Sergeant's latest acquisitions – works by Jacob Cats, van Goudhoeven and Scriverius, as well as books imported from England and Germany.

I propped the broom against the wall and went to take a closer look. Whoever had drawn it must live in the sky and looked down on the city from there. He'd drawn not just streets, but every house, garden, market and church; almshouses and city monuments too. There were ships on the quayside; the tiniest of people in a line outside Noorderkerk; cattle grazed in the fields beyond the city wall. Each house seemed to stand up from the page. I touched my finger to it, to be sure it was flat.

My eye was drawn to ever smaller details: apples in the trees; linen shirts left to dry in the sun; windmills no bigger than my fingernail. I traced along Prinsengracht until I found Westerkerk. I counted the houses in the street, stopping when I reached Mr Sergeant's house. *Mr Sergeant's house! Ha!* I half expected to see myself airing bedding out of the window.

'Blaeu,' came a voice from behind.

Mr Veldman! I startled, the same as if he'd said *Boo!*

'Blaeu's finest, in my opinion. Absorbing, isn't it?' he said, not looking at the map, but at me. His moustache quivered. 'By all means, look.' He held out his hand in invitation, but I took a step back. I followed his eye to where the broom rested against the wall, then to the floor, still littered with papers and clearly unswept.

He stepped closer, close enough now for me to feel the edges of his words against my cheek.

'Haven't you work to do, Helena? Shall you return to Mr Sergeant with only a quarter-jug of brandy?'

'No, Mr Veldman, yes,' I said. I curtsied, picked up the broom and set to sweeping while he watched.

I wished I had Betje to talk to on my way back. I had to be content with my own company. At least I was used to it, knew the questions I liked to be asked and the answers best avoided.

– *How was your day, Helena?*

– Well, thank you for asking, it passed tolerably well – *tolerably well*: that's what Mr Sergeant said when what he meant in all honesty was *grim*.

– *And is that a full jug of brandy I see?*

– It would have been but I was docked.

– *Docked?*

– Docked.

– *And why were you docked?*

– For looking at maps.

– *Helena, Helena, will you ever learn?*

– (*ignoring myself*) An Amsterdam map, as it happens . . .

I blew out my cheeks. Then I saw him. *Thomas!* Ahead of me by about thirty strides, hands in his pockets, slouched down.

'Thomas!' I shouted. 'Thomas!' Brandy slopped from the jug as I ran. 'Thomas, stop!'

'Thomas!' My poor chapped hands prickled and stung. When I sucked on my knuckles, the brandy set my mouth aflame too.

'Thomas!'

He heard me at last and stopped. And I stopped too, though I'd not reached him. Had he grown taller? And lost most of his hair? As he turned to look over his shoulder, I saw a man easily twenty years older. A man who did not know me, who'd never set eyes on me in his life.

'Oh,' I said and took three or four steps back.

I turned away, the jug still clasped to me, its contents mostly spilled. A smell of brandy rose from my skirts.

All of Mr Veldman's maps surfaced in my thoughts at once, one over the other, becoming an impossible place.

Thomas could have made his way anywhere. Perhaps he had made Batavia his home. He was gone.

I threw what was left of the brandy – the jug, all of it – into the gutter.

AMSTERDAM, 1634

Wax

THE KNOCK AT the door was hard and ill-tempered, a *Get here quick* knock. It came again just as I reached for the handle, and fell into air as I yanked the door open. The man on the step held a book wrapped in cloth. He looked as though he'd run the length of Prinsengracht.

'Monsieur Descartes' lodgings?'

'It is.' I hooked a stray hair behind my ear.

'I have a book for him.'

'I'm afraid he's not here.'

His shoulders slumped.

'He will not be back until this evening. Is the Monsieur expecting you? I can give the book to him, if you like.'

He hugged the book to him. 'No! It is for Monsieur Descartes.'

'But Monsieur Descartes is not here.'

'I'll wait then, until he returns.'

'The book will be safe.' I held out my hand but did not open the door wider.

He snapped round at the sound of a carriage. He scratched his forehead, then the back of his neck, all nerves.

'I came as soon as I could. I know him, *have known him,* for years. *Please.*'

Please? I tried to remember when anyone had said that

to me – no man I knew. It did make me nervous to look at him, but it was obvious he was not going to go.

'You had better come in, Mr—'

'Beeckman. Thank you. Yes.'

Once inside, he went to the window and glanced left and right. He flinched when I went to take his cape.

'Forgive me,' he said and held it out to me. 'Is there somewhere I can sit?'

With Mr Sergeant away in Utrecht, I could not leave Mr Beeckman alone in the study. I led him across to the dining room, but when I turned to leave him, he followed me into the kitchen. He put the book on the table in front of him and rested his hands on top. Even sitting down, he seemed ready to spring up.

'Have you travelled far, Mr Beeckman?'

'Dordrecht,' he said. 'Via Haarlem.' He cast about the kitchen, his eyes settling on the remains of a loaf.

'Are you hungry?'

He nodded. 'Famished.'

I offered him salad and cheese to go with the bread. He ate with one elbow on the book, not breaking contact with it.

'Do you have wine?'

I poured him a half-glass from the jug. He motioned to me to leave the jug on the table.

'So, Descartes, will he be staying long?' He took a long drink from his glass, spilling a little on his shirt as he did so.

'That I do not know, sir.'

'*Sir*, is it?' He laughed.

He took another slice of cheese and tore a chunk from the loaf, leaving the crust. He filled his glass, drank it back and filled it again. If the Monsieur did not come soon, there'd be nothing left. But it relaxed him, enough at least for him to move his arm away from the book. When he caught my eye, I looked down. My attention did not go unnoticed.

'I expected him here. He knew I was due. I've come all this way. And now I've had to impose on your hospitality.'

He shook his head as if the three glasses of wine he'd drunk in quick succession were all the Monsieur's fault. Crumbs covered the book now, but he seemed neither to notice nor care.

'I suppose he has other visitors?'

I shook my head. In fact, now that I thought about it, Mr Beeckman was the first.

'That comes as no surprise!'

He stared at the book without blinking. I thought he was going to turn the conversation in another direction, but then he said, 'I hadn't thought I'd have occasion to see him again. I've known him for years; taught him once – a long time ago now. He'd tell you it was nothing more than *idle fancies*.' He tapped his head with two fingers. 'It is all his, you know. If he had anything from me, that is coincidence – how very *Descartes*!' He emptied his glass and filled it to the brim again. 'Thirsty, I apologise.'

'No, no, please . . .'

'We all begin somewhere. Me. Him. Even you.' He drew a line across the table with his finger. 'A nudge, a chance meeting, a conversation – so many ways to set a life in motion. There it is and now I am married with seven children. Then one day something stops you: perhaps the way the light is, on that morning of all mornings, and you think – is this my life? Is this what I'd intended?' He stabbed at the table with his finger. 'I'm sorry. Seven children, a good wife: I am fortunate.'

He was a little drunk, I thought.

His eye met mine. 'What is your name?'

'Helena, sir.'

'Well, Helena.' He patted the book and opened the cloth to reveal it. 'You do not know what you have in your kitchen. This is an extraordinary book.'

I looked at it. It looked like a book.

'Quite, quite extraordinary.'

The drink had slowed him, but he was in talkative mood, so I could risk a question. 'Is it a Dutch book, sir?'

'Dutch? Oh, no, no, no.'

'French?'

He laughed. 'Spare me! No. *Italian.* By one of the finest minds alive – Galileo Galilei.'

Galileo? I'd heard the name before, but could not think where.

'Your French guest pales somewhat by his side.' He leaned back in his chair. He had the certainty of someone who could say what they liked to someone like me in a place such as this. 'He is terrifying, don't you think?'

'Who?'

'Descartes, of course!'

'Well . . .' It was true he shouted at Limousin most days.

'I thought so. And still we do his bidding.' He stroked

the book as he thought. 'I've not seen him for years, have had nothing but insults from him, yet here I am with what he needs. Remarkable, really. What do you think that makes me?'

I shook my head.

'Either an extraordinarily faithful friend, or a colossal fool.' He emptied his glass in three gulps and wiped his mouth on the back of his hand, then kicked off his boots.

'Damned if I know the difference between the two. I will rest now. The Haarlem barge always exhausts me.'

I shut the door to the kitchen. What choice had I but to let him sleep? I could not cook with a man asleep in the kitchen. Dinner would have to wait.

Limousin returned first.

'*Mon Dieu*,' he said, when I told him who was waiting. He peeped around the door, then closed it again. '*Mon Dieu*.'

'Should I have sent him away?'

Mr Sergeant trusted me to manage the house whilst he was gone. He'd not wag a finger at the Monsieur, but I could see him wagging a finger at me – It is not as it should be, Helena.

The Limousin paced up and down, one hand on his forehead. 'There's nothing to be done about it now.' He peeped around the door again. '*Mon Dieu*.'

Nothing to be done? I could ask him to leave. Mr Beeckman too.

The Limousin waited for the Monsieur in the *voorhuis* and

was on him as soon as he came in the door. He fussed about, took his cape and hat and brushed at his shoulders. 'Monsieur, Monsieur. *Avez-vous passé un bon promenade?*'

The Monsieur shrugged him off. '*Arrête!*'

As I went to speak, the Limousin stepped forwards, straight as a pulpit. 'You have a visitor, Monsieur. *Mr Beeckman.* I did not say he could stay.' He flashed me an accusing look.

The Monsieur tilted his head as if he had not heard correctly and turned in a circle. 'Beeckman! The rascal! He came then! Ha! Where have you hidden him?'

'I'm sorry, Monsieur . . .' Then I stopped. To my surprise, he was smiling.

He opened the door to Mr Sergeant's study. 'Not in here.' He was across to the dining room in three or four strides. 'Nor in here . . .' He appeared to be enjoying himself. I remembered Beeckman's jumpiness. What had gone on between these two before?

'Ah,' he said and went down the steps to the kitchen. 'I might have known he'd be in here. Beeckman!' He swung the door shut after him with a bang.

The Limousin and I looked at the door, then at each other. We stood there for a while, not talking, waiting for a shout or a cry maybe – or for the house to fall down about us.

When the Monsieur came out again, he had one arm around Mr Beeckman's shoulders, the book tucked under the other. Mr Beeckman seemed to have shrunk.

'The wine, Beeckman, has fuddled your brain.'

Mr Beeckman shook off the Monsieur. His next words came out as if he had measured the weight of each one.

'You have until Monday morning, first light. That should give you plenty of time to take what you need from the work. All of us start somewhere, remember that. Some have the courtesy to acknowledge it.'

Then he bowed and went out, leaving the door ajar behind him, gaping like an open mouth. No one made a move to close it.

The Monsieur laughed, but shook his head. 'He's lost none of his charm since we last met. *All of us start somewhere?* Hear that, Limousin? And plenty remain where they began!'

He turned and went upstairs, Limousin still fussing two steps behind. As I closed the front door, I wondered what could bring a man so far, with such little prospect of reward.

There was no moon that night, the house so dark it seemed filled to the eaves with soot. A terrible clatter woke me, tipping me out of sleep. I could hear a scuffling sound, then a sharp crack as a pot splintered on the floor.

'*Merde!*'

The Monsieur! I let go of the clog I had hold of and clambered out of bed. A candle, nearly burned down to the stub, gave the only light. I could just make him out on the far side of the kitchen, crouched down, looking for something on the floor.

'Monsieur?'

He stood up, broken pottery in both hands, his legs bare

97

to his knees. He had a sheet wrapped around him, fastened at his waist with a strap; the strap, if I wasn't mistaken, was one of Mr Sergeant's belts.

'I need a candle, one candle, that is all. I cannot read without it. They're not where they usually are.' He brushed pieces of pottery under the table with the side of his foot. 'You have moved them?'

'Careful,' I said, taking hold of the broom, 'you'll cut yourself.'

He made no attempt to cover himself, nor move away, as I swept around his feet. I reached for a large pot on the mantel.

'Now that I think of it, four or five. Six is sufficient.'

I counted out six candles. Six was a good many more than one.

'Here,' I said and passed them to him. I thought of the pewter plate, covered with waxy thumbprints. Candles were not just for reading.

He lit a candle from the stub of the old one, twisting the end in the melted wax until the two joined together. 'I have made a discovery this evening. The effect can be seen only in the dark.'

A *discovery*? The word seemed made of sparks.

He set the candle down on the table and went around to the other side. 'See, there?' He pointed at the flame, his finger so close I thought he would burn it. 'Look. Can you see?'

I crouched down and squinted, not sure what it was he wanted me to look at. I stared into the flame and saw him on the other side of it. His lips parted as he concentrated.

'The flame is brightest at the very centre. There are two distinct coronas – blue, and red, then yellow – *c'est belle.* Beautiful, no?'

Corona – I whispered it, to be sure I had it. The night would not have the word off me like it had my dreams away. I stared at the flame until my eyes stung, but I could not see the colours he said were there. I saw him, and the flame between us, blue, shimmering. Then I saw that the flame was not just blue, but clear in the middle, above where the wick glowed red. I liked how candlelight gathered the room in, like a room inside a room – a much smaller place. The flame swayed. One breath would put it out.

'It's not the same as the colours we see around stars, the reverse, in fact.'

I wondered how he knew about such things, about starlight. He could not find his way around the kitchen in the dark.

'Candles can tell us much.' He picked up one from the bundle and tapped it against the table. 'Solid,' he said. 'What happens when I light it?'

'It lights a room.' I felt a fool for saying it.

'Indeed it does!'

Anyone who had lit a candle knew that! He seemed pleased I had said it. Did he think me stupid?

He stroked his chin, waiting for me to go on. 'Anything else?'

'It melts a little.' It was painful to say something so plain.

'*Oui!*'

He nodded gently, as though trying to draw the answers from me. So far, I'd said two simple things.

He held his hand over the flame then pulled it away.

'It becomes hot!'

'Yes. *And* . . .'

I shook my head. It was the middle of the night. My head felt full of moths. Moths with singed wings.

'Wax is solid, like this,' he tapped the candle again, 'or it can be melted – as you said. When wax melts, the colour, the smell' – he sniffed, running the length of it under his nose – 'all these things, *these properties,* change too. The properties are different and yet . . .'

I thought about it, about what was plain and simple, rolling the light and heat back into the candle before it was lit. Then I had it, as bright as the flame in front of me.

'It is still a candle!'

'It is still *wax* . . . and that is important.' He leaned forwards, letting the thought open up.

'Yes,' I said, but I was doubtful I had said anything of sense. He was still looking at me. I blinked and looked down.

'Enough about candles. It is late. You need your sleep, and I must read if I am to get Beeckman's book to him on time.'

He picked up the candle he had lit and went out, taking both discovery and light with him, leaving me to feel my way in the dark.

When I was back in bed, I thought of all the candles I had seen burn down to the stub. Discoveries must be all about us, waiting to be found, in the most ordinary places of all – even in candles and flames. I opened my eyes wide. Even this darkness must be *something,* I thought, and the thought came out as a laugh.

I yawned, tired after all. But when I closed my eyes, I could still see the candle burning. I couldn't wait to tell Betje.

There was no sign of the Monsieur the next morning, and he was still in his room by late afternoon, his lunch untouched on the tray by his door. When the Limousin knocked, he was shouted downstairs again.

'He says he's not slept. I thought I heard steps in the night.'

Limousin frowned. He was bored without his instructions for the day. He went out to the courtyard, then came in again. As soon as he sat down, he was up on his feet once more. He poked at the fire and sent soots across the floor. Then, not finding anything else to do, he slumped at the kitchen table and watched me chop onions for a soup.

He picked up a spoon, polished it on his sleeve and studied his reflection. 'Did I tell you I know the principles of mathematics?'

I ignored him. I halved an onion and chopped it into quarters.

'The Monsieur is teaching me his *method*.' He smirked and leaned back with his hands behind his head.

I wiped my hands on a cloth. 'Will you share it? Or perhaps you've forgotten? Well, never mind, if you have.'

That made the smile fall off his face. 'Most certainly I have not forgotten!'

He reached for a bowl of eggs, cleared a space on the

table and set out four eggs in a square. He took a ladle and placed it across the square from the top corner to the bottom, cutting it in half. When he was done, he stood back and admired his work.

'Triangles,' he said. 'They are not only the same, they are equal, in fact.'

'Oh,' I said, as disappointed as it was possible to be.

I considered the shape he had made. I had seen drawings in the Monsieur's room – lines that cut through circles, lines described by letters, triangles nested within squares, and everything neatly labelled.

'There's more to it than that, isn't there?'

He scratched his head. If there was more to it than the makings of an omelette, he did not know it.

I picked up a handful of flour and sprinkled it in a thin line, halving each triangle again and then again. 'The pattern repeats.'

'The soup will spoil at this rate.'

He swept the flour into a cloud, knocking an egg off the table. I had a mind to tell him to clean it up, but then word would get back to Mr Sergeant. Better to have no maid at all than one who argued and squirrelled away quills and turned good beetroot to ink. He'd sent Gerarda away.

Limousin carried the Monsieur's correspondence. He must have seen the Monsieur's papers when he was in his room. I wondered what he understood of the Monsieur's work. Very little, it seemed, from what he had just shown me.

'I have known the Monsieur since he was young. I know his tempers, his moods, his *foibles* . . . in these regards he is a man like any other. But he is different. *Exceptional.* I have travelled with him all over.'

Here came one of his army tales perhaps, or maybe the strange story about a dream the Monsieur once had, which sounded more like a fever to me. When I'd suggested that to him, Limousin had slapped his hand on the table and crossed himself.

'A turning point, more like! Nothing short of a revelation!'

I went over to the fire, and stirred together onions, vegetables and stock. Having my back to him meant I didn't have to talk and he could tell the story without interruption. He would be happy talking to a tree if he thought it was listening. Well, I could be a tree. A tree might be rooted into the ground, but didn't the wind that moved through it, the birds that nested there, come from afar? I'd never go to France, nor any of the places he mentioned. But I had eyes and ears – I'd seen maps and read Mr Sergeant's frontispieces. Little by little, I could bring these places to me.

But I mustn't interrupt, nor offer any thought or opinion, because then he'd shut tight as a mussel, tapped against a pan. So I listened to him tell me about Poland. Again. Sometimes a tree had to weather a grey day.

When the soup was ready, I poured it into a bowl. 'I'll take this up.'

'No, I'll do that,' he said, already on his feet.

'Yes, Limousin.'

If he wanted to balance the soup on a tray up two flights of stairs, then that was up to him.

*   *   *

I didn't know what was in that book, but all was not well. The Monsieur stayed in his room for two days and refused to see Mr Beeckman when he came to collect it. The Limousin had to give back the book on the Monsieur's behalf and make his excuses. No, Monsieur Descartes could not see him and would not discuss – he should write a letter if he had anything further to add. Beeckman tucked the book under his arm and scowled.

'Some call it plagiarism!' he shouted from the pavement towards the Monsieur's window.

'He outgrew you years ago, and you know it!' Limousin shouted back.

'I'll write then!'

'Write? *Allez vous faire foutre!*'

And with that, the Limousin slammed the door. He walked past me without a sideways glance. I'd never known such a carry-on; not even Mr Veldman's daughters behaved like this.

When the Limousin went up with food for the Monsieur, he was chased out again. I heard what sounded like a candle-stick being thrown and the door to the Monsieur's room close with a bang. Then silence. I had heard quieter thunder before.

I met him on the stairs as I took up a chamber pot. He looked as if he'd not slept for a week, one sleeve rolled up, the other down, and his shirt flapping loose at the front. He'd nothing on his feet. He came clattering down at such a rate that I thought he'd not seen me, and I had to flatten myself to the wall. But when he was by me, he stopped. 'Where's that imbecile, Limousin? Is he in?'

'*Non*, Monsieur.'

He turned to me in astonishment. '*Non*, Monsieur? *Non?*'

My heart jumped as if a hundred more hearts were jumping in it. '*Non*, Monsieur.'

I swallowed. His shirt had slipped at his shoulder. He was still trying to get his breath.

'*Tu est certain?*'

I nodded.

He looked at me, then at the pot. 'Ah,' he said. '*C'est mon pissoir?*'

I nodded again and held out the pot, feeling a complete fool. He took it from me, turned and bounded back upstairs.

'*Merci!*' he shouted over his shoulder, followed by something else about Limousin. I knew those words too, some of them.

'Where've you been?' Betje asked.

'Oh,' I said. I lifted my arms and let them fall back to my sides.

'Oh? What does *oh* mean?' She lifted her arms, higher than I had, and let them drop too. 'I waited today, I waited yesterday.'

'Well, sometimes,' I said, '*sometimes*, I am needed for other things.'

'I see.'

'Yes.' I turned away. I'd wanted to tell her about candles and wax and Mr Beeckman, but now hadn't good mood left in me for it.

'Will you come to market tomorrow?'

'Yes,' I said.

She looked so downcast all of a sudden. I swallowed and nudged her arm gently to show I was sorry, but she did not budge, not even a little bit; there was no give in her at all.

'I'll see you then, then,' I said.

'See you then, then.'

It was our way of saying goodbye. It always made us laugh when we said it, then laugh again, for laughing.

Now the words sounded as if we'd both had our fill – of each other, and of them.

Invitations

MR SERGEANT HAD plans in mind for a party. A soirée. He had been desperate to show off the Monsieur since he had arrived, but so far the Monsieur had slipped free, giving excuses that kept him away.

'I have a new strategy! A *fait accompli*, Helena.' He handed me a bundle of invitations he had prepared. 'He won't be able to refuse.'

I sorted the invitations quickly, building a picture in my mind of where I needed to go. I took a deep breath. Mr Sergeant's party would send me halfway around the city.

'Wait. Wait!'

I turned at the voice behind me and saw the Monsieur come running down the stairs, his cape on crooked. He struggled with the fastening on his glove; it was a wonder he did not trip and fall.

'I need a walk. I will walk with you.'

I looked at the invitations; there were so many to deliver. I pressed them between my hands.

'What is it you have there?'

He was talking for both of us, I realised. 'Party invitations, Monsieur.' There was no good hiding them behind my back, not now he'd seen.

He smiled. 'Aha. A *party*. Making plans without me?'

'Yes, Monsieur,' I said and flushed.

I looked at the half-tied ribbon on his cape. It surprised me to see him go out like that. When I glanced up, I caught his eye and saw mischief.

'Well. *Allons-y*. Lead on.' He held out his hand, palm side up, waiting for me to go ahead.

We stepped into the street. Once out of Westerkerk's shadow, we stopped to take it all in: Prinsengracht, bright and glittering – nothing still in the warm breeze. Barges, rafted together, bobbed and rubbed on their moorings; ropes slackened, tightened, chafed. Women walked by in light linens, sleeves and bonnets so fine they seemed made of mist. I shrugged off my shawl, suddenly too hot.

Swallows skimmed above the water, twisting and turning, tipping and dipping, before soaring into the heavens. I followed one until it was gone, envying it the blue width of the sky.

'This sunshine, after so much time indoors . . .'

Oh, I know. I knew what it was like to have a day go by and not see it. I stretched my arms, enjoying the feel of the sun. What was the hurry? Once the invitations had been delivered, that was not the end. There was always, *always* more work waiting for me, no matter how quickly I went, or how quickly I returned.

We stood there a while. I heard him breathe out.

'Shouldn't we go?' he said. 'We should.'

But though he said it, neither of us moved.

'There! See that?'

He pointed to a swallow as it came down and turned to follow it as it swept along the canal.

The pearl buttons at his neck caught the light. I knew from washing his collars that the buttons were there. Underneath, hidden away, his shirt fastened with three buttons more. I knew that as well. Knowing these things gave me a funny feeling. I glanced down, along the length of his arms to his hands. His sleeves narrowed in pleats at the elbows and tied at each cuff. I'd pressed the pleats flat only yesterday. As I looked up, he looked quickly away. Perhaps it was the sunshine, but I thought I saw more colour in his cheeks than before.

His hip touched mine as he shifted his weight. I stayed as still as I could, though where we touched raised a furious itch.

'The swallows are low today.' He looked at me and seemed waiting for my reply.

'They're feeding, Monsieur.'

'Well, yes, of course, feeding. I can see that.' He searched the sky, as if I had missed the point entirely. 'But see how they've come down?'

I nodded. This was something I knew without having to be told. Then I realised: *But he does not know why the swallows have come down.*

'They do, Monsieur.'

His eyes became bright with question. 'They do?'

We each seemed as surprised as the other. I thought everyone knew this much about swallows.

'There's rain on the way, Monsieur. First the wind brings the flies down, then the swallows follow them, and then comes the rain.' I brought my hand back to my side as I realised I was wiggling my fingers to show it raining.

He held up his hand, feeling for the wind. '*Un, deux, trois.*
I didn't know that. *Fascinant.*'

'Monsieur?'

'*Fascinant? Fascinerend* – fascinating.'

He pulled off his gloves and wove his fingers together as
he thought, then pulled them apart, gripped his hands into
fists and released them.

The wind had got up, driving the water on the canal into
small ridges. Not one of Mr Sergeant's invitations was
delivered yet.

'Monsieur . . .'

'*Bien.* Let's go. We'll see what weather those swallows
bring.'

Soon we were walking in step.

*Fascinant, fascinating, fascinerend; fascinant, fascinating, fascin-
erend.* I liked how the words were different and the same
– like brothers and sisters in a family. By the time we reached
the turning for Leliegracht, he was a little out of breath and
I had to slow down. He spent too much time in his room.

'Why so quiet? You need to be careful. Do you want to
end up like me, with nothing but thoughts for company?'

'No, Monsieur . . . yes,' I said, not sure if I had said the
opposite of what I meant and startled to realise he had been
thinking about me.

Apart from when I was with Betje, I had only my thoughts
for company too.

Then I remembered – *Betje! Oh, no.* I had left her waiting
again. There was nothing I could do.

I gripped the invitations and pointed to where we needed
to cross the road towards Herengracht. Once we reached

the other side of the road, we cut through a narrow alley onto Langestraat and came out again into bright sunshine. Two doors down, I stopped in front of a small townhouse: painted on the door, the name of Lemmens, the bookseller. That was the first of the invitations delivered.

'You know your way.' He sounded impressed.

'Yes.' I turned in a neat half-circle and my skirt swung out. 'I do.'

'Are you from Amsterdam?'

'Leiden, Monsieur.'

'Leiden?' He seemed cheered by this. 'I know it well.' He looked at Lemmens' door, then back to me and smiled. 'But don't you see what you have done? I can't extricate myself now.'

Extricate? I thought for a while what it could mean. And then I had it, the meaning of it. There, in the words around it.

'No,' I said, the word seeming to lift me off my feet. 'I don't think you can.'

He held out his hand for me to take the lead again. I did not need further invitation; it was all I could do not to skip. I took him along Brouwersgracht, where we crossed to the Jordaan.

'Read the names to me, let me see if I have the pronunciation right.'

'Noorderkerk,' I said, as we reached my church.

'Noorderkerk,' he repeated.

I thought he said it well. I liked how he rolled his Rs. I wanted my Rs to sound like that.

'Anjeliersstraat.'

111

'Anjeliersstraat,' he echoed.

'Tuinstraat.'

'Tuinstraat. Do I make a good pupil?'

'Dutch is not easy, Monsieur.'

He made a small bow. I had the feeling he was trying not to laugh. 'I'll take that as a compliment.'

I blushed.

He brought his hand to my cheek, but did not touch it. '*Et en dessous?* What is below? What brings such a pink? So many emotions: embarrassment, shyness, happiness.' He paused for a moment. 'Pleasure.'

My colour deepened. When I glanced up, he smiled. His eyes had a way of smiling too. I had thought him so serious, but maybe he kept something hidden in him, just like me. Were we, in some way, alike?

'Egelantiersstraat,' I whispered.

'Eg-el-ant-iers-straat,' he repeated, his voice dropping to a whisper too.

The argument over the book still troubled me. 'I'm very sorry about Mr Beeckman, Monsieur.'

'*Pourquoi?* You are not responsible for his behaviour. He was disagreeable then and is disagreeable still.'

'I should have made him leave the book.'

'The book? The book was the least of it. Maybe a little less wine is what he needs.'

'He drank a whole jug!'

'Sometimes one must tolerate *les idiots* to get what one needs.'

Idiot? It was just the same in Dutch as French. He must know I understood.

We had reached the flower market. Petals littered the ground, bright on the dull pavement. I thought it pretty and took a higgledy path so we did not trample them. Some stallholders had started to pack away; others were busy selling off their last flowers for a few stuivers. One pressed a yellow rose to the Monsieur's chest, but he held up one hand to refuse it. A man barged past us as he chased after his hat, blown off his head by the freshening wind.

'Bloemgracht.'

He did not reply.

'Bloemgracht, Monsieur.'

He looked around him. 'Do you know what draws me to this city, Helena?'

Helena? My name. He'd said my name. I'd never heard it said like that: *He-lena*. For a moment, I wasn't sure he meant me.

'Monsieur?'

'No one cares.'

Oh! I had not expected him to say that. Perhaps he saw my look, because he shook his head and laughed.

'No, you misunderstand. What I do, *who I am*, is of no concern: not to that flower seller over there, nor the merchant on his stoep. I am a nobody, lost in the crowd – safe in my bed when I sleep.'

He went up to a man, bundling together the last of his unsold flowers onto a small cart, and tapped him on the shoulder. The man, caught off-guard, wheeled round. I thought the Monsieur lucky not to be shoved aside.

'Excuse me. Do you know who I am?'

The man stepped back and considered him. 'Do *you* know who you are?'

'Ha! Good answer! Yes, I do.'

The flower seller shook his head and went back to what he was doing.

'And what if I told you the earth moved? That it was not at the centre of the universe? What would you say to that?'

It was the way he said it – a challenge, and no doubt about it – that made me worry. The man narrowed his eyes. He looked at the Monsieur, then me, taking in details now.

'Seriously?'

'Yes.'

He thought for a moment, leaned in and sniffed the Monsieur's breath. 'I'd tell you not to drink so much at lunchtime.'

'Is that it?'

He shrugged. 'That's it.'

The Monsieur turned back towards me, certain he had made his point. He linked his arm through mine, spinning me around and away – and any objection I had, any word or thought, all of it spun away too.

'Words, Helena, words are another matter. Words pin me to the page.'

His eyes searched mine, as though trying to decide what to say or whether to say it. *Please keep talking*, I wanted my eyes to say. *Please don't stop*. Then, with no warning, he swept his arms into the air. Whatever he was thinking seemed to be running ahead of him – and had made him wild.

'What's a book? Thoughts in my head. *Les mots*, written in ink, printed. Pages, gathered together and bound. Hawked by Mr Sergeant and his kind, but once let go into the world, a book is *incroyable*, Helena, an incredible thing – it has *force, consequences*. It can expose old dogmas, upskittle the stoutest clerics, split thoughts apart . . . *vlan!* A book: it can, *it must,* astonish.'

I had never known a book like the invisible one he was waving about. Mr Sergeant sold nothing like it.

He dropped his arms back to his sides as though suddenly exhausted.

I thought of the papers scattered across his desk. 'Are you writing a book, Monsieur?'

He laughed, but his laugh sounded hollow all the same. 'I was. Four years' work. But I cannot publish, not now. I suspected it last year; now I know for certain.'

What was he saying? It was terrible to think that nothing would come of his work.

Then an awful thought came to me. *It was my fault.*

'Is it because of Mr Beeckman? I'm so sorry, Monsieur.'

'It has nothing to do with Beeckman.'

If it was not Mr Beeckman, then it must be the book he had brought – why had I let it into the house? I scuffed my toe on the ground as I tried to remember what Mr Beeckman had said. Then I had it, and I remembered not only who had written it, but when I'd first heard the name too. Mr Veldman had mentioned the same to Mr Sergeant all those weeks before the Monsieur and Limousin arrived.

'Galileo!' I said, a little too loudly, so taken by surprise by knowing it.

'Galileo? What do you know of Galileo?'

I faltered. I knew nothing about Galileo, but I told the Monsieur what Mr Veldman had said.

'Mr Veldman is interested in Galileo?'

'He wanted to know what you think.'

'I'm sure he did! Anything else?'

I looked down. I'd already said too much.

'*Hmm?*'

'He wondered if you would publish, Monsieur.'

'Did he venture an opinion on that?'

I shook my head, not wanting to say it.

'Well, he was right! Suffer the miseries Galileo faces? I think not.'

'Monsieur?'

'He's under arrest. All copies of his book are ordered to be burned. I cannot place my words alongside his. Defend my words against the authority of the Church? That flower seller over there might not care, but if I wrote a word the Church disapproved of . . .' He shook his head as his thoughts took over.

I could barely keep up with what he was telling me. I thought of the glasses filled with water in his room, the candle stubs, his papers. I couldn't imagine anyone wanting to hurt him for writing about *wax*. And what of the sketches I had seen on his desk, the lines and circles: what harm was there in any of that? I wondered what was in Galileo's book for him to have been arrested and it burned. No wonder Beeckman had looked nervous – and I'd allowed the book into the house!

I looked at the Monsieur. His world was not mine. It went beyond Amsterdam and Holland. It pressed in too. It could reach in and touch him, here on the street, as flower sellers packed away their wares and swept their rubbish into the canal.

He lifted his hands and shrugged. 'I'll have to burn it.'

'Oh, Monsieur! No!'

I knew nothing about the meaning of his work. If the Church disapproved, then what was he involved with? Suddenly, Mr Veldman's warnings to Mr Sergeant all those months ago did not seem so misplaced.

'Or cut out the offending parts, mutilate the work to satisfy the *hawks*. I'm not prepared to do that.'

'Then keep it awhile, put it to one side, Monsieur.'

'And where do you propose I keep it?'

'In a box.' Where else did he think?

'A box?'

'Yes.'

'Hide the sun in a box? It's not possible!'

'It is if you keep the lid shut.'

He had no answer to that and there was not much more I could say about it.

We had reached Mr Veldman's house – his was the last invitation left to deliver. I heard within the unmistakable sound of an argument; the shouting could be heard from the street. I slipped the invitation under the door and dashed down the steps again.

As we made our way back, it started to rain – a small shower, nothing much, then the sun returned as bright as ever. The swallows had gone from the water.

'See,' I said, as we reached Mr Sergeant's step, 'now that the rain has gone, the swallows are back in the sky.'

We stood on the threshold. On one side of it, behind us, lay our walk together and, on the other, the day ahead and the work I had yet to do. It seemed such a thing to be standing there, as if I could see my life from all sides at once. One more step, and I'd be inside and on my own again. But this time would be different. I'd still have everything he'd said with me and for as long as I could remember.

He looked back towards the canal, into the distance – at nothing in particular, or perhaps at it all. He seemed not to want to go inside either.

'I needed this walk. It has done me good. I have learned something today – about swallows *and boxes*. Thank you, Helena.'

I was looking at his mouth as he said this. He'd said my name again.

He turned to me and smiled. Inside, all of me smiled back.

Crows

I WOKE IN the night and pulled the covers to my chin. Then, too warm, I huffed pillow and me to the edge of the bed where it was cooler. I rolled over. I dangled my arm out, then both my feet, and watched a panel of moonlight track across the floor and slowly fade as dawn lifted a grey, dull morning to the window.

It was no good. I had no sleep left in me. I kicked off the covers, swung my legs out and stood up. Embers still glowed in the fire from the night before. I threw on kindling, sending up strands of smoke and a flurry of sparks. Apart from the crackle of sticks, the house was still. The men would sleep for hours yet.

I drew my arms around me. I had an off-balance, unquiet feeling, the same as when I'd arrived in Amsterdam. I touched my hand to my forehead, but my skin was cool. I was not sick.

There was not enough light to read, but I held my Bible in my lap for comfort and closed my eyes. And then there he was, before me – *the Monsieur*. I pulled the memory closer and held it at the moment he looked up, the moment before he smiled, when his eyes were serious and then softened and . . . *and what?*

Stop it, I thought, and sat up straight. *People smile. They* smile when they're happy; some smile when they're not. Was the Monsieur any different? He had managed a smile for awful Mr Beeckman at one point, although that man clearly caused him pain. The Monsieur had smiled at me, and here I was, behaving as though I had found a guilder on the ground.

I stood up. But as soon as I was standing, I wanted to sit down. He would not leave my thoughts.

I went out in my bare feet and gathered up peat, stacking it along the length of my arm. I could carry twelve blocks at once like this, enough to keep the fire going until after break-fast. Today, I would need more – many times more than that. Today was Mr Sergeant's party. I dropped the blocks in a pile by the fire and went out to collect more.

Try as I might, though I counted the peat blocks out loud, and loudly at that, I could not push what the Monsieur had said from my mind. Books had force, he'd said. Books had consequences. Some books were burned and those who wrote them were arrested or worse. I had never thought he might come to harm.

It was not a *meal*, but a *banquet*, and help had to be hired in to prepare it. Help, when it came, arrived in the shape of a stout cook and her daughter, who was as pale and thin as an offering candle. They brought their own pans and ladles, and a cart laden with meats, fruits and vegetables. Any relief I felt went up the chimney with the steam from the stock pot. I was set to peeling and chopping: apples, carrots, parsnips, turnips, onions and garlic, plunging it all into buckets of water. By the time I had finished, my hands were chapped red; not even sucking on my knuckles could warm them. The cook found fault with everything and lashed out with her ladle, but by early evening the dishes were finished and set out on the kitchen table.

I stared at my hands, at the hot, cross cook and her beaten, sullen daughter. It was hard to believe that our miserable combination had produced this food: pork stuffed with prunes; minced ox tongue with green apple sauce; chicken with spices; oysters on a pewter platter; a porcelain plate piled with fat crimson pomegranates and rosy peaches. There were dishes of buttered carrots and golden parsnips, and nuts and candied ginger for the evening's end. It was as if we had managed to gather an ingredient from each of the ships docked on the IJ – and served up the whole world on a plate.

Then the cook and her daughter packed up their things and left. I was glad to have the kitchen to myself again, though I would be the only one serving and would have all of it to clean and put right once it was over.

I heard the sound of Mr Sergeant's guests gathering in the *voorhuis*. They brought in with them smells of tobacco, damp leather and a musty horse smell from their boots. Mr Sergeant's laughter sounded out above all the others, like a standard hoisted to the top of the house.

The meal started with a salad, followed by the meat and vegetable dishes. I served, then cleared, and kept the glasses filled with wine.

'Monsieur?' I offered the fruit to him, but he was in

conversation. He chose a pomegranate without looking at it. He went to place it next to him, missing the table with his hand.

When I came to Mr Veldman, he took his time, then selected a peach. He took a bite and sucked the juice from his wrist.

'Books are our trade. Words are what matter to us,' he said, in answer to a question from a crow-like man next him. Mr Crow waved me away without looking at the fruit; his hands held the edge of the table as a bird might a branch. He scowled.

'Without our money crediting their pockets, I think you'd find half your customers could ill afford books.'

'Without my maps to guide them, those captains would having nothing of worth to deposit with you.'

'Which came first, the maps or the money?' asked Mr Sergeant, leaning in, his smile rising higher as the faces of both men fell. He laughed. 'Neither, gentlemen, neither! Poetry came first and that is a most glorious truth!'

A cleric, who had spent most of the meal writing notes and then reading them back to himself, raised a hand and coughed. He coughed again and waited until the chatter either side of him fell quiet, clearing space for what he had to say. He shuffled his notes and began to read.

'Tell me, would I be correct in my understanding – that it is your belief – that everything is to be questioned, Monsieur Descartes?'

'Yes.'

He glanced up from his papers, as if he had not heard correctly. *'Everything?'*

'Yes.'

A murmur lifted around the table. Someone joked, 'Any fool can ask questions!'

'True,' said the Monsieur. 'But those who are open to learning, who question everything, are the better judges. They assume nothing.'

'Your work is for fools?' the jester persisted.

'No. I write so that even people who have not studied can understand my method. They can progress their understanding incrementally, step by step, starting with the simplest elements.'

'Ah, your *method*. The method of *doubting*.' Mr Veldman refilled his glass, took a mouthful of wine and swilled it from one cheek to the other. 'If everything is in doubt, what can be believed?'

'Truth – that which can be proven. God directs our minds to truth. Knowledge is insufficient. Knowledge is nothing without understanding. Doubting frees us from our doubts and takes us further than you may think. From this universal doubt, as from a fixed, immovable point, it is possible to derive knowledge of God, of yourself, of everything in the world.'

Mr Veldman tapped his fingers on the table; either what he had heard, or what he wanted to say, had made him impatient. 'Such *modest* claims, Monsieur Descartes.'

Someone sniggered.

Mr Veldman raised his eyebrows and smiled. 'Can everyone learn from your *admirable* method?'

The Monsieur folded his napkin, placing it on the table. 'Yes. Everyone. Certainly.'

'Everyone?'

'Yes.'

'Women, even?'

'Yes, even women.'

A roar went up around the table. A glass was knocked over; red wine ran across the cloth like a gash.

'What, even this maid?' Mr Veldman pulled my sleeve, bringing me up sharply to the table. He tightened his grip. 'Come here, Helena, tell us what you know. You are an expert on maps, I believe.'

Another roar of laughter. I glanced up. The faces seemed to run into one another, and all of them laughing except the Monsieur and Mr Sergeant, who looked startled at the turn of events. Some slapped their thighs, others banged their hands on the table. Shame flooded me. The room pressed in, smelling of wine and smoke, and bitten fruit. It smelled of men, and all that was theirs.

'Mr Veldman, please . . .' said Mr Sergeant, struggling to be heard above the hubbub.

'Yes, even a maid,' said the Monsieur, his voice rising.

Mr Veldman snorted but let go. 'Ah, women,' he said. 'Tell me, how do you find our women, Monsieur? Do they compare favourably? Plain, humble and honest, would you say, or too cold-blooded and dampened by our northern climate for your liking?'

'*Pour qui vous prenez-vous?*' The Monsieur pushed his chair back from the table.

Mr Sergeant stood up and tried to pat down the row. 'Gentlemen, gentlemen,' he said, 'there are many questions in this world to which we do not have answers. Least of all the question of women.'

As laughter erupted again, Mr Sergeant's face shone with relief.

'Now, *Messieurs*, please join me in thanking our honoured guest, Monsieur Descartes.'

He raised his hands above his head and clapped. As all around the table joined in, the Monsieur rose from his seat and bowed. I turned and was out of the door before the clapping had stopped.

And then, the evening was done with and I was not needed any more. I was glad of it. One by one, sometimes in twos or threes, I heard them go and then, finally, Mr Sergeant and the Monsieur on the stairs as they went up to their beds. I had the pans to scour before I could sleep. The fire had settled to a deep amber glow. I stifled a yawn, tugged open a sack of straw, screwed up a fistful in my hand and started on the largest pan.

'So here you are.'

I startled and turned, seeing a man silhouetted in the courtyard door. *Mr Crow*. He pulled up a chair and straddled it. The silver buttons on his cape glinted in the candlelight – a line of eyes watching me.

'Have you forgotten something, sir?' My throat felt as dry as the straw in my hand.

He picked at his fingernails, then held out his hand to inspect them. 'Remind me of your name, maid.'

I continued to scrub and did not look up.

'Let me guess. Maria, Catharina? *Hagar?* Ah, I remember now. *Helena.* What ambition your mother must have had, giving you a name like that. Such a pity to squander it in a place like this. I've been watching you, Helena. Let me take a good look at you.'

His stare was blunt, flattening. I drew my arms around me, huddling into myself.

'You are not what I would look for in a maid.'

He shuffled the chair towards me, close enough now to lift my chin with his finger. I jerked my head away.

'Now then.' He caught hold of my skirt, yanked it, tipping me off balance. 'That's no way to treat a guest.' He pinched a finger and thumb either side of my face and trailed a wet kiss down my cheek, his mouth like a slug.

'No!' I twisted away, but he lurched forwards, his chair clattering to the floor. He grabbed my hands and stepped me backwards until my head hit the wall. He turned the heel of his hand on my breast, making me buckle under his weight.

He groped at the fastening of his breeches, then pushed my hand in, squeezing my fingers around the lump.

'Take hold,' he said. 'Hold it, damn you.' He held his hand over mine to lock it in place.

'*Qu'est-ce que vous faites?*'

It was Mr Crow's turn to startle. As he clutched at his breeches, I staggered away from him.

'Helena?' said the Monsieur. He came towards me, his brow furrowed with concern, but I shook my head and drew back into the shadows. What had he seen? What would he think?

126

'*Helena*, is it? Been here before me, have you?' sneered the crow.

The Monsieur spun round on one heel. 'Mind your mouth!'

'Fuck off, Descartes. This isn't France.'

I pulled at my sleeve where it had ripped. I rubbed and rubbed my hand on my skirts to get the feel of him off.

'*Morceau de merde!*' The Monsieur ducked out of the way as crow man swung at him.

'*Please*,' I said, horrified. 'Mr Sergeant will hear.' If he came in and saw this, it'd be me out on the step.

The Monsieur threw open the yard door. 'Go home, *fool*.'

Crow man stuffed his shirt into his breeches. 'Me the fool? Look at you. The pair of you. A maid who would know everything, and the French doubter. The world has gone mad.'

At that, he grabbed his cape, elbowed his way past the Monsieur and went out.

The Monsieur picked up my shawl from the floor and held it out for me. As I went to take it from him, he wrapped it around my shoulders and only after some time did he set me away from him.

'You won't tell, will you, Monsieur? Please, Monsieur, say you won't.'

He shook his head. 'No, nothing.'

And then he went back to his room and only afterwards did I wonder. The door had been closed. He'd not have heard what was happening from the top of the house. Why had he come down to the kitchen?

* * *

My shadow had more to it than me, as if my ghost had been set to work in my place.

I moved through the house when everyone else was busy so I would not be seen. When Mr Sergeant was in his study, I tidied his bedroom; when the Limousin and the Monsieur went out, I found the dirty clothes and washed them. I prepared a lunch that could be left at the table and cleared away only once I had heard the last chair pushed back into place.

I hated my hands. I scrubbed and scrubbed them, but they felt no cleaner. I thought of the Monsieur. Then I thought, *Can a man who is gentle also be unkind? Weren't all men threaded from good and bad? But Eve had sinned; all suffering came from her. Weren't women the most wicked of all?*

And when Sunday came, I went to church and stood in the straight light. It passed over me as though I was not there.

When I next saw Betje, she wanted to know all about the party. I told her there had never been food like it – the fruit must have cost more than my wages for a year. She laughed as we worked out my worth in pomegranates. But Betje knew something was wrong. I had tears in my eyes, without a word being mentioned about the crow man, or Mr Veldman's unkindness.

'What happened, Helena?'

I shook my head, my hand on my chin to stop it trembling.

'Helena, Helena,' she said, but that only made me cry.

When I told her what had happened, all she said was, 'You had a lucky escape.'

Escape? I thought of Gerarda and shuddered.

'Will he tell Mr Sergeant?'

I shook my head. 'No.'

No. The word silenced us.

Betje squeezed my hand and let go. 'He sounds very . . .'

'Kind,' I said, finishing the sentence for her.

'I was going to say, *gallant.*'

Where had she found a word like that? We laughed, and I cried some more.

I did not tell her the Monsieur had held me. I did not tell her I'd heard his heart.

Words

I WAS NOT to go to Mr Veldman's house again, Mr Sergeant said. From what I could learn, it was not his treatment of me that had caused offence, but his *refusal to desist* when asked to do so.

'I do not care to be made to bawl like that . . . He's made me quite hoarse.' Mr Sergeant gave a small, high-pitched cough and patted his chest. 'See?'

When Thursday came round, I went out to find Betje. I did not want to leave her waiting.

'How will he manage without his brandy?' she asked.

'The Monsieur has found him another supply.'

'The Monsieur, *the Monsieur*.' She winked.

'Betje!' I was shocked she could think such a thing.

She nudged me with her elbow. 'You've gone red.'

'I haven't!'

She skipped ahead, then turned so she was skipping backwards. 'Have so!'

'Haven't!' I made a dash for her, but she was off, running, her laughter about all I could catch.

Mr Sergeant would be away for two weeks, he said. He would travel with the Limousin to Leiden. He had publishers to meet and the Limousin would see to the Monsieur's affairs. Mr Sergeant would then go to Utrecht; Limousin would stay on in Leiden.

Leiden? My heart lifted. I'd let Leiden drift from me, had done nothing to pull it back. Mr Slootmaekers, when he came by for his fee, brought no news. *You'll hear soon enough if there's a problem,* he said. I thought about all I had to tell Mother. There was so much to tell – and just as much I wanted to keep to myself. But I wanted her to know I was well, and I wanted to know how she fared.

'Excuse me, Limousin?' I tapped him on the shoulder. 'Limousin?'

He shrugged my hand away. 'What?'

'Can you take word to my mother, let her know I am well? And bring me word back?'

He frowned.

'Please, Limousin.'

I did not like to ask anything of him. He needed everything to balance – if not at the end of the day, then at the end of each week – as if he carried a scale in his head to keep tally.

'You have this in a note?'

I had no paper. He knew that. I shook my head. 'She cannot read, not without help.'

'Then no, I don't think so.'

'She lives on Hoy Gracht, on the corner with Lange Nieustraet.'

'The Monsieur's schedule allows no time for diversions. A note can be delivered. A conversation – especially with a stranger, in another tongue – is difficult. It takes time.'

'Please, if you can. Hoy Gracht,' I repeated, in the hope he would remember.

'Limousin?' The Monsieur came running down the stairs with a bundle of letters. 'Here,' he said and handed them to him.

I looked at the letters with bitter envy as the Limousin slipped them into his satchel. If only my message could slip in there too. How easily their words moved. Mine were stuck here with me, glued to my tongue.

The Monsieur embraced him. '*Bon voyage. Portez-vous bien, et à bientôt!*'

Then, in the time it took to turn the horses around, the Limousin and Mr Sergeant were gone. I went back to the kitchen. My mood darkened, gathering in black and heavy. I broke a plate, cutting my hand across the palm. The water pump was stiffer than ever, and I soaked my feet and muddied my hem. I emptied the chamber pots. This was my life: blood, shit, mud, and there was no escaping it. I banged the copper pans together over the fire. There was thunder in the house, though the sky was as bright and blameless as a high-summer's morning.

I set the Monsieur's place with a knife and spoon in the dining room. I placed him at the head of the table, where Mr Sergeant normally sat. At dinner time, I brought him soup, then a plate of dumplings in cream and parsley with mushrooms.

'Smells delicious. And you? Are you not eating, Helena?' He motioned towards the seat next to him.

'I eat later, Monsieur.'

'But I insist. Bring your plate,' he said, not letting his hand drop.

I shook my head. 'Mr Sergeant has rules.'

'Mr Sergeant's *English* rules! What other Dutch house behaves like this? I don't wish to eat on my own. Come, Helena. A plate of food. The world will not stop turning. I'll not tell Mr Sergeant if it does.'

Oh! Did he say these things to vex me? *The world does not move!*

Still he held out his hand. He looked at me, not minding, quite patient, as I considered for and against.

I could not ask Mr Sergeant, he was not here. He'd never said, *Helena, you are not to eat at this table.* But neither had he invited me to do so. Who'd made the rule, then? Him or me?

I nodded and went to fetch my plate, sitting one place further away than where he showed me. If I ate quickly, I could be done with it and gone. I perched on the edge of the chair, my feet flat to the floor, to be sure I did not tumble, should the ground suddenly fall away. I glanced up at him, at the picture on the wall behind. Neither had shifted, not a bit. He was still where he was when the meal began. Every time I looked up to check, I saw him watching. In the end he said, 'You're frowning.'

I went back to what was on my plate, chopped a dumpling in half with my spoon and scooped it up.

'You'll give yourself hiccoughs. Slow down.'

And now he would tell me how to eat! I shifted on the chair a little, eased out my legs. I tipped out what was in my spoon and took a sip of the sauce instead.

'Ha!' He made a great fuss over a sliver of mushroom, eating it as though it were a dainty treat. After that, he broke off a chunk of bread and swooped it around his plate, picking up sauce and mushrooms and the last of a dumpling, and ate it in one. He licked his fingers in turn. I'd never seen the like of it, not from a lodger.

'See, I'm not finicky like Mr Sergeant.' He sat back and pushed the empty plate away from him.

I blinked. The plate shone. 'Monsieur?'

He picked up his knife and pretended to slice something smaller and smaller, until only a morsel remained. He peered at it, then held it from him, as though he had fished up the last herring from the bottom of a barrel.

'*Kieskeurig!*'

'*Exactement!*'

'*Fin-nincky!*' The word seemed made of prickles. What he'd said of Mr Sergeant was true. He did like everything to be *just so*.

But now the meal was done and all eaten. I sat there, and he sat there, both as empty of something to say as our plates were empty of food. I should clear the table.

I would clear the table.

Clear the table, I told myself; he would be waiting for me to.

I rose to my feet and reached for his plate.

'Please, there's no rush.'

I shook my head and sat down.

'I—'

'Are you recovered, Helena?'

Recovered? I had to think. Then I realised: *crow man*.

'Yes, Monsieur,' I whispered.

'Good. Good.'

He looked at me for a while. I hoped he wasn't thinking on that night. Perhaps he was considering what to say next. Did he think in French first? Then in Dutch?

'I've heard you can write, is that true?'

Goodness! Who ever had told him that? 'No. No I can't.'

'No? I had quite a story from Mr Sergeant when I asked about the quills in his room.'

Oh. After all the fuss, Mr Sergeant had thought them too pretty to throw away. He'd kept them in a glass on his desk, and that helped keep the story fresh. From what I'd heard, he'd told half of Amsterdam, seemed eager to remember, when I'd done my best to forget. And now he'd told the Monsieur.

'I can't. Not really.'

'Not really? Either you can, or you can't.'

I thought of the papers in the Monsieur's room, scattered over the table. His careful handwriting; important words that needed wax to seal them.

'Only like this.'

I wrote a word on the palm of my hand with my finger. Was that writing? It was a nothing word, that's what it was. Invisible. Were any of Mr Sergeant's books written with invisible ink? No, they were not. I closed my hand over it.

He picked up the salt cellar, tipped the contents on the table between us and spread the salt out quickly with his hand. *Helena*, he wrote, with the tip of his finger, then smoothed it over.

'Here,' he said and invited me to do the same. I was glad Mr Sergeant was not here to see. 'Show me.'

Dekart, I wrote. I did not know how to spell *Monsieur*.

He smiled. 'See, you can write.'

I scooped the salt into a small pile. 'It's not the same.'

'No?'

'I don't have paper . . . nothing to write with.' I felt a flash of anger as I thought of the quills Mr Sergeant had taken from me.

'Where did you learn? School?'

I shook my head. 'Girls are not taught that.'

'How, then?'

I looked at my hands. 'I taught myself, Monsieur.'

'Well, that makes you remarkable.'

I pushed back my chair and stood up, stacking plates and bowls in an untidy tower. No one had ever said anything like that to me before. 'I must do my work.' I hadn't meant to sound sharp, but I felt as if I had a bird in me, a bird that now insisted on taking flight.

In the kitchen, I put it all in a bucket, then sat on my bed. On the shelf was my Bible, the brooch and the drawing of the rose stem in the glass. I reached for the drawing and looked at it again. He had given me this and something more besides – a feeling I could not explain. I imagined what it would be like to write all day, for the day to be filled with words. How incredible to spend your days like that. Not to have to draw water, or lay fires, or cook, or polish or sweep or scrub.

I sat up with a start as the Monsieur came into the kitchen. He had paper and ink and quills and he set them down on the table.

'Here,' he said, without looking at me.

'Monsieur?'

'Here. Come here.'

I went over to the table and sat down in front of a blank piece of paper.

'*Prends!*' He held out a quill. 'Take it.'

I let it rest between my fingers, enjoying the slight feel of it.

'You're going to learn,' he said. 'Write.'

I dipped the quill in the ink so that it took up a black bead of liquid, as bright as bird's eye. I wrote my name. My writing was not as clumsy and ugly as it used to be, but still not what I wanted, what I knew it could be with practice. The nib caught on the paper.

I slumped over the page. 'I can't . . .'

He slapped his hand on the table, making me jump. 'I will not hear that word! Write!'

I closed my eyes and thought. How did I write, before all this? I thought about each letter and searched my mind for their shapes. I had to make the quill become my finger, and the paper the palm of my hand. I opened my eyes and started again.

'An improvement,' he said, when he saw it, though he still did not sound pleased. 'But you can do better. You can read more than street names, I take it?'

'Yes, Monsieur.'

He went across to my bed and took the Bible from the shelf. He opened it in the middle and tapped a finger on the page. 'I want to see a fair copy of this by the morning.'

'All of it?'

'Every word.' He pointed to the ink and quills. 'These are yours. You are to tell me if you need more. *Compris?*'

I nodded, too surprised to say anything.

I worked into the night to finish. In the morning, he seemed happier with the result. He set me another task, then another – each time more satisfied with my progress than before. I wanted to show him I could do it. The feeling it gave me bloomed inside.

I worried about the paper I used, how much it cost.

'It is my work,' he said. 'There is no cost, not to you. I want to know whether you can do this, if you are *capable of learning*. That is all.'

I put down the quill. I had not thought that – that he would study me.

'When I look at what you have achieved, it is remarkable.'

'There's nothing remarkable about me, Monsieur.' I said this with more bitterness than I intended. I did not want it: him studying me. I pushed the chair back from the table and stood up.

He let me stand. He did not tell me to sit down. 'I bring you these things so you can write. . . and *you* are angry with *me?*'

I gripped the table to stop myself from saying any-thing I shouldn't. I sat down and picked up the quill. *I'll show you*, I thought, and I realised I'd seen exactly the same stubbornness in Betje.

'Good,' he said. 'Continue.'

He asked me to calculate numbers, quickly in my head, and seemed surprised that I could – but it was no different to what I did each day at market. He talked about knowns and unknowns. Some things were certain, he said – a square having four sides, for instance.

'But the world is not only made up of squares!'

His eyes brightened. 'Indeed.'

Many things could vary. He called these *variables*. *Unknowns.* He sat beside me and opened a sheet covered with his neat writing.

'Limousin struggled with this. Let's see if you can make more sense of it. Let's work out what your cost is to Mr Sergeant. How much are you paid?'

I looked away.

'Any number will do. Let's say six guilders.'

Guilders! I liked these numbers of his; he'd made me head of the household!

'This is a known. Let's call it a. a equals six guilders. Now, how much does it cost Mr Sergeant to feed and house you, do you think? Let's call that x.'

I had to think. It would cost more in the winter than the summer, when the house had to be heated and meat was expensive. I needed a new woollen stole to keep warm. He watched me as I tried to work it out. But it was a struggle. I didn't want him to think me stupid.

I shook my head. 'It costs less in the summer than the winter, Monsieur.'

'*Exactement!* So the cost is variable, depending on the time of year.'

Now I understood. 'Different in the summer and winter!'

'Yes. x describes a *variable*.'

He unrolled a page of shapes – circles with lines running through them, each point labelled with a letter.

'What is interesting is when we apply this further to lines and shapes, to *geometry*. We can use *a, b, c* for what is known; *x, y, z* for the unknown.'

His hands moved across the page, drawing shapes as he explained. I didn't understand much of what followed. I looked at the numbers and letters, and saw how they brought him alive.

He came into the kitchen when he wanted, papers bundled in his arms. Never in the mornings, sometimes quite late in the evening. I had to stop what I was doing, pay attention, write. Mr Sergeant, still on his travels to Utrecht, could not be asked for his say-so.

He adjusted the quill in my hand. 'Centre it, like this. *Oui, comme ça.*'

He was determined.

'Like this, see.' He turned the quill again.

After a week, he said, 'You have made progress.'

I looked up from what I was doing and pulled a face.

'You think you haven't?' He slapped his hands on his legs. 'Oh, what a look! Have you nothing to say? Talk to me, Helena! You do not need permission. I like it when you talk.'

I put down the quill and held my hands in my lap. I would have talked, but my words had fled. *What am I doing here?* I thought. *Learning? Is that all?* No, Monsieur, it was not all. If he wanted me to talk, I would say it.

'I want to learn, like my brother, like any man does.'

'I have met many foolish men! And worse than a foolish man is the man who believes himself wise, having learned only foolish things. Much of what is taught – much of what I was taught – is useless.'

'I do not want to be a foolish man!'

'You'll never be that!'

My cheeks burned as I realised what I'd said. I felt as foolish as I ever had.

He took a breath and let it out slowly. 'But maybe I am. I do not put myself above anyone. I've never supposed my mind was beyond the ordinary. We need to be more open to surprise – to wonder. I include myself in this. The learning is mine, but it's yours too. Let's see what can be done this next week and what I might learn from you.'

Him, learn from me? Only by turning everything upside down. Stand it the right way up again, and I was the maid who cooked his food and he the Monsieur, with time to think. And yet, when I looked at what lay between us, at the line on the ground that separated us, I saw it fast disappearing.

We had a week before Mr Sergeant's return. The Monsieur must know, as well as I did, that all of this – this learning – would have to stop.

'Mr Sergeant . . .' But to say what I needed to would be to say too much.

'Mr Sergeant is busy enough without being troubled further, don't you think?'

So that was it. This was ours, between us and no one else. I picked up the quill and turned it to centre it.

'Très bien,' he said, when he saw what I had done.

'*Merci,*' I replied.

Had I known, before I said it, how it would make him smile? And how his smile, when he smiled it, would make my heart lift?

Snowflakes

WINTER ARRIVED EARLY on an easterly storm. I woke the next morning to snow. When I went to fetch kindling, I found the sticks frozen together. I chipped away at the pile until I had freed a handful, but barely enough. They'd have to do. If I stayed outside much longer, I'd freeze into the wood pile too. The fire, when I lit it, took an age to take hold. Cold pressed in from the corners of the room. I went to the window and looked out. It was still early, but already children were throwing snowballs. I folded my arms and turned my back, but their laughter kept pulling me round. They looked so happy. I longed to be out there too. No, I told myself, I ought not. It was contrary to want to – hadn't I only just managed to get warm?

Then, I could bear it no longer. I pulled on my boots, grabbed my shawl and pinned it with my brooch. I wouldn't be long. I'd just take a look. If I didn't throw a snowball, I couldn't be accused of playing.

I dashed to the door and threw it open. The sight of Westermarkt, covered with snow, stopped me on the step. I looked left, then right. Everything sparkled – windows, railings, the stone step at my feet, even the brass knocker on Mr Sergeant's door. My breath drifted away from me in clouds, and if I could have caught it again, I'm sure it would have sparkled too.

I took a step and felt the snow cuff my ankles. I slid my feet slowly forwards to find my grip, like a small child just walking. I held out my hand as I went and watched the snowflakes settle on it.

'Like ice flowers. Or ferns, or feathers. Each one has branches,' said the Monsieur, coming up by me. I dropped my hand to my side, but he lifted it again.

'Look,' he said.

He still had hold of my hand as I brought it close to my eye. Yes, I could see branches; tiny, tiny branches of ice. 'Four, five . . .'

He levelled my hand with his eye and blinked to focus, but he was too close and his breath melted them.

The snow fell more heavily, clumping in large, soft flakes.

'Keep your hand there,' he said. 'That's better. Four, five, six. Six radii. Perfect hexagonal structures.'

Hexagonal – what a word. If it had a taste, it would taste of cherry.

Children slid past on icy paths; a snowball just missed my ear. We were the only ones standing still. Now I felt cold. It gripped at my shoulders through my shawl. I shivered. He continued to watch the snow fall – and seemed more interested in these scraps of frost than anything else. My arm ached as I held it out, but there was something about his attention and the soft snow falling that kept me there.

'Done!' he said, making me jump. He turned and headed towards the house, slipping and sliding as he went. 'Come on,' he called. 'You'll freeze if you stand there much longer!'

I watched him make his way back. I crouched down, scooped up snow in both hands, took aim, and threw. The snowball fell short, as I meant it to, but skittered between his feet.

'Ha!' he said and turned round to see me brushing snow off my hands and guilt all over my face. He gathered up snow into a larger ball, laughing as he came closer. The snow, when he threw it, caught my shoulder.

'Oh!' I said, already crushing snow into another ball. My breath burst out of me as laughter. And between there and the door, I laughed for all my Amsterdam days.

Once we were inside, he kicked off his boots, leaving a trail of footprints and half-thawed snow across the floor. He bounded up the stairs, two at a time.

'Bring a foot-warmer,' he shouted over his shoulder, then I heard him go up the second flight of stairs and the door to his room clatter shut.

I went down on my hands and knees and mopped up the mess. I stood his boots by the fire to dry, took embers from the fire and slipped them into the foot-warmer box, and closed the lid. I could still feel where the snowball had hit me. Outside his door, laughter bubbled up in me again. I swallowed it down, took a deep breath and knocked.

'*Entrez!*'

As I went in, he pulled a second chair up to the table and motioned to me to sit down. He took the foot-warmer from me and, once I was seated, slipped it under my feet. He placed a sheet of paper in front of him and set his ink pot to one side. He started to draw – six-sided snowflakes with tiny, feathered lines. He worked in silence, and when he had covered the sheet with twenty or more shapes he turned the paper towards me. Snowflakes. I had seen them fall from the sky and now here they were, fixed by ink to the page. It gave me a tingling feeling to see them.

'They're beautiful.'

'Yes,' he said, looking straight at me. 'They are.'

I studied the page again, taking in what I'd already seen, what I thought I knew. 'They're all different.' I hadn't expected that.

'Yes, indeed.'

'Is every snowflake different?'

'I think so. They must be.'

I thought of the snow outside, all the snow that had ever fallen. 'How can you know – for certain?'

He smiled and shrugged, but said nothing.

'What I mean is, there might be no two alike. But how can we know? We can't see every snowflake fall.'

'Indeed.'

'Some things can't be known.' I frowned. 'Can they? No two people are the same and we don't think that's strange. But there are twins . . . Are there twin snowflakes too?'

It was a muddle. I'd lost the thought I had begun with. I understood now why he wrote so much down.

'It's an interesting question – perhaps the most interesting question of all. It is possible to understand in the end and be certain. Many things are simply imperfectly understood.'

I shook my head and shivered.

'Is something the matter?'

He reached across and took hold of my hand, turning it over to its pink palm.

'You're cold,' he said. 'And that is my fault.'

He took my hands between his, brought them up to his mouth and blew on them gently.

'Better?'

I felt his breath on my fingers, the heat of his hands around mine. I nodded.

He blew again. 'Warmer?'

'*Oui, Monsieur.*'

'Good,' he said, 'good.'

He placed my hands back on the table. Then, and only after some time, did he lift his hands away.

Betje said, 'I saw you, you know, with him. *Your Monsieur.*'

'He's not mine! You're not to say that!'

'Standing in the snow.'

'He asked me to help.'

'*Asked you to help?* Who stands in the snow like that? For *ages?*'

'Wasn't ages.'

'You were there when I went to fetch eggs, and you were there when I came back!' She sounded triumphant. And she hadn't seen the snowballs I'd thrown!

I hated how she managed to needle under my skin and place her mark on everything I did. I pointed to the paper and quills we had been using – the first writing either of us had done for some time. I'd drawn what I could remember of the snowflakes and written *hexagernal* alongside. But she wasn't interested, I could tell.

'You realise,' I said, pulling myself straight, 'without his generosity, you would not have paper and ink to write with.'

'*Generosity?* Listen to you! You always expect me to be thankful.' She pushed the paper away.

I felt the hurt rise in my throat. 'I don't.'

'You can keep it. Keep it all.'

'If that's what you want,' I said and gathered everything up. I had the feeling she wanted to go so far, but no further. It was an unkind thing to think, but I thought it.

She'd miss this. She'd change her mind. I knew she would.

It was too cold to write anyway.

When I got back to the kitchen, I found the Monsieur at the table, waiting. He'd built a good fire and the room was filled with orange light; a deep warmth had settled over everything.

'Hello,' he said, getting up. His eyebrows raised in question when he saw what what I carried.

I put the quills, ink and paper on the table, sat down opposite him and waited for his scolding. He picked up a sheet of paper and nodded as he considered it.

'You have a student? A good one, I hope?'

I pushed my unkind thoughts of Betje away. I remembered how she'd smiled, how her face had lit up when the words made a sentence, a paragraph, a page. I knew that feeling too.

'Yes. Yes she is.'

'Where do you teach her? Not here, it seems.'

I could see no hint of displeasure in him. He wanted to

know. And then, at that moment, the line between us went.

I told him about Noorderkerk and Lindengracht. What he'd heard from Mr Sergeant about the purple quills wasn't the half of it. And when I told him about the ink I'd made, and the crusts I'd baked, he laughed so hard and tipped so far back in his chair, I thought he'd fall on the floor.

Then I told him about the place we used in winter – a storeroom attached to an outhouse where Betje worked. *No one hardly ever goes in*, Betje had said, brandishing a key.

The risks I took for her. The risks she took for me.

'It is a good thing you do for her,' he said.

'It's only what you have done for me, Monsieur.'

And at that we looked at each other. Words weren't needed.

I went over to the fire, wanting the heat on my face. He came up beside me and reached for my hand, and we stood there as though it was our fire, our kitchen, our home. At that moment, it was.

And then I turned to him and we kissed.

The door to his room stood open. A light flickered – he was awake. I tapped on the frame.

'*Oui?*'

He was sitting at the table. He had undressed for bed, his legs bare, his shirt loose to his thighs.

'I've brought you a foot-warmer, Monsieur. I saw you were working . . . it is cold tonight . . .'

The room was still. The candle flame stretched upwards.

He stared at the candle without blinking. 'I wasn't working, Helena.'

I knelt down and placed the foot-warmer under his feet. As I went to get up I saw a cut on the side of his foot. He flinched when I touched it.

'It's nothing, *rien*,' he said, and tucked one foot behind the other.

'I have salve, Monsieur.'

Before he could say no, I was on my feet and downstairs again. I returned with a small bowl of water, a cloth and the pot of salve.

'Here.'

I settled on the floor in front of him and lifted his foot into my lap. I dabbed at the cut, cleaning away the dried blood, then towelled it dry. As I smoothed in the cream, his foot relaxed in my hands. And when I was done, I did not ask – I reached for his other foot and laid it in my lap.

'Helena . . .'

I washed it and dried it.

'Helena. Look at me.'

His foot flexed as I rubbed cream along the instep, where his skin was whitest. A foot seemed like such an ordinary thing, as did a hand. I looked at his foot in my hands, at how my thumb fitted the dimple at his ankle. The arc of my thumb matched the arch of his instep; my fingers the same length as the furrows bridging his foot. Even my fingertips seemed shaped for the grooves between his toes. Hand and foot, made to fit together.

'Helena, look at me.'

I shook my head.

He lifted his feet out of my lap and stood up, reaching down to help me stand too. I took a couple of steps back.

'Take off your slippers.'

I hooked off my slippers, pushed them to one side with my foot.

'And your shawl.'

I pulled my shawl from my shoulders, held it by my side, and dropped it to the floor. I looked at his mouth, then at his shoulders.

'Come closer.'

I took a small step towards him, the floor cold under my feet.

'Closer.'

Another step.

He reached out to touch me, his fingers moving to my cheek in the gentlest of circles. I closed my eyes.

'Helena,' he whispered, 'open your eyes.'

I turned towards his touch.

He lifted my chin, tilted it with his thumb. He smoothed my brow. How could something so soothing plunge into me so deeply?

'Open your eyes.' He kissed my forehead, his hands cupped either side of my face. He kissed both cheeks, then my eyelids. 'Open your eyes.'

I should not be here. I could hear my breath and his. I bunched my chemise in my hand.

'Monsieur . . .'

I hardly dared say his name, afraid of what it would mean

if he heard. I felt the cool slip of the ribbon between my fingers as he freed it.

He kissed my neck and the shoulder he had bared. His fingers trembled as he tugged at a second ribbon, pooling my chemise at my feet.

He pulled me onto the bed so that I was underneath him, his legs between mine. He arched his back and groaned. His hands moved under, then over, his kisses on my mouth, my neck and ears.

'Open your eyes.'

His hands went between my legs. He lifted one leg higher and the other wider, and pushed into me, and as he went deeper, I felt such a sharp sting. I snapped up towards him, my breath stopped in my throat.

And then I saw him. His hair on my shoulders, his eyes searching and serious. He kissed away my tears, then pulled his shirt over his head. There was nothing between us. He moved, murmuring in French, words I did not know. He took my hands, palm to palm, and gripped them. My mouth went to his shoulder and I did not care how or why, all that mattered was the kiss I had for him.

'Helena,' he whispered and closed his eyes. 'Helena. Helena.'

Slowly, slowly he became still, with all of his weight on me. His hair, silvered by moonlight, fell across my breast. I listened to him breathing, long warm breaths along my arm.

The candle flickered. I stared at it. In the centre, the brightest light of all. Dreams and memories shifted their shadows across the wall. I felt the black dissolve of sleep.

The Monsieur stirred and nuzzled my neck. From the distance somewhere, I heard a faint cry, my own voice perhaps, as my mouth closed over his.

In the morning, I went to the kitchen, not caring that my feet were bare. Grey light fell across the floor. I poured water from the jug and washed myself.

'Helena . . .'

He came up behind me, his hands on my shoulders, then his arms went round me and I felt his warmth across my back.

'Helena. I need to know. Do you have your courses, do you bleed yet?'

I shook my head. 'No, Monsieur. Next year, perhaps, Mother said.'

'How old are you?'

'Seventeen. Eighteen.'

He turned his face in my hair. 'Come to bed.'

'I have to fetch water.'

'For whom? Do you need it? I don't.'

'Breakfast to make . . .'

'I am not hungry. We can eat later.' He kissed the nape of my neck.

'Peat to bring in . . .'

'The bed is warm.'

'I've to keep the fire lit, Monsieur.' I pulled away from him, turned my hands palm-side up and stared at them.

'No you don't. Not for me.' He took hold of my hands.

'Not today. Not tomorrow. There's no other besides us. You don't have to be a maid for me.'

I reached for him then, and held him, as he had held me, and I kissed him and I kissed him again.

For the rest of that week, Mr Sergeant's house was ours. We laughed. We kicked the sheets to the floor. October sunshine filled the Monsieur's room, as if every day in May had been threaded together and put on display just for us. He came with me to Noorderkerk – watched from the doorway as I prayed. The light fell straight as a sword, but it could not hold down the giddiness that danced in me.

Then came the day of Mr Sergeant's return. The Monsieur helped me dress, fastening the buttons on my bodice, threading the ribbon on my sleeve. He pulled on my stockings, placing kisses between my ankle and knee. Then it was my turn to dress him and, when every button was done up, I pressed my ear to his chest so I could hear his heart. He smoothed my hair across my brow. At first his heartbeat sounded in my ear, but then it seemed to surround me, and I the smaller thing, encompassed by it. What was small was now big, and what was big was now small. Everything at a tilt.

He cupped the side of my head to him.

Oh, what had I done?

But there was no more time. I heard the rattle of a carriage as it pulled up outside and the restlessness of horses reined in on the spot. The door to the carriage slammed shut, followed by a laugh I knew well: Mr Sergeant.

'We have harmed no one,' he said gently. 'You have to love life, Helena, without fearing it, without fearing death.'

He kissed my forehead. I felt shy, and as if I were burning, and I held him to me to keep the feeling close.

We broke apart. I tucked the last stray strands of my hair under my cap. The Monsieur coughed to clear his throat and nodded at me.

'I'll find you later.'

Then, like that, his attention switched and he opened the door and went out.

I smoothed the creases from my skirts and, after a moment or two, followed after him.

'Mr Sergeant!' I heard him call. 'What news of Utrecht?'

I went to the kitchen and rested my back against the door. From the other side, I could hear the Monsieur's laughter. Monsieur and maid. Who would know, if they looked at us, how we had changed, what level had tipped and could not be set straight?

Antje was waiting with the letter when I came back from the market. I knew, as soon as I saw it, who it was from. I had not seen Betje for more than a week. A new maid, who wanted nothing to do with my greetings, now hung out the washing with Antje instead.

I took the letter to the kitchen and read it standing up.

Dear Helena

I am leaving for Alkmaar I know my way I read the rest of the letter from the Orphanage myself and know where my Mother lived

I am unhappy here And Amsterdam is not my life And I need to know if she lives and if she will have me Please do not say where I am gone Do not cry too much if Thomas is gone too

I am sorry for my writing but I think it is good even so Be happy for me dearest friend and Thank you for all you did for me and you will be in my prayers

I wrote this on the Hoeks paper and with their ink and I think I am owed that for what they did

Betje

'Betje, Betje, Betje,' I whispered. I rolled up my sleeve, but her name, where I'd written it, had long since worn off.

I pinched my skin, raising a red weal. I pinched again, harder this time. I nipped where my skin was whitest; I nipped where it hurt most.

Swifts

'I AM A grey man,' he said. 'You are a goldfinch, *Madonna del cardellino.*'

He came to my bed. He took me to his room. He found me when I was out walking. To my shame, I led him to alleyways and to the garden at night. *Helena*, he whispered, and I could not have enough of him saying it. Each day had the chance of him in it, but when we were in company I had to be as I was before. We knew what was between us. He'd touch his fingertips to mine when I went to fill his glass; I'd let my hand rest against his as I took his plate.

Most times, I did not see him, I could not, but I felt him near by. When I tidied capes and boots in the *voorhuis*, he seemed to be there too, as though he'd kicked off his shadow along with his boots and left it there for my company. Then, he would be back and me on my knees, helping him on with them again, hands gripped either side of his calf, until his foot jolted into place. And when he had gone, I was left wondering how the air, the space he had been in, still held the shape of him; to feel as if he'd not left it, nor me.

I knew which of the sounds in the house were his. His laughter made me ache. When I heard his footsteps on the floor above the kitchen, I stopped. I pictured him standing there. Had he heard me as I worked? Did he look down as I looked up?

What I felt was not smooth nor flat. Happiness welled up in me, making me giddy, but sadness pressed in too. Thomas had gone, and now Betje. Most times I was alone.

I was not myself. I no longer knew who I was any more. I was both the old Helena and this strange new Helena rolled up in one. Some days, a terrible fear pushed up in me and the floor seemed to heave and pitch. I worried that the windows, if I looked at them, would lose their glass. But the floor remained level, the glass stayed where it was.

Then a day came and I woke with blood between my legs. I took valerian steeped in milk as Mother had told me to and after two days it stopped. I had expected more, something worse. This was very little, almost nothing. It did not come again and I forgot about it.

The Monsieur pressed his thumb gently to the middle of my forehead.

'*Mio cardellino*. Raphael's goldfinch is a symbol . . . the red spot, the sign of Christ's suffering.'

I was not sure I liked that. My hand went up to where he had touched me. I frowned.

'You do not like the comparison? Raphael's madonna needed no throne. A madonna of the field, and very beautiful.'

It seemed to me, as I listened, that Raphael had painted a real woman. I wondered who she was.

He kissed me where he had touched me. 'Perhaps life is like a painting for others to stand before and judge.'

And then he wrote. He worked furiously, page after page, as if the words had at last found a way to escape. New papers appeared on his desk, alongside letters from Mersenne. *Mersenne* – Limousin had mentioned him only once, and then to remark that he thanked God that he was in France and his Monsieur in Holland. He'd be at the door every day if not. Limousin had crossed himself at the thought. But judging by the number of letters that had Mersenne's seal on them, distance had done nothing to deter him.

I regarded it all and remembered the papers the Monsieur had wanted to burn. 'Is this what you were working on before, Monsieur?'

'No, the world is not ready for that.' He pointed to the sheet in front of him, and then to a large number of pages, many worn and creased. 'Something new, and older work. I want to combine them into a history, a history of the mind.'

A history of the mind? We all have thoughts and memories, but it seemed to me that he meant something else, that he was not simply writing a history of *his* mind. He wanted his thoughts to journey far from him to see what stories they might tell when they returned.

He rubbed his eyes and picked up a page. *Toutefois il se peut faire que je me trompe.*

'I don't understand.'

He translated, 'After all, it is possible I may be mistaken, and it is but a little copper and glass, perhaps, that I take for gold and diamonds.'

'You're writing in French?'

'Yes. I want everyone to read it.'

Everyone? His words made me bold. 'Teach me French, then I can too.'

'Who is this?' he said, turning to wrap his arms around me. 'This maid who would learn French?'

I liked how he made me feel, as though anything was possible.

I turned in the circle he made as it tightened around me. 'Teach me. Will you?'

Mr Sergeant worried. 'I see nothing of him these days. Is he writing? It would be good to discuss. He's always in his room, or out. Or asleep.'

The Limousin complained. 'I may as well go back to France. He has no need of me any more. He sends me on pointless errands. I think he wants me out of the way. You see him more than anyone.'

'I see his room.'

'He seems *préoccupé*. Have you noticed anything different about him?'

'Nothing at all!' I said, feeling myself blush when I saw his eyebrows arch. 'I don't notice him.'

But the Limousin was right. I did see the most of him. I saw him at first light. When I went in, he came up behind me, urgent, silent, his hands on my breasts and lifting my skirts, his mouth over mine to stop himself or me, I did not know which, from crying out. His need overwhelmed me. Was this what it was like to drown? We lay back on the bed, his eyes heavy but not drowsy, and there, in among his papers, he pushed until I thought we were so far joined we would never break apart. He lifted me onto him and moved me over him until the moment when everything stopped, even breathing. And then we were the same.

When he was done, I wanted to hold him but he turned back to his writing: *Discourse* together with earlier work – *Optics*, *Geometry*, *Meteorology*. I recognised the sketches of snowflakes on his desk; a passage about swallows caught my eye:

It is because of this wind that the swallows' flying very low warns us of rain; for it brings down certain gnats on which they live, which normally buzz about and cavort high in the air when the weather is good.

I blinked – they were not my words, but I knew them. He'd painted them in Raphael's blues and reds. I had not realised his work sprang out of the day, from the time we'd been together, from what I'd said to him. Through all of it, he'd been thinking, and he had made those thoughts into words and written them down.

Then I recalled our time together and him over me. I swallowed. I had to hope he would not write about that.

Sometimes, when he was working, his gaze rested on me for a moment or two, but it was not me he was thinking about, not me he could see. To look at, he was no different. He went on as he had before.

He never told me to go, but he had his work and I had mine. I wanted to hold him, but how could I? Who was I to do that? I wanted to talk, but what had I to say *to him*?

I tried not to disturb him. I slipped off my shoes and worked round him.

But when he did not look up, not even as I took my leave and went out, it made me think: what was this world I was in? A world he had made to please himself – beyond the rules and the reach of the one I knew? Would I be surprised if I woke one day to find the world turned after all and God had vanished as well?

I could not take his hand, not in the open, but I knew a path that narrowed and narrowed until the wall brushed against my arms on either side; the sky a blue line above us, falling to darkness at our feet. The path used to frighten me, but now, for thirty-two steps, I could reach behind and take his hand and no one would see. I could stop, turn, kiss him and his mouth would open to mine.

At the end of the path, we found an old church. A small side door had been left off the latch – not an invitation to go in, but neither was it locked. I heard music coming from inside. It was not Sunday. Whoever was playing was not doing so for God.

We were not the only ones: an audience of the uninvited, avoiding as best we could one another's eye. Few candles had been lit, making the people about me appear pale and dreamlike. I made out the shapes of shoulders and how they went down, as mine did too, as the first clear note sounded out.

'I know this!' I said, but I had not heard it for such a long time. It came back to me with a memory from Leiden – sitting in church before the service began, holding Father's hand.

The music drifted down from above. Quietly at first, then louder. It was in my feet, and I felt it inside me, where I breathed; it ran along my cheekbones to the top of my head. Did the Monsieur feel it too?

He turned to me with a frown. 'Who's the composer?'

When I shook my head, he turned away in search of someone who knew.

I did not know and I did not want to know. It made me think about a man hunched over a desk, a maid tidying up behind him.

He'd not settle until he had the answer. His question was passed behind us and to both sides, through shrugs and upturned hands, before whispered word came back: *Ricercar*, by *Sweelinck*.

Only then did he lean forwards, hands held together under his chin. I watched him as he listened, but not in the way I watched him at Mr Sergeant's house. Here I was not afraid of being seen. In this half-light, and half drowned by music, I could drink him in. Then the music stopped and the last notes faded away into the rafters. Silence folded over us and we sat there awhile, as though held fast.

As soon as we were outside, I kissed him.

A scraggly man veered up behind the Monsieur. 'Aye, aye!'

The Monsieur drew me to him, turning his back to block the man out, his mouth on mine, our kiss not breaking. In my head, I could hear the music rise to its final note. I still had hold of his hand.

Swifts massed into black clouds, mapping the shape of the wind. All of Amsterdam restless, as the last leaves fell. When the sky emptied in November, I was sick. Although I took valerian, it did not help. I had no fever, but I felt I'd been weighted with stones. All I wanted to do was sleep.

'You're looking well, Helena,' Mr Sergeant said. 'If a little pink. Not beetroot-related, I hope.'

Beetroot, I was certain, it was not. However, I was at a loss. For all I felt wretched inside, when I caught my reflection in the mirror in Mr Sergeant's room, I had never looked better. Then the tiredness passed and the sickness stopped.

One morning, the Limousin stopped me on the stairs. 'Where are you going with that?'

I had a tray with breakfast things for the Monsieur. 'It's for the Monsieur,' I said and held his eye. It was trouble, I could feel it; he was after knowing something he already knew.

'He's not to be disturbed at this hour, you know that.'

I had to think quickly. 'He's started to take breakfast.'

The Limousin stared at me, as if expecting me to say something more. The house was so quiet and my heartbeat so loud, I was sure he could hear it. Sometimes, I thought, he expected the answer to his questions would be found in these silences, in arguments he had already had, and won, in his head.

He was not going to budge.

I had to be careful what I said. If the wrong words came out, those were the words I'd have to live with.

'You take it,' I said, keeping my expression flat.

Whatever it was he was looking for in me, some sign of defeat perhaps, he must have seen, because he reached out for the tray and said, 'Yes. We would not want an *embarrassment* if the Monsieur is not dressed yet, would we?'

'No, Limousin.' I turned and went downstairs.

It didn't take long before the Limousin was back without the tray. He sat on a chair, tilted it and began to rock on its legs, all the while watching me. My hands wouldn't work properly with him there. I dropped a knife, just missing my foot, then knocked a candlestick onto the floor with my elbow.

'It seems there is more than one distracted person in this house.'

I poked at the fire. The damp peat hissed miserably like an old cat. Rock, rock, rock he went on the chair. I wanted to grab it, to make him stop.

'The Monsieur was in bed. I've left him with his breakfast. I suggested I should bring his breakfast in future.'

'Yes,' I said, doing my best to sound disinterested, still with my back to him. I unhooked a pan of water and carried it over to the table.

He studied his fingers and picked at his nails one by one, making the most of whatever it was he had to say. 'But that's not what he wants. He wants you to bring it to him.'

'You should take it.'

'You are not listening. It's you he wants, not me.'

I tried to laugh him off, but the Limousin did not smile. He made a great show of standing up and brushing down his clothes, then went out, closing the door hard enough to rattle the latch, leaving me in no doubt as to his thoughts on the matter.

A week later, he caught me coming out of the Monsieur's room.

'That was a long breakfast.' He stood in the doorway to his room, opposite the Monsieur's. 'Do you always wait for him to finish eating before taking the tray?'

How long had he been standing there? Had he been listening at the door? I swallowed. 'I cleaned whilst he ate.'

His eyes widened. His jaw went slack, as though about to take a bite. '*You cleaned whilst he ate?* Strange. The broom and pan have stayed outside all this time, exactly where you left them.' He pointed to the broom resting against the wall.

'I cleaned the windows.'

He looked at the tray and then at me. There was no cleaning cloth, only the remains of a small breakfast the Monsieur had eaten in a hurry.

'You look flushed, Helena, is something the matter?'

'No. Nothing at all.'

'You seem quite changed to me. Larger too.'

'Well!' I wasn't going to stay and listen to his insults, valet or not.

'I'm not stupid. *Pas stupide!*' he called after me, his words, like wasps, stinging my heels.

Lines

I LEARNED ABOUT him. He told me.

'Mother died when I was born. Father was seldom there, so my grandmother took me. Then I was sent to school. Limousin no doubt imparted the rest.' He drew a circle with his finger on my stomach.

'Do you miss France, Monsieur?'

'*Non.* France is gone from me. I try not to concern myself with it. What value in missing something I cannot have, nor easily return to? I'd be a stranger there. Being away is the only way I can be at home, I think. Or as near as my father can bear me. But it's true I miss my sister.'

The candle guttered. It was the first I'd heard tell of a sister. I knew there must be someone somewhere, but it was strange to think of his family.

'Why do you think I live like this? In rooms such as this?'

I heard tiredness in his voice. I shook my head. He did not need my answer.

'I can live without the demands of others.'

He was not telling me anything I did not know, and that was very little. But each small detail sank a little deeper into him like a plumb line; I had begun to fathom him. The rules he lived by – rules that had brought him to me – would one day take him away. I knew he was not thinking of me.

Why should he? I thought of my little bed in the kitchen downstairs. When I'd arrived, I'd imagined myself there for years. Thinking about it now made me want to draw into myself, like a snail whose shell had been given a sharp tap.

'Besides, it's all sold, apart from the title: 'sieur du Perron. What value in that? Ha! Such vanities! Still, my brother is what I am not.'

'Monsieur?'

He touched his shoulder. 'My father . . . his disappointment sits here.'

It was remarkable to think that his father did not approve of him. 'What's France like, Monsieur?'

He gripped his temples. 'Like a cage, like a cage. The France I remember, *the France I love*, is from my childhood – the happier parts of it – summer hayfields running down to the river. Even the memory brings back the smell of grapes, warming in the trough.'

'Will you go back?'

'For warm grapes?'

I did not know what to say. I felt nipped by his reply. My eyes stung and I blinked.

But when I went to leave, he turned to me and said, 'Stay. Don't go.'

'Loneliness is not the same as being alone; one can choose to be alone, seek it out, desire it perhaps. Loneliness asserts itself . . . The feeling, it is a weight, here.' He pressed his hand where his ribs met. 'It is *suffocation*.'

I placed my hand over his and he let me lift his away.

Sometimes, when I was with him, I felt I'd been given a cup and told to scoop up the sea.

Then a day came when he seemed surprised to see me. I had gone to his room when I was not expected and had stopped his work.

'Yes?'

That one word, the sharpness of it, told me I had been wrong to come.

'What is it, Helena?' he said without looking up. 'I am working.'

'Monsieur . . .'

'Yes?'

I heard a small sigh, and the *tap, tap, tap* of his quill on the desk.

'Mr Sergeant . . .'

The tapping stopped. I glanced up, only to be met with a frown.

'If he—'

'What? If he what?'

He placed the quill next to the page he was working on.

'He does not know, if that's what concerns you.'

'I—'

'What is it you want to know, Helena? Why are you here?'

I flushed, my cheeks hot. 'Are you—'

'Am I what? Married? *No.* Is there another? *No.* Has there been another? *Yes.*'

The silence grew. By now it was quieter than the quietest part of the night.

'Is that why you are here? To ask ridiculous questions?'

'No!'

He stared at the page, turning the quill between his fingers. 'Anything else you would like to know?'

I shook my head, my hand at my neck, on the line of my collarbone.

'Good.'

He was setting me in my place. I looked at my toes, peeping out from under the hem of my dress. There was the line, right there, in between us again. I had thought myself certain before all of this – *clever me*, I could find my way around Amsterdam on any of Mr Sergeant's errands. This house had been my home long before it was his, and now look at me.

I clasped my hands together. *Sorry?* Wasn't that what I was supposed to say? *Curtsy?* Wasn't that what was I supposed to do? Why shouldn't I come to his room and ask questions of him, when he'd had so much of me?

I glared, I think, a little, enough at least for his mouth to open, as if to say something. But I was already turning away, sharply on one heel, so quickly I felt the air slip over my cheek.

He'd study me, if I wasn't careful, mark out the parts of me in a list; pin me to the page, cut me open, peer inside. *Imperfectly understood*, he'd write in the margin, draw a line through me and then snap the book shut.

* * *

By February, the Limousin knew. I saw him looking and watching. What didn't come to him this way came by instinct, it seemed. He knew without asking. He knew without being told.

He found me in the washroom.

'I know what's with you.'

'Know what?'

He grabbed my wrist. 'I'm no fool.'

'Limousin, please.'

'You've been with him, haven't you?'

'No!'

'Don't lie. All those late mornings. Think I can't hear? Think I can't *smell*?' He leaned in, sniffed and pulled a face. 'You've been with him, haven't you?' He shook my arm. 'Haven't you?'

I nodded and shrank away from him. He did not care that he was hurting me.

'For how long?' He tightened his grip and shook me again. 'Tell me!'

'Four months.'

He fell back, as if I had slapped him. 'No! Not him. He would not.'

'I'll leave, return to Leiden.'

'And let everyone know the child is Descartes'?'

'Child?' My hands went to my face, then my stomach. *'Child?'*

'What else did you think would happen? Look at you,' he sneered and flicked at my skirts. 'Filling out.'

I put my hand over my mouth, the breath knocked from me.

He shook his head. 'This will ruin him. Is that what you want?'

'No!'

He let go of my arm. 'He will have to be told.'

I shook my head. Panic flooded me. 'No, please.'

'Do you think you can hide it? That it will just disappear – *disparaître* – poof?'

I looked down at the curve of me, horrified.

'It must be got rid of.'

'No!' I clutched my stomach.

'What then, the *spinhuis*?'

'No!'

'Did you think he would marry you?'

I said nothing.

'*Madame* Descartes? Is that what you thought? You? A little nothing of a maid? Two years in Amsterdam and you think you know how the world is . . . You are no more than a *distraction*. I have to talk to him. He has to know.'

'No! Please,' I begged, and now I clutched at him, but he shook me off.

'An arrangement must be sought that finds a way for him. Do you understand?'

Then he turned and went out, without waiting for my reply.

DEVENTER, 1635

Sketch

EVERYTHING WAS FROZEN and everything was dead – the town sunken and sallow. I glanced over my shoulder at the road behind. Our tracks were already hidden under the snow: a white road, bordered by white fields, ran to a white horizon; Amsterdam, far beyond it, lost from sight.

The slowing of the carriage nudged the Limousin awake. He looked out of the window and frowned. The driver brought the horses to a walk as we crossed the bridge into the town. I peered down. The river below, solid ice; fog hugged the surface.

The driver threaded the coach through the shuttered-up streets. We crossed a deserted square and then passed by the church, the streets growing narrower the further into the town we went. It was too cold to stand by windows, watching. If anyone saw us arrive, they would have glanced out for no more than a moment, then turned away, thankful to be inside.

The Limousin leaned forwards, wanting a better view. 'At last,' he said, as he recognised where we were. 'We're here.'

The coach stopped outside a small townhouse. Only the shutters at the very top were open, the rest had been closed against the winter.

The Limousin rapped sharply on the door. The noise took me straight back to Mr Sergeant's front step and Mr Slootmaekers. As I struggled to straighten, to ease the chill from my shoulders, a feeling ran inside me like fingers. I held my stomach, looking for the pulse that beat alongside mine, but it was gone almost as soon as I felt it.

A woman opened the door. This was Mrs Anholts and she was to have me to stay. An arrangement, the Limousin had said. She was a widow, like my mother, but looked older by several years. Silvery hair poked out from the sides of her cap. Her mouth pulled in, but with age or disapproval, I could not tell.

'Clément!' she cried and embraced the Limousin. He had not told me they knew each other.

'Mrs Anholts – a delight!' He kissed her hand, then stepped to one side. 'This is her.'

'Aha, here she is. Helena.'

I kept my hands together under my cape and bowed my head.

The Limousin threw down my bundle from the coach and followed Mrs Anholts into the house. We passed through a darkened passageway into the kitchen beyond. The room glowed with candlelight; a large fire reached up the chimney.

The Limousin warmed his back. 'You keep a good fire, there's none better in Holland.'

I looked about for a sign of the Monsieur, his gloves, or boots, or cape, but there was nothing I could see that was his.

'He's not here, if you're wondering,' she said, when she

saw me look. 'He's been gone a week already.' She poured the Limousin a glass of wine and ladled out a bowl of soup for him. Then she guided me to a chair and put a bowl of soup on the table in front of me. 'Sit down, eat.'

'I'm not hungry. Thank you.'

'You look half perished. Sit down.' She patted the back of my hand.

Now that I looked at her, she appeared softer, her mouth fuller, as though all she needed to do was to come inside and thaw. I sipped the soup, too pinched by cold to notice anything other than its heat. Despite the fire, I shivered.

Mrs Anholts and the Limousin slipped into easy chatter about old friends and life with Mr Sergeant. I was the stranger, and talked about as if I were not there. The conversation kept coming back to me, as if Limousin had me tied to him by a length of string that he kept tugging to see if I was still attached. Perhaps it was because we were away from Amsterdam, or because the Monsieur was not there, but distance loosened his tongue. He seemed not to care what I heard.

'I said we should get rid of it, but the Monsieur said no.'

'Clément! It is as well.'

He snorted.

'It would have been a terrible thing to do, Clément, and you know it.'

He pulled a face, but did not seem inclined to argue further. The fire crackled as the peat sank in the middle, sending a shower of sparks up the chimney. I wondered what had already been said, what would be said when I was not there. I glanced across at Mrs Anholts – she nodded, as though to signal some small understanding.

He stared at his hands. 'You have the story?' He tapped his ear and angled it towards her, waiting to hear.

Mrs Anholts turned to me. 'Helena, from Amsterdam—'

'No!' I interrupted. 'I'm from Leiden.'

I didn't like this, not at all. What had been ours, between the Monsieur and me, was theirs, the curtains pulled back, the shutters thrown wide.

'My great-niece from *Leiden*,' she began again carefully. 'Her husband killed after a fall, leaving the poor girl carrying their first child. *We must look to our kin, before looking to others.* Satisfied, Clément?'

The Limousin nodded. 'And no mention of the Monsieur by name?'

'Certainly not!'

'Good. Because if his name came out—'

'I know. I know. But if I am asked? Have you agreed a name?'

He thought for a moment. 'Reyner Joachim. His name, in Dutch.'

'Jochems,' she corrected him. 'Reyner Jochems.'

'Reyner Jochems.' He turned to me as he said it and I nodded to let him know I'd heard. *Reyner Jochems.* Two words. It seemed to me then it was all I had left.

His attention switched back to Mrs Anholts. 'He is not to be troubled further by this.'

'Clément! No one will know but . . .' She glanced at me again.

'But?'

I could hear the impatience in his voice, the annoyance at being questioned.

'When the baby is here – what then?'

He didn't even narrow his eyes; the thought, and thinking it, seemed to have worn him flat. 'He should never have taken this route. I told him . . .'

I was hearing things I should not hear. He watched me now, wanting my reaction, but I kept still. This was how it would be – I would be talked about and would have to keep my feelings inside.

I wondered what Limousin saw when he looked at me. A simple maid in rough clothes? He thought he was better than me, no doubt. But I carried the Monsieur's child and the Monsieur wanted to keep it – that much I knew. All the Limousin could ever be to the Monsieur was his valet. I did not need to tell him that. I was sure he realised it himself. Limousin. Conduit. *Valet*. Three words that meant the same thing.

After the meal had been cleared away, Mrs Anholts held out a bucket to me.

'We have to be our own maids in this house. For as long as you are able, you will empty your soil every morning in the back pit. Your room is to be kept clean. Strip your bed fortnightly on Tuesday and wash the sheets. All meals will be eaten in the kitchen with me. I will provide as well as the Monsieur's allowance and this winter permit. God willing.' She thought for a moment, seeming to go over what she had just said to see if there was anything she had forgotten.

We went up to the top floor of the house. She opened the door to a small, cold room. The room contained what was needed and no more: a narrow bed and a dresser tucked under the eaves, with a bowl and jug for washing. A table stood under a window, and on it a small box. I scraped a circle of ice from the glass and looked out over the rooftops. They angled steeply, gathered, as if in prayer, around the church we had passed on our way.

'What church is that?'

'Grote of Lebuinuskerk. But you'll not be going there as you are.'

It was a shock to hear it so bluntly put; I had never missed church unless I was unwell. She gave my shoulder a gentle squeeze. Her eyes were grey, the colour of ashes; her cheeks dusted with pale freckles, the colour of ash too.

'It's best you don't go for now. There will be time enough after.'

I clutched my stomach as the feeling came again.

'Is there movement?'

I nodded.

'October, was it?'

He must have told her. She would know all of it, every-thing. 'Yes.'

'There will be no hiding it soon.'

'When will it – *she* be here?'

'*She?* She will come when she's ready.' She counted on her fingers, first one hand, then the other, until she reached nine. 'If October, then the summer. July. Pray it is no sooner.'

'The Monsieur will be here by then . . .' My voice trailed away, each word softer than the one before.

'Well, well,' she said, neither agreeing nor disagreeing.

'And you will stay with me, and we shall have time to get to know one another better.'

She crossed over to the table, picked up the box and held it out to me. 'Here. He left this for you.'

I turned my back to her as I opened it. Inside was a sheaf of paper, a bottle of ink and several quills, sharpened with nibs. There was a letter on top, sealed with a ribbon and wax. My hands trembled as I broke the wax seal and pulled the ribbon free.

Deventer, 24 February 1635

H—,

I am not able to stay. I travelled ahead to make these arrangements and tomorrow travel on to Utrecht, where I shall lodge for a while.

Mrs A—will care for you and ensure you have what you need.

I have provided paper, ink and quills. You can leave letters for me at the Athenaeum Library, if you wish. Mark these for Professor H R—, Utrecht, with my initials, and they will find their way to me. I lodged with him only a year ago and any correspondence can be trusted to him. Write and tell me how you are, what changes you have – I am interested.

Utrecht is not too far away – a visit, possible.

Your humble servant,

R—D—

Postscript: L—can bring your first letter to me if you write by return.

It was a letter, but not the letter I had hoped for. *Changes?* Did he want to make notes on my condition? Questions crowded my head. If L—was the Limousin, and I was H—, then who was Professor H R—?

I turned to Mrs Anholts. 'I need to rest.'

When she had gone, I read the letter again. It offered no comfort, nor hint of his feelings for me: he might as well have written to an elderly aunt, or a distant cousin, or, I realised with a jolt, *a servant*. He had me on stepping stones and not one of them steady. There was no mention, for certain, of a visit, yet he wanted me to write. As hope rose in me, doubt weighed it back down.

I counted twenty small sheets of paper in the box. I sat at the table and rubbed my hands to warm them. But if they were cold, my thoughts were colder.

Dear Monsieur, I began, then crossed it out.

Monsieur . . . I scribbled this out too.

I opened the letter he had sent me. He had signed it *R—D—*.

'René.' I said his name for the first time, the sound of it strange to me. *René.* I had never called him that. It did not seem right.

I started again:

> *Monsieur,*
> *Thank you.*
> *Am I here till summer? And then?*

I read back what I had written and tore the paper in half. I closed my eyes and took a deep breath.

The changes I have? I am half myself without you.

No! I screwed the paper into a ball, staining my fingers with ink. He had left me twenty pages; at this rate they would not last me this first day.

My gaze rested for a while on the page, on the quill in my hand, then travelled up to the window. Sparkling ice fanned out across the glass, like feathers frozen to the pane. *Be more open to surprise,* wasn't that what he'd said? I dipped the quill in the ink and touched the side of the well to remove the spare. I looked at the glass, then at the paper and started to sketch. I was better at drawing than writing. I had not expected that. I wondered what he would see when he saw it. A simple sketch? Or would he see me, through the paper, drawing it? Would he know I'd tried to see him too, from here, through this circle of ice?

I left off his name, it wasn't needed. When I had finished, I dipped the quill in the ink and wrote:

I am certain she is a girl.
Helena Jans

I was not afraid to sign my name.

I stared at the page – at the neat sketch and the uneven writing. I folded the letter quickly before I changed my mind and took it downstairs.

Wine and the fire had warmed the Limousin through; I could hear it in him before I reached the kitchen again. He was telling Mrs Anholts about the army in Poland. He would tell the story to anyone who would listen. If she had heard it before, it did not seem to matter. She laughed loudly, her laugh as bright as firelight on copper.

As she brushed past him, he reached for her waist. I looked at them, their easy company, with a terrible envy. The smallest touch that went between them, I felt its shadow – emptiness and loss.

I held out the letter to him. 'For the Monsieur.' I had no choice but to trust him.

The Limousin slipped it into his satchel without a second glance. 'I'll take it with me to Utrecht in the morning.'

I stood there a moment, expecting him to object, to make some unkind remark about *a letter, from a maid, to his Monsieur*. Instead, he poured the last of the wine from the jug into his glass and patted Mrs Anholts on the waist, all attention on her.

'Marry me,' he said, his eyes half closed, his neck curved back to show the hard small lump in his throat.

She pushed his shoulder, lifted his hand and dropped it back in his lap. 'And what would your French wife say then?' she said, laughing her bright copper laugh.

'I tell you, there is no French wife! I'll make you my *Dutch* wife, my *favourite* wife of all. *Vous êtes la plus belle de toutes.*'

'To accompany the Polish wife and the Italian wife?' She cleared his glass from the table. 'You've had enough, I think.'

'You are cruel, Mrs Anholts.' He took hold of her hand and kissed it, while reaching for his glass with the other. 'But more wine! After what I've had to endure these past few days, it's the very least of what I am owed!'

Later, after I had gone to my room, I heard him on the stair and the soft click of the latch on her door. I heard no sound of him being sent away. I thought of my little drawing in his satchel, and ice melting, and ink bleeding. I turned to the wall, curled up under the blankets and hugged what small warmth there was in the bed to me.

I held his letter.

I closed my eyes and tried to conjure him from the darkness, but when he came, the man who stood before me had no warmth, no weight, no breath.

List

MARCH ARRIVED. HE did not come. No letter came in reply to the one I had sent. Days stretched into weeks. I wrote letters I did not send, crowding several onto a single sheet – word after word, like knots tied on a lengthening piece of string, marking time.

The days stayed cold. I walked out, alone, veiled by my breath. Deventer. I could map it quickly on the palm of my hand. Ten, twenty such places could have fitted into Amsterdam. I had to be careful where I went. There were soldiers in this town. I wondered where they had travelled from and where they'd next be sent. Some of them just boys, still with growing to do: cuffs down to their fingers; boots that flapped at their knees. Hadn't I been sent to the edge of the country too – the furthest I'd been in my life? Did I look as lost as their youngest? Was I as ignorant of the Monsieur's plans as they were of theirs?

Why here, why send me here?

The weeks passed and still no word. What had I done to be so ignored? Then worry set in. I imagined illness and accident; saw him gaoled for his work. But Limousin would have come with such news, and he as scarce as his master.

I thought, *He is thinking.* I thought, *He forgets.*

Then I thought, *Why give me paper? Why ask me to write?*

I missed Betje. If she were here, she'd have something to say. I missed our walks. I missed our chatter. I could walk around Deventer, without a word to anyone, and still have time to be by myself with no one to talk to before lunch.

I stopped writing letters – it wasted good paper. I wrote a list instead. I titled it:

What is it you want, Helena?

For her to be born well and the birth be a good one
For her to be named before God
To make a living for us both
To give her a home, when she comes
So I do not have to give her up
Not for her to be a maid like me
Not for her to be a maid like Betje – not knowing
To go to Leiden again
For him to know her

When I'd finished, I looked at what I had written.

I showed the list to Mrs Anholts and she read it under her breath, nodding or frowning as she made her way down it. I wasn't to worry about the birth, she said, she'd help with that when the time came. What kind of living did I think I could make with an infant, what did I think I would do?

'The Monsieur has provided for you, Helena. Not many would do that.'

'I'm considering, Mrs Anholts,' I said, as though I had a basket of eggs and could choose any I liked.

'Considering?' She looked at me as if it was the most ridiculous thing she had heard.

'I was a good maid, Mrs Anholts.'

'And how will you be a maid again? Have you thought of that? Will Mr Sergeant provide a reference?' When I said nothing, she went on, 'You need to think of these things, Helena.'

She moved on to the next point. *To give her a home . . .* but your home is here. I'm taking good care of you.'

'Yes, Mrs Anholts.' I stared at my hands.

'I shan't shoo you out,' she said, seeming to read my worry.

On she went down the list. 'Oh, no, Helena. What a terrible thing to suppose. The Monsieur's child *given up?* He would *never* allow that. And no son or daughter of his would ever be a servant.' She fanned herself with the paper and patted her chest.

I wanted to believe her, but how could she be so certain of his opinion?

'Betje? Who's she? Never heard mention of her. Leiden? That's where your family live?'

'My mother.'

'Anyone else?'

I shook my head.

'For him to know her.' She didn't say anything for a while. 'I'm certain he will, in good time.'

She held out the list to me with a sweet smile.

'I should have had a list like this when I lost Mr Anholts

and was left with my two little ones. There was *assistance.*' She said the word as if she had the taste of something bad in her mouth. 'But charity is not always without favour or cost. Becoming a mother changes everything – you'll find that out soon enough.'

'Why are you helping, Mrs Anholts?'

'Well,' she said, surprised by my question. 'Because the Monsieur asked and I thought I could help. And because I understand. My sister, Hendrika . . .'

She paused as she remembered.

'Hendrika was a little older than you when she was with child to a farmer's son. He would marry her, he said, but he didn't. He beat her and said the child was not his. Father would not have her in the house – the shame of it, you see. There was no *arrangement* for her. Mother begged him not to send her away. Hendrika went down to the river one morning and did not come back.'

'Oh, Mrs Anholts.'

'It was a long time ago, Helena, but such things happen and can't be forgotten. The Monsieur provides when many wouldn't. I will do what I can.'

'Did he ask for me, when he was here?'

'Put him from your mind! He has *means.* He has a *valet.* He's *French.*' She said this as if it were the biggest obstacle of all. She gestured to my stomach. 'He has made an arrangement.'

'And what will happen when the baby is here? What then? Will he come?'

'It is not for us to speculate. A walk, Helena, will do you good.'

A walk was her answer to everything. It was her way of saying she did not want to talk.

'Wrap up, cover yourself. You will feel better for it.'

'Yes, Mrs Anholts.'

It was only when I was some way from the house that I realised Mrs Anholts had not asked about everything on my list. She had not asked me about her name.

I traced the path the carriage had come in on, and found my way back to the river and the road that ran west to Amsterdam. As I went, I thought about what Mrs Anholts had said and how different my position was to hers, and to my mother's. They were both widows, but I wasn't. The Monsieur lived. They had been married. I hadn't. Not every family could be a father, a mother and their children, and if a family fell on misfortune then God would provide. But to hide away as I was doing here?

I had been told to tell no one, to guard the Monsieur's name. Keeping this from my mother was a lie and that was a sin. But how could I tell her? If word had got back to her about Thomas, how would she bear the shame of me as well? Wasn't it better to be lost? To disappear? To hide?

I thought of Betje and her strength. I had the family she'd craved and now I shunned it.

It did not matter how far I drew my hood over my head, God could still see me. Every way I turned, I fell into shadow.

It started to rain, pulling the sky down in a lank sheet. When I reached the river, I watched the ice break from the far bank. Great, grey chunks tipped and rolled to start their slow journey downstream. Winter, even when it froze twenty feet into the ground, could not put a stop to spring.

He did not write.

I felt her move in me more and more. *Girl. Baby. Darling.* I rubbed small circles into my skin where her elbow, foot or hand pushed out. *Baby girl, my darling.* I wrote the name I had for her across my stomach with my finger.

I used his paper. I sat in the kitchen and sketched. I drew pots and pans, and the plates on Mrs Anholts' mantel. I drew apples in a bowl.

'You are thinking in circles,' she said, when I showed her what I had done. Then she looked again, from it to me, and said, 'You have a good eye, Helena.'

At night, I considered my list. That list, and her kicking, kept me a good deal from sleep. I thought: *How can I make it be?* Underneath, like a nightmare beneath a dream, tugged the fear of the opposite – of not being able to give her the simplest things needed for life; the fear of one day making the journey Betje's mother had made.

I screwed the list into a ball and threw it into a corner. Then I smoothed it flat and slept with it under my pillow.

I slept without sleeping. He surfaced, heavy, soft, coaxing. I pushed him away.

I pushed him away. I pushed him away. He found the softest part of my ear. He would not go.

He would not go.

'Mrs Anholts? Did he say when he'd come back?'

'No, he did not,' she said, putting down her embroidery. She snapped the cotton between her teeth, patted it and seemed satisfied.

Beeswax

NO WORD FROM him. April came, bright with blossom. Patches of ice clung to the ground and thawed into puddles in the low sunshine. I said I was tired. I spent days in my room. I needed to think.

I took out my list. The words, where I left them, no nearer answering the questions that crowded in.

> *For her to be born well and the birth be a good one*
> *For her to be named before God*
> *To make a living for us both*
> *To give her a home, when she comes*
> *So I do not have to give her up*
> *Not for her to be a maid like me*
> *Not for her to be a maid like Betje – not knowing*
> *To go to Leiden again*
> *For him to know her*

I pulled out my bundle from under the bed and tipped out all I had. I sorted through my things: my Bible, Mother's brooch, the linen headscarf, the sketch of the rose stem. I'd brought a small roll of papers, the work I'd done with the Monsieur in the kitchen whilst Mr Sergeant was in Utrecht. Page after page I'd copied from the Bible. Words, words,

words, words. Numbers. Algebra. It had seemed like another language then, but, looking at it now, I could see patterns, as though the puzzle had sorted all by itself.

I picked up the slate Mr Sergeant had given me. I saw him alone, at the kitchen table, cutting into a cheese. I hoped Mr Slootmaekers had found him a new maid. But I could not make myself think kindly of the replacement me. She'd be a little clumsy, I thought; she'd spill his tea. She'd not make ink from beetroot. Mr Sergeant might be a little disappointed, I thought.

I opened Betje's letter, touched my fingers to her words.

I stood for a long time, staring out of the window, and listened to pigeons skitter on the roof. What had he said? *You have to love life without fearing death. Well,* I thought, *he's not stuck in this attic, with only pigeons for company.*

I left everything where it was and fastened my shawl around my shoulders with the brooch.

'I thought you weren't feeling well,' Mrs Anholts said, looking up in surprise as I clattered down the stairs.

'Thank you.' I walked past her without stopping. 'But I'm much better.'

'Helena—?'

I closed the door behind me, rattling the knocker as it shut, leaving her question unanswered.

How peculiar to walk and have no place to go – nothing to fetch, nothing to carry, nothing to do. I had no basket, no jug to fill. I saw maids rushing home from the market, laden with as much as they could carry. My hands, horribly empty.

I could go where I liked. I could stop, look, watch. I could take my time and did not have to think, *I must get back.*

I made my way along Lange Bisschopstraat. I usually avoided this street. The Monsieur had lodged here a year ago, Mrs Anholts said. I thought of him walking these streets and seeing the things I now saw. I glanced up at the windows, but what good was there in imagining him there, looking out? What did I think he would do? Come and greet me? Or, seeing me, turn away?

I passed the house as if it were any other and on I went to the end of the street. I'd spotted a bookseller there before. *This time,* I thought, *I will go in.*

It was unlike Mr Sergeant's. It was unlike Mr Veldman's. It was unlike any bookshop I had been in before.

The room was small and dark; the smell of beeswax tickled my nose. I had the impression that nothing had moved for a very long time; it was all a little dusty. 'May I help you with something?' The voice seemed made of shadow at first, but then a man stepped out of darker shadow behind. He must have been there all the while, and had watched me come in.

'I am only looking, sir.'

'For anything in particular?' His eyes slipped over me, taking in details, stitching them together into a likely purse.

There were a number of unbound books on a desk. 'Theses,' he said when he saw me notice them.

Each had a different frontispiece. They were not as grand as those I'd seen in Mr Sergeant's study. One had a picture of a hare, its face more like that of a sheep. *I could do better,* I thought.

'Do you have a children's alphabet?'

He tilted his head, as if to scoop up what I'd said with his ear. His moustache twitched. He held up one hand and then turned in a slow circle. 'As you can see, I have many, many books. Unfortunately, I am unable to count a children's alphabet among them. Sorry.' He waited a moment. 'Anything else I can interest you in?'

'All children have to learn, sir.'

'They do indeed.' His gaze dropped lower. 'And in God they find wisdom, truth, grace.'

'A pity you have no book.'

We considered one another for a moment. He held himself still, his eyes a little too open, as if trying not to frown.

And then I had it.

What is thought? What is hope?

It is shadow and beeswax and dust. It is the letters I first learned.

I thanked him and left.

I started the Alphabet that day. But I had only five sheets of paper remaining in the box and regretted the paper I'd wasted.

I had to get a letter to him, to ask for more. I will take it to the Athenaeum Library, I thought, and if they will not take it, I will walk to Utrecht myself.

I propped a pillow behind me and set a sheet of paper

by my side. I studied my hand and drew a fingernail first, then the palm, my fingers relaxed and curled into a C. I smoothed my dress over my stomach and drew its swollen crescent. Each sketch traced the slow curved growing of me. *See, Monsieur, this is my condition, these are the changes I have.*

I angled a small mirror against the pillow and caught my frown briefly reflected as I concentrated. I eased the laces on my bodice. I cupped my breast and ran my hand over the darkening nipple. In two, three lines, I had its shape on the page. I remembered the shape of his shoulder in my hand. He wasn't just thought and thinking. I could *feel* him still. When I had covered the page in sketches, I wrote:

> *I have no more paper.*
> *The river is thawed. The road is clear.*
> *Helena Jans*

I folded the letter, sealed it and took it downstairs to Mrs Anholts. I found her, polishing copper, her sleeves rolled up to her elbows and the table piled high with pans. Her cheeks shone red from the effort. She'd taken off her cap; strands of silvery hair framed her face. I could see her younger self underneath – the high cheekbones that still made her pretty.

'Mrs Anholts.'

When she saw the letter, she wagged a finger at me. 'It will get you nowhere. And don't ask for postage, I haven't money for that.'

'But—'

'Taking you in is one thing; funding an exchange of letters is another. Your allowance doesn't pay for such things. Besides, where would you send it? Did he leave an address? I don't have one!'

'He said, take it to the Athenaeum Library.'

'That's on Klooster.' She thought for a moment. 'There's nothing for you there. Monsieur Descartes worked there last year when he was staying with Professor Reneri; Clément lodged here. He had such a wretched time carrying books and papers and—'

I stopped her before she had firm hold of the memory. 'Professor Reneri?'

'Yes. He's a good friend of the Monsieur's. He was the reason he came to Deventer in the first place and—'

'And his first name?'

'Well,' she thought for a bit, 'Henri, I believe, but I'd never call him that.'

Henri Reneri? *HR.* He was the HR in the Monsieur's letter. I grabbed my shawl and made a dash for the door.

'But Reneri is with Monsieur Descartes in Utrecht,' she called after me.

'I know!' I shouted back.

I could not stay a moment longer and rushed out into the street. I knew where to go.

I made my way quickly. Each step towards Klooster quickened my heart. For the first time since I had arrived, I felt the possibility of him. It was as if a thread had been wound in a little and had shortened the distance between us.

Library

THE LIBRARY WAS not hard to find. Without realising, I had passed by it before on my way to the river. But once I arrived, I stopped, no longer certain what I should do. I stood to one side of the courtyard and watched. There were men with books and scrolls and sheafs of paper; men in velvet gowns trimmed with fur, wearing feathered, triangle hats; men in small, murmuring groups. Hunched, shuffling men bundled in silence; and young men, shoulders back, arguing. Clerics and professors. Researchers and scholars.

I stepped back as one man caught my eye – but it was as if he had seen through me to the wall behind. I heard Dutch, and French, and languages I did not know. The whole world seemed to have been called to the library. But no woman crossed the threshold, not even a maid sent to sweep the floor – perhaps thinking made no dust at all. I looked at my letter. It was not a scroll. It was not a book. I was not a man.

I rested one hand on my stomach. All I had to do was to take a step.

I slid one foot forwards a little. One step. Then another. Then another. I could not look up, only at my feet, as I willed myself across the courtyard – step by step by step. Then I was at the door, standing in the entrance and in the way. The door opened and I was caught in a gust of men, swept along in a dispute about polders. The door clicked shut behind me.

I found myself in a brightly lit corridor. Between the windows, bookcases ran from floor to ceiling. Desks had been placed in front of the windows, where the light was best. I had never seen so many books – or men so silenced by them. Were these the same books the Monsieur had spoken of? Books that could split thoughts apart? If so, these men were completely unscathed, the only sound being the occasional dry cough.

I made my way along the corridor to a table at the end. A man glanced up from behind it, then went back to the papers in front of him. He had a neat white beard, and both it and his moustache were twisted into points. Oddly, it focused attention on his very small mouth. He continued to write though I stood there before him and only the desk between us. But I was not here to converse with it.

'Excuse me, I have a letter for Professor Reneri.'

The man shook his head and waved me away.

I considered the bald patch on his head. In that moment I had to decide what to do. I hadn't time to think, to consider for or against.

I said, 'Excuse me, sir, but who are you?'

It was no way to address a man of his position and well we both knew it. 'The Athenaeum librarian!' he said, the words shocked out of him before he'd considered for or against answering me either.

I had the right person. I bowed. 'I have a letter.' I held it out so he could see. 'Where should I put it?'

He blinked. 'Professor Reneri is not here. He teaches at the Illustrious School, Utrecht.'

'This letter is for him.'

He gave me a scornful look. 'This is a library, not a postal service.'

'I was told I could leave it here.'

'Well, you can't. Go away.'

I stood there and watched him write – word after effortless word stretched across the page.

He stopped what he was doing and frowned. 'Who told you that you could use the library as a post office?'

I swallowed. If I said Reneri, he might ask me how I knew him and I wouldn't know what to say. I couldn't risk that. Mrs Anholts said the Monsieur had worked here last year, so perhaps the librarian knew him.

'Monsieur Descartes.'

His mouth snapped shut. Now I had his attention. 'Descartes! I might have known.'

'You know him?'

He gave a laugh, but not a happy one. 'I've had the pleasure of meeting him but not the cow's head he was butchering at the time.' He did not seem pleased to be reminded.

'Please, this letter is important.'

He looked at my letter, the lines on his forehead deepening. 'Those papers there are going to Utrecht.' He pointed with his quill to a pile on the corner of his desk. It was clear he did not want to touch it. 'Leave it there and it will find Professor Reneri that way.'

'One moment.' I reached for his quill, turning it to be

sure I did not damage the nib. I wrote *Professor Henri Reneri, Utrecht*, and the letters *RD* underneath.

'A most peculiar arrangement,' he said.

But one that works, I thought, and I put the letter on the pile. He looked at me as though he thought me quite peculiar too.

Outside, the sun shone brightly. I had solved the Monsieur's riddle and the letter was on its way. I stretched out my hands in front of me, turning them over in the warm sunshine. My skin had softened and paled. They were not a maid's hands anymore. They were ink stained, like the Monsieur's.

Alphabet

A LARGE AMOUNT of paper arrived for me. He had included a letter:

Utrecht, 15 May 1635

H—,

Thank you for your sketches.

I would like to be able to draw as well as you can – how much more a well-executed picture tells me than the words needed to describe it. I envy you that; my drawing skills frustrate me. You have put the paper to good use and that pleases me. I am happy to provide more.

I am making progress on my Meteorology and revising completely my little treatise on Optics. It takes all my attention, for I need it to say what I mean and I need to be clear on that. Life should be a good deal more certain when I am done; I hope, at least, to have time . . .

There followed two more pages about life in Utrecht, most of it concerned with an argument with an unnamed senior cleric. He wrote that he was under pressure 'from all directions' and needed to find a publisher; his illustrations were 'woeful'. *Mersenne hounded him,* he went on.

I did not sleep with this letter, unlike the first he sent. I read it, folded it and slipped it into the pages of my Bible, next to the note I'd had from Thomas.

I took longer walks, out to the river, over the bridge and on into the fields until all I could see of Deventer were church towers in the distance, blurred in the haze. Each dusty step sent up a cloud of mayflies, the world brought down to the path at my feet. I walked as though I had somewhere to be and returned to Mrs Anholts' house exhausted.

I tried not to look at his letters – they made me feel I'd lost what edged me.

I no longer went as far as the fields and then I stopped going out altogether.

The summer hay grew high.

I had grown so big, I did not know how I would be delivered. I knew from stories my mother had told, stories she'd come back with from neighbours, that sometimes the pain was too great; sometimes the baby could not be freed. Sometimes it was too much.

'Is it hard, Mrs Anholts?'

'The first time, yes. It is no good telling you otherwise. But I will help you.'

She'd helped deliver babies before, was still called on to help from time to time.

'Do you have a name for her yet?'

I nodded, but would not be drawn.

'And if it's a boy?'

'It's a girl!'

'You cannot know whether the child is a girl or a boy, Helena,' she said. 'If it's a boy, he'll need a name.'

'It's a girl! That's what I feel.' I felt stupid saying it, then angry for feeling stupid.

There had not been a baby in the house for years, but Mrs Anholts gave me what she had. She fashioned a crib from a drawer, making it ready. She gave me the contents of a small wooden box from under her bed – tiny clothes speckled with mildew and deeply creased after years of being folded away.

She muttered a little as she did this. It seemed the Monsieur had not thought to provide these items; no allowance had been made to buy new in the money he had sent. Although he could look deeply, he had not looked far. Not for the first time, I thought, he has not looked ahead.

I worked on my Alphabet. I did not want Mrs Anholts to see. I said I was tired, and spent more and more time in my room.

I knew what I wanted to do: letters, decorated simply, with a verse underneath; a number of pages that would make a book. As I worked, the gap between me and the page seemed to get wider and wider. It was as well he had sent so much paper. I would need it. I found it best to have a separate sheet for thinking. It was only once the idea was there, and had worked its way down to my fingertips, so close to the page it might jump on it, that I felt I could begin.

Sometimes I had two or three pages by the end of the day and worked without a break. Most days, nothing – the work shambling, awkward, wrong.

There were days when I imagined a copy of my Alphabet in the hands of every Dutch child.

And then I realised. The child I was imagining was mine – my little girl, reading. Perhaps I should do this only for her, for the love of it? I remembered Mr Sergeant's house and all that books had afforded him. I thought of my list. I had to finish the book and then I would sell it.

He came to me into my dreams.

Let me look at you. At this little mountain we have made.

He laid his head against me.

Let me see . . .

Nuzzling, nuzzling, slipping fabric from my grip.

Let me see . . .

Kissing my temple, soothing, words in my hair.

Let me see.

And I turned to him and brought him to me – the need I felt, a rage almost.

Air

THE DOOR OPENED into a large, square room. Light flooded in through a window at the far end, throwing into silhouette a man, the church deacon, who was sitting at the large desk in front of it. A high-backed chair with scrolled arms had been set on the far side of the table, facing into the bright sunshine – all the better to lay bare the faces of those who would be brought before him.

'Sit down,' he said, as I approached.

Suddenly, I saw him to my left as well. I startled, then realised it was his portrait. His pale face, even paler against the black background, looked down on me – a lifetime's sternness in a single expression. Mrs Anholts said he had more children than were easy to count. I imagined how it must be when they gathered together, no child daring to speak; smiling only when he went out and then only to remind themselves that smiling was possible.

Once I was seated, he pressed his fingertips into a peak and studied me in silence for a while. How white his hands; like hands that had stayed too long in water – they would be cold if I touched them. The thought made me draw back. He laid them palm-side down on the table, spreading out his fingers. He did this slowly, as if everything he considered, every movement he made, added weight to him and he was wary of adding more.

'Yes?' He said this in a way that made it seem he had been waiting for me to speak first.

'I—'

'You have a baptismal request, I believe.'

'Yes.'

'You will have to speak up.'

The chair I was sitting on was low. I looked up at him. 'Yes.'

He brought his fingers together into a peak again and tapped them as he thought. 'What *you* would like is irrelevant, you realise?'

I looked down.

'Tell me about the child.' His gaze slipped to my stomach. 'When was it conceived?'

I tried not to fidget. I locked my hands over my stomach to shield her from his questions. 'Last winter.'

'Where?'

'Amsterdam.'

'And the father?' He raised his eyes, waited.

'I . . . he . . .'

I had not expected this. I thought of what the Limousin and Mrs Anholts had agreed. I could not lie to the deacon.

He tapped his fingers together. 'Let me help you. Unmarried?'

I nodded.

'I see.'

He studied me for a while. 'A child is from God. Even those born, let's say, to one side – *onecht kind* – have a place.'

'Yes,' I whispered. 'That's what I want for her. To have a place. More than anything.'

He stood up and went over to the window. 'Any prospect of marriage?'

'No.'

'Pardon?'

'No. None.'

'Tell me, has he abandoned you?'

I shook my head.

'Is he feckless? Married already?'

'No.'

'Is he insane? Imprisoned? Awaiting execution? *Dead?*'

'No!'

'I see.'

He stared out of the window for a while, then seemed to tire of it. He came round so that he was in front of me and sat on the edge of the table. I could smell a perfume on him – rosemary and clove. He smelled of death.

He leaned towards me.

'So tell me, Helena Jans, about the father. What is it that prevents him?'

I drew my arms around me and away from him.

He leaned in closer still. I could smell his breath now. 'Tell me.'

'He cannot. I'm—'

'What?' he said. 'Beneath him?'

Beneath, less than, below. I sank in the chair. I nodded.

'And his church? Tell me.'

'Catholic,' I murmured.

'Ah, a *Catholic.*' He tutted and shook his head as if he had

209

been expecting this all along, and we had finally reached the true depth of my misfortune. 'And does this *Catholic* have a name?'

'Reyner.' I looked down. It was not quite the truth, nor was it quite a lie, but he moved on before I could dwell on it.

'Reyner, the Catholic from Deventer?'

I shook my head.

'Apeldoorn?'

'No.'

'Amsterdam?'

'No.'

'Delft? Groningen? *Amersfoort?*'

'No, no . . . France.'

'France! Reyner, from France? Most *peculiar.*'

I flushed.

He went back to his desk and wrote down the name, then held the quill above the page, waiting. He wanted the father's family name too.

'Jochems,' I said. I watched as he wrote, my heart sinking further with every scratch of his nib.

'So, Reyner, who is French, prefers a Dutch name, correct?'

I heard how he said it, the disbelief in his voice. 'Yes.'

'I see.'

'He provides . . .'

'He provides? But where is his provision now?' He cast about the room, raising his hands in the air with his question, and shrugged. 'Where is he?'

'He is away.'

'Ah, a *travelling* provider. I see. And he is educated?'

'Yes. He is.'

'Virtuous?'

I nodded. 'Yes.'

'So, the debauchery is yours, correct?'

I looked down.

'If he is virtuous, the debauchery must be yours?'

'Yes,' I whispered, 'mine.'

'And now you seek the child's legitimation through baptism?'

'She *must* be baptised.'

'*Must?*' He put down the quill and considered me. 'His Catholic God would not be so understanding. If you were in France . . . but then you wouldn't be, would you?'

This seemed to amuse him and he laughed.

He picked up the quill again. 'Tell me about you.'

'I am from Leiden—'

He raised his hand to stop me and shook his head. 'But that is where you should be making your request. Where the charity begins. Leiden. Not here.'

I could see the calculations he was making. 'I don't want charity! He provides!'

'So you tell me, but if I had a guilder for the times I have heard that . . .'

I tried a different approach. 'She will be born here, in Deventer. She *belongs* here, with this church.'

'And your parents?'

'My father is dead.'

'Mother?'

I shook my head. 'She does not know.'

'But you will tell her?'

'Yes.'

He slapped his hand down on the table. 'I will not tolerate lies!'

'No, please. I have not been able—'

'You will tell her, is that clear?'

'Yes,' I whispered.

He seemed satisfied. 'Good. We cannot know what God intends for us. I have a duty to bring the child into the Church, so that *he* may gather around the fountain of His Good Grace – the Grace of Christ reaches further than the sin of Adam. *Let the children come to Me and do not hinder them; for to such belongs the Kingdom of Heaven.* Bring the infant here and the minister at Grote of Lebuinuskerk will baptise him. Will your travelling French provider attend?'

'I do not know.' I felt as though my voice was about to slide out of me.

'Let's see this as a test of his *provision*, shall we?'

I nodded, then stood up, bowed and turned to leave.

'Helena Jans,' he called back to me, 'baptism is only the beginning, you realise that, don't you?'

I bowed again, lower this time.

He waved me away and went back to his writing. No amount of bowing would make me taller in his eyes.

In the night, it was on me. It approached with fingers, then teeth. It nipped me and bit me, then skulked in the shadows for a while.

'Mrs Anholts!' I shouted, as water ran between my legs, soaking the sheets. 'Mrs Anholts!'

She came into my room, and when she saw what had happened she went out returned with jugs of water and bundles of old sheets. She rolled up a piece of cloth and put it on one side. She made me stand, then lean over. She held me as I rocked against her.

'Child, child, child, child, child, child.'

'No, no, no . . .' I moaned, as the pain locked in me.

I wanted my mother, but in the black distances that rolled in my mind, Leiden was as far away as the East Indies. He had set her from me. His fault. His fault entirely.

Mrs Anholts rubbed my back in circles. She led me to the bed. 'Open your legs.'

I lay back, shook my head and drew my knees together.

'It'll not come out if you don't!' She put her hands between my knees and prised them apart. 'There,' she said, 'good.'

When I arched my back, the pain pushed me flat.

'Get it out of me,' I cried. It would eat me, tear me, rip me; it did not care if I died.

'Helena . . .' She went to wipe me, but I knocked her hand away.

It came at me with knives, then beat me.

'Monsieur,' I wept.

I wanted him. And then I no longer had words, not even his name, just sounds that came from a place I did not know was in me.

She placed the cloth roll between my teeth. 'Bite.'

I turned my head away.

'Bite!'

She knelt between my knees, pushed my legs apart, then took hold of my hand and gripped. The pain ran at me with a final crashing blow, driving my breath from me until all the air had gone. Then I felt her coming, a blinding, twisting pain and the sudden rush of her.

'She's here, Helena, look,' Mrs Anholts said and she was crying too.

She lifted a small, pale baby onto my stomach.

'The rest needs to come out.'

She clamped the cord, picked up a knife and cut my baby free.

A girl. Dear God. A girl. Pink and wrinkled and limp. Her tiny fist stretched open.

'Sweet darling,' I sobbed and kissed her cheeks. Her hair was dark and bloodied. She blinked at my touch.

'Beautiful, beautiful girl,' I said. 'My darling, Fransintge. *Francine.*'

Francine opened her mouth, as if breathing for both of us, and cried.

Water

SHE HAD HIS eyes and his hair and it curled at her ear just like his. I drew a picture of her asleep, snipped a tiny lock of her hair and folded it into a letter. She would be baptised on 28 July – it would give time for the news to reach him and for him to come. I wrote the details in my best hand. I told him his Dutch name would be entered onto her baptism record. Once baptised, she would be legitimate. If he objected, he would need to tell me by reply.

I wrote the letter as though to someone I had known long ago, as though writing to my past. I gave the letter to Mrs Anholts to take. Before she went, she fiddled with a piece of lace she'd taken from her pocket. She examined it, trying to decide what to do, then held it out.

'Here.'

I opened the lace panel and laid it out on the bed, my fingers following the patterned edge. It was a *kraamkloppertje*.

'I used it for my children.'

'It's beautiful,' I said.

I thought of it wrapped around the door knocker on the front door, the simple proud announcement of her birth. I placed the cloth on the table next to a small pile of baby clothes.

I lifted Francine from the bed and held her to me. I kissed

her forehead and whispered, 'We know you're here, that's what matters.'

'There's soup and *kraamanijs* on the tray there. Drink it up, it'll do you good.'

The soup smelled delicious, but the *kraamanijs* was revolting – a vile, bitter concoction the colour of tar.

'If he saw her, he would never leave.'

'Oh, Helena. What do you know about him?'

My shoulders went down.

'Well? You are lucky he has provided.'

'Provision! Is this what it is?'

'Helena!'

'Why doesn't he come, Mrs Anholts?'

She held her up her hand. 'Enough. There's no more to be said.'

Once she had gone with the letter, I picked up the *kraam-kloppertje* and slipped a piece of paper into the front pocket. I waited until I heard Mrs Anholts go out, then tied it around the door knocker on the front door, knotting it tightly to keep it in place. I hoped Mother would have done the same and her fingers, made a little clumsy by love like mine, would fumble as she tied the knot. I lifted the knocker gently and let it drop, the cloth muffling its sound.

Now no one would be in any doubt. A baby girl, born here – knock quietly, lest you wake her.

No objection arrived from him; my relief brought low by his silence.

The morning of Francine's baptism crept over Deventer's rooftops, slow and heavy with mist. The sun rose in the sky, as flat and pale as an old guilder. I had not slept well, but I had not stayed awake to listen for him. There was no need. I'd not hear his foot on the step. He would not come.

Francine stirred in her crib.

'Sh,' I said as I lifted her.

She nudged against me for milk. I carried her over to the edge of the bed and stroked her hair as she fed – both of us still drowsy. I loved her. I loved her. I loved her. I felt the line between us – an invisible thread that connected her to me and to my mother and to her mother before her. There was another thread too, one that ran to a family she would never meet – *his family*. There was something of my mother in her, I thought, but there was much more of him.

When she had finished feeding, I dressed her in her baptism dress. Mrs Anholts had bleached it to remove the mildew and the black dots had faded to brown.

We walked to the church in silence. Mrs Anholts fiddled with her shawl. I straightened my shoulders and held Francine close to me. The streets became busier and busier as we approached the church. I felt I had been pitched into a sea of starched collars – white-tipped waves that rushed towards the shore of Grote of Lebuinuskerk. Women and girls came out of the houses wearing the prettiest bonnets I'd ever seen. The lace gathered in tiny pleats across their brows and fanned out behind each ear. Everywhere I looked, great blossoms of lace seemed to have flowered in the sunshine.

All the town would be in church. Those who did not already suspect would know; *where's the father then?* Today, my dark-haired girl – so painfully, clearly *other* – would join with them in their church. But it was Francine's church too, I told myself, and she would not be kept from it.

There was a bustle at the door, a jostling for position. Mrs Anholts went up on tiptoe, but shook her head to say no, she'd not seen him. I pressed back into the shadows as far as I could. I could hear the church filling – people shuffling, clogs banging; the few who had seats sat down.

My arms ached from holding Francine. When I looked up, I saw people whispering, words hidden behind hands, blunt stares above.

We stood at the back, with soldiers and beggars: many propped up on crutches, or huddled against the wall, sniffing and wheezing; some moaning in pain. I could not see the minister from here, but there was something familiar about his voice. It was impossible to make out; the sounds broke apart before they reached me. I could not tell where one prayer ended and another began. Mrs Anholts swayed a little. Her lips moved with her own prayers.

I had never felt more awake, so aware of where I was, who I was and why I was here. He had not come; he was gone from me. My throat stung when I swallowed; my heart hurt when it beat.

When the service was over, the church sexton approached. 'We are ready for you now,' he said.

I followed behind him, his shadow almost, with Mrs Anholts by my side. The church so quiet, I could hear the swish of his robe on the floor. He walked slowly, in no hurry – each solemn step took us closer to her baptism and to God. To either side, heads turned, people stared. He was not among them.

When I saw the minister, I stopped. The Athenaeum librarian! His frown deepened when he saw me; he looked briefly at Francine. In that moment, no more than a flicker, he knew my worth. He nodded stiffly to dismiss the sexton. He leaned in, his face so tight his mouth barely moved, the words so faint I hardly heard them.

'I hope this has nothing to do with Reneri, that he is not implicated in this.'

'No!' My astonishment made me vehement. 'Nothing.'

He continued to stare and I feared he would turn me away. Then without dropping his gaze, he brought his hands together and prayed. Only then did he close his eyes and release me.

Our help is in the name of the Lord . . . All these graces are conferred upon us when He is pleased to incorporate us into His Church by baptism . . . to us the remission of our sins . . .

I looked down. The minister wore shoes of the softest leather, polished bright. His robe had been edged with neat stitches and cloth-covered buttons, pulled so tight they shone. His collar, crisp white, pressed. I knew the work needed to make men like him clean. I had polished shoes and made buttons and pressed linen flat. I tucked my feet under my hem.

And for this cause, He has ordained the sign of water, to signify

*that, as by this natural element the body is washed of its bodily
odours, so He wishes to wash and purify our souls* . . .

'Who are the witnesses?'

Mrs Anholts stepped forward and curtsied.

'Who presents this child for baptism?'

'I do,' I said.

'And the father?' He looked beyond me, addressing the
congregation behind.

There was a murmur. I heard people shift about.
Restlessness bloomed.

'No,' I said and shook my head, but the minister waited,
as if expecting a voice to come from the back.

'The father?' he said, louder this time.

When no reply came, he turned his attention back to me
and held out his hands to take Francine.

'Then we shall have to proceed without him.'

I kissed Francine's forehead and passed her to him. He
held her awkwardly in one arm, cupped water in his other
hand and held it above Francine's head. And as he did so,
light poured in through the window, as if God had moved
the clouds away. I saw light on the water, and God's blessing,
there in his hand.

'Helena Jans, will you bring this child up in the nurture
and admonition of the Lord?'

'Yes.'

'Her name? How is she to be baptised?'

'Fransintge.'

Water trickled between his fingers.

I thought he had not heard. '*Fransintge.* That is her name.'

He dripped water onto Francine's head. '*Repent, and be*

baptised every one of you in the name of Jesus Christ for the forgiveness of your sins; and you shall receive the gift of the Holy Spirit. For the promise is to you and to your children and to all that are far off . . . Fransintge, I baptise you in the name of the Father and the Son and the Holy Spirit. Amen.'

There was a fleeting silence and then a thunder of amens echoed around the church, as though a flock of birds had gone up, startling at a clap of hands.

Fransintge – Francine. She had her name. She was baptised. I thought I would die from the beating of my heart.

The church sexton brought the register. 'Names?' he asked. 'Father first.'

'Reyner. Reyner Jochems.'

I watched him write. Even at this point, I thought someone might stop him, might stand up and protest. But he wrote without interruption.

He tapped the quill on the ink pot. 'Mother?'

'Helena Jans.'

He took his time writing *Fransintge* and I was not sure he had the spelling right.

I looked at the register, at our names at the bottom of the page: his name, my name, hers – side by side – and the ink not yet dry. We were the same as any other Dutch family listed there. I wanted to press my palm against the wet ink, to soak the words into my skin. She had her name. She had been brought towards God.

The minister took a cloth from a curate and dried each

finger, knuckle by knuckle, as if he wanted to remove every last trace of water.

'It is done,' he said with no warmth or joy. 'My responsibility in this matter is towards the child. Everything will out, in the end, before God.'

'Yes,' I said, and bowed. 'Minister?'

He turned to me.

'Your name. I don't know your name.'

'Jacobus Revius.'

He dropped the cloth back into a bowl the curate held out, then turned and walked away. He wanted nothing more to do with me, or Francine, or Reyner Jochems. Reyner Jochems? It was him and it wasn't. Not a lie, but not the truth either. I was holding a curtain in front of God's eyes, here, in His house.

The church started to empty; the aisles filled with chatter, piety loosening as quickly as a belt after a large meal.

'Did you see the child?'

'I did. So *dark*.'

'You know where it came from . . . She found it . . . in among the peat!'

'Ha!'

'I'm surprised the minister allowed it!'

'*Hoer.*'

I rubbed my thumb on the back of Francine's hand. She blinked and sucked her knuckles. Every time I looked at her, I saw him. *He would love her if he saw her.*

I knew he would not come, but that had not stopped me from imagining the day differently. I was a fool for doing so. I had wanted him to see her. But he was in Utrecht with his thoughts and his books and his candles. *Yes, Monsieur, I thought, I know what happens to wax after it melts – it cools and greys and hardens.*

I'd made discoveries too.

A box had been delivered whilst we were gone. Mrs Anholts shook her head, but pushed it towards me. 'Well, go on. Open it.'

I pulled at the string that held the lid in place. Inside was a sheaf of paper and a small bundle wrapped in tissue. I unwrapped the paper, revealing a slither of gold. Attached to it, a note:

For my daughter, Francine, on her baptism day.

I let the note drop. *I have this life, no other,* he'd told me. I should have listened. I should have known. He should have been here.

But I'd had enough of shoulds.

I would not write again. He would come if he wanted to.

Dream

I HAD REACHED the last three letters of my Alphabet when news arrived of the plague in Leiden. I was anxious to have news of my mother. I had no way of knowing if she had survived, or how she coped if she lived. I prayed – desperate, pleading prayers, even though I knew it was not my place to question what would be. God knew who would be saved. Every morning, when I woke, the worry was there where I had left it, as if it had stood by my bedside all night, waiting for me to open my eyes again.

And then, one day, after months had gone by, the Limousin arrived. He wanted to see Francine.

'What do you want?'

He ignored me and squeezed Francine's arms in turn as if he were at market, examining livestock. At first he measured her against the length of his arm and then awkwardly along the length of his leg. Now that she had a tooth starting, he prised open her mouth to see. She struggled on his knee and tried to get free. He would deserve it if she bit him. He gave me no news of the Monsieur and I did not ask.

'You've heard of the plague in Leiden,' he said, his eyes bright and knowing. 'Isn't that where your mother lives?'

I nodded. He knew she did.

'If she had sense, she'd leave. But that's not what your Church preaches, is it?'

The Limousin had brought another present for Francine from the Monsieur – a girl's dress, of the darkest blue silk, with an embroidered hem. It would have fitted a child twice her size: a reminder that the Monsieur had not seen her yet. I wondered what little of Limousin's news reached him.

'Oh,' said Mrs Anholts, when she saw it. Her hand hovered above the cloth, not touching it. She brought her hand away, her fingers curled into her palm, as though it might burn her. 'Beautiful.'

And it was. Blue, the most precious colour of all. Were they tiny white flowers that had been embroidered at the hem? Or stars in a night sky? But I could not see how Francine could wear it. It was for a different child – a merchant's child, not one brought up in attics and alcoves.

I pushed the dress back at him. 'No, thank you.'

He held my eye as he pushed it back. 'I don't know who else you think it will fit.'

Mrs Anholts picked up the dress and tucked it under one arm to stop any further dispute. 'Tell the Monsieur thank you.'

I arranged the loose sheets of my Alphabet – thirty in all – imagining the book it would be, how it would look once bound. At first I thought, *It's not good enough, he won't want it, I'll keep it.*

I drew the frontispiece last of all and titled it, *An Alphabet with Verse – for the Instruction of Small Children.* Underneath the title, my name, *Helena Jans van der Strom, Deventer, 1636.*

I set the pages in order, placed them between two thin boards so the paper would not crush and bound it all with a thin leather strap. I walked down Lange Bisschopstraat without a glance left or right. The bookseller seemed not to have moved and was in the same place I left him last – as though he spent his days attached to the bookcase like a bat.

I cleared space on his desk, moving the theses to one side, and placed my package in the centre.

'I have something for you.' I did not unwrap it immediately. I wanted him to think, to wonder what was inside.

His fingers lifted in anticipation. 'Well?' he said, after a short while. 'Will you open it, or shall I?'

I untied the strap. 'An Alphabet. With instruction,' I explained.

I opened it at the letter A and turned the sheets, so he could see the work on each. He leaned in, stopped my hand as I turned and leaned in closer.

'Hm,' he said.

We reached the end.

'Interesting work.' He looked at me. 'Where did you get it?'

'Does it please you?'

'Yes, very much.' He rubbed his chin. 'Show me the letter D again.'

I turned back to it.

D

~ *Dream* ~

And they said unto him, We have dreamed a dream, and there
is no interpreter of it. And Joseph said unto them, Do not
interpretations belong to God?

Genesis 40:8

He looked at me with his wide-open eyes. 'Are you taken
with dreaming?'

I dropped my gaze. 'Do you think it will sell, sir?'

'I can see a market for it. But how did you come by it?'

I closed the Alphabet, to reveal the front page. I
thought it the loveliest page and had combined all the
letters in miniature around the border. Wasn't that what
a frontispiece was for – to describe the work about to
be read?

'Oh.' He blinked, then frowned. He tapped his finger on
my name. 'Is this you?'

'Yes.'

'*You* did this?'

'Yes.'

He seemed dazed, still a little lost in the work. 'It is good.'

My heart swelled. 'Thank you.'

'But why have you brought it to me?'

'I want to sell it.' His question surprised me. Why did he
think I was here?

Without needing time to reflect, he said, 'I'm afraid I can't
buy it from you. As it is, it is worthless.'

'It can't be *worthless*.'

'Let me demonstrate.' He picked up the title page, turning it over to its blank side. 'Now it might sell.'

I looked at him, not understanding. He turned the title page back, revealing my name.

'Now it won't,' he said.

Then he turned the page over again, so that my name was hidden.

'Now it will.'

'Oh.'

'No man buys a book written by a woman. And I am in the business of selling books – to men. Sorry.'

'But I need to sell it, sir.'

He placed the frontispiece on one side. 'I would need a new frontispiece. Something anonymous.'

I nodded.

'I'd give you a guilder then.'

'It is worth more than that!' I thought of the work I had put into it.

'By an *unknown*?' He shook his head. 'A book like this is always a risk. I would have to find a publisher. Add to this the expense of cutting plates. Printing costs. Binding. *Distribution*.' He shuddered. 'Bring me a new frontispiece and then I might reconsider.'

In the end we settled on two guilders. I had wanted four. Many of Mr Sergeant's books sold for many times that.

'I do not doubt its worth,' he said, 'but worth is not the same as *value*.'

I could not allow bitterness to temper what I had. I had money, more than I had ever had before. And when the plague in Leiden lifted, this money would take me home.

I left Mrs Anholts a letter and thanked her for her kindness. I waited until she was gone to Apeldoorn for the day, then gathered my things, dressed Francine in a new wool coat, pulled the door to behind me and went.

I told her I could not stay, that I needed to find my own way. I could not live, waiting for him, when he never came. I said I was headed to Leiden, but gave no address.

Before I left, I took out the list I'd written when I had first arrived.

For him to know her

I picked up my quill, drew a line through it and crossed it thoroughly out.

LEIDEN, 1636–7

Wool

'WATCH HER FINGERS!' Mother shouted. Francine had crawled over to her spinning wheel and was pulling herself to her feet. 'Watch her, Helena!'

Francine startled, sat down with a bump and began to cry.

'I'm not to blame if she loses her fingers!'

I scooped Francine up and kissed her cheek. As soon as she was in my arms, she twisted away, wanting to be on the floor again. I carried her over to where I worked.

'Here, play with these,' I said and stacked a tower of old bobbins.

Francine took a swipe and scattered them. She clapped her hands and shrieked, her tears forgotten.

'Now you do it.'

I put a bobbin in each of her hands. She clacked them together and grinned. I crouched down in front of her, dropping my voice to a whisper as I spoke.

'You need those fingers. One day, I'm going to teach you to write.'

Mother cocked her head towards the basket of wool I had carded that morning. 'She needs to learn useful things.'

'Promise I am,' I said, ignoring her, as I stacked the bobbins again. I kissed Francine on the nose.

'Shall I spin for the both of us?'

Mother hunched lower over her work. The yarn seemed part of her, as if she unwound it from an endless spool somewhere inside. There were hunched women all over this town – women who would never straighten again.

I steadied my stool and set my foot on the treadle, but my mood darkened as soon as I started and the yarn tangled into knots. I slumped over the wheel. I could not spin wool like this. Wool had to slip through your fingers with the gentlest touch, else it would snarl and hitch. Lumpy yarn wasn't worth the money in a pauper's pocket. I drew the wool back, blew on my fingers to warm them and started again.

Apart from spinning, Mother took in sewing – hemming or repairing sheets or longer pieces of cloth. We worked in silence by candlelight, late into the night. I knew what had happened in Amsterdam still turned in her mind, that she was looking at it this way, then that. When she did speak, what she said came at me as if with the flat of her hand.

'Some drunk from the *kermis*?'

'No!'

'Well, who then?'

I shook my head.

One evening, after we had put our sewing away, Mother took a letter from the mantelpiece and held it out to me, then settled herself in her chair. I recognised the hand immediately. *Thomas.* I looked at the date, *16 February 1633* – sent before his return voyage.

The letter had been opened.

'The Joostens' boy read it to me – but he reads so quickly, it was hard to take in. Read it to me, Helena.'

I shuffled my stool closer to the fire and angled the page into the light. Even so, it was a struggle to see.

Dear Mother,

I'm arrived in Batavia. What a place! I wish you could see it. A great wall is being built – people from the world over are building it. I hear Dutch spoken all parts about – seems half of Holland is here. Some are staying, making this home. Imagine! Tis hard, but there is work to do, work for men like me – walls to strengthen, canals to dig, houses to build.

Makes me think I'm a land man after all. I'm sick of the sea and the sea is sick of me. Would Father be ashamed to hear it? Don't be sad – I'm well as can be, I reckon. But I miss home, Mother, and I wishes I was back.

God be with you –

Thomas

I rested the letter in my lap. *Absconded.* It was there, between the lines. The reason why. He didn't need to write it for me to understand.

'There's been no word since.' She touched tears away with a finger. 'I've heard of terrible fevers there.'

'Oh, Mother.'

I tried to think of words that might comfort her. Should I tell her that Thomas's ship had made it back to Amsterdam? Wouldn't she want to know why he hadn't come home? She looked so worn down by worry. I did not know if he lived. Would he not have made his way back here by now if he did?

So I told her instead about Mr Veldman's maps, about the tall trees, tufted with giant leaves, and cats as big as sheep, and all other amazements Thomas must have seen. Her hands fell open as she listened. She stared at them as though she had lost something, but was not sure what.

We sat in silence. After some time, she said, 'You need to know something, Helena. I'm going to Zeeland, at Martinmas, to stay with Margriet. I'll return after Easter. It is decided.'

Margriet, her sister, had an ague that had stopped her left arm and leg years ago and they had not moved well since. Mother had never seemed too concerned before – Margriet had family to care for her.

'Oh.' I had not expected this news. Martinmas was still weeks away.

'That's to be done first.' She pointed at the sacks of wool piled in one corner. 'You can stay whilst I am gone.'

Stay? I swallowed. Now it was I who looked at my hands.

'Yes, Mother.' My voice dropped to a whisper.

'When I come back I do not want to find what I left.'

I looked up and met her eye.

'You need to find your own way, Helena. Somewhere to live, work to support you; a man who will not object to the child – there are men like that, widowers and the like. But you're not to bring them here. I'll not allow it.'

Her words fell through me to my feet. Is that what she thought of me? I felt tears in my eyes, hot and stinging.

'By Easter, Helena. A new beginning. I am giving you time.' She touched my shoulder as she stood up. 'When you've finished, put the letter back where it was. I will sleep.'

I turned my head as she undressed. I heard her clamber into bed and draw the curtains closed. I placed the letter back on the mantelpiece, tidied the threads into a basket and swept up the ashes. Tiredness weighted me, but I had never felt less like sleeping. I had a pain in my head like a binding being wound ever tighter about it.

I went to the window to close the shutters – the summer night not black, but a deep inky blue. As I stood there, I noticed people with their arms raised to the heavens. I recognised neighbours, wrapped in blankets; others in nightgowns – strange twins of their daytime selves, faces pale as milk in the moonlight. I gathered my shawl around me and went out.

'St Lawrence's tears,' said a weaver from the house opposite, when I asked him why everyone was there.

As if I didn't know this myself. But with all that had happened, I'd forgotten. Had I no room in my mind to remember such things any more?

His wife elbowed him in the ribs to shush him. 'You're not to call them that. If the minister hears, we'll be in trouble. He'll think we're with the *Catholics*.'

'Has the minister got a better name for them? Has he? Well, then.'

I left them to their argument and gazed at what was above. I had never seen so many stars – nor such a clear night. I searched for the star Father used to navigate by. I drew a line, as he had shown me once, from a group shaped like a pan. And there it was: *Polaris*, the brightest star – *it shows the way north.*

Just then, pinpoints of light started to shower down: one or two at first, then many, many more. Some people covered their heads. Others dropped to their knees and prayed, there in the street, not minding if they muddied their clothes, nor caring what would be said of them in the morning.

But these were not like sparks from a blacksmith's anvil. I closed my eyes and felt the night air on my skin. I missed him then – but the feeling, like a moment of light, like a star falling, was gone as soon as I felt it.

I shivered. What would I do? I thought of the man, the widower who might want me, and shuddered.

And then I had it.

I can make a life here. I will make new drawings, a selection this time, not a book. Something that will show what I can do. There were plenty of booksellers and publishers to choose from in Leiden – writers who needed pictures for their books. I would draw anything they asked me to; anything to make a guilder or two. And with guilders I could have a room of my own. I thought of my list and all that was on it. I could do it. I could provide.

I looked up once more. I did not know what held the stars in place, why some fell and others didn't. No doubt the Monsieur did. I did not need him to tell me the stars were bright only because the sky was dark. They needed the night to be seen.

* * *

238

The answer was no, and no again. No, no, no, no, no. Every bookshop I went in, every publisher I saw. Many would not see me. One or two said sorry. They all said no.

'I cannot take it.'

'You realise what you are asking me to do?' said another, drawing a line across his throat.

I was shooed from a third, as soon as I showed him a map I had sketched, as though looking was curse enough and mapped his certain demise.

'Oh,' I said and rolled up my work again, tying it with a ribbon and taking my leave in a hurry.

I told the story of my Deventer Alphabet – but that did not help and merely made their indignation burn brighter.

I thought of my little Alphabet as a fire starter and swallowed.

'The trouble is of two kinds,' said one, taking time to explain. 'The first being your sex, which is – *ha* – an unfortunate and obdurate fact. The second being your non-membership of any guild. We employ draughtsmen, artists, etchers of the highest order – men with the best skills. To procure work from *others* would be a *dilution*. A betrayal. Do you not see?'

He flicked through my work again, shuffling sheets, squinting, and picked up a sketch of Francine. I'd drawn her showing her back, sitting in a pool of sunshine, holding a bobbin. His mouth turned down as he looked at it. He dropped it on his desk with the rest of the papers he held – the slap of paper ending his assessment of my work.

'Mostly amateurish.' He picked up the sketch of Francine

again. 'I will buy this for my wife; it is the kind of thing she likes. If you are selling.'

I nodded.

He dug in a pocket, sorted through his coins and held out what was left. No guilders among them.

I took what he offered me, rolled up my work, tying the ribbon a little too tightly, crushing it all in the middle.

I kicked my way home. The wind had got up. Didn't they know I had used the last of my paper on this work? The new paper I wanted, bought with money I'd never have, blew about my head, tumbling like leaves in a gale. I saw birds, caught in the storm, taken higher and higher – quills blown to the top of the sky.

I remembered what Mother had said. I had to find a way.

Peat

I SAW HIM before he saw me. The air, too thick to breathe. I pressed myself against the wall, turned my head a little, as much as I dared, and looked again.

There he was. Without doubt. The Monsieur, talking to a man I did not know. Limousin was nowhere to be seen.

I had come out to the butter market, as I always did on Tuesdays, and now there he was, less than the width of the street away. Although it was busy, all he had to do was turn and he would see me. I did not dare move. I stayed absolutely still, flattened against the wall – as if a horse had passed by too close.

He shook hands with the man he was speaking to and went through a door with a heavy brass knocker on it. It was a merchant's house, or a publisher's, perhaps; the same as the houses Mr Sergeant had sent me to in Amsterdam.

The Monsieur. In Leiden. Perhaps I was mistaken. It wasn't the first time I thought I'd seen him, only to get closer and find it was not him. One man had smiled, mistaking my intent.

My shoulders fell as my breathing slowed. Once I had regained my nerve I hooked my basket into the crook of my elbow, brushed down my skirts and started off again towards 't Sant. I was already late.

Just at that moment, the door opened and the Monsieur came out. He could not avoid seeing me, I could not avoid being seen.

'Helena!' His face mirrored the shock in mine.

I couldn't speak, and that was as well.

'My goodness, it *is* you.' He took a step towards me and held out his arms as if to hold me. I brought my basket in front, so it was between us.

He stepped back, his breath went from him as though he had been winded. 'Helena. Let me look at you.'

He must have thought me stupid, standing there with nothing to say.

'How are you? *And Francine?*' Although he smiled, I saw him falter.

I could not believe it was him, or how he had changed. He had grown thin. His hair had greyed, the curls pulled straight by the long need to wash it. I saw a man who lived alone, not expecting to meet anyone he cared for.

'She is well, Monsieur.'

'Helena,' he said, still taking me in. His gaze dropped lower, to my side. 'But where is she?'

'Francine? With Mother. She's too small yet to bring to market.' How normal I made this sound; a different truth lived inside my words.

'Yes, yes. Certainly so.'

He cast about and seemed in search of somewhere else we could go. But the street was full and jostling; there was no quieter place.

'Mrs Anholts sent me the letter you left for her, but there was no letter for me.'

I heard the way he said it, the scold in his voice. I shook my head at the unfairness of his words.

'I knew you were here, but you left no address.'

I flashed him an angry look. I'd not be made to feel like a child. This from the man who'd had me solving riddles and using a library to forward his post! Besides, Limousin knew my mother lived in Leiden. Hadn't he thought to ask?

'Francine must have grown.'

'Yes, Monsieur. She has.'

People passed by with their chatter and laughter; mothers with children, couples arm in arm.

'What brings you here, Monsieur?' I said, making it sound as if he had no right to be in Leiden.

He gestured towards the house he'd come from. 'I'm in discussion with a publisher about *Discourse* . . . Everything's late. I couldn't risk coming here until I knew it was safe, after the plague, that is.'

His book. Of course. That came first.

'I'm lodging not far from here, on Rapenburg, at Gillot's house.'

I shrugged. What was it to me where he stayed? He had on the same shoes as in Amsterdam, now shabby and worn; his stockings muddied too. I'd always thought him so neat and fine.

'Helena.'

I held his eye. His countenance had softened, but I had to harden myself against it.

'Why did you stop writing? Did you get the paper I sent you?'

Hurt rose in my throat. 'You did not visit, Monsieur. Not once.'

'I could not, Helena. I thought it best.'

Best? Best for whom?

'Then I heard from Mrs Anholts that you had gone.'

Hearing it from him only brought it all back. But I'd lived it, not him. What was past was past – it needed to be held under water, drowned if needs be.

I hugged my basket closer to me. 'I am late, Monsieur.'

'Let me walk with you.'

I shook my head. All I had to do was take a step, then one more, and show him I meant what I said.

'You realise why I had to . . . When *Discourse* is finished, when it is published—'

'I have to go.'

'But Francine? Can I see her?'

I shook my head. 'No.'

'*No?* Helena, *please*.' He fumbled in his pocket and held out a handful of coins, dropping several on the ground. 'Here. It's all I have – but I can get more to you.'

I looked away. 'I work, Monsieur.'

'Helena, please.'

I took one step and another and another.

'*Helena!*'

In that one word, the way he said it, he thought me lost. But I walked away and carried on walking.

She looks just like you, I wanted to shout. *She can say* bloem *and* melk *and* kaas, *Monsieur. She can say* Mama, *but not* Papa *– and why should she? Why should she ever?*

I crossed over towards Borstelbrugh where men beat

fleeces in the river, hanging them to dry over the wall. I watched the sodden wool drip – like dull white flags surrendered against the city's red brick.

I knew it was only a matter of time before the Limousin found me. I had told him Mother lived on Hoy Gracht. Once it was all I needed him to remember. Now the most I could hope was that he had forgot, and would not work his way down the street, house by house, until he found us. For days afterwards, I expected a knock at the door. At night, I imagined him in the room, watching from the corner. I had to close my eyes tight, to make the thought go away.

I thought I'd be prepared when I saw him. He didn't surprise me; he didn't jump out of the shadows; or appear on the step. He just let himself be seen, let me sense he was there. It was not until afterwards I realised: he must have been there all the while.

I was at the peat market on the corner of De Oude Vest.

'Hello, Helena,' he said, as he approached. 'The little runaway.'

He took his pipe from his pocket, pushed tobacco in with his thumb and puffed at it until it was lit, then released a slow stream of smoke. He was in no hurry. He was not here to buy peat.

He did not offer his hand in greeting and I would not have taken it if he had. I could not bring myself even to say hello. I felt him watching me while I looked at the peat. He trailed behind as I made my way along the sellers to where the cheapest was to be had. It was horrible stuff, loose and damp – it would not burn well. He stood there whilst I haggled.

'Take it or leave it,' the peat seller said and shrugged. 'You'll make my house cold just so yours can be warm.'

I handed over the money I had, half filled my buckets, then turned to go. The Limousin took a step, blocking the way.

'Looks heavy. Before you go, I have to give you this.'

He held out a letter.

Neither of us moved. I glanced at the letter, then at him. He held his hand steady.

'Not wishing to burden you further.'

'Not at all,' I said, making it sound as if it didn't matter.

He wasn't going to go until I took it, that much was plain, and I hadn't time to waste on staring games. I set the buckets by my feet and tucked the letter away.

'See how much easier it is when you are *amenable*,' he said and stepped to one side. Then he turned and went, leaving me with my filthy hands and the buckets of peat to carry home.

That evening, after Mother had gone to bed, I took out the letter and studied the writing on the front – written in the Monsieur's neat hand. I thought about throwing it on the fire, but then what? The Limousin would only bring another. Keeping it sealed wouldn't change what he'd written inside.

I broke the seal and opened it.

14 August 1636

My dear Helena,

I am sorry our meeting ended as it did. I am nearing the end of my work on Discourse. I shall be on a firmer footing then. For years, I have been uncertain where fate might take me, where my foot might rest. I want a quieter life. My thoughts turn from the towns I have made home these past years.

I want to see Francine and ask that you bring her to me. My address: Rapenburg, Gillot's house. Send word so I know to expect you. I have matters to discuss.

Your most humble and affectionate servant,
René Descartes

An apology, then, before his attention returned to himself. I touched my finger to his signature – it was the first letter I'd had from him that he'd signed.

I held my hands out in front of me. I could hold them steady too if I tried.

When Francine could walk, I would take her.

Questions

THE DRESS HE'D given her was too big, but I hemmed it and gathered the waist with a length of linen, trimmed from a sheet I had recently edged. I tied a longer length to Francine's wrist and grasped it tightly.

'We're off!' I said.

She looked up at me with serious eyes and pulled at the knot. When she realised it would not come undone, she set off in a zigzag across the street, stopping every few steps to pick up fallen leaves. By the end of the Hoy Gracht, she had a fat posy bundled in one hand. I scooped her up and carried her, then set her down again when she grew too heavy. Up, down, up, down, up, down she went, from my arms to the ground and back again.

We'll get there when we get there, I thought. It will give him time to think. He'd let months pass. What was another morning?

'Mama!' she said.

'Francine!'

'Mama!'

'Francine!'

'Mama!'

'Francine!'

This was our game and I liked to play it. I did not want

to think closely about where we were going or what might be said.

'Ap-pol.'

'Apple,' I corrected. It was her new word. I smiled, brimful with pride.

'Appol!'

'Pear.'

'Pip!'

'Pop!'

She squealed and clapped her hands.

'Careful, Francine,' I said, as she lost her balance and tripped.

She picked herself up and wiped her hands on her dress. 'Mama!'

'Francine!'

We reached the fish market and then Pieterskerk, passing a man in the pillory. He had no coat and was barefoot. A sign had been placed alongside him: FORNICATOR.

I gripped the line holding Francine and hurried by.

The house on Rapenburg was squeezed in between two much larger ones. It seemed smaller than Mr Sergeant's: the doors and windows narrower. I wondered if there was room for the Limousin here, or if he lodged elsewhere. I hesitated before I knocked. Hadn't I become like the Monsieur too, moving from place to place because I had to? Now we were both in Leiden with only this door between us.

An elderly, stout maid answered the door and ushered me into a wood-panelled room where I was told to wait. Three chairs had been set together by a low table, facing away from the door and towards the hearth. The furniture was plain and heavy. There were no ornaments, books or pictures – nothing to make it feel homely, or as though it belonged to a family; nothing that suggested a child lived there. Perhaps it was what the Monsieur wanted. I doubted he noticed or cared. I heard the murmur of voices outside, then it went quiet again.

A fire had been lit, the room stuffy after the cold outside. I had grown used to much cooler rooms, to far smaller fires. I took off Francine's hat and coat and shrugged off my shawl. She toddled over to one of the chairs and clambered up, tugging at her skirts when they got in the way.

I stared into the flames and listened to my breathing. Gradually, the ache in my arms from carrying Francine grew less.

Helena, I thought, *you've got breath in you and you are strong. Not strong like an ox, because an ox can be stubborn, but like the wind, filling a sail or lifting roof tiles and tumbling hats from heads.*

I was so drawn into the fire's orange glow and my thoughts, and the gale I'd set blowing in my mind, that when the door finally opened, I startled the same as a sparrow. If the window had been open, I'd have flown straight out of it. I turned, expecting the Monsieur, but the man who came in was a stranger.

I lifted Francine onto my hip and cradled her.

'Helena! And this must be Francine!' he said, as he approached.

How could he know me when I did not know him? We had not been introduced. I curtsied out of habit, then flushed. I was not a maid. I was no one's maid any more.

Francine turned her head when she heard her name. She looked at the man, then back at me, burrowing her head into my shoulder.

He held out a chair. 'Sit down, please, sit down. I'm Henri Reneri.'

Henri Reneri? The man I had sent the Monsieur's letters to? Reneri of the library, Reneri of Utrecht, Professor Reneri – the Monsieur's – what: *go-between*?

'So, Helena . . . *Helena*. In some regards I feel I know you already.' He turned his attention to Francine. 'Will she play whilst we talk? René, Monsieur Descartes, has asked me to intercede.'

'Where is he?'

'I have some questions – just a few.'

I had not expected this – could the Monsieur not ask his own questions? I placed Francine on the floor, then wound the linen strip quickly around my hand and tied it into a ball.

'Here, Francine,' I said and rolled it across the floor for her to follow.

I brought my hands neatly together in my lap and waited for him to begin.

He walked over to the window and looked out, lost in thought. 'It's always so hard to believe that the weather will warm again once autumn's here, don't you think?'

Nothing could be as bad as that winter in Deventer, I thought. It was hard not to think of Reneri and the

251

Monsieur, their easy company together; how different those months must have been for them to those I had lived through in Mrs Anholts' attic.

'You are well, Helena? And the child, no ailments?'

Ailments? 'She is well, we both are.'

'Good. Good.'

My answer appeared to please him. He did not speak for a while. I had the feeling he was trying to find a way towards whatever he had to ask me and needed to order the questions he had. His next one caught me by surprise.

'Your age. How old are you, Helena?'

'What's that to you?' The words were out before I could stop them.

He thought for a moment. 'Your father went to sea, I believe? Perhaps he told you that even a small hole will sink the greatest ship, given time. However, if we know the hole is there, we have the chance to do something, to cover it, to effect a repair.'

What did he know about boats and holes? 'My father's ship sank in a storm. Nothing to be done about it.'

'My analogy was a little clumsy and I am sincerely sorry for your loss. But your age, Helena . . . I need to know.'

I shuffled to the edge of the chair, keeping my back straight. I gave him the number in my head. 'Nineteen. Almost.'

He nodded slowly. I could see him counting the months backwards. 'You have told no one who the father is?'

'No one, no.'

'Not your mother?'

I shook my head. 'Mrs Anholts knows. And Limousin. No one else.'

'Minister Revius?' He raised his eyebrows. 'He conducted the baptism, I believe?'

I wondered how he knew. Perhaps Mrs Anholts had said.

'Minister Revius knew about the letters because they went from the library – but they were addressed to you. He does not know the Monsieur is Francine's father.'

'I see. Good.' He looked relieved.

As he watched Francine play, my eyes took in details. He was smartly dressed, but not as smart as some – his shoes were scuffed and his shirt frayed at the cuffs. His shoulders were rounded, his back curved, like many of the reading men I'd seen at the library; all had seemed burdened in some way. Reneri's tiredness seemed deeper, to come from the heart of him.

'My wife, God keep her, could not have children.' At the memory, he became still and stared at a point at his feet.

'I'm sorry,' I said, as I realised his wife was lost.

He turned, so that he faced me. 'A child is a gift from God. You are fortunate.'

I did not need him to tell me what I already knew, but I was surprised he had said it. If I had met him on my way and our paths had crossed in too narrow a place, I would have stepped to one side, to let him pass. I knew nothing of him, other than what had just been said. But having said it, something had opened between us and he had stepped aside for me.

'You work?'

'Yes.' I had a feeling he already knew what I did. 'I spin wool. I sew. And—'

He waited for me to continue.

'Draw. I draw.'

'The spinning and sewing, do they provide? Are they sufficient?'

I nodded. I could not admit the truth, or tell him I would soon have to provide on my own.

'And there is no other, how shall I put this – no other *interest?*'

I frowned, not knowing what he meant.

He fiddled with a button at his cuff. 'Forgive me, no other *young man?*'

'I wouldn't!'

'Why is that, Helena?'

I didn't like these questions. Is this what the Monsieur wanted to know? 'I don't want another.'

He thought for a while. 'Is there anything you want from Monsieur Descartes?'

Was this why I had been brought here? To lay claim to the Monsieur in some way? Did he think I had demands? I could care for Francine myself.

I shook my head.

'And would you want to see him again?'

That was not for him to know. I wondered what he did know. He was the Monsieur's friend. His only friend, perhaps.

'The letters you sent affected him.'

I flushed, suddenly angered. 'Letters? What can you know of a child from paper and ink?'

He did not need to be a father to understand that much. He considered me then, with what? A sympathy I'd not seen in him so far.

'He is her father. He should have come.'

He dropped his gaze. 'Where's that maid got to?' he said, not addressing me, nor even looking in the direction of the kitchen.

The flames had died down; he gave the fire a poke, sending sparks across the floor. I was unsure what else to say, or where I should go, but was relieved the strange interview seemed over.

I held out my arms to Francine, feeling the sudden need to hold her. 'Francine, here . . . *Francine.*' She looked up and carried on playing.

'She has her own mind.'

I twisted around at the Monsieur's voice. I had little expected it, had forgotten the reason I had come. There he was, standing by the door. Perhaps, since we'd met last, he had thought more on what he wanted, because this time his eyes held mine, all hesitancy gone. His attention turned to Francine, taking her in at once – a famished man, feasting.

He went over to where she was, knelt down and placed a wooden puzzle in front of her on the floor.

'See?' he said, as he showed her how the pieces went together to make a fish. He broke the puzzle apart and handed her a piece, but she pushed it away and chose another.

'That's it,' he said, as the first two pieces went together.

She slotted another piece into place and beamed. His smile reflected hers.

'Vis!' she said, the word breaking into a giggle.

'*Oui, c'est un poisson.*'

'Vis!'

'*Poisson.*'

'*Vis!*'

'Yes, *vis*, if you say so.' He threw back his head and laughed. I had never heard him laugh like it before.

In a blink, Monsieur, you will be in love.

The maid came back into the room and placed a tray on the table, covered over with a linen cloth. When she saw the Monsieur playing with Francine on the floor, her mouth fell open. A slice of cake could have fitted in there. Instead of looking down, which would only have confirmed my shame in her eyes, I stared back. Then Reneri thanked her, and she bobbed a stiff curtsy and went out.

The tray of food reminded me Francine needed to be fed and I needed badly to relieve the milk in me. I felt heavy, hot, swollen. My clothes fitted me well when the day started, but by noon they felt made for someone smaller and I had to ease out the laces. I could not do that in front of Reneri and the Monsieur.

'Is there somewhere I can go? Francine needs feeding.'

Reneri lifted the cloth from the tray. 'There's cake, if she would like.'

A laugh, mostly nerves, burst out of me.

He frowned, not understanding. Why should he know what I meant? He was not a father. And what did the Monsieur know about such things? Families like his used wet-nurses for their children.

I tapped a couple of fingers on my chest as discreetly as I could. 'She needs to take from me first.'

'Ah!' Reneri said, as he realised what I meant. 'Let me call the maid back.'

The Monsieur stood up. 'No. Not that.' He turned to me. 'I'll take you where you won't be disturbed.'

I gathered up Francine and followed the Monsieur out. I expected him to show me to a corner, where I could sit, but he turned to go upstairs. He was taking me to his room.

As we went in, he stooped to pick up a shirt from the floor. I recognised his books and the wooden case he kept his clock in. I had not thought I would see it all again. It made me sad. He was free to go, and nothing to hold him, and that's what he wanted. But what a life: to lodge in one room, then another, with only himself for company, or the company of men and their letters – Limousin, Reneri, Mersenne.

His papers were piled on a small table, pushed up against a wall. The maid here did not care. I would have placed the table in front of the window where the light was best. I turned away. It was not my worry any more.

'Sit down, Helena. Here.' He smoothed the bedcover flat. 'It's comfortable. And clean,' he said, when he saw me hesitate.

I glanced at him; he seemed just as anxious as me.

We're not so different after all, I thought, *we both have hold by our fingertips.* Did he expect me to turn tail and run? I had Francine to feed first.

And now she pulled at my bodice, not understanding the delay. 'Mama!'

'Monsieur.' I battled to keep Francine's hands from me.

'*Ah, oui*,' he said and turned his back as I unfastened my bodice. Although I turned my shoulder to hide myself as I started to feed her, he came closer, until he was sitting by my side on the bed.

'She has beautiful eyes,' he said, as he watched her feed.

I wound a curl of Francine's hair around my finger. In a year or two, it would be to her shoulders, like his. Did he see himself in her too?

Francine gazed as she fed, her hand cupped in his. I looked at his hand, at his neat crescent nails. I had always thought his hands beautiful. Little by little, I felt her go limp as she slept. Her mouth broke from my nipple. And then, without asking, he lifted her from me and placed her with great tenderness in the middle of the bed.

I had not minded him watching when she'd been feeding, but now that she'd finished, I did. My hands shook as I fastened my bodice. I saw him look as I brought the ribbons together.

When I went to get up he said, 'Stay a while, please,' and walked round to the far side of the bed. He patted the mattress. 'See, I will be here.'

I tucked the pillow behind me and leaned back, and we sat, side by side, with Francine between us. I could have slept too if I had not been so intent on keeping awake. He turned, so that he faced me, and touched my cheek. I closed my eyes. The cool room, his cool hand, a relief.

'I did not think I would see you again.'

Oh, I wanted these words from him, but I hated them too. He had let months go by without a visit.

'You could have come to Deventer, Monsieur. You were only in Utrecht.'

He reached for my hand, but I laced my fingers together so he could not have it. At that, he moved down the bed a little, onto his back, and stared up at the ceiling, lying straight as a furrow. If he thought I would take pity, he was mistaken. I kept my hands where they were and we stayed like that a good while, tented under the silence. It was his silence, not mine, and I wasn't going to break it. I'd speak, if he did. Then, in the end, I had to, because we'd have been there until springtime if not; we'd have rooted right through the bed.

'Why Deventer, Monsieur? My home's here, in Leiden.'

A sharp laugh burst from him. '*Vraiment?* And if your mother had turned you away? What then? I could not – *cannot* – take that risk. With *my* child? *Non.*' He closed his eyes. 'I needed you to be . . .' He thought for a moment until he had the word he needed. '*Safe.* And I am known here.'

So that was it. All turned about him.

I did not look, but he'd not moved, so nothing had changed with his mood that I could tell, and it all stuck in his head. Well, I would not hook his thoughts out of him, and I would not let him judge me by the sorry way he lived his life.

But then a thought came to me, making me feel horribly uneasy. *Helena, have you a home any more?*

I glanced at the window. The light had started to grey; the day to darken. I stretched my legs. I remembered our feet touching – my toes finding the dimple at his ankle. I drew my feet together, as if I'd stepped into cold water.

'I have to go.'

'No, Helena, *please.*' He rubbed his forehead with one hand. 'I'm leaving Leiden. I've decided.'

I did not want to know. I pushed myself off the bed.

'Helena, Helena . . . please. *Wait.*'

'Why you are telling me this?'

He came round the bed and held out a blanket.

I looked at it. 'I have a shawl, Monsieur, Francine a coat, downstairs.'

'Take it. Take it. *Please.* I have another.'

He wrapped it loosely around Francine.

'Do you think I want this? To continue, like this?'

He seemed not to be talking to me, the thought emptying out on its own. He shook his head, answering his own questions, despair thinning his voice. But despair at what? This was his life. I made no claim on him.

'I am looking for a house in the north, no more than a day away – towards the sea, among the dunes, with a garden. Certainly, of course, somewhere to work. Somewhere *où il est possible d'être.* Somewhere peaceful. Can you imagine such a place, Helena?'

I swallowed. Yes, I could. I could see a small cottage and the sea somewhere beyond it, and the wind high in the trees, a place where nothing stayed still. He could go anywhere he wanted. Had only himself to take care of, and Limousin to help him with that.

I stroked Francine's cheek to get her to wake. It was time to go. I'd leave him to his dreaming and I would walk home in the dark.

'If I found such a place, would you come with me and

bring Francine?' He stepped towards me, took hold of my hand and pressed a kiss to my knuckles, as though to seal a promise.

'We could be together, Helena. No one need know.'

I let him walk with me. He carried Francine, the puzzle pieces still clasped in her hands, the blanket draped over her back. Smoke lifted in pale lines from the chimneys. I tasted peat in the air. He hoisted Francine higher in his arms. No one carried her other than me. She'd been reluctant at first, but now her head nestled on his shoulder. It gave me a freedom I'd not had before. A freedom, at that moment, I did not much want.

'Here,' I said, and I reached to take her from him as he hitched her higher once more.

It was an awkward way he had of carrying her – one arm under and another across her back, clasping her to him like a breastplate.

'Like this, Monsieur,' I said, one arm at my hip to show him how to carry her there.

'I have her,' he said and lifted her again.

I felt a flick of annoyance. He'd learn. I let my arm fall back to my side. I felt restless, walking like this.

'Have you thought yet?'

When I didn't answer, he said, 'Come with me, Helena.'

I fretted a ribbon on my cuff. *No one need know.* Even the thought of it made my stomach tighten and roll.

'Helena?'

261

I heard how he pleaded. He had plenty to say now. But I felt I'd been chased from one corner into another – first by Mother, now by him.

'No, Monsieur, I won't.'

'No? What? *No?*'

Was the word new to him? Had he not heard it before?

'No. Sorry.'

He shook his head, still not understanding. 'Sorry?' Then, 'No? You cannot say no!'

I stamped my foot. 'No!'

He had hold of my arm now. 'Stop it! Stop saying no! You would stay *here*?'

'No, no.'

'What are you saying? You won't come? You won't stay? Not here, not there? Where then? Where?'

And then I told him all Mother had said. I looked at my feet and at his. We might have the same ground under us, but different paths had brought us here.

'So it is decided! Come! You must!' In his mind the matter was settled. 'Helena?'

Was this how it would be with him? Did he not see? But if I were to go with him, then this time, at least, the arrangement would be mine.

'You said there's no reason why a girl might not learn. I showed you I could. Francine can too. I want her to, Monsieur.'

His laugh was more startled than happy. 'But she's still so small.'

'If she were your son, would you think that?'

I knew it was a risk talking to him like this. It had become

262

so still; the trees we walked under had hushed, as though waiting for what would be said next.

'Reading and writing, she can have from me. But she needs numbers, Monsieur, like you showed me. And to learn about candles and snowflakes and rainbows and stars and—'

His laugh stopped me. 'Is that to begin with?'

My heart thumped, pushing what I said next into my chest. 'Will you teach her?'

I twisted my foot in the grit and drew my shawl tighter. There was more I wanted, more I needed to say.

'And if I came, I would not be your maid, Monsieur. I will not be that.'

'No. No. Certainly.' Hope, now, in his voice, but I'd still not had the answer I needed.

'Will you teach her, Monsieur?'

It was dark, his face in shadow. He took a breath and let it out slowly.

'I have my work, Helena.'

'Monsieur?' I would not let this go.

'Yes, yes.'

If I heard impatience in his voice, I let it be. I turned to him – the moonlight full clear on me so he could see.

'Then I will come.'

Hearth

THE SEA, *IMAGINE*. I had never seen the sea.

I looked at people differently. I wondered what they kept hidden – what they held inside. I knew what it was like to have secrets; to feel as if the ground wasn't where it should be.

After Martinmas, Mother went to Zeeland. I did not need reminding I must be gone by her return. I knew I would go, but I did not know when. I sold two more drawings to the publisher who had taken the first. Limousin brought small parcels of food and, when the Monsieur saw my work, more paper and ink too. The Monsieur visited only after dark, when the neighbours would not see him. As the days lengthened it was hard to keep Francine awake long enough, or in a good enough mood. If she howled, he went almost as soon as he arrived.

Slowly she grew to know him. Mister Vee-veer, she called him, after the feather in his hat.

'*Je suis Monsieur Plume!*' he joked and tickled her nose.

He spent what time he wanted with her, then Limousin came to collect him and they left. We could not leave Leiden until his *Discourse* was published, but he did not know when that would be.

'I thought you were *certain*,' I teased.

'I am!' he said and slapped a hand to his forehead, keeping it there. '*Ce n'est pas la même chose!*'

He explained he was waiting for a licence from Mersenne. 'He's intent on doing the opposite of what I want.'

I saw the book as the object he had once described, pages that were bound together. A book needed paper, ink, a press to print it, but why a licence? Why Mersenne?

'It has everything and nothing to do with Mersenne. I need a licence, *royal privilege*, from France, which he must arrange – it's the price for writing the wretched thing in French – to stop it being pirated there.'

When spring came, I no longer teased him about it. I had my own worries. In a month, Mother would return.

And then, one day, he came running. 'It is done,' he said, quite out of breath.

He laughed and so did I. His book was published. We could go.

One night, not long after, a knock came at the door. The man who stood on the step swayed a little, as though he'd been pitched there by the sea. He gripped the door frame – perhaps afraid he'd be swept away.

'*Thomas!*' And even though I said it, I could not believe it was him.

'*Helena?*'

He blinked hard, to be sure it was me. The question in his voice – the look on my face: neither of us had expected the door to open to the other. He wiped his mouth with the back of his hand and I smelled the thick fug of juniper coming off him. *Jenever.* He'd been drinking.

He looked as though he'd been left out all winter in the rain. How thin he'd become. His clothes were little better than tattered sailcloth; holes had worn through his breeches, showing scabs underneath. I was glad Mother was not here to see him.

Mother! My hand went up to my mouth to stop myself saying it.

His eyes grew guarded, watchful. He cocked his head towards the inside. 'Is Mother there?'

I shook my head; a single, stunned *no* came from me. Still I took in his condition.

He frowned, but I saw relief too and his shoulders went down. He let go of the door frame, then stopped. I was on the threshold, in the way. What would he think? But the Monsieur and Francine were within. I did not know where to begin to explain them.

'It's true I've had some rough nights . . . that boat is terrible hard.' He brushed at his jacket, thinking the fault lay with him. He looked up and I caught a small, boyish smile on his lips. He laughed. 'Better? Now can I come in?'

But no amount of brushing would make the cloth cleaner; there was no word rough enough for the state of him.

'Oh, Thomas.'

I could have wept. *Boat?* I thought of what he had gone through, the ditches he'd slept in, all that had brought him to this.

Just then, a cry came from behind – a shriek and then a

giggle; we both started at the sound. *Francine.* She would not settle until she had the feather from the Monsieur's hat, which he had been trying to free from his hatband when the knock came at the door.

Thomas frowned. 'Who's that?'

Francine giggled again, then came the sound of furious whispering.

He went up on tiptoe and tried to peer over my shoulder. 'Am I not to come in? Am I not welcome? In my own home?'

'*Arrête!*'

Thomas didn't wait to hear more, but pushed past. For a moment he looked lost, unsure where he was, as he tried to take in what was before him. The Monsieur was crouched down in the corner by a small mattress; Francine was tucked under the quilt, holding the feather in one hand. When she tried to see who had come in, he hushed her and stroked her forehead to get her to sleep.

Thomas shook his head, as though the house and everything in it had been turned upside down and he was the only one left upright. He turned. Any softness in his mood had gone.

'Who's this then? Where's Mother?'

'Thomas, I—'

He held up his hand to silence me and dropped the remains of his coat over the back of Mother's chair. He walked around the room, touching the bowl, the table, the edge of the mantel – bringing the place back to him, piece by piece. All the while, his gaze flicked back to the Monsieur. Finally, he lifted his hands in question.

'Where is she?'

'Gone to Zeeland. Thomas—'

'When?'

'Martinmas.'

He drew himself up to his full height and jutted out his chin the way Father did. '*Martinmas*? But that's last year?'

'Yes.'

He frowned as he took in the news, glancing back at the Monsieur, then at Francine. 'Weren't you in Amsterdam?'

'I was.'

'Made yourself at home here, I see. *With him*.'

I flushed.

'So it's like that, is it?'

'No!'

'No? What's he doing here then?'

'There's no harm.' But I knew, as I said it, I had gone against Mother's wishes.

'When's she back?'

'Easter, she said.'

He swept his arms wide. 'Puts me in charge, until then, and I am sore in need of a bed.'

He was not asking. I had not thought he would be so blunt in his claim. But there it was, I was being told. The brother I'd lost was not the one who had returned. But I wasn't the same sister he'd left behind either.

'Why did you come back, Thomas? What do you want?'

He ignored me. When he looked at the Monsieur again, he was not afraid to stare. 'So who's this?' he said, his voice rising. 'I want to know.'

The Monsieur pressed a finger to his lips, addressing him for the first time.

'Sh. The child tries to sleep.'

'I like that! Shushed in my home, and me just come back from the sea! A child? Whose child?'

Could he not see? Would he make me tell? 'You are an uncle, Thomas.'

'Since when?' He swivelled on one heel, turning back to me. 'And the father? *Him?*'

'*Bien sûr*, him,' said the Monsieur.

Thomas took a step back. 'A *Frenchie?*'

At this, the Monsieur was up on his feet. 'I have a name. You would do well to remember it.'

'A name?' Thomas sneered. 'Well, that much we have in common.'

'*Je crois pas!* There is a difference.'

Thomas spat into the fireplace. 'I'm not seeing it. So tell me. What is it? Your name?'

'Descartes.'

'Descartes?' He considered him. 'See his clothes, Helena? He's above us.' I heard the scorn in him. 'Maybe so. But, from what I reckon has gone on here, not by much.'

'Thomas!'

He spun round to me. 'I know men like him – walking on their elbows just so they can keep their noses out of the muck.'

'And you, Thomas?' I said, my voice shaking.

'*Me?*' He glowered. 'What about me?'

I felt the heat of what I had to say rise in me. I had words that could scald him. 'Well, you know.'

He laughed. 'He would ruin our name, yet I am the one accused!'

I swallowed back my fury in great gulps. *Just come back from the sea?* I would pull off his mask! 'I found out, about you. In Amsterdam. At the VOC.'

He looked at me then, surprise laid bare on his face.

'They keep records, Thomas. There to see, if you know where to look. Did you think I'd not? You asked me to! *Look out for me*, you said. *I'm on the Aemilia!*'

'You? What do you know of the VOC?'

'*Absconded*, Thomas, that's what it said. *Absconded.*' I felt triumphant saying it, letting the power of what I knew take flight.

He shook his head.

'Well, well, well,' said the Monsieur, as the meaning of what had happened became clear. He threw back his head and laughed. '*C'est l'hôpital qui se moque de la charité!*'

'Absconded, Thomas.'

Thomas took several more steps back; his strength seemed to have ebbed from him. And then I saw Thomas for who he was: my brother, made desperate by untold miseries on board that wretched ship. The soaring triumph I'd felt fell at my feet. I wanted to hold him, and him to hold me, but we weren't children any more.

'And Mother?' he said, managing to gather himself at last. 'Does she know?'

I shook my head. 'She thinks you are still in Batavia. Or at sea. She longs for your return . . . it's you she wants.'

'Then I'll be here, when she gets back. I have nowhere else.'

'Won't they be after you? The VOC?'

'Said I was from Utrecht when I signed up; they'll be looking there, if they're looking anywhere at all.'

That much must be true. No one had come to the door, asking after him.

'And Mother? What will you tell her?'

'Stories. What else? The truth?'

I turned away. It was Thomas she wanted, I knew that. He would be welcome, no matter what. Would she want the truth from him, even if she thought him telling her a lie? The thought made me suddenly bitter.

Thomas considered the Monsieur with cold regard. 'I am the man in this house. Remember that.' Then he shouldered his way past and clambered into Mother's bed, yanking the curtains closed.

'Mama?'

Francine clambered out from under her quilt. She rubbed at her eyes, and held out her arms to be picked up. I went over and scooped her up, kissing all along her brow. 'Shush now, shush.'

In the morning, when the Monsieur returned, I gathered what was mine and left. We would not speak of Thomas again, he said. He took me to a small rented room where I would stay, whilst he went ahead, with Limousin, to arrange a cottage near Santpoort.

And then he went. And in the days that followed, I thought of these men, the men whose names mattered so much; names I had done my best to guard.

On the day I left Leiden for Santpoort, I returned to the house one last time. Thomas came to the window and saw me. He did not open the door but stood there and then turned his back.

SANTPOORT, 1637–9

Seeds

THE CARRIAGE STOPPED at the end of a dusty track. Francine, who had been all chatter since Santpoort, fell silent. I hadn't been able to answer her questions, not properly.

'Are we here yet, Mama? Mama, are we here? Are we? Is that the sea? There, Mama?' as she pointed again and again to the horizon. 'Over there?'

I didn't know. I hadn't answers to my own questions: *Where were we going? What welcome awaited?* And now that the carriage had stopped and I peered out of the window: of all the places I had imagined between Leiden and here, this was not it. But one thing was certain: we could not go back. The place where we found ourselves was home.

We stood there, hand in hand, and looked at the little house. It was not slim and tall like those in Amsterdam. The roof dipped in the middle and came down almost as far as the ground. It had four dusty windows on two floors. The front wall bulged at the base as if rooted into the ground. Land stretched around, fenced in by a ring of trees and dense, overgrown thicket. I listened, but heard nothing. The sea nowhere near by.

The carriage driver unloaded the bundles we had and carried them to the front door, where he knocked and waited.

I gripped Francine's hand in mine as we waited for it to

open. After some time, and a second sharp knock from the driver, Limousin came out. He took in our things without acknowledging us, as though taking delivery only of them. The driver scowled as he climbed onto the carriage seat.

'A glass of something would've been welcome . . .' He flicked the reins sharply, pulling the horses round in a tight circle, and was gone.

'Well, come on! *Vas-y!*' shouted Limousin, coming out again. He clapped his hands as though shooing chickens, then went back inside.

We found him waiting in the kitchen. 'There are beds either side of the alcove,' he said. He looked pleased with himself, as though the decision had been made for me. I ignored him; I knew where I would sleep.

'I can't stand here chatting,' he said, going out, with not a word for me about the Monsieur.

Francine let go of my hand, ran over to the alcove and clambered through a narrow gap in the curtains. She poked her head through and grinned.

'Come on, mischief.' I held out my hand. 'Let's see what we can see.'

The kitchen was bright and sunny. Off to one side, we discovered a small, stone-lined pantry and a laundry room with a water pump. In the pantry, I found a sack of flour and several large earthenware pots with butter, sugar, raisins, eggs. A single, thin rabbit hung from a hook. What was anyone supposed to do with that?

Next we went upstairs. There were two rooms – the larger, at the front, the Monsieur's. I knocked first, in case he was there. Hearing no sound, we went in. Francine ran

276

over to the window and peered out. His cape hung on a hook, his shirts draped over a chair; I ran my fingers along its back, wanting the feel of him. Francine pulled at my hand, eager to explore. We peeped around the door of the second room. Limousin had made it his. His trunk, at the end of the bed, underlined the fact.

The downstairs room at the front was the most peculiar, having no furniture, other than a large table. It was cold and damp and badly needed airing. I opened the window as wide as it would go, hooking away a cobweb with my finger. Although I searched both the downstairs rooms, I could find only four chairs. What an odd arrangement. One for each of us, but if he had guests, we'd have to take it in turns to sit.

Back in the kitchen, I unpacked the clothes I had brought with me into a drawer under the alcove bed, placed my Bible and brooch on the shelf, and Francine's bobbins and puzzle in a small basket. Still no sign of the Monsieur.

'My bed,' Francine said, when she saw me place my night-dress on the pillow with hers. She folded her arms. 'My bed.'

'We have to share, sweetheart.' Three lots of sheets to wash were enough.

'Where's Grootje?' she asked.

'Grandma's in Zeeland.' She would return to Leiden soon and find the child she wanted waiting for her.

'I want Grootje.' She frowned. She didn't yet have the words to argue.

'This is our home, Francine. You can play outside now! Lucky Francine!'

'You're to tell me if anything is lacking,' the Limousin

said as he came back. 'I did my best to provision the house. There's a new broom, washcloths, vinegar for the glass.'

'And the Monsieur?'

'Oh, walking.' He looked as vague as he sounded. 'He has his routine.'

I thought of the rabbit on the hook. 'How will I get to market?'

'Anything you need, you ask me. I will fetch it.'

Was this how it would be? Most of what he said told me nothing. But I didn't know if he was being difficult or simply telling me what he had been told.

'Yeast.' I had searched in each of the pots in the pantry, but had not found any. 'I need it if I am to make bread.'

In Amsterdam and Leiden, I had got what I needed from the markets – freshly baked bread, and fish and cheese.

We had passed through a small town on our way to the house – Santpoort, I guessed – but had not stopped. There would be a market there, twice weekly at least. I'd tried to keep the journey in my head, but the countryside stretched away in all directions. I noticed the sky. So much sky. Neither rooftop, nor steeple, nor ship's mast crowded the view.

And then we'd come upon field after field of cloth, pegged out on frames. Linen, I guessed, as we drew near. What an extraordinary sight – and such a white with the sun flat on it. It made me squint. No one raised a hand in greeting as we passed by; the women and girls who worked there had already turned back to their labours. The place smelled worse than de Oude Waegh's fish market on an August afternoon. I put a hand to my mouth and drew back into the carriage.

Apart from farmhouses and windmills, there had been

little else to/see, no means to remember our way. I had lost count of the windmills somewhere after twenty. Everywhere was flat as far as I could see – rolled out and on show. What a simple map this would make: a narrow track, making its way to the coast. And I thought, *What does he want, being out here, with it all so open?*

Then, as we'd approached the coast, the ground had heaped into dunes – small ones at first, just sweepings and dust. But they soon pushed up in strange, lumbering shapes, like the shoulders of giant hunchbacks. Higgledy fir trees grew up in between, twisted this way and that, as if in a mad dance. When I had pointed them out to Francine, she'd shrieked. I had clapped my hands, as much taken by surprise as she. She had looked how I felt; this place had made us both giddy.

Further on, the carriage driver had stopped to let us stretch our legs. The ground felt different somehow, as if I needed to grip with my toes to stay steady. Francine pulled off her shoes and socks and ran around in the sand at the side of the track. I had to call her several times before I could get her to come back.

Somewhere here, tucked away in the middle of nowhere, the Monsieur's house. I knew that nowhere had to be some-where, but at that moment I was lost.

I turned in a circle. The house had been furnished by men for men. Did it matter that the Limousin had no eye for comfort other than the Monsieur's and his own? This was our home now. I touched the old oak mantel above the fireplace, sooted black over the years. I liked its warmth, its strength.

'Helena!'

I spun round at the sound of the voice. 'Monsieur!'

He held out his arms. 'You're here!' He said it as though he could not believe I was.

I nodded. A furious shyness beat in me and I did not take his hand.

'You do not have to sleep here,' he said, when he saw where I had put my things.

The Limousin looked up, all ears, while trying his best not to be seen. But I knew he was there even if the Monsieur seemed not to.

'Francine needs me,' I said and gathered her to my side.

'Of course. Yes, of course.'

I stood there and I hadn't the words. But then, I realised, *neither had he.*

Had the lines that separated us been lost on the journey? Could we leave them there, behind on the track?

I glanced at the Limousin and saw him scowl.

I doubted it very much.

The house had been empty for a year or more, but the Monsieur did not seem troubled by the way things were – by the holes in the fence, or the thatch that had slid off the roof.

'There will be flowers at the front, a vegetable and herb

garden at the back,' he said, as he showed me around the outside.

'A garden?' I stood there, grass to my knees. Pollen lifted in clouds where Francine charged about. The only way to see a garden was to close my eyes and imagine it. 'Can we grow lavender?'

And roses and honeysuckle and daisies too, and after that I didn't know. They were the only flowers I could think of.

He thrashed at some brambles growing by the front window. 'Limousin will need to clear this. I need as much light as possible into this room.'

At the back of the house, we found several old fruit trees, their branches grown into a tangle. Plums, apples, pears? Neither of us knew. We'd have to wait until autumn to see what fell.

'It should give us what we need.'

I looked at him, then at the garden, and could see the weeks, no, months, of work ahead. In this garden then, his plan to settle.

Beyond the trees, the path disappeared into bushes.

'I've not had a chance to walk it,' he said, when he saw me look. 'It runs towards the sand dunes and, after that, the sea.'

The sea! The thought of it surfaced, clear and blue. I picked a dandelion clock and blew the seeds into the air. We watched the wind carry them across the garden until they were lost in the grass.

Later, he needed me to help him fix the fence. Limousin was off setting rabbit traps.

'*Bon, ça va mieux.*'

He waggled the post. Pale sunshine fell in soft drifts through the clouds. I gripped the fence post as he hammered in one nail, then another. The knock of the hammer shook my arm, the shock of his strength running the length of it.

The Monsieur spent the afternoons that first week clearing land to the front and back of the house. I had only ever seen him formally dressed before; sleeves to his wrists; stockings to his knees. Now he worked with his shirt unbuttoned at the front. It was heavy, hard work in the heat and we all had to help. I raked weeds into piles and Francine carried them in her arms to a compost heap at the bottom of the garden. Once the ground was cleared, the Monsieur and Limousin set to digging, turning over large clods of black soil. Not a word passed between them as a large rectangular plot appeared.

The rest, it seemed, was up to me. We needed onions, cabbages, carrots. I stood there a while and wondered how I could get anything to come out of the earth.

I sowed seeds for tender crops – lettuce and herbs – then chased away the sparrows that flocked down. Francine collected worms in her apron pocket and I found them again when I came to wash her dress.

My hands blistered and calloused and cracked. I went to bed aching and woke the next day stiff and sore, only to end it aching even more. I planned to sketch the plants as they grew, but there was too much to do. I managed a picture of a few seeds before I planted them – but they were little more than dots on a page.

Limousin brought back strawberry plants from market and young leeks as thin as blades of grass.

'See, this is how you do it.'

He poked a hole in the soil with a stick, placed a leek deep in it and poured in water.

'The trick is not to fill the soil in around it. It will grow in the hole, and the end of the leek stays white. I like leeks cooked in butter. Cooked slowly until they soften.'

I planted it all and the whole patch covered over green until no soil showed through. I hadn't expected so much so quickly. There was more growing than I had sowed, but how should I know what was what? I went back and looked at the dots I'd drawn. Nothing linked plant with seed: that I could see. I could only guess what were weeds.

The pale green beans grew fastest, stretching up above everything else, then shrivelled up brown and black. When I looked closer, I found each stem collared with flies, some green, some black; sweaty and sticky, and each tiny fly fat with what it had feasted on, and about to pop. I dug the whole lot in and started again, and when the flies came back, it made me think God did not want us to have them. Were the flies a test – of the beans and of me?

I asked God to forgive me for what I was about to do, then stripped the flies off between my finger and thumb, trying my best not to break the stems or show my disgust. I hated the feel of them on my skin as they bunched up; the foul stains on my apron where I wiped my fingers clean.

When the Monsieur saw what I was doing, the shuddering, the green-black smears on my apron, he laughed.

'You are a surprise, Helena.'

My mouth was open, because I shut it. I wondered what I must appear like to him, standing there in that scraggy patch – skirts hitched up, weeds as high as my waist, fingers fouled with flies. I pushed the hair back from my face. And then it started to rain – a fine, warm rain, just what was needed to make it all grow.

I surprise myself too, Monsieur, I thought, and turned to the beans and the flies I was about to squash, feeling the rain already come through at my shoulders and back.

I could have danced among the beans when they came into flower – four rows made purple and heavy with bees. We would have beans. And I would dry them. A good crop would keep us this winter. After that, I walked a bit taller, as though I had mastered the art of balancing beans on my head.

Kneeling one day in the garden, I laid my hands on the soil and closed my eyes, thinking I'd feel what grew beneath them, but I couldn't, only the tickle of a beetle as it scuttled across my hand.

Monsieur. I wrote the word in mud on my palm, then rubbed it away with my thumb.

Weeks of rain swelled the fruit on the trees – we would have apples, plums and a hard knobbly fruit I had no idea of. I bit into one, thinking it ready, and spat it out. The

Limousin said it was *coing* – *kweepeer* – quince. He was surprised to see it this far north; quince was as French as lavender and needed the sun.

'Most things will grow here,' I said, somewhat primly.

'That tree must be hardier than it looks. One tree does not an orchard make,' he retorted and gave me a look as sour as the fruit on it.

Over the weeks, the fruit ripened to a deep custard-yellow, with a rich honey-sweet smell. I remembered my first taste and was not fooled. I decided to harvest it last.

We ate strawberries, salad and tiny carrots cooked in butter on Francine's second birthday, silenced by the sweet taste. I saw how Limousin saved his fattest strawberry until last.

'Delicious,' said the Monsieur, as he ate the last of the carrots on his plate, mopping up the butter with a chunk of bread.

Yes, they were. I was already thinking ahead to what would have to be planted next. We would need turnips and beets to see us through the winter. And kale and cabbage and spinach.

I knew what I felt when I saw him, and the feeling jumped this way and that.

At night, when all I had were my thoughts, I had to stop myself. I had to stop my thoughts running ahead. *This* is what we have. A little house, among the dunes, with holes in the thatch and black lines in the carrots where the grubs had burrowed in.

Blood

I DID NOT understand how so many people could know the book was his, when he had not put his name to it. The Limousin collected letters twice a week from Santpoort; sometimes when he returned his satchel was filled with them: replies, objections, praise. Mostly objections, it seemed.

The Monsieur had set aside afternoons for thinking. The front room would be used for observations and practical work, and that was morning work. But I seldom found him in there. He spent most days in his room upstairs, replying to the letters the Limousin brought. In the evenings, if Francine was still awake, he read to her. Sometimes, I heard him sing, French songs that drifted down the stairs; or the rattle of pebbles on the floor – small stones she'd dug out of the soil that he was using to teach her to count.

'I am getting white hairs on my head,' he said.

I did not like to tell him he'd had these for a while.

'I have never been less in the mood to write than at this moment,' he said, when Limousin came back with another bundle of letters. Yet it did not stop him; he replied to each one.

I took him bread and soup late in the evening when he

wanted it; found him, night after night, huddled over the page, reading by dim candlelight. He showed me what he worked on: a long piece on cogwheels and pulleys, with badly drawn pictures. Sometimes, I found him asleep.

'Monsieur.' I rested my hand on his shoulder.

He angled his head towards my touch, turned and drew me to him, his head on my stomach, his arms going around me to hold me there while he nuzzled his cheek against my skirts.

As he brought me closer, I pushed away from him. 'No. Monsieur, no.'

I left him at his desk and went into the garden. Autumn had made it cold, and the stars shone in the dark. I heard him come up behind me. His mouth sought mine as we stumbled into the shadows. My back hit a tree. He hitched up my skirts and I felt one hand between my legs as he pressed himself against me.

'No.'

'Helena.' He rested his forehead on mine. 'I see it in you too.'

'Monsieur, not this. Francine . . .'

'I need you. I need you.'

I closed my eyes; my throat hurt when I swallowed. And if I had another baby? What would happen then? But what if I refused him?

He kissed my neck, then along the line of my collarbone, his kisses not stopping. 'Share my bed. *Viens.*'

I would not be that, not what he wanted, not in front of the Limousin. What of Francine?

'I can't.'

His kisses were on my ear; his voice, roughened, pooled there. 'I told you. Not those words, not with me . . . and if not in my bed, then here.'

Then he knelt. He lifted my skirts over him and put his mouth where he had pressed. His hands moved my legs apart and he kissed me. God would see us. I screwed up my eyes. And then all was darkness, and the feeling that grew in me when he kissed me. He pushed with his fingers, and he kissed, and the darkness opened and I fell backwards into it.

After some time, he stood and he held me until I was still.

I brought my arms around him and pulled him to me and then I felt him in me, and the tree, hard, under my back. *Oh God, there will be a baby, there will be a baby, there will be—*

Three days later, my courses came. I bled.

I tried to understand what this blood meant, why I felt so wretched. It had stopped when Francine was growing inside me and for some time after her birth. *That's what happens when you're feeding*, Mrs Anholts had said. Then the bleeding came again. I counted the days so I knew when, so I was prepared with cloths and did not bloody my skirts.

It was a man's seed that brought the baby to life – like tinder catching alight – and then the monthly blood ceased. What the baby was before it came out, I didn't know.

Something tiny, but perfect, perhaps the size of a pea. Did that mean there were lots of these pea-sized babies in me, waiting for their time to grow?

I looked at the blood on the cloth. There would be no baby. Had his seed died? Would the pea baby die too?

My back ached. I cried when I broke the milk jug, even though it was already cracked and no real loss. Then I laughed because I had cried. Perhaps it was the wrong time; perhaps there was something unfavourable in me just before my bleeding began, so that the baby could not be, even if his seed was in me. My father's brother and his wife had no children; Reneri neither. Mr Beeckman's wife had seven.

I counted the days – a little over three weeks until my next bleeding would start. That would be the next time. The time when his seed would not take hold.

'Not yet,' I said when he came up behind me and his hands slipped over my breasts. He had to learn too, know the patterns and what they meant.

By late autumn, he understood. He sent the Limousin away on errands the week before I bled, to Utrecht and Amsterdam, and when Francine was asleep I went to him.

I hated the bleeding, but I understood it. It was not just a man's seed that made a baby. Something happened in me too.

I counted the days. I did not refuse him.

Tulips

THE DOG CAME back with the Monsieur from Haarlem market in November.

'He found me,' said the Monsieur and rubbed the dog's ears. 'Followed our carriage for a good distance out of town before we allowed him to hop in. He has adopted us, I think.'

The dog wagged his tail and sat down. He scratched his ear, then lay on the floor with his nose between his paws.

'My dog? Please!' said Francine. She sat on the floor beside the dog and circled his scruffy head in her arms. 'My dog.'

The Monsieur laughed. 'If he decides to stay, then he's yours.'

Francine squealed and laid her head on top of the dog's. 'What's his name?'

The dog licked his paw, then scratched his ear again.

'*Il s'appelle Monsieur Grat*,' said the Monsieur. The Limousin laughed.

'Monsieur Grat! Monsieur Grat! Monsieur Grat!' She jumped to her feet and skipped around, singing his name. 'Monsieur Grat!'

'This one's not for cutting open then, Monsieur?' said the Limousin. 'You're not going to look inside?'

'No!' Francine's eyes widened with horror.

'Oh, he would!' The Limousin leaned in, enjoying himself. 'He will slit open the belly, pull it apart and—'

'*Ça suffit!*' said the Monsieur, so sharply we all startled.

The Limousin tensed. '*Je m'excuse, Monsieur.*'

'*Êtes-vous complètement fou?*'

'*Pardonnez-moi.*'

The Monsieur gathered Francine to him and crouched down so he was at her height. 'Monsieur Grat, he's yours. Do you know what Monsieur Grat means?' He lifted her chin a little.

She looked at him, still mistrustful, and shook her head.

'Mister Scratch.' He smiled and touched away her tears. 'Don't cry. Do you think Mister Scratch is a good name? That it suits him?'

'Yes,' she sniffed.

'You will need to teach him good manners because I am certain he has none and will steal your dinner from your plate. You will need to train him to come when called, else he will take himself off back to Santpoort. Limousin will find some rope and make a leash for him.'

'Monsieur Grat,' she called and patted her leg, 'Monsieur Grat, *viens.*'

The dog stood up, stretched and wandered over to her. He stood as tall as her shoulder. But our eyes were not on the dog. Francine had spoken her first French word. She twisted away, not understanding, made shy by our attention.

The Limousin thrust his hands in his pockets. 'Come with me, we'll sort out a lead.'

'He is a fool sometimes,' said the Monsieur after they had gone.

I wished we could do without him. I knew we could not.

* * *

Francine quickly outgrew her clothes. With winter coming, she would need boots. The Limousin complained about the errands he needed to make. I gave him her old shoes to take with him to market so he could buy larger.

'I did my best,' he said and shrugged as I unwrapped a pair of clogs that would have fitted a ten-year-old. The cloth he had chosen was little better. I wanted to make a new dress for Francine. I ran the wool between finger and thumb; coarse, working cloth, suitable for a maid.

'No lace,' he added, before I could ask.

He went out, then returned with another crate.

'I nearly forgot. Items the Monsieur wanted. For you.'

I was not expecting anything from the Monsieur. I opened the crate. At the top was a small copper pan and a blue and white jug, patterned with sailboats. There were eight new dishes, with the same pattern. Tucked away alongside them I found a pomander filled with lavender. At the very bottom of the crate, a small box. I gasped as I opened it. Inside, in a nest of straw, three tulip bulbs.

'Well, well, well,' said the Limousin, and I did not know who was more surprised, me or him.

A note tucked around them told me to plant them a hand's depth in September. They would need all of autumn and winter to grow. I folded the note away. He was looking ahead to spring.

The Limousin chose an apple from the dish and took a bite.

'I should go to the market next time,' I said. 'That would be best.'

'I doubt that's possible, but it's not for me to decide.

Discuss it with the Monsieur.' He dropped the half-eaten apple back into the dish.

The Monsieur did not say no and he did not say yes. I understood we had to be careful, that he guarded his peace.

'It took time to find this place. I would not want to risk losing it.'

I had to step back from what he said to understand his meaning. We would be noticed. Even if I went with Francine, questions would be asked. People would want to know who we were, where we were from, why we were here. One question was never enough.

'Be clear with Limousin what it is you need. He will bring it.'

'Yes, Monsieur.' I did not want to seem ungrateful.

Most days I was very happy.

Letters continued to come. He listed those who sent them and kept copies of his replies. He wrote to Mersenne and others too: Plempius, Vatier, Huygens, Reneri, Pollot, Morin, Hogelande, Debeaune. Their names seemed to come from the far corners of Mr Veldman's maps. I imagined them, lined up, like a row of spice jars. Debeaune was vanilla; Morin, clove or mace; Vatier, something sharp and tangy, like tamarind or pickled lime. Plempius, may God forgive me, I could associate only with goose fat.

I cooked and cleaned and looked after Francine. Limousin ran errands. He went fishing with the Monsieur; they set eel traps and snared rabbits. Once the water froze, there would be no more eels until it thawed. I baked bread in the morning; afternoons were for the garden and readying the ground for the spring. We had six chickens in a coop now and enough eggs for cake. Once a week, I made soft cheese from the milk Limousin brought back from market.

Monsieur and the Limousin walked every day. I had to swallow my envy as I watched them go. I wondered how far it was to the sea.

I still could not go to church.

'It does not mean that God is not in us,' said the Monsieur, his hand to his chest. 'And in our words and our deeds.'

I read my Bible and I read to Francine; we prayed together and sometimes with the Monsieur too. Although our prayers were different, they drifted into one another, like smoke into fog. Francine learned both.

In the mornings, she spilled out of bed before I could catch her, charged up to his room and jumped on his bed. She'd drag him downstairs, still heavy with sleep, chattering for them both.

'Breakfast,' she said, bringing yesterday's bread to the table. 'You can't stay in bed all day.' She chewed on a chunk of bread as she considered him. 'It's a waste.'

'Francine!' I said, but I could not dispute it, nor scold her much. She was only saying what she had heard from me.

He held up his hand in defeat and yawned deeply.

In the autumn, I planted the tulips under the apple tree. They would be beautiful when they flowered. I told myself I was lucky to have them.

* * *

The announcement that Reneri would visit sent our little house into turmoil. It was as if everything had been knocked up into the air and I had to catch it all again before it fell. The Monsieur ordered wine and brandy from Amsterdam and had it delivered at great expense. He made detailed plans for what they would do together and in the week before he arrived could not settle to anything.

'We need to give him the warmest of welcomes. He has suffered since the death of Anna.'

I thought back to when I had met Reneri in Leiden. There was sadness in him, but kindness too. Perhaps his kindness came from his loss. He had not judged me.

He would be our first visitor. A guest – any guest – meant that the Limousin's room would need to be made ready and Limousin would have to take the other alcove bed in the kitchen. I'd not be able to avoid him. I hoped he didn't expect me to chat. Or drink.

The Limousin drank in the evenings. He took a jug of wine up to bed and always brought it back empty in the morning. It warmed his blood, he said. Where would he drink now? In the kitchen, with me.

Reneri arrived with a winter storm. Snow covered the garden, burying the winter cabbages, kale and leeks, and then froze into a hard, white crust. The chickens refused to come out of their coop.

'Reneri! Come in, come in!' The Monsieur hugged Reneri to him as he stepped over the threshold.

I had not seen him since Leiden, but was not prepared for the sight that met me at the door. He looked ten years

295

older and stooped like an old man. I took his coat and scarf – to find a much thinner man underneath.

'Helena,' he said, holding my hands between his and patting them. 'How good to see you.'

His touch felt so light, as if his hands were the gloves and had lost what filled them.

The Monsieur was all questions.

'Come through, come through. You've brought no one? Told no one?' He turned this way and that, from Reneri to me and back to Reneri again. 'Good, good. Helena, bring drinks. We'll eat after that.'

'Yes, Monsieur.' I was quite laden by this time with our visitor's heavy winter coat, fur scarf, gloves and a blanket besides. Of Reneri himself, I wondered what, if anything, would be left.

The Monsieur showed Reneri into the front room. I had lit a fire in there, closing the door and the shutters to keep the heat in. I brought two chairs from the kitchen, so they could sit together. I brought them hot drinks. Then I left them. And the thought came to me as I went out: *Nothing changes; I do what I do and he is happy with that.*

The Limousin shouldered Reneri's trunk upstairs, then carried up a number of books. 'I don't know how long he reckons he's staying for.'

I knew. The Monsieur had told me. I was surprised the Limousin didn't know.

'Five weeks.'

'Five weeks?' He looked pained.

'At least,' I said, knowing it would pain him more.

That night, the Monsieur and Reneri ate together in the front room. They sent for more wine, then closed the door. In the kitchen, Limousin kicked off his boots and sat by the fire with his legs thrust out in front of him. He cracked nuts, dropping the shells onto the floor. I pulled up a chair as far away from him as was polite. Francine clambered onto my knee and leaned back against me. Her hair tickled me under my chin.

'Tell me a story, Mama.'

'Well . . .'

I glanced across at the Limousin, but he seemed lost in his thoughts.

'One long time ago,' I whispered, 'there was a little girl.'

Francine sighed and relaxed in my arms. This was our story, her favourite story.

'She was a happy little girl – the happiest girl of all, and everyone loved her.'

'Where did she live?'

'She lived in a little cottage with her mama and her—'

'Was she a good girl, Mama?'

'She was a very good girl. She was kind and helpful, and her mama loved her, and Monsieur Grat loved her, and the chickens loved her. The chickens loved her especially and laid the biggest, tastiest eggs just for her.'

'Did the worms love her?'

'Yes, even the wiggly wiggly worms loved her.' I wriggled my fingers in her hair. She squirmed on my lap and giggled.

'Did Monsieur love her too?'

'Yes, he did,' I whispered.

'What was her name, Mama?'

'That's a very good question. Her name was Francine and she looked a lot like you.'

She stopped wriggling and sat straight as a thought sprang up in her. 'Francine!' she said. 'Like France!'

'France?'

She twisted around on my lap. 'I'm France.'

'You're not France!' I laughed, then hesitated when I saw her frown. I had been certain of her name when I chose it. *Francine – from France, free one.* 'It's French and Dutch.'

She clapped her hands. 'Like Monsieur! Like Mama!'

'Oh for goodness' sake!' said the Limousin. 'I'm not listening to this.'

He stood up, pulled on his boots and bundled his coat around him. He thumbed tobacco into his pipe and went outside, clattering the door shut behind him.

'I don't like him.'

'Sh, now. It's his way. It's time for sleepy girls to go to bed.'

I helped her into bed, drew the curtains across and cuddled up close.

'Mama,' she whispered. 'Monsieur's my uncle now.'

'Is he?' I tried to keep the surprise out of my voice. What had he said to her? Uncle? *Uncle?*

'Monsieur Uncle.'

'Just uncle, Francine, if that's what he said. *Uncle.*' I said the word as if I had firm hold of it, but I could feel it already struggling free.

'But you call him Monsieur?'

'Yes.' These questions, I had not expected them so soon.

Francine turned over to face the wall. 'Uncle,' she whispered, 'Uncle, uncle, uncle . . .' She sat up and threw her arms wide. 'France is big, Mama, like this.'

'Is it?'

She nodded. 'Uncle said so.'

She thought for a moment. 'Can I go, Mama?'

'To France? It's a long way, Francine. A very, *very* long way.'

'I'll come back.'

'Sh, now. This is your home.'

'Mama?'

'Sh, Francine. Sleep.'

Sometime later, the Limousin came back. I heard him pour a glass of wine from the jug, and the bed creak on the far side of the alcove as he climbed in and turned over. Upstairs, Reneri coughed, and there followed such a quiet, as though we'd been snowed into our beds. But I could not sleep. France – it was as far away as the moon. It was as close as the lavender in the garden.

Francine snuffled beside me and I realised I was holding my breath.

The new year came in, bright and sunny, the sky such a blue it hurt my eyes. There had been no snow for some days and the track to the house was passable with care. The Monsieur and Reneri had spent the previous week in the front room, talking, and in the end I think even the Monsieur wanted to escape. They said they would go sledging and take Francine.

'If those books of yours don't kill you, Henri, they'll be

the end of me,' the Monsieur said, as he came into the kitchen. 'How many now?'

'A thousand or so. One more, with yours.'

'A thousand or so books and one! Damn you! And you complain you've no money!' The Monsieur flung open the back door. 'This is my library!'

'There's no doubt you look well, René, on a library of snow.'

I belted Francine's coat around her and slipped mittens over her hands. I pulled a hat I had edged with rabbit fur around her ears to straighten it. 'That'll keep you warm.' I kissed her on the nose and stood her away from me at arm's length. I wanted to keep her all for myself.

I held out a blanket to the Monsieur.

'She won't need that.'

He reached for Francine's hand. She skipped across and took it, swinging around.

'All children should sledge. Some are made to stay in bed in case they catch a chill – imagine that! I say we run around as fast as we can and the chill won't catch us!'

Francine squealed and jumped up and down. She still had hold of his hand and nearly toppled him over.

Limousin came in and stamped snow off his boots, hands thrust deep in his pockets.

'*C'est prêt*,' he said. I had never seen anyone less inclined to go sledging.

I watched them go, Reneri and the Monsieur. Monsieur Grat bounded along after them, biting the snow, and Francine ran after him. Last of all came the Limousin with the sledge. I'd not been asked. Who'd bake the bread and cook and do the rest if I went too?

The bread did not prove well; the crust split and burned on top as it baked. I'd been heavy-handed with it and now had a line of loaves frowning at me to thank me for my efforts. The kitchen was hot in the sunshine, but when I opened the back door the cold air made my ankles ache. I kicked it shut. I hated days like these, with everything set against me.

Uncle? Uncle? With Reneri here, I'd had no chance to ask him about it. I trailed about, letting my miserable mood fatten. I knew this feeling. My courses were due.

I left the bread to frown on the cooling tray, then went upstairs to make the beds. Reneri left his folded back and I had it straight again in a moment. The Monsieur's bed was a tangle, as it always was, sheets bundled on the floor, everything knotted with sleep. As I shook the pillow to air it, a letter fell out of the case. I shook it again and several more tumbled out. I could see what they were even before I picked them up – my letters from Deventer.

I sat down on the bed, my stomach-ache forgotten. As I sorted through them, I found copies of letters he'd sent me and other letters too – letters not sent. Some looked as if they had been sealed, then opened again. I saw him reading, rereading, changing his mind, deciding against.

I chose one and smoothed it open.

12 February 1635

Dearest Helena,
   This is my fifth attempt at writing. I struggle to find the words . . . I can rationalise my feelings, but that does not make it easier to live with them.

I shall do whatever is necessary, to keep you and my infant child – when he, or she, arrives – safe; to protect you both from unwelcome attention.

The nature of love is difficult to understand, but I am trying. I value love so highly – and I think whatever we go through for the sake of it is pleasant – so much so that even those who are ready to die for the good of those they love seem to me to be happy to their last breath . . .

I read that letter and another, and another, but startled so much as a bird went up from a tree that I did not dare read more. My fingers shook as I folded the letters again and tucked them back in the pillowcase. I finished making the bed and went downstairs.

Back in the kitchen, I stood at the window and stared into the garden until my eyes hurt and all I could see was white become whiter. He'd written the first letter as I was leaving Amsterdam, but had not sent it.

Love?

I tipped back my head, letting my hair tumble free, and stretched my arms wide. I went on tiptoe and turned in a circle, faster and faster. I stumbled and grabbed hold of the table to steady myself as the room continued to spin and everything in it took flight.

When I heard them coming back, I smoothed down my skirts, tucking away my feelings as surely as I tucked my hair under my cap.

'Mama!' Francine said and charged straight at me. Her boots and mittens were sodden, the skirts of her dress stiff with cold. 'I sledgedid! From the top to the bottom!'

She shivered violently, her teeth chattering as she spoke.

'Look at you! You're frozen!'

Letters forgotten, I pulled off her coat, then layer after layer of cold clothing. I grabbed the blanket he'd refused to take earlier and wrapped it around her, then stood her in front of the fire so she'd warm, muttering cross words all the while.

The Monsieur and Reneri tumbled into the kitchen, giddy and breathless, like boys just home from playing.

I turned on him with such a fervour. 'I told you, I did. The blanket, I said! Look at her!'

He held his hands up, more to shield himself than to deny the sorry truth before him. 'She'll warm soon enough.'

Francine looked up and grinned. As I turned, I thought I saw him wink.

'Did you not think?'

'Helena, please. Consider our guest.'

'She could have caught her death!'

'She hasn't.'

I folded my arms. He didn't know everything. 'Next time, a blanket.'

His mouth fell open a little and Reneri stifled a laugh. Francine wiggled her toes and sneezed and sneezed.

He came for me that night. He placed his finger to his lips as he listened for the Limousin's snore, then helped me from my bed. Reneri slept lightly; we could not risk the stairs. He took me through into the front room, where the fire still glowed. There was a blanket on the floor.

His fingers freed the ribbons on my chemise, his hands on my breasts. I kissed him as I drew his shirt over his shoulders, my breath already betraying my need. He circled my nipple with his thumb and then drew it into his mouth. He tilted my head towards him.

'What are you that I cannot last a month without you? That you have me counting the days . . .'

Later, I stroked the inside of his arm, from elbow to wrist, circling the violet shadow that pooled in the palm of his hand. The dark made us quiet. His fingers curved and went soft under my touch. I was shy of him then, the plain truth of him – the white of his arm, his hair on the pillow, his pulse flickering at his neck.

I thought of the letters I'd found. Why hadn't he sent them? Why had he left me so alone?

'Francine calls you uncle.'

There was no need to say more. He moved his hand away from mine.

'I needed to recognise our relationship in some way. It is right.'

Monsieur, Reyner Jochems, Uncle – *sly gubbins,* that's what Betje would say.

We lay there, not speaking, the crackle of the fire punctuating our thoughts.

'Will you tell her?'

The soft firelight framed him and threw his face into shadow.

'Will you?'

Eels

MARCH BROUGHT THE Monsieur's birthday. Francine helped decorate a cake. She poked raisins into the top of it, to make the letter U.

'Forty-two,' he said, when she asked him how old he was. He widened his eyes in surprise. 'And I have at least forty-two white hairs!'

It was the first time he'd mentioned his age. I measured the years between us – so much life before me; so much of his used up. I jumped my age forwards to make it match his.

Francine held out her hands and counted her fingers. I'd not counted past twenty with her before. 'Se-ven, four, three. I'm forty-two too, Uncle!'

He laughed. 'That's a fine age for one so small.' He counted two of her fingers and then bent one gently at the knuckle. '*Un, deux . . . et trois quarts*. You're two and three quarters.'

She grinned. 'Cake,' she said and pointed to it.

'*Un gâteau? Pour moi?*'

She nodded.

'Shall I tell you something?' He crouched down and whispered as though sharing a secret. 'This is my first birthday cake. Shall I keep it safe, until next year?'

'No, eat it! Now!'

'But I'll need another cake, next year.'

'I'll make it!' she said. 'Eat it!'

He laughed. 'Later! I have work to do.' He pulled a sad face to match hers, then lifted her chin. 'Go play now, Francine,' he said. 'And you must be quiet whilst I'm working. *Comme une souris.*'

'*Oui!*' She squeaked in a way that made him flinch. '*Souris, souris.*'

'Look, here's Monsieur Grat, he'll play with you. Cake later, *je te promets*. And remember, *sh.*' He held a finger to his lips.

'Monsieur Grat, no barking,' she said to the dog as she led him away by his ear.

I followed the Monsieur into the front room where I was to help him. The Limousin had left that morning for France and would be gone for two months. The larder was stocked up and peat piled high against the wall. Two months! I was happier than I had been in weeks.

Before he left, Limousin had showed me how to bait eel traps – I'd have it do whilst he was gone. He took me out to the dyke where they were set. He used a small boat, with rough planks for seats, staked at the bank. With us and six baited traps, there was little room to move.

He knelt on the plank at the front. The bow dug into the water under his weight and pitched dangerously as he centred himself. He held the paddle in front of him and twisted it from side to side, sculling the boat through the black water. Once across, he let the water stream out of the traps before hauling them over the gunwale. I had to pull up four of the six, to be sure I could do it, my dress saturated by the time I had done. He flipped the baited traps over the side.

'You're taking us back,' he said and held out the paddle to me.

Back on the bank, he loaded what we'd caught into a small handcart.

'Please,' he said, standing to one side and inviting me to take it.

The words I had, I kept to myself. I would have it to do whilst he was away; there was no good complaining. I put the strap across my shoulders and heaved the cart home.

I tried not to think unkindly of Limousin. He'd fetched in the eel traps that morning before he'd set off for France and they littered the floor where he had dropped them. I looked at the muddy puddles he'd left – the whole floor would need scrubbing. His every assistance seemed to come with a hindrance attached to its back.

I helped the Monsieur carry the table across to where the sunshine slanted in, warm and golden. We had until late morning, when the light was best, before the sun passed behind the gable and beat down on the back garden for the afternoon. The Monsieur poured the contents of a bucket into a larger barrel. I peered in, then shrank back. The water writhed and heaved, thick with eels. He rolled up his sleeves, reached into the barrel and swirled his arm around. Water slopped onto the floor and soaked his feet.

'*Voilà!*' he cried and lifted an eel above his head. The creature dangled limply, then gave a sharp flick. It thrashed again, sending a crescent of water across the room. He had to grab it with both hands to stop it jumping free.

'*Parfait!* Good and strong.'

He took the eel over to the table where several knives and empty dishes had been set out, and selected a knife with a thin blade – not a kitchen knife, but a paring knife he'd had sent from Amsterdam. He pinned the eel down and panted with the effort.

'Take the tail. Hold it.'

I clutched the tail. The eel jolted beneath my palm.

'Now take the head. Quickly! Do you have it?'

I gripped the eel and nodded. The Monsieur angled the knife, but it slipped as he made the cut. He grimaced.

'No,' he said. 'That's no good.' He threw the eel into a bucket.

Six more eels quickly followed the first.

'Damn! How is it possible, without killing it first?' He sucked his thumb where he had sliced it. At this rate he would run out of fingers before he ran out of eels.

'Here, let me try.'

I held out my hand for the knife and then fished an eel out of the barrel. Father had shown me how to kill eels, with a quick cut to the back of the head.

'I don't want it dead, Helena. Nor the innards mangled. I want to study its heart. A light cut, like this.' He drew his finger across the palm of his hand.

'I know what to do,' I said.

I did not know where an eel's heart would be, but knew

308

well enough where the guts were. I felt along the eel's belly and made a shorter, swift cut. The eel split apart, the insides gorged out, shiny and pink. The poor creature arched and bent; I wondered what he wanted from it to make it suffer so. I put the knife on the table, then placed my hands by the Monsieur's so I had tight hold of it once more.

'See?' I said, pleased I had done it first time.

He hunched over the eel and poked at the insides with the knife. He moved a small flap of pink flesh so that it rested on the blade of the knife. He leaned in closer. I felt his breath along my arm.

Francine ran in from the garden, her dress no cleaner than the floor she stood on. She stopped when she saw us. She looked at the Monsieur, at the knife he had hold of and then at the eel.

'*Viens.*' He beckoned to her.

She peeped over the table top, pulling herself up onto her toes.

'No, here,' he said and patted the chair, 'then you can see.'

'What's it?' she asked, as she clambered up.

He made a small cut, so that the heart was on the blade, then slid it into a dish. The eel twitched and was still. He took hold of her hand and placed it on his chest. 'There, can you feel that?'

She nodded, her eyes wide open, all play gone from them.

'Do you know what it is?'

She shook her head.

'It's my heart.' Then he placed her hand over her own heart. 'There, do you feel that? That's your heart.' He pointed to the small pink flap in the dish. 'And that is the eel's heart.'

'It's very little,' she said. 'Too little for me.'

'Perfect for an eel, though.'

'It must hurt it.'

'Animals do not have feelings as we do.'

I stared at the eel. I hoped for its sake what he said was true.

Francine still had her hand over her heart. She considered the heart in the dish. 'It's dead.'

'Well, the blood is cold, but if it is warmed carefully, a heart might beat again.'

She frowned. She had a way of looking that was his. 'No, Uncle. It is dead. Just like Squirrel.'

And then, just like that, with a tilt of her chin, she hopped off the chair and ran off.

The Monsieur turned to me. '*Squirrel?*'

In that one word, and the way he said it, the difference in our ages. I flushed.

'A squirrel, Monsieur. Monsieur Grat had it. We buried it last week at the bottom of the garden.'

He wiped the blade of his knife on a cloth. 'I see. Do you think it proper to accord a burial to a squirrel, Helena?'

I shook my head. I did not think it proper that an eel's heart should be made to beat again after it had been cut out.

He turned back to his work, making rapid, untidy notes and sketching a poor idea of what was laid out before him. I could draw it better. He only had to ask. These notes of his were unlike the letters he wrote, with their wide, neat margins. He would burn these papers. He had one eye on the future; he was not writing just for himself.

I washed the gore off my hands, wiped the worst off the table and started to scrub. I'd the floor to do after that. Then Francine's filthy dress.

The knock at the door startled us both. He flashed me a questioning look. I shrugged. I did not know who was there.

Another knock, louder this time, then a man's voice. 'Hello?'

A floorboard creaked. The Monsieur winced, as if he had stepped on a splinter. Our unknown visitor was now in the house. I tucked my hair away to make myself tidy. *Tidy?* With my apron so smeared with blood? It was all I could do not to laugh.

'Hello? *He-llo-o?*'

We could pretend we were not here, but what if he came further and found us? What then? Would we both have to pretend to be deaf?

The Monsieur rolled down his sleeves. He smiled, to re-assure me, but I saw his smile fade as he turned. He went out to greet whoever was already halfway into the house.

'Hello, hello!' I heard the Monsieur say. 'Forgive me, I was working.'

'No, no. *Forgive me*. The door was open.'

I did not know what to do. Keep quiet? Carry on tidying? I wiped the bowl I held on a cloth and placed it gently on the table, all of a sudden afraid I would drop it. A muddy smell hung in the air. Such a quantity of eel festered in the bucket. What had seemed normal now appeared not. I could see how strange it all looked, revolting, even. Who kept eels in their front room? Who thought that a proper way to behave?

At that moment, the Monsieur returned, followed by a stout man in black. There was no need for introductions His clothes gave him away. A minister. Likely from Santpoort.

'This is where I work,' said the Monsieur. He held out a hand, palm side up, pointing to nothing in particular. 'And this is Helena, my maid. Helena, this is Minister van Agteren.'

I stepped back, catching my leg on the corner of the table. Fear cartwheeled in me. *Maid?* I'd not heard the word in so long, it took a moment for it to become clear and to realise he meant me. Maid. What else could I be? With my red hands and scrubbing brush and filthy, bloodied skirts? What other reason would excuse me being here? Working like this? *With him?*

'Delighted to meet you, Helena.'

He took one look at my apron and did not offer his hand. I could see him becoming aware of where he was. He peered into the bucket of eel remains, his expression rearranging as he tried to control his disgust. He sniffed and wrinkled his nose.

'Curious work, Mr—'

'You know perhaps of William Harvey's work on circulation of the blood?'

He stepped away from the bucket and wiped his hands on his coat, though he had touched nothing. 'No. Should I?'

I leaned against the table as the Monsieur steered him out, feeling behind me for support. My leg throbbed where

I had bumped it. I counted for as long as I could, then went through to the kitchen and peeped out of the window. I could see the Monsieur and the minister outside, by the vegetable patch, but where was Francine? I went on tiptoe, casting left and right, back and forth, until I spotted her at the bottom of the garden, under the fruit trees. *Stay there, stay there, stay there*, I thought. *Stay put.*

As they came inside, I lowered my head and busied myself peeling an apple. Once the peel was off, I turned it in my hand and pared away scabs that weren't there. I would end up with only the core and then the pips if the minister did not leave soon. I pretended I wasn't interested in what was being said. *I am a maid, being a maid, peeling an apple.* But inside, I felt like a rabbit chased out of the long grass.

'Fascinating, Mr . . . I had heard this house was occupied and wanted to extend my invitation to you to attend church.'

'Well, yes. Thank you,' said the Monsieur. 'I travel frequently, but shall keep your invitation in mind.'

'Travel, you say? I thought I detected an accent.' He tapped the side of his nose and seemed pleased. 'I was in Gouda this last—'

'Uncle, Uncle!'

Francine ran into the kitchen, heading straight for the Monsieur. When she saw the minister, she stopped, ran across to me and buried her head in my skirts. She wriggled in closer, in search of a cuddle, but I did not reach down to her as I normally would.

The minister crouched down and held out his hand.

'And who is this little girl? Your niece?'

'Yes. My niece.' The Monsieur glanced at me.

'A pretty girl too,' said the minister, 'and you do look alike!'

Francine tugged at my apron.

'Not now,' I said and gently pushed her away.

'But *Mama!*' she cried and tugged my apron again. 'You *must* come. Monsieur Grat has cut his paw.' She turned from me and ran across to the Monsieur. 'Uncle, please come. Monsieur Grat has hurted hisself.'

The minister straightened up, his look all knowing as he took us in afresh. The Monsieur drew Francine to him, cupped the side of her head with his hand. Nothing was said. I lifted my chin, then raised my eyes, trying to steady myself with each of these small movements.

'I didn't catch your name, Mr . . .'

'There is no need,' said the Monsieur, all pretence gone.

'Well, I see how it is. Most irregular, and shocking, I must—'

The Monsieur held up a hand to silence him.

'As you wish.'

The minister bowed; suddenly he seemed dipped in starch.

'I will see you in church.'

He glanced at the bucket and shuddered. He waited for a moment, but when the Monsieur did not return his bow, he went out without another word.

After he had gone, we stood there a while. Eventually, Francine twisted free of the Monsieur. She stepped away from him, a little fierce, and said, 'Animals do have feelings.

Monsieur Grat cried. I heard him.' She turned on her heel and ran out.

He pinched the bridge of his nose. Outside, I heard Francine call for the dog and, beyond her somewhere, the sound of gulls as they came inland.

I glanced at him. He shut his eyes as he thought, perhaps to close out what had happened.

'A soup with those eels later, I think.'

'Yes, Monsieur.'

People did not need to be told he was here; they would find him anyway. The apple had browned in my hand. I went out into the garden and threw it away from me as far as I could.

We did not go to church. Not that Sunday, nor the Sunday after that.

'I miss my church, Monsieur. Can I go?'

'We carry God in us, Helena.'

That gave me no comfort. I had heard it before. His weary patience only annoyed me more. *An internal God, hidden from sight?* That was not my God.

'That's not enough!'

'It has to be. We have no choice.'

We? Why did he include me in this?

'It is through our *practice* that we are good to others. If we do not have that, if we do not *do* that, can we call ourselves Christian?'

'*Practice?* Practice makes us seen, Helena. It gives us a face and then a name. Many men speak God's word, and those with authority over us are ready to level accusations of atheism or heresy at those who do not *exactly* conform . . . I am a Catholic. You are not. As we are, here, *nous trois*, we cannot go to church.'

'Then I will take Francine.'

'What welcome do you think awaits you? Will Minister van Agteren be pleased to see you? Is that what you want for her?'

'Oh!' I spun away from him, my arms crossed against my chest to stop my anger flying out.

'I know a priest, in Alkmaar. He does not, of course, proclaim his vocation, but he might provide counsel . . .'

A priest? Alkmaar? How did he think this helped me? I glared at him.

And then, in a flash, my anger was gone. *Betje.* Of course! Betje was in Alkmaar.

I could send Betje a letter as long as I did not give our address or *indication of our whereabouts*. The letter could be trusted to the Alkmaar priest, who would do his best to find her.

'She can't reply without an address,' I said.

'A reply can be left with the priest. He will fetch it when he next visits Santpoort.'

I saw each painful, unhurried stage of the journey, slowed down to the pace of a shuffle.

'It will take *for ever*, Monsieur.'

'It will not take for ever. A week or two, at most.'

I bristled. Three or four, at least.

'No address, Helena. That is the condition.'

'But what if I want her to come?'

The look he gave me! Had I asked the king of Spain to visit?

'She cannot, not here. *Absolument pas.* Out of the question.'

'Cannot?' I took a step back. 'Why not, Monsieur?'

'Do I now find myself in the position of having to explain myself to you, Helena?' He shook his head.

'Reneri came.'

'Reneri is a different matter; and, let me be frank with you, in no way comparable.'

I knew then he was angry. He was using more words than he needed.

Then he said, 'You are not to mention me.'

'Should I send her a blank sheet of paper, Monsieur? Would you be happy with that?'

He slapped the desk. *'Tu est impossible!'*

'Et vous, et vous êtes—'

'Oui? Quoi?'

The word came to me, quick as the animal I saw dart in my mind. *'Une souris!'*

That made him sit back.

I wiggled finger whiskers at him. *'Oui.* Monsieur *Souris.* Hiding. Like a mouse.'

I turned and went out, rattling the door behind me.

When I had calmed down, I took the letter I had written and gave it to him, and not a word was said about priests or mice or anything else.

Now all I had to do was wait for a reply. Three years, if the priest was sprightly.

I did not mention going to church again. I waited for Betje's reply.

As the weather warmed, Francine grew more restless. She turned three. Worms no longer entertained her. She scuffed about the house, elbows and shins turned out.

'Monsieur Grat is bored,' she complained and picked at a scab on her knee.

She no longer slept in the afternoons. She bubbled up like hot milk in a pan.

'You *must* be quiet, Francine, when I am working,' said the Monsieur.

It was impossible for her to be quiet. If she played inside, the sound of her feet on the floor annoyed him. Outside, her laughter distracted him and I heard him bolt the shutters to keep out the noise. She could not be silenced, just like that, when he wanted.

Fending off arguments and tantrums, I tried to get Francine to hush. But I could not stop the days from lengthening, nor tell the sun to stop shining. Francine charged about the garden with the great lolloping Monsieur Grat barking by her side. Birds went up from the trees, unripe apples tumbled to the ground.

'*Tais-toi!*' he bellowed down the stairs, then to me, 'For goodness' sake, make her shut up!'

'Not the clock!' he shouted, chasing Francine from his room. 'You are absolutely forbidden to touch it!'

In the end, I went to him. 'Monsieur, she needs exercise. A walk? We'll not go far.'

Without looking up from what he was doing, he waved me away with his hand. 'Yes, take her. I need to finish this today.'

He called me back as I reached the door. 'I nearly forgot. This came for you.'

He handed me a letter. After weeks of waiting – Betje's reply.

'You can open it, you know,' he said as I went out and I thought I saw him smile.

I went straight to the kitchen with the letter.

dear Dear Helena

    oh I am happy to have your news and to hear you are well but sorry to hear of your brother and I think your mother will be happy in Zeeland though I am glad it is not me that has gone there

    well I was <u>surprised</u> to hear you are not with Mr S and I had to read your letter again to be sure I had it right because I was <u>even more surprised</u> to hear you are a mother Your little girl – <u>does she have a name</u> – She sounds beautiful

    your story about the book made me laugh I would buy it I am now married His name is Henk and I will have a child myself soon and if I have a girl I am calling her after my mother and if I have a boy he will be called Henk and if I have another girl I will call her after you my dear Helena you should see me I am like a whale

    I did not find my mother She died but I found her sister and her family are kind to me

*I heard Mr Hoek was angry about me leaving like that
and Mrs Hoek more so I feel sorry for whoever came after
Did you know what happened to Antje*

*Your letter came <u>as such a surprise</u> and brought to me at
such a late hour But he was kind and gave me paper for this
reply and will fetch it from me He left me more paper so I
can write again if you like*

*I am sorry about my writing I have not done it for so
long a time but I read whatever I can*

your friend

Betje

*write and tell me your girls name Who is the father <u>I
cannot believe you are a mother before me</u>*

I read the letter again. Dear, dearest Betje. I missed her.
She'd used her learning to leave. And here I was, stuck.

I called Francine in from the garden.

'Go find your shoes, sweetheart, we're going for a walk.'

Linen

WE TOOK THE path from the garden. It twisted through the dunes, narrowing a little as it forked, until it came down to the width of my foot. Then it disappeared into a thicket, banked on either side by prickly bushes. Francine ran on before I could stop her and wouldn't come back. I had no choice but to follow. I ducked as low as I could, hands over my head, elbows in, and prayed I would not tear my dress. On the other side, the path opened out into a circle of light; tall grasses stirred in the soft breeze. A pair of startled skylarks flew up with a shrill cry. Grasses, kale and sea pinks tufted the dune tops – a ragged hem to the sky.

The walk had taken us further than I expected. I could already hear Francine's complaints on the way back. I took a deep breath and pushed the thought away. I untied my cap and shook my hair free.

'Francine?'

I clambered up a dune on my hands and knees, following a trail of her footprints, the wind already smoothing them away. At the top, a great gust blew my skirts between my legs. I dug in my heels so I wouldn't topple over. And there it was: the sea – stretching away to a clear, blue horizon. Gulls soared and swooped above the white-capped waves.

I shaded my eyes against the glare of the water. My mouth formed the only word I had in me – *Oh! Oh!*

Great waves tumbled inland and fanned into foamy sheets over the sand. And there was Francine, down on the beach below me. The wind pushed knuckles into my back. *Go on*, it urged, *run.*

I ran down the dune, giddy and off-balance. Sand streamed away from under my feet – there was no way to go slower even if I'd wanted to. I picked up Francine's shoes – one here, one there – that she'd pulled off and abandoned at the bottom. She jumped up and down in a shallow pool and pointed to the sea to be sure I had seen it.

'Mama, Mama, Mama!' Then she threw her arms wide and brought them together to hug it all to her.

I kicked off my shoes, lifted my skirts and watched the wet sand ooze between my toes.

Francine knelt down and started to dig. She found one shell, then another, and rubbed them clean on her skirt.

'She-shells,' she said and held them out to me, squinting into the sun through her fingers and curls.

'Pretty as you!'

I kissed her cheek, but when I tried to catch hold of her, she wriggled free and scampered off. She was like Monsieur Grat, running backwards and forwards. She dropped a wet pebble in my hand and I watched it dry from shining silver to pale dove grey.

We walked down the beach and scratched words in the sand with a stick as we went. Then, I needed to rest and sat down while Francine continued to play. The sand felt warm under me. I lay back and closed my eyes and listened to the waves on the shore. What did it matter if my hair was loose, when only the sky could see?

So, this is what the sea does – it loosens things, it lays them flat.

A sharp tug at my skirt woke me. I sat up and looked around, for a moment unsure where I was. The breeze raised goosebumps on my arms. White mist rose up from the sea's edge, from bigger waves that now crashed on the beach.

'Mama?'

I rubbed my eyes, seeing Francine. She tugged my skirt and pointed out to sea.

'Mama? Why's it blue?'

I followed the line of her hand.

'Mama?'

I blinked and tried to clear my thoughts. 'God made it that way.'

She tugged my skirt again. '*Why*, Mama?'

I batted her hand away. 'Stop that, Francine. I don't know. You do not ask questions of God.'

She looked at her toes and wiggled them. The beach was covered with her footprints – circles and lines – like a giant page of the Monsieur's notes spread out on the sand.

She cocked her head on one side. 'Uncle will know.'

I levered myself up. 'I think you'll find he will agree with me – about not asking questions of God.'

Francine frowned. 'But—'

It was my turn to frown. 'Look at you!' I brushed the sand from her skirts.

She dropped the shells in her hand. 'Is Uncle your uncle too?'

'Of course he isn't!'

She still clutched a feather. 'Plume,' she said and held it out to me.

'Plume?' I scanned the dunes and grabbed her hand. 'It's time we got back.'

'P-lume.' The word bounced out of her as she struggled to keep up.

The closer we got to the dunes, the less certain I was of the one we had come down. They all looked the same. Nothing to tell them apart.

We walked around and around; I climbed dune after dune, looking for our path until my legs ached. My hands stung from clutching at grass to stop me sliding down again. It was no good. Our path was lost somewhere in a warren of paths. The only place I recognised was a white patch in the distance, where the linen fields were. The house was not too much further on, that I remembered. I'd be able to find my way from there.

The linen fields were as strange as the first time I'd seen them. From a distance, the ground seemed planted with clouds – but there was nothing cloud-like about the place. As we drew near, the air filled with the same sickening stench. I covered my mouth and nose with my hand, breathing in as little as I could. Francine buried her head in my skirt.

We passed several groups of women huddled over wooden troughs, each trough brimful with what smelled like sour milk. Some women stirred; others pulled lengths of cloth from the troughs and passed the sodden bundles to a group of girls, some not much older than Francine. The whole wretched business was carried out ankle-deep in green-rimmed pools of milk. The girls carried the cloth to a wheel where it was wrung out. A man pegged the cloth onto low platforms and frames, and women walked up and down with watering cans, either rinsing it or soaking it further with the foul mixture, I could not tell. Cloth was pegged out at various stages of the process, showing how it changed from grey to the brightest white.

A woman watched us approach. I nodded to her and carried on walking, motioning to Francine to keep up.

'Here, girlie,' she called to Francine. She cupped her hands together and scooped up a handful of liquid. 'Thirsty?'

Francine shook her head. The woman laughed and let it trickle between her fingers.

'That's a shame. It makes the best linen; only for the cleanest, fairest necks.' She turned her attention to me. 'We don't get many people along this way. Are you lost?'

I shook my head, allowing myself no more than a glimpse of her. 'I know where I am, thank you.'

'We live with my uncle. He's French! He knows everything,' said Francine, all in one breath.

It was the most she'd said to anyone, other than the Monsieur and me, since we'd left Leiden.

'And I have a dog, and I—'

I gave her shoulder a sharp squeeze. She twisted away and scowled at me.

The woman wiped her hands on her apron. 'Isn't a French uncle the fanciest thing to have? Fanciest thing I've heard of.' Her gaze snagged at my waist.

I held out my hand to Francine. 'Francine, come now.'

'*Francine?* Well, that's a fancy name too. I've not seen you in church. I'd have noticed a little girl like you, especially one with a *French* uncle. But as you know where you're going . . .'

The woman nodded slowly and plunged lumps of grey cloth below the milk's surface, squeezing the material as if kneading bread.

'This your little one?'

I gathered Francine to me.

'Thought as much. But you're not French, are you? You don't look it. You don't sound it. Bit of a mystery, I reckon. I don't know many families with Dutch sisters *and* French brothers. None at all, now I think of it.'

I took Francine's arm to get her to come. The smell of the cloth made me retch.

The woman continued to stare. She ran her tongue over her teeth.

'I bet you're wondering how we do it, make something white out of something so . . . *disgusting.* Know what I think when I see you out walking with your little girl and your hair undone, when everyone else around here is working hard to make grey cloth white? Too fine to be a maid, not fine enough to be the wife, that's what I think. What does it make you if you're not one or the other?'

'Well!' I said.

'Ha! I thought as much. I have an eye for these things.'

'I'm a mother. She is my child!'

'Mama,' Francine cried, trying to pull free from my grip. 'Mama!'

'Mother?' The woman sneered. 'Spare me. There are places for mothers like you' – she cocked her head at Francine – 'for children like that. I might work in this slop, but I'm cleaner than you'll ever be. *Miss.*'

I pulled Francine after me. 'Come on,' I said.

As soon as we were out of sight, I knelt down in front of her, so that we were on a level. I took her by the shoulders and shook her.

'You are not to talk to people, or tell them your name, do you hear me, Francine? Not ever!'

Tears welled in her eyes.

I shook her again. 'Do you know what will happen? *Do you?* The Monsieur will send us away. Is that what you want? Is it?'

'No, Mama.'

'And if he does that, then what? Where will we go?'

Tears trickled down her cheeks.

'Tell me!' I shouted.

Her hands shot up and covered her ears.

I sat on the ground. When Francine came to me, I pushed her away, then when she went, I clutched at her.

'I'm sorry. I'm sorry. I'm sorry, I'm sorry, I'm sorry.'

And we stayed like that until my crying stopped, and

then for a time longer. I caught up my hair into a loop and pushed it under my cap, fumbling with the ribbon. My hands shook and I couldn't make it tie.

We stood up. Francine took my hand. We walked in silence until we came to a windmill drawing water from a dyke. I watched the sails turn, flinching each time the sail cut through air, passing over my head.

'Mama? Is Uncle your brother?'

'Not another word, Francine.'

Sand skittered across the path, blown by a freshening wind. On one side of it, the bank had been scoured away completely, baring the roots of a tree. A length of fence had lost its footing and started to collapse.

Nothing in these parts had a firm foundation. Everything shown for what it was.

The sun was low in the sky by the time we got back. Our shadows stretched ahead, as though longing to be at the door before us. A horse and carriage stood in front of the house with several wooden crates stacked by its side. It meant only one thing: Monsieur Sour Lemon had returned.

Francine grabbed a handful of marguerites and ran on ahead. I closed my eyes and when I had counted to twenty, I followed her. Blisters flared between my toes where the sand had rubbed them raw.

The Monsieur came out of the house with the Limousin and patted him on the back. 'Look who's here!'

The Limousin acknowledged the Monsieur with a small

bow, then continued with what he had been saying. 'Mersenne keeps well, but he's more concerned about your health than his.'

'Uncle?' Francine tugged at the Monsieur's coat.

'He wanted to know everything – *everything* – what you are working on—'

'*Uncle?*' She reached up with the flowers in her hand.

The Monsieur knelt down and took them. '*Pour moi? Merci.*' He passed the flowers to me. 'Is Limousin's room prepared?'

'It can be, Monsieur.'

'Please. If you would.'

No word for me. No comment on our lateness. I went in with my orders, loosely arranged the marguerites in a glass of water and put them on the sill in the Monsieur's room. Francine trailed after me, her bare feet slapping against the wooden floor, each step protesting her tiredness.

'I'm hungry, Mama.'

'Later, Francine.'

I went into the Limousin's room, turned back the covers on the bed and smoothed the sheet flat with my hand. A faint trace of Reneri's perfume still hung in the air from when he had stayed.

Francine twisted the hem of her dress. 'Thirsty, Mama.'

I heard footsteps on the stairs; a trunk knocked against the wall.

'Downstairs, Francine. Now.'

She turned her foot and shook her head.

'*Now!*'

The Limousin backed into the room, dragging his trunk between his legs. In a slip, Francine was past him and off down the stairs. He pushed the trunk into a corner and sat down on the bed, prodded the mattress, then lay back, dust from his shoes marking the cover.

'You look well, Helena. And the child is calling him *uncle*. How *gentil*.'

'The Monsieur wanted it.'

'She has more and more a look of him, it's true. Looks less Dutch every day.' He rubbed his hands on his trousers. 'Seems she belongs with him after all.'

'But she is—'

I knew, as soon I said it, he meant something else.

He closed his eyes and folded his arms over his chest. 'It is always so pleasing to see you, Helena.'

'And the Monsieur is happy at your return,' I said and went out, closing the door behind me.

As I turned to go downstairs, the Monsieur came out of his room.

'Eels,' he said as he walked past, 'provide the perfect analogy for water.'

Echo

'MERSENNE HAS IT wrong,' he said, and dropped the letter he had been reading into his lap. He covered his eyes with one hand. 'Why do I have to explain everything twice?'

I glanced up from the picture of a cogwheel I was sketching – my third attempt. He had not asked me to do it, but if I waited for his word on everything, nothing would be done. His drawings of a cogwheel looked squashed flat. My first two had come out the same, until I realised I was seeing it wrong. I drew an oval instead, making the cogs at the front larger and those furthest away, at the back, smallest of all.

'Not bad,' he said, when I turned it to show him.

'I'm not finished yet.' I already knew it was better than anything of his.

He was up on his feet again, pacing. He slapped Mersenne's letter against his thigh. It was impossible to work with him like this.

He picked up a book and weighed it in his hand. 'Why is it heavy?'

He dropped the book with a thump on the table and went to fetch the broom from the corner of the room. He held it front of him, first by the middle, then by one end.

'Why does it appear heavier when I hold it like this? It's the same broom.'

He placed the broom back in the corner, then strode over to the window. He swept his hand along the windowsill and into the air, watching the dust he had set dancing.

'What can dust, this *chaos*, tell us about air, about subtle matter?' He rubbed his hands clean. 'What I want to know is: will Mersenne ever understand *a word* I write?'

Dust? Brooms? Books? There was nothing to say when he was like this. Nothing he wanted me to say.

He went back to where he had been working, the table piled with unopened letters and half-written replies.

'Three letters to reply to from Mersenne alone . . .'

He picked them up and let them drop. He slumped down in the chair, leaned forwards and rested his head on the table. He pushed outwards with his arms, sending letters and quills tumbling off both sides. He did not stop until all was on the floor.

'Monsieur!' I cried and leapt to my feet.

The ink pot toppled over and pooled in a puddle. He'd shouted at Francine for spilling less.

He looked at me and at the ink, as though trying to fathom how it had got there.

'Fetch water, Monsieur!' I said, my voice rising, anything to get him to move.

I looked at the ink, aghast. The stain would never lift from the wood. He had regard neither for me, nor for the ink he'd wasted.

'It's never you has to do this,' I said, as he returned with a small glass of water and a cloth. 'That's not nearly enough!'

I stormed into the kitchen to fetch a bucket. He came after me, but I was already on my way back.

I took the cloth, went down on my knees and started to mop it up.

'Oh, just look at it,' I said, as I rinsed the cloth in the bucket. 'It'll never come out.'

'Leave it,' he said. He crouched down beside me and gathered up papers, not caring to order them, shaking off ink drops.

'Leave it?'

I scrubbed at the floor ever more furiously but managed only to drive the stain further out, blackening my hands with it too. I didn't know why, but at that moment I wanted to cry.

'Petty posturing by halfwits and sycophants ...' he muttered, as he sorted his papers. 'It was stupid to publish in French ...'

'Enough, Monsieur.'

'I need to translate it, then it will be read.'

I slapped my hand on the floor. 'Enough, Monsieur! Enough.'

My shoulders sagged.

'It has been read. You have the replies to show it. *They* take up your time. You spend all your time replying to letters Limousin brings – questions, complaints, questions, complaints. A translation would only bring more.'

'But the work is not *understood*. If it were translated ...'

Would he ever listen? I picked up a handful of the papers and thrust them at him, then levered myself up off the floor.

'Instead of writing these replies, explaining the same thing, first to this person, then to that, you should write something that explains what you mean – *clearly*.'

'A new work?'

'Yes.'

I could see the thought working in him.

'What else will you do? Spend your days writing replies? Teach – *like Reneri?*'

That made him wince. I pointed to the letters on the table. I'd had my fill of them. He'd no time for Francine any more.

'I think you waste your time. And,' I added, now that I had his ear, now that he had turned to me and was listening, 'this time you should put your name on it. Then there will be no doubt.'

I threw the cloth in the bucket and went out. I thought I'd said too much, but then I heard him call after me, 'You're right. I should listen to you more.'

Yes, you should, I thought, as I threw the water into the garden. Without thinking, I wiped my hands on my apron to dry them, only then becoming aware of what I'd done. I looked at the inky handprints that now covered it. My apron, brought new from market a week ago, was ruined.

Reneri visited again. He had spent the summer teaching and had not been outside once during the day. I was happy to see him, but distressed that he had grown thinner.

'Tell me everything, tell me everything you know, I want

to hear it all,' said the Monsieur, desperate for news from Utrecht. 'Spare no detail!'

After we had eaten one evening, we went into the garden to watch the sunset. The Monsieur and Reneri took chairs out with them. I sat on a stone to one side, with my back to a tree. Limousin came out and stood far enough away so he would not have to make conversation with me, but close enough to the Monsieur, if required.

They turned to watch Francine run up the garden.

'Here,' the Monsieur said, 'watch this.' He called to her, 'Francine, *écoutes!*' and clapped his hands, then cupped his hand to his ear. 'Hear that?'

She stopped, listened, then jumped up and down. '*Arn-cor!*'

'*Encore, petite fifille?*' He clapped again and this time a faint sound came back. 'You'll have to be quick – go catch it!'

At that she was off down the garden, where the weeds had grown high, charging into the tall grass. She came back again, hands clasped together, grass seeds tangled in her hair.

'I got it! I got it!'

He leaned in to listen as she opened her hands a crack, pulled a face and shook his head. 'It's escaped, I think.'

He clapped again and off she went, her skirts kicking out on either side as she chased after it.

The Monsieur turned to the Limousin. 'Did you hear it, the echo? The long grass, the trees overhead – just right.'

'I see that,' said the Limousin, cheerlessly. He was like the grey edge of night nudging the day away.

Reneri clasped his hands together and stared at the sky.

The Monsieur leaned forwards to pick a grass stem, rolling it between his hands.

'So, what do you think of this garden I have made?'

Reneri considered him for a while before he replied. 'I don't think you need me to tell you how fortunate you are, René.'

'See the gardener I have become?' He plucked another piece of grass, studied it for a moment, then threw it away.

'Indeed, René. I did not foresee that. *De toekomst is een boek met zeven sloten.*'

The Monsieur did not answer.

We had come out for the sunset, but it had passed. Dusk was already upon us, darkening blue above the trees. Moths lifted from the grasses, like butterfly ghosts. I closed my eyes.

De toekomst is een boek met zeven sloten – *the future is a book with seven locks.* Who knew what the future would bring?

Reneri and the Monsieur's voices had dropped to a murmur and, somewhere beyond them, Francine's laughter in the distance. Doves cooed and settled in their roosts.

Have you thought more . . .

when she is older . . .

matters we discussed last time . . .

certainly not, but I am prepared . . .

. . . love, if it's that . . .

Voetius . . .

I never intended . . .

I opened my eyes to darkness. They had been talking,

the Monsieur and Reneri. I shook my head. Their words had gone. The garden was empty. I was alone.

I woke the next morning to the sound of chickens outside the window. At first I thought a fox had got them. It was just after dawn, the sun a faint pink in the east. There, at the bottom of the garden, I could just make out the Limousin with his shirt-sleeves rolled up. I saw a flash of silver, then another – grey light on a blade. He had a scythe and was cutting the grass in wide sweeping arcs. Back and forth, back and forth he went. He sliced through the grass until all of it had been levelled.

When Francine saw what he had done, she ran in and threw herself at me.

'I can't find it!' she wailed.

'What, sweetheart? What can't you find?'

'My echo! It's gone. I *hate* him!'

'The Limousin says that long grass harbours ticks,' said the Monsieur later. 'We must keep it short. It's for our own good.'

Down by the apple tree, where the grass had been longest, I came upon the three tulip bulbs, which had flowered for the first time that year, dug up.

'Monsieur Grat,' said the Limousin, when I challenged him. 'That's the trouble with dogs, I'm afraid.'

The day burned hot; the heat sank deep into the ground as though the sun had anchored there. Francine and the

Monsieur were under the shade of the apple tree; she'd made a pillow of his arm and was asleep. I sat with them a while, then went to fetch paper, a quill and some ink. Back outside, I rested the sheet of paper on the back of a chopping board and started to sketch. He watched me and did not move until I was done. Only then did he pick up a feather from the grass and touch it gently to Francine's arm. She twitched and giggled in her sleep, gradually coming awake. When she realised what he was doing, she grabbed the feather and wriggled free of his arms.

'My feather!' she laughed, and ran off.

He came up behind me and rested his hands on my shoulders. 'Very good,' he said, leaning in closer to see. 'When did you learn to draw?'

'When you weren't looking,' I said.

I didn't know why those words roused such a revolt in me, but my fair mood suddenly rubbed foul. I dipped my nib in the ink, taking up too much, covering my fingers with it. I dropped the quill into the bottle and folded my hands in my lap.

His hands were heavy and though I shifted away he kept them there.

'Do you know what I think, Monsieur?

He straightened up, still behind me, only now his hands fell to his sides.

'What do you think, Helena?' The weight of his hands now a weariness in his voice.

'I think you would rather be in Utrecht.'

Sand

SOMNOLENCE: THOSE SUDDEN hot days; clouds piled so high I thought they would topple out of the sky. If I said the word slowly, it reminded me of the sound a marble makes, rolled around a bowl.

We had been in Santpoort for nearly two years. Limousin brought fewer and fewer letters in reply to *Discourse.* I added *lassitude, languor* and *lethargy* to the list of words I kept in my head. I liked it when the Monsieur said them in French; it felt as if he were circling the words on my hand. I gave Francine old quills to play with. She knew some words from the Bible and when she picked them out with her finger she yelped with delight.

The Monsieur had more time for her. At the end of the mornings, he called for her to come through into the front room and showed her what he had been working on. Rabbits replaced eels on the table; Limousin kept the tails for her, but she did not want their feet. The Monsieur spoke to her more and more in French. I found her with chalk one day, writing numbers in a crooked line on the floor. Her seven, like his, had a line through it.

She pointed to a number in the middle of her row. '*Neuf,*' she said and underlined it.

They made paper kites and flew them from the top of the

highest dune they could find, catching the wind that ran fastest there. Her adventures came back to me at bedtime. She had outgrown the curve of my arm. She wriggled and kicked, cutting the air with her hands, colliding French and Dutch into a language of her own.

'Mama,' she said, 'I like it here with Uncle.'

The Monsieur still sent the Limousin away each month for three or four days. He returned with letters, with news and, increasingly, with gossip.

One evening, I went to bring them a warm drink, but I was delayed by needing to build up the kitchen fire. It was late and night had come on. Perhaps they had forgotten me. As I came back, the door to the front room stood open a little and they were talking.

'There are rumours again in Utrecht, Monsieur.'

'What now?'

'About a child.' He cleared his throat. 'Forgive me . . . *a French liar's* child.'

I stepped closer, pressed myself against the wall. I could see the Monsieur through the crack in the door. He was seated and Limousin stood near by, to one side.

'Who is it this time? That cretin Voetius? Revius?'

'You realise what will happen if this comes out? All you have worked towards—'

The Monsieur shook his head. 'I'll deny it.'

'The child . . . the child is only part of it; the difficulty is also with her, with *Helena*. You must see that?'

The Monsieur shrank back, sinking lower in his seat. 'I did my best.'

'You did, you did, I know,' said the Limousin, his voice soothing, consoling. 'You did what you could and more. Some would be surprised you did so much; they would read it as evidence of attachment. Some may even go so far as to call it *guilt* – and that presents a difficulty, because it requires explanation. Some things are beyond your control. Word is out in Haarlem—'

'In Haarlem?'

The Limousin nodded. 'Among the linen bleachers.'

The Monsieur waved his hand, dismissing the remark. 'That does not concern me.'

'But it shows, Monsieur, how easily word travels. And if word gets as far as Voetius, as I am almost certain it will if matters continue as they are, what then? You would want me to be frank with you, Monsieur?'

I did not know who Voetius was, but the Limousin was a leech. He had latched onto the Monsieur and would not let go.

'If what you tell me is true, if Voetius finds out—'

'Rumours, rumours, Monsieur. They have a way of becoming *truth*. Of course, she's not the first maid to bear a child and will not be the last. But her age, Monsieur . . . Then there are differences of church, your status.'

'I regret that, certainly.'

I covered my mouth. *Guilt? Regret?* Was he ashamed? Ashamed of himself, ashamed of me, of *Francine*? Everything I thought I knew of us began to unravel – a thread pulled back to the beginning, a story taken back to the first word.

He had said he wanted us. Said he could not be a month without me. His letters – *he had written of love.*

I rested my head against the wall and closed my eyes. I remembered the letters I'd found. *Words.* Words he had never sent; words he had not wanted me to see. Words were what he was good at. He could present whatever face he wanted to the world. *Love?* The word thickened in my throat.

'The child could be anyone's.'

'She's clearly mine! Have you no eyes in your head?'

'Forgive me, Monsieur. Yes, she is yours, *clearly so.* But you have a duty to yourself and to your work. You would risk that? *Il y a parfois des petits accidents,* a child or two with some pretty young thing. With kings and princes, one might even say it is *normale* but the protection of kings is not yours to share. This would be used against you. Those Utrecht crows would delight in bringing you low.'

'I will never win approval from them.'

'But *disapproval* is another matter, Monsieur, another matter entirely. Think of how they would feed on this.'

'Damn it! I never swore a vow of chastity! How far do I have to go to be rid of this? Into the sea? I thought here at least, *in this godforsaken place,* I could be away from that.'

The Limousin shook his head. 'You do see the problem, Monsieur?'

'Yes. Yes, I do.'

'The risk to your work, you see that?'

'Yes, yes.'

'It cannot continue.' His voice, when he said it, hopeful.

'Where? Where, if not here?'

The Limousin paused. 'France, Monsieur . . . at least for a while.' He rested his hand on the Monsieur's shoulder, as though to comfort a grief. 'You tried.'

'And Francine? I have a duty.'

A duty?

And then Limousin's words came back to me – *maybe she belongs with him after all* – and I understood. The Monsieur had hidden me, *his shame*, in Deventer and was hiding me still. Now he was talking of leaving and would take Francine with him. Hide her instead. All that mattered to him – himself, his work. His reputation.

I could not listen to another word.

Later, when he came to find me, I turned from him.

He touched his fingers to my elbow. 'Helena what is it?'

I shrugged his hand away.

'Helena?' He went to stroke my cheek.

I drew back. Anger had made me darkly bright. 'I am not your maid, Monsieur.'

He startled a little. 'No, Helena, of course not.'

Monsieur? Why was I still calling him that? Why did he let me? Did he not have a name? Did he not want me to say it?

I spun away from him. He could close the shutters himself.

I went out into the garden. I could barely make out the path that edged the vegetable patch in the dark. It was cold, but I did not care.

'I'll tell you what a garden needs, Monsieur,' I shouted back towards the house, yanking handfuls of lavender from a bush and hurling them into the air. 'It needs attention, Monsieur. It needs care. It needs love.'

I went over to the carrots and pulled at those, snapping off the tops.

'Not ink, Monsieur. No. Not words. Not thoughts and thinking. Love!' I hoicked out a row of beans and threw them over my shoulder.

Seeing him come out, I took aim and kicked at a lettuce, shattering it.

'*Qu'est-ce que tu fais? Helena?* What's happened?'

'Learning, Monsieur! Knowledge! That's what's happened.'

'Helena, please. Come indoors.'

'A garden needs love, do you hear me? *Love!*'

I wheeled around, snatching at whatever was to hand – beans, onions, mint, nettles, dandelions – and threw it at him. 'It needs strength, Monsieur! And someone with a kind heart to tend it! And effort! It needs *work*, Monsieur, did you not know that?'

He cowered under the bombardment.

'You think you know everything!'

'Helena, please—'

'Go away!' I shouted. My fingers stung where I had cut them. And when he took a step towards me, I screamed. 'Leave me alone! *Laissez-moi!*'

Ditch

I WALKED WHERE I wanted, when I wanted. I took Francine with me. I did not say where we were going nor when we would be back.

I avoided the path towards the linen fields and walked along the polder towards Santpoort instead. It took me past a farm, where children played outside. When Francine ran down the bank to say hello to them, I did not stop her. I walked on. She could catch up with me or wait until I returned.

I could see in all directions from the top of the dyke. Santpoort, Haarlem and, in the far distance, Amsterdam. If I looked south, there was my childhood. To the north, my life with Mr Sergeant; east, Deventer and Mrs Anholts. And here I was in the west. Everywhere I looked brought me back to where I was standing. Should I fill my pockets with stones and step into the dyke?

'Hey, hey!'

I turned. A young man hurried towards me and had hold of Francine's hand.

'Oh!' I said, as I realised how far I had come. 'I am so sorry.'

Francine twisted away from him and ran the last few steps. 'You left me!' she wailed.

'Sweetheart.' I hugged her to me and kissed her hair; her cheeks damp from crying.

The man coughed. 'Well, she's returned to you.'

I looked up at him. 'Thank you.'

'Well,' he said and blushed. 'I'll go then.'

He made no move to leave.

'It's a grand day,' he said. 'I've seen you before.'

He folded his arms, then unfolded them, as though he had only just been given them and didn't know what to do with them yet. Everything about him angled out, awkward.

'I don't think so.' I was not in the mood for chatter.

'Well, we have honey for sale, you know. It's the best there is. You could have some if you like.'

His chin was stubbled, his hair rough – cut with a blade by candlelight. He was freckled already, had spent all his summers in the sun.

'Thank you.' I straightened Francine's shoulders and touched her nose to raise a smile.

'I like honey,' she said.

The next time we headed out that way, he was waiting. The time after that, he had a pot of honey in his hand. The next time, he came with us and showed us where the bilberries grew. The time after that, I let him kiss me.

His kiss held no surprise. It did not start with something soft nor become something softer; it did not open inside me. It pushed against me, as flat as the palm of a hand.

Perhaps I did not want it, perhaps there was no place for it in me. He did not disgust me. But he was not the Monsieur. He reminded me of the wet fleeces in Leiden – limp white flags of surrender.

He placed his hand on my breast, and seemed astonished that his hand could make a shape that could cup it.

He never asked about Francine.

I did not like his mouth. I turned away from him when he was on me, so that his breath went into my neck, or the grass beneath us. I left Francine at the farm and she played in the hay, cracking a tooth when she tumbled from a tree. We both walked home dishevelled in our own way, bruised, bitten, soiled.

'Where have you been?' asked the Monsieur, grabbing my arm as I passed by him.

'Nowhere,' I said.

He did not let go.

'You're hurting me.'

'You will tell me where you have been.'

'Nowhere!' I yanked my arm free.

I wanted him. I wanted him. I wanted him. I hated every part of him.

'What's your name?' I asked.

'Daan,' he said.

'Daan.' He might as well have said ditch.

'I think you are very pretty, Helena.' He patted my hand, as he might a dog. 'I think you would be happy here.'

I heard the hope in him. I was the first woman he had kissed.

'Yes,' I said. But I wanted to be sick.

I looked at Daan, at his dusty skin; the soil under his nails; his fair eyelashes. There was nothing more I could know, nothing inside to unwrap. Everything about him was on the surface and could be seen – *this is who I am*. He reached towards me. He needed me and that was enough. I unlaced my bodice, pulled the fabric away from my shoulders so my breasts were bare. I turned to him, brought his mouth to my nipple and as he sucked, I cried. I would not kiss him. He bit my shoulder instead. When he was done, I pushed him away. I fastened myself up, staggered to my feet and walked back towards the farm for Francine.

I did not turn, nor did I heed him when he called for me to stop. Once I had Francine again, we made our way home without talking, without rest.

I found the Monsieur in his room. I wanted him to know. I wanted him to see.

I stood there in front of him. My chin trembled.

'Oh,' he said, when he saw the state of me. 'Helena . . .'

The love in his voice nearly broke me.

I stepped away. I stepped away, until my back bumped the wall.

'I want you, Helena.'

He caught hold of my hands, pinning them above me in the air. But I was stronger than him. It was me who carried the peat; me who dug the garden; me who heaved the sodden sheets from tub to wringer.

'No.' I brought my arms down, shaking with the effort. 'No, you do not.'

It was the Limousin who told me Reneri had died. The Monsieur left for Utrecht that day.

'Scholars' disease,' he went on. 'Such a short life. Forty-six. Not much older than the Monsieur.'

Each detail, as he said it, worse than the last. It was not that he enjoyed telling me, but he was watching me closely. His eyes flickered over mine while he clicked a finger and thumbnail together. He seemed strangely agitated, as if Reneri's death brought him alive in some way.

'For the Monsieur it is terrible ... they were like brothers.'

'Yes, I could see that. Poor Reneri. God keep his soul.'

'So it's just you and me until the Monsieur gets back. You are my responsibility while he is gone. And the girl.'

'Her name is Francine. And I can take care of her myself.'

'I do not doubt that. I do not doubt that at all.'

His tone was cold, as it often was when the Monsieur was not near. But I'd had enough.

'Why don't you like me, Limousin?'

He made a face of complete surprise, opening his eyes wide, as if this was the most ridiculous question he had ever been asked.

'I don't *dislike* you, Helena.'

'I heard you ... with the Monsieur.'

'Ah, *that*. Seems the walls have ears.'

He said nothing for a while, in no hurry to say more, tapping his fingers on the table.

'I have known great danger at times. Have marched to the front line of wars far from here; have travelled vast distances and seen unspeakable cruelty. Life *vanishes* in such places; there are times when that is all you wish for – to vanish and never have to see such suffering again. And here we are, in this blessed sanctuary, and you are concerned if I like you? Do you know what happens to people in places like that? Do you have any idea what is done to them? *Do you?*'

He shook his head as he spoke.

'I don't know what you heard. You will reach your own conclusion. There are men who would destroy the Monsieur. Not just ridicule him, though that is bad enough. No, they would take him outside, pile stones on him until he repents or his body breaks. They would not care if he died. They would enjoy it. I think he should be done with you and I said so. He is of a different opinion. Before you, it was me. I saw the life go from the animals he cut open. Watched them struggle even as death was certain. I wiped the blood from his table. And after death? Nothing. We live, we die. *C'est tout. Rien de plus.* I have learnt too, Helena.'

I thought his words went against God. I had taken his place with the Monsieur and he was jealous.

'His work will outlast us. Mersenne, Huygens: they know his worth. You? What are you? Little more than nothing.'

'The Monsieur does not think that.' Then I had to correct myself. 'Of Francine.'

He smiled faintly, but still looked sad. 'Helena, Helena
... we all know our place in the end.'

I stopped going out. I stayed with Francine. I drew letters
for her to trace and wrote her name so she could copy it.
The Monsieur came back from Utrecht, but the door to his
room stayed shut. Silence shrouded the house; even
Francine spoke in whispers. It was worse than the time
Beeckman had visited in Amsterdam. This time there was
no book to return. No shouting that could be had on the
step. He shut his door to me and kept it shut.

'There's talk of a stranger about,' said Limousin. 'A man's
been spotted watching houses and chased off more than
once. Sounds like a spy to me. We cannot be too careful.'

A week or two later, a movement in the garden caught
my eye. My heart lurched. Whoever it was had darted
behind a bush near the apple tree. The branches shook, and
then a fair-haired man stood up and made a dash for the
tree – *Daan*! He peeped out from around the trunk and
then tucked himself behind it.

I grabbed my shawl and hurried outside. He popped up
like a startled rabbit when he saw me.

'Helena!'

I had my hands out in front to keep him back as he
stumbled towards me. He frowned at me, not understanding. I stepped back as he stepped forwards.

'How did you know I was here?' I glanced over my
shoulder.

'I didn't,' he said, still coming towards me. 'I've been to every house hereabouts, looking for you. Where've you been? Why didn't you come?'

'You need to go. Go away. Right now.'

He shook his head. 'I'm not going until I've said what I've got to say.'

'No! Don't.'

At that moment, the Monsieur came out. He stopped when he saw Daan. 'Helena? What's going on? Who's this?'

Before I could say anything, Daan was past me and had offered his hand to the Monsieur.

'My name is Daan.'

'Daan?' He stared at Daan's hand and at the flowers he had hold of.

'Yes. Well, I live in a farm a mile or so from here. I am the eldest and the farm will be mine.' He pulled his shoulders back.

Then the most awful thought occurred to me – Daan must be confusing the Monsieur with my father and was presenting himself as a suitor.

'Indeed,' said the Monsieur, his attention no longer on Daan, but me. 'So you have land, or will have, is that what you are telling me?'

'Yes!' said Daan, brightening, but still seeming uncertain. His jaw became slack as he studied the Monsieur. He held out the flowers to me.

I hesitated, then took them. 'Daan sells honey,' I said.

The Monsieur frowned.

'And I don't mind about the child either,' Daan said, turning to me and fumbling for my hand.

The Monsieur tensed. 'That's remarkably generous of you.'

Daan bowed, clearly pleased with how well he thought the conversation was going.

'Daan, thank you. You have given me a lot to consider. I did not know Helena had a suitor.'

'You didn't?' His shoulders sagged. He looked at me then. Everything inside me wanted to run away; everything rooted me to the spot.

'Come in, Daan, let me show you where we live, so you can know us better.'

He linked arms with Daan and steered him inside, sitting him down at the kitchen table.

'A drink for Daan, Helena, don't you think? Some of our brandy perhaps.' He went to fetch the brandy himself.

'No, no. I don't drink.'

The Monsieur put a glass in front of him and poured a good measure of brandy. 'Drink up,' he said. 'It will do you good. It's *French*. The best.'

Daan took a sip and pulled a face, struggling to swallow. He looked about him, seeing the place properly for the first time – broken quills in a glass, bird skulls on the mantelpiece, ink stains on the table where we ate. In among the clutter, portraits I had drawn of Francine and the Monsieur.

The Monsieur followed Daan's eye, shook his head and laughed. 'Striking, don't you think? The resemblance?'

A look of complete astonishment came across Daan's face as he realised what the Monsieur meant. He stood up, knocking a bowl off the table as he did so.

'God alive . . .'

353

He snatched the flowers from me and threw them on the floor, gave me one last desperate look, then turned and fled.

I knelt down and picked up the broken pottery, gathering the pieces up into my apron. Flower petals strewn among the broken shards.

'You are a cruel man,' I said.

'What would you have me do? Give you to some idiot?'

'I am not yours to give. You do not own me, Monsieur.'

'No, I do not. You are free to go. Be a farmhand's wife, if that's what you want. Francine stays with me.'

When I next went walking, ten days later, Daan was by the farm gate as usual. I was alone. The Monsieur would not let Francine outside, not even to play in the garden.

'Do you wait here each day, Daan?' I asked. The wind had unpicked my hair around the edges of my cap and it blew in long strands around my face.

He shrugged.

'You shouldn't wait for me.'

'I wasn't waiting,' he said, then added quickly, 'I thought you cared.'

Cared? I laughed. 'Daan. Why are you here?'

'Is it the farm? The land is good, I told you.'

I carried on walking. He jumped down from the gate and caught up with me.

'Where are you going? Stop!'

He grabbed my arm and pulled me off balance. My ankle

twisted under me and a sharp, hot pain flashed up my leg as I fell.

'Did you laugh, the both of you? *Stupid Daan*, is that what you said?' He spat the words at me. 'You're shit.'

I tried to stand up, but he still had hold of me and he pushed me down. Then he was on his knees in front of me.

'No, Daan.'

I tried to scrabble away from him, but he was stronger and dragged me back.

'Daan, no . . .'

'I hate you!' He threw me to one side. 'Who'd want a whore for a wife?'

Then he was over me, his knee in my ribs, one hand at my throat. My ribs would break. He wanted to break me.

'You're shit. Shit.'

He picked up a rock.

'Shit,' he said. 'Shit.'

I arched my neck, gasping for air. Then he hit me and the sky fell down on me, purple and black.

Soot

WHERE'S MY GIRL, *the girl with black hair? My little girl? My darling child? And my love, where are you, the man I love? Let me draw you. I'll draw our days and make a fine book. In the winter, when flowers are promises curled under snow, I'll spin a thread to make you a cloak and edge it with fur. I'll plant our garden with apples and cherries and quince. I'll bring you sweet strawberries.*

Where is she, the girl from the shore, with shells in her pockets and seaweed hair? Draw me a rose, draw me a stem, draw me a snowflake you've caught from the sky and I'll bring you a candle, love; I'll bring you my kiss in the night.

I am water. I am mud. I am stone. I splinter. I sink. I break. Sludge fills my pockets, my mouth, my eyes. Paper, rag; words, crows. I am rotten and rotting. My bones, brittle and broken. I am sticks – tinder for the fire, soot in the smoke. I am the chimney's black burning throat. Every breath I take chokes; the air I make is poison.

AMERSFOORT, 1640

Clock

THE LITTLE HOUSE overlooked the Lange Gracht. The canals were narrower here, the streets quieter – wide enough for couples to walk arm in arm and for children to run in front. It reminded me of Amsterdam, but an Amsterdam so small it might be folded away and slipped into a pocket.

Francine clambered out of the carriage. As I stepped down after her, pain flared in my side. The carriage driver went to steady my elbow, but I shook him away. I closed my eyes and waited for the pain to ease.

Before we had chance to knock at the door, it swung open and a familiar face peeped out – Mrs Anholts.

'Helena!' she said, with the brightness of someone who'd spent the day waiting. 'It's good to see you. And Francine! Look how tall you are! How old now?'

'I'm very almost five!'

'Very almost five! Well, that's the best age of all. Until you are six, then you'll wonder what all the fuss of being five was about.'

Francine grinned and reached for my hand.

Mrs Anholts came down the steps, took my basket and linked her arm in mine. Although her smile didn't waver, I could see her taking me in, the concern in her eyes.

'I'm to look after you. I have instructions from the Monsieur. He was quite specific. Call it an *arrangement*, if you will. Come in, come in. This way. Look.'

She opened the door into a day room, her chatter going ahead of her as she went in. It had been newly furnished. Each chair had a cushion; on the floor, a patterned rug. There was a table by the window where books, papers and a pot of ink had been set out.

'See, I said I had instructions!'

She made a tour of the room, pointing out a picture on the wall, a vase on the mantel, lacework she had started.

I picked up a quill from the table. It was quite smooth – whoever had prepared it understood. The barb had been stripped back; *no reason for a thought to tarry or trip*. The nib was clean. No words from it yet.

Mrs Anholts walked around the edges of the rug, looking doubtful. 'It's what is done these days, I'm told.'

I went over to the fireplace, to a stove decorated with Delft tiles. Each had a picture of a boat scudding along. I turned around the room. Though small, it was full of light. Happy, cheerful, bright, and Mrs Anholts in the middle of it, hands held out either side of her, waiting for me to say something, for some word of thanks, anything at all.

'Limousin's not allowed,' she said, in answer to a question I'd not asked. 'Who'd want such a grump in the house? If he behaves, I might let him visit.'

I chose the chair furthest from the window and sat down, content to let Mrs Anholts talk. A warm breeze blew in through the open window, carrying with it sounds of the street – a horse as it approached. I listened for it to go and whatever Mrs Anholts had been saying faded away with it too.

She chose the chair next to mine and patted the cushion. She folded her arms as she settled in it and seemed pleased. 'So how is he, the Monsieur?'

I looked across to the window, wanting it closed, turning as Francine came in with Monsieur Grat. She led him by the ear, a habit she'd not lost since he had first arrived with the Monsieur from Santpoort market.

'Mama?' She touched my sleeve with her fingers, careful in every way. She no longer tugged at me, or clambered up. It was no way for a child to be. 'Can Monsieur Grat sleep in my room?'

The dog hung his head and studied me with sorrowful eyes.

'*Please*, Mama.' She twisted her foot on the floor.

I had such a longing for her then and hugged her to me, but when I felt her resist, I let go suddenly, as though I had burned her, or she me. She stumbled and stood there, not knowing whether to come to me or not.

'Go find your room, Francine,' said Mrs Anholts, up on her feet and chasing her out. 'Upstairs and upstairs again. Go on. Off you go.

'She's the very picture of him,' she said, as she came back in and sat down again, folding her hands together neatly in her lap. She blinked rapidly, as though struggling to pin down a thought in her mind.

'You need time, Helena. We'll walk a little each day. The Monsieur has a tutor for Francine and that will keep her busy. He chose this house well. The carriage can draw up under the arch. No one will know. You're not to fret. You've to get your strength back and that's what you're going to do.'

I saw the weeks stretch ahead of me – a length of cloth, mine to pattern as I wished. But I didn't want to walk, or talk, or draw. I didn't want the horse in the street, the rug on the floor, or the cushions on the chair. I wanted to close my eyes and not see Daan when I did.

Mrs Anholts leaned in closer. 'Did the Monsieur make mention of a visit?'

I looked away, then down. I shook my head.

I learned every sound in that house, was awake when I should have been sleeping. I knew which knock at the door I could trust: Francine's tutor; the fishmonger coming by, twice weekly. I knew whose foot was on the stair; which window had been opened; the slow clop of the peat merchant's poor, worn-out pony.

When we went out, I tried to close my ears to it all – to the din that pressed in from all sides. I walked as quickly as I could, the sooner to be home again, Mrs Anholts out of breath by my side, taking two steps for every one of mine.

'Helena?'

She brought me to a sharp stop in front of a tree. I'd had my head down and would have gone straight into it, had she not prevented me. I stepped briskly to one side and carried on.

*　*　*

shoulders. 'I have decided to keep it here. You will have to wind it when I am away.

'Let me help,' he said, as I began to undress. He stood in front of me and unlaced my bodice, slipping the sleeves down my arms and unfastening the skirt at my waist. He touched the scars on my stomach and, when I was naked, went to drop my nightgown over my shoulders.

I shook my head. Then he undressed and when he was naked we lay down together, shivering a little until the air warmed between us. I took his hand and curled my fingers in his. He nuzzled against my shoulder and slowly I felt him slip away from me, into sleep.

I listened to the clock for a long time. I had never realised how easily each moment went, nor how eager the next was to arrive.

France

THE SUMMER DAYS burned hot, then showers came in from the north and the temperature tumbled. One day we had all the windows flung open; the next we needed a fire in the grate.

'I don't care for this weather one bit,' said Mrs Anholts as she fanned herself with a cloth.

Francine didn't like it either, and complained that her room was stuffy. She slept badly and then stomped about, all fists, arguments and stamping feet. The Monsieur's mood was no better; his *Meditations* brought out in him the opposite of what the book proposed. He kicked Monsieur Grat, slammed more doors than he shut, threw a sheaf of papers out of the window into the yard. And then, in July, the draft was done and the days settled back on their haunches.

He sent the draft to Utrecht, to seek objections before it was published, unlike poor little *Discourse*. The trouble that book had caused. I was certain it was what kept him in Leiden. I knew he would have preferred Utrecht, but complaints against him – against *Discourse* – had started again. Everything he did seemed to create a wake that threatened to pitch him off his feet.

'Pedants, fools, pseudo-theologians! So-called experts!

Bullies, more like. They speak with confidence, but only idiots think they are educated. Don't worry, I won't stir up the hornets,' he said, with a wink. 'They are quite capable of stirring up themselves.'

There was no pattern to his visits. He stayed a few days; he stayed for a week. With his moods, it was enough. And there were times I was glad he was gone again. He talked about visiting France, at the end of the summer, but when he next mentioned it he said he wouldn't go after all.

The days became hot. It was hard to think, or to settle; thoughts burned away as easily as morning mist. He wrote a new work on tides and something seemed to ebb and flow in him too, as if he could not decide what to do.

'I have an aunt,' he said, after dinner one evening, after Francine had gone to bed. He had been unusually quiet through the meal and had avoided my eye. We still had not risen from the table and a good portion of his meal remained uneaten.

I considered telling him that an aunt was not too remarkable a relative to have, not even for him, a man who, to all intents and purposes, seemed to have no family at all. I could see it would be wrong to tease – he had something to say.

'I think Francine will be old enough . . .' He circled his finger on the tablecloth as though chasing an idea around with it.

'Monsieur?'

'I promised you she would be educated. She'll be five soon. She's a bright child.'

'She has the tutor twice weekly.'

'And I believe there is no obstacle to learning – for a girl.' He continued to circle his finger. I wanted to stop his hand and for him to tell me what troubled him. 'Did I tell you about Anna Maria van Schurman? Ruined completely by Voetius, but quite brilliant.'

'Francine, Monsieur?' I said, trying to pull him back to where he had started.

Still he chased whatever he was thinking in circles. 'A tutor, once or twice a week? Hardly enough, I think.'

Did he think it not worthwhile? That it should not continue?

'But she's doing so well!'

He nodded. 'But what of the world can we know if all we do is live in one room?'

Oh. I saw then how small this room must look to him. How small this house. How small Amersfoort.

Well, I thought, and I tilted my chin up a little as I did so, with God to guide us, we did not have to go far to know what was right and true.

But the thought made me sit no straighter. I was no taller for having thought it.

Then he looked at me. 'I have made a decision. Francine will go to France in the autumn. She will stay with my aunt, Madame du Tronchet. She will be educated there. Properly so.'

'*France?*' Had I heard him right?

'Indeed. France.'

And then it was as if he had beaten what he'd said out on a drum: *Boom! – Boom! – Boom!*

I pushed my plate away.

'When?'

'In October, or soon after.'

October? I counted the weeks – *a handful* – and saw them already flown by, used up, gone. I searched his eyes for any trace of doubt, but he held my gaze. Not a blink. He had made up his mind. *October.*

'I've considered it for a while. Limousin confirmed it in my mind.'

'*Limousin?*'

I slapped my hand down on the table, anger catapulting me beyond the boundaries I had stood behind all my life, the invisible lines that said, *Know your place.*

'You were guided by *Limousin?*' I had risen from my chair without realising. I remembered what I'd overheard between them in Santpoort, the discord Limousin had tried to sow.

'Helena, *Helena.*'

Helena, Helena? I saw him stiffen as he said it. Oh, he might seem to listen but I would be told in the end. Nothing changed with him.

He reached towards me, but I pulled away. 'No!'

And then it was as if the sea had surged over the dunes and was swirling about our feet. *Can you swim, Monsieur? Can you?* I was away from the table, pacing across the room and back again, not even addressing him any more.

'*Limousin!* He's a snake! A slithering snake, *slithering!*'

He leaned back in his chair with his hands behind his head. 'A snake?'

'Yes. A snake.'

He had started to smile. 'Do you think I need a snake for counsel? That I cannot think for myself?'

I ignored him. 'You want to take her from me. And hide her, so no one knows.'

'Have you finished?'

'And me? Am I to be sent away too? Has Limousin decided that for you as well? Where next? Won't you run out of places to send me?'

He held up a hand to get me to stop and kept it there until I did.

'You misunderstand, I think. Why would you leave, unless you wanted to? Of course we could continue here, as we are, and as for hiding . . . Francine will go to France as my ward. She will not – *she could not* – go as my niece. How could she?'

He paused for a moment, his smile gone.

'I have told them. My family know.'

Paper

I WOULD WRITE it all in a letter to Betje and see what she had to say in reply. But the paper was no longer on the table. Nor the ink. Nor the quills. I stared at the table top and blinked. I blinked again. As though blinking might bring it back! I pulled out the drawer underneath, in case the paper had been put away there, and emptied it of pebbles and shells. Not a scrap.

'Mrs Anholts? Mrs Anholts?'

I found her in the kitchen, making cinnamon bread.

'The paper, *my paper*,' I said, correcting myself, 'do you know where it is?'

'Paper?' She carried on kneading the dough, adding a handful of flour to the mix. 'What paper is that?'

Her neck had flushed quite pink.

Which paper did she think I meant? There was no other paper in the house than the Monsieur's, which he kept locked in his trunk. My mood from last night spiked up hot, the argument I'd had with the Monsieur still speared on it. I had to steady my voice when I spoke again.

'My paper, the paper in the front room. It has always been kept on the table. It's not there.'

She scratched her neck, floury fingerprints only making the pink pinker.

'Ah,' she said, suddenly seeming to remember. 'Francine has it.'

'Francine?'

'She had need of it.'

'*My paper?*'

'Yes.'

'And you let her?'

'It hadn't been touched.'

Was everything conspiring against me? Could I not have a sheet of paper when I needed it? Did no one think to ask me first – about paper, Madame du Tronchet, France, *anything*?

'And where is it now?'

'In her room, I suppose.'

'Her room, you suppose?' I was doing my very best not to shout.

She looked up from what she was doing and managed a cautious smile. 'Do you need some?'

'If there's any left!' I said and spun around quickly, going out before I had a chance to say worse.

Francine was occupied with her tutor and, as angry as I was, I could not disturb her. I went upstairs, and upstairs again, taking the stairs in twos, up to her room. There was no paper on the shelf, on her dressing table, or in the drawer where her clothes were kept. I turned back the bedding, half expecting to find it sheeting the bed or squir-relled away under the pillow, but there was nothing apart from a small dimple in the mattress where she had lain.

I sat on the bed and formed further argument for when I went downstairs. Then I saw it: a box, tucked behind the door, with a pair of Francine's shoes placed on top.

A box. I don't know what I expected when I opened it. To find it in tatters, screwed into a ball, scribbled on, used up?

As I lifted the paper out, I saw that several sheets had been cut into. *My paper,* I thought, with a sinking heart, and was immediately ashamed. I opened them out, scattering little scraps on the floor: one, two, three, four – four paper snowflakes. I held them up to the window and, in the light, they were lace.

I turned my attention to the pages underneath and found several more covered with letters, where she had been practising her alphabet over and over. In among the letters I had learned myself as a child, the alphabet I had taught her in Santpoort, were letters I'd seen only the Monsieur write; the C with the piglet tail and others that simply looked surprised:

à è ç é

On another sheet, she'd copied out her name, again and again, the word seeming to skid apart as it went down the page:

FRANCINE
FRANCINE
FRANCINE
FRANCINE

And, on a third sheet, a list:

mama
franseen

375

chiens

poolay

frnscene

belle

monsur grat

Francene

daykart

deycart

descarte

de scartes

francine Des cartes

At the bottom of the box there was paper to spare, paper she'd not touched. I put it all back: the box by the door and her shoes on top.

She'd not taken the paper, but neither had she asked me.

What she'd written – it wasn't hidden, but neither had she shared it.

Hers, not mine – part of her, apart from me.

Francine Descartes.

I looked at the box. I did not need the Limousin to tell me. I knew my place.

Shadow

'*VIENS*, FRANCINE.'

The Monsieur held out his hand, and spun Francine in a brisk half-turn as he lifted her onto the table, so that she perched on the edge with her legs dangling over the side. He fished in his pocket and brought out something that at first glance looked like a flat, oval pebble. It fitted perfectly in the palm of his hand. I'd seen no pebble like it – it was gold and silver and very finely etched, attached at one end to a long gold chain. He held it out so we could see. Curved around the top, where his fingers held it, the outlines of two women. Both wore skirts, but skirts of such scant substance that the line of their legs, from hip to bare, arched foot, showed clearly. And then, I realised, neither wore anything more.

'It's a nocturlabe, a nocturnal watch. Look at this.' He touched a catch and the lid flipped up.

'Oh!' Francine sat back, caught by surprise.

He smiled. 'Do you want to hold it?'

She shook her head, but leaned in towards it at the same time.

'No?'

She shook her head a little less.

'Here.'

He took her hands and, cupping them together, gently placed the nocturlabe in them. She looked at it, then back at him, not moving, her arms held out awkwardly in front of her, perhaps remembering being shouted at for touching his clock.

'What's it for?' she asked.

'It tells the time. It has a sundial for the day and can read the stars at night. See how small it is? Small enough to carry in my pocket, so wherever I am, I can know the time. Incredible. I couldn't do that with my clock, could I?' He mimed carting his clock about and struggling to pull it from a pocket.

She giggled and shook her head.

He took the nocturlabe from her and pointed to a ring around the outside.

'See here? This is used for the date; that tells us which day of the month it is. And here, inside the lid, a *table*, see – longitude: *Lyons, Marseilles, Grenoble*.'

He lifted a silver ring inside to reveal a pin in the centre and angled the nocturlabe towards the window.

'The light is not so good today . . . No, it's not possible. Too many clouds.'

Francine craned her neck. We couldn't see from where we were.

He brought it up to his eye and squinted through a tiny hole pierced through the top, no bigger than a pinprick.

'Then, at night, if we look through this and find the North Star, and turn the pointer like this – *voi-là!* – we can know what the time is then too.'

'But we're sleeping then! In bed! Sleeping!' Francine kicked her legs, not bored, but losing patience with him.

He flipped the cover shut and closed the shadow inside, then held it out to me.

It was heavier than I expected. I turned it to the reverse. Inscribed underneath, À *Monsieur René Descartes*.

'A gift, Monsieur?'

'Yes,' he said, rubbing finger and thumb together, his thoughts elsewhere.

I flipped the catch to open it and looked at the needle in the centre. I could not say what the time was, but already, even though the day was dull, the sun had moved on. I did not want to be reminded of that, of time passing, of her leaving. Because then, one day soon, she would be gone.

'Here,' I said and returned it to his hands.

The trunk he had brought with him from Leiden did not contain clothes. As well as paper, he kept his letters there; letters he had received and copies of every letter he had sent. My own were in there too. He kept the trunk locked and the key in the dresser. He made no show of hiding it from me.

Of all the places I had lived, I decided I liked Amersfoort best. As Mrs Anholts had said I would, I grew stronger each day. After another hard winter, the heat of summer bore down on us bluntly. Mrs Anholts did not like it; she thought the canals stagnant, the air bad. In August, she decided she would return to Deventer.

'You're well enough to be on your own now, Helena,' she

said. 'I need the IJssel, the breeze it brings. There's not enough air in this town.'

After she had gone, I continued my walks with Francine instead. We went out each day, sometimes managing the whole of Lange Gracht. As the leaves fell at the end of August, they settled in drifts on the water and the canal became like a gold ribbon, winding around the town.

My thoughts turned to the weeks ahead and Francine leaving. I saw her at a desk. She would learn French, I knew that, and a new language too, one without words, a language made up only of numbers and shapes – geometry. Would she wonder at the stars in the sky? And at the darkness between them? Who would she be like? Me? Him? Would she remember, or would she forget?

'I'm going to France,' she told me at bedtime.

'Yes,' I said and tucked the covers around her, her pale arms at her sides, anchoring her there for the night. My slip of a child, tucked up in bed.

'Can't you come, Mama?'

I turned away so she did not see the anguish on my face. I made my voice bright. 'I have to stay here and look after Monsieur Grat.'

'Monsieur Grat can come too!'

'Sh, now.' I kissed her forehead. 'Monsieur Grat needs canal boats to bark at.'

'I want you to come, Mama.'

'Oh, Francine, darling . . .' I was at a loss what to say.

'You've to tell me all about it when you come back, will you? *Promise?*'

She nodded and turned her head away, nuzzling under the blanket. '*Bonne nuit*,' she whispered into her pillow, as if trying out a bedtime far from here.

'*Bonne nuit*,' I called from the doorway.

I left her door half open and went to my room and sat by the window. I stayed there like that, quite still, until the candle had burned to its stub and the shadows had soaked into the night.

Fever

'WE'RE GOING FOR a walk.' I held out my hand to get Francine to come.

She and the dog were on the steps outside the house. She'd been teaching him to sit, though from what she'd shown me of his new tricks, he seemed most capable when on his feet, barking.

She ignored my hand.

'You can't stay here on your own.'

She hopped from one foot to the other. 'I can. Monsieur Grat's with me.'

'A short walk, Francine, that is all.'

She stopped hopping. 'I don't want to.'

I saw the change in her already. She stood a little taller; her hair – though I'd combed it – seemed tied higher at the back. I liked our walks; so few remained until she went. I waited a moment for her to change her mind, but she shook Monsieur Grat's ears between her hands and pretended I wasn't there. I hadn't thought I'd ever feel envious of a dog. I dropped my hand back to my side.

'I won't be long.' I pointed to where I would walk. 'I'll go along here and come back on the other side, in a circle. You're not to go near the canal. Stay put. Don't move.'

She widened her eyes and grinned, as surprised as I

was that I'd relented. I was too annoyed with her to smile back.

I walked the circle as quickly as I could and was out of breath as I returned. My hip ached; my mood no brighter than when I had set off. Francine jumped up when she saw me, as if I'd been gone a month.

'Mama!'

She threw her arms wide but tripped on her hem as she came down the steps, tumbled over and landed with a bump at my feet. Apart from a few scratches, she wasn't hurt that I could see, but howled as if she had broken a bone.

'I've told you and told you about these steps,' I scolded, licking my thumb to rub at a cut on her hand.

She grabbed my skirts, to wipe her tears away.

Pain flared in my hip. I needed to sit down. I shook her off and shooed her indoors.

'For goodness' sake, child, out from under my feet!'

There was so much to do before she went. I knew his family had means, but I would send her away properly dressed. I sewed clothes and made skirts that could be lengthened in the months to come, the hem being let down as she grew. I thought of the people that bordered Mr Veldman's map, but couldn't remember how French folk dressed. The Monsieur was in Leiden, so I did not have him to ask. Should I add a ribbon, or not?

Francine stood on a chair as I worked around her, pinning the hem of a new skirt. She picked at the scab on her hand.

'No!' I said, when I saw what she was doing. 'You need to remember your manners.'

'Yes.'

'Yes, what?'

'Yes, Mama.'

'Good.'

I turned her a little as I continued to pin.

'And you're to ask if you want something. *Always*,' I said, as I remembered the paper in her room.

'Yes.'

I despaired. 'Yes what, Francine?'

I patted her to show I'd finished and she could take the skirt off ready for me to sew it.

'Yes, thank you,' she said and jumped down from the chair.

She skipped away, was out of the door with the dog before I could stop her, and gone.

'Francine,' I called after her, 'come back with that skirt!'

In the evening, she came to me. She rubbed at her head. 'Mama, I feel scratchy.'

I put down my needlework and took her back upstairs. It was the third time already she'd come down and it was late. She looked tired, grey shadows thumbed beneath her eyes.

'You need to sleep. You can't do that if you keep getting out of bed.' I tucked her in, and smoothed her hair across her brow. 'Are you worrying? Is that what it is?'

'No,' she said.

'Good. There's no need.'

She swallowed and pulled a face.

'I'll let Monsieur Grat stay with you, but you're to go to sleep now, Francine. If I hear any mischief between the two of you . . .'

'No, Mama.' She brought the bedcovers up to her chin.

I opened the window in her room, but the air outside was no cooler. Mrs Anholts was right, there was something about the air here.

'Sleep well.'

Then, in the night, a ghost. I sat up, suddenly awake.

Francine? Monsieur Grat, by her side, nuzzled at her ankle. She wavered, on the point of falling.

'I'm goosebumpy, Mama . . .'

'Francine? Darling? *Francine!*'

I jumped out of bed and took her into my arms. Her eyes flickered open, then closed, neither awake nor asleep. All of her damp and clammy, as though she'd been out in the rain. I touched my fingers to her forehead, feeling heat there. I scooped her up and carried her over to my bed. Shutting the window tight, I lit kindling in the stove and threw on peat. Heat needed heat to draw it out.

I lit the candles so I could see. Even in that light, she looked flushed. I lifted her nightgown. All of her, blotchy red with a rash – it covered her tummy, went up her neck and along her arms.

What to do? What to do? What to do?

I'd never known anyone so unwell so quickly. Thomas, Mother, Limousin, the Monsieur – they'd had sneezes, cuts, a boil, a bad tooth. Daan had done his best to break me, but even my bones had healed in time. Whatever was in Francine had crept under her skin and was trapped there. I couldn't see how it could ever come out. I had nothing to help soothe her, nor anything that might make it stop.

In the morning, I sent for the physician for his opinion. He hooked a finger into her mouth to look at her tongue – overnight it had become swollen and red. He felt the rash and showed me where it was raised at the edges. I snatched my fingers away. Her skin was as rough as an eel's.

'A sure sign. Scarlatina. Scarlet fever,' he said.

Scarlet fever? And then, in whispers and shadows, I remembered what I had long forgotten: children I grew up with who had been lost to this, and children who had recovered and lived: Isaak, without hearing; Griet, without sight.

He brought out a knife from his bag; a knife with a thin blade, like the one the Monsieur had used in Santpoort. I saw a pink flicker of flesh – an eel's tiny heart – and everything in me shrank back.

'No!'

'But the blood is bad, it must come out.' He held up the knife and inspected the edge, then rubbed it on his sleeve.

'Please. No.' I had hold of his arm now.

'It offers the best chance of recovery.' He looked at my hand on his arm and waited for me to let go. 'I have done it many times. Children do not feel pain as we do.'

'She's too small . . .'

An eel without blood died. Take the blood from a rabbit and it would die too. I'd seen it.

He pulled away from me and, stepping up to the bed, ran his thumb firmly down the inside of her arm. When he reached her hand, he prodded at the palm.

'When was she born?'

'July.'

'No, no. Gemini? Cancer? *Leo?*'

I heard the impatience in his voice. 'Cancer.'

'Then taking from her arm is quite useless.' Drawing down her nightdress to bare her shoulder, he felt above her collarbone. 'A little more tricky, but . . . aha, that's it.' He hunched over her. 'A little cut is all that is needed.'

As he pressed with his knife, Francine heaved on the bed.

'*Mama!*' she shrieked.

Her breath shocked from her, short and ragged. I took her hand and held it tight. I did not know where to look – at the horror of what rushed between his fingers, or into her eyes, as black as the stain that seeped into the bedclothes. What had I allowed?

'Sweetheart, I'm sorry. I'm sorry.'

'If you are not strong, how can she be?' he scolded, muffling her cries with his hand and bearing down on her with his weight to hold her still. Her blood came quick and fast. I counted to twenty. I counted to thirty. And yet he let it flow. When was enough enough?

'That's it, good,' he said, watching her, as she struggled less and less. Then his mood became urgent. 'A cloth, here, now. Goodness, woman, hurry up.'

He pressed, first with one hand, then with both, as he

tried to stem the blood. He scrabbled about, grabbed a cloth from me, bundled it into a ball and pressed it into the wound. 'Another, another!'

One cloth followed another onto the floor. Several more were thrown down before he was done. Then he wiped his hands clean and dabbed at the sweat on his brow.

'See how she's calmed? You had no reason to doubt me.'

When he had tidied away, he took a glass of brandy in the kitchen.

'Her father, where is he?'

'Leiden.'

'Send for him. That's my advice.'

'But the treatment?'

He glanced at me and took a large drink, holding it in his mouth before swallowing. 'There are times, *unfortunately*, when the effects do not last. We see this mostly in children, the infirm, the weak of spirit.'

He fumbled in a pocket for a scrap of paper, which he held out to me.

Saartje & Daughters ~ Amersfoort
Wakers
Mourners
Makers of shrouds

I looked from it to him. Though I understood each and every wretched word written there, they were needed for someone else, *not Francine*. I shook my head.

He took another drink and finished what was in his glass. 'They can help . . . with preparations and such like. Should it be necessary.'

'No,' I said.

He took my hand and closed my fingers around the paper so it was held tight. 'Nothing would make me happier than if in a day or two I heard you had thrown it on the fire and burned it. Keep it. Burn it. I don't want it back.'

After he went, she slept. She looked peaceful, her red cheeks the only sign of what raged within. I sat by her bedside and sewed. I made a broth and, hopeful, brought her a whole cup.

She would not take it when it was hot, nor later, when it was cold.

She had nothing inside her. Hadn't eaten all day.

'You must eat. *Francine . . . eat!*'

She pushed my hand away; the spoon clattered to the floor.

Is she sleeping? Will she wake? Should I wake her?

*   *   *

I would hem this skirt. She would need it. I threw it down. I could no longer see for my tears.

She had to drink. But I struggled to lift her head and tilt the cup at the same time. She would not take it. The water poured down her cheek. I spooned water into her mouth, but that made her choke. I dripped water from a cloth. She turned her head away.

She did not want it. She would not take it.

She vomited. She shivered. She cried.

Her rash broke into sores.

I went to find the book. *His* book. There was a copy in the trunk, loose bound. He knew what made a body work, how blood moved; he knew about eels and rabbits. He could make cold blood warm so that a heart could beat again. I took the key from the dresser and opened the trunk. There it was:

DISCOURSE ON THE METHOD FOR RIGHTLY DIRECTING ONE'S REASON AND SEARCHING FOR TRUTH IN THE SCIENCES

I turned to the introduction, my eye jumping between words, then between lines; I turned one page, then another, dropping to the floor pages I didn't need. *Branches of knowledge, principles and rules, morals, arguments on the existence of God.*

Then I saw it: *The Fifth Discourse, the order of the problems of physics (particularly the explanation of the movement of the heart, and of some other difficulties of medicine).*

Some other difficulties of medicine? That must be it.

I had to stop my eyes from skipping ahead as I read. He described a heart, page after page after page, describing a heart. I knew this work, could see it before me. I had scrubbed the blood from his table, scraped the animal remains into the pan. I read it all. There was nothing on *other difficulties of medicine*. It ended with some differences between men and animals. *The soul is not subject to death along with the body . . .* I looked at the next page: *The Sixth Discourse*. No, Monsieur! I turned back a page. That couldn't be all there was, all he had written? *All he knew?*

Francine whimpered.

I turned through the remaining pages in chunks. *Optics, Refraction, The Eye, Telescopes, Geometry, Hail, Salt, Clouds . . .* No, no, no, no, no! I threw the book down and leaned forwards, my head in my hands. There was nothing in what he had written that might help.

Whatever it was that I was rushing towards was rushing as quickly away.

Where was he? When would he come?

He arrived that evening, saw the papers on the floor where I had dropped them and left them there. That night, we spoke in whispers. Neither of us slept.

In the morning, he sent me to another room to rest.

'I will stay with her. I will wake you if . . .'

But he could not say it. Neither could I. The words had gone from us.

It was impossible to believe she was dying, that she would die. Even though she had worsened, I thought, *This is what happens, she'll come through. In a little while, she'll take a sip of milk, then sleep, and be better.*

When I returned, the Monsieur's face told another story, revealing what I was trying to deny. He looked ashen and drawn. But, worse than that, he looked lost.

We held one another in our arms, each needing the strength of the other to stand. When he had last been here, she'd squeezed in between us, her face pressed into my stomach. I could feel her still, standing there, the memory worming between us.

'Do you remember the swallows in Amsterdam? *Un, deux, trois.* As the wind brings the rain, so the swallows. Swallows? I wasted my time! Let me never see another one! Oh, I can understand *birds,* but a fever – *a common fever?*' He stepped away, his hands at his temples. '*Mon Dieu,* is this my punishment?'

Punishment? I covered my eyes as a sob heaved in me. How could I live if she died?

God have mercy. God have mercy. Spare her, I beg you.

Francine woke that afternoon.

'Mama . . .'

'I'm here, darling.' I stroked her cheek. 'Would you like a story?'

She nodded weakly.

'One long time ago,' I said, and the tears streamed down my face, 'there was a little girl. She was such a happy little girl and her Mama loved her dearly.'

I thought I saw her smile. I thought I felt her fingers lift in mine before her eyes closed.

I rested my head on the bed as she slept, and the hours that were left went by, and the light that was there was lost. Night came on. The day snapped shut.

Ash

THERE COMETH ONE of the rulers of the synagogue, Jairus by name, and when he saw him, he fell at his feet, and besought him greatly, saying, My little daughter lieth at the point of death: I pray thee, come and lay thy hands on her, that she may be healed.

Francine's chest rose – a small breath, but not enough for a child. I curled her fingers in mine and willed my life into hers. I held my breath until all of me hurt, until my body insisted I breathe.

Saartje moved around the room with small, shuffling steps. She shrouded the mirror, covered the clock, draped a cloth over the water bowl. Once every shiny surface had been cloaked, she swung the shutters inwards and, with a single, sharp twist, bolted the window to close out the light. She lit the candles. The thin flames flickered. Our shadows hunched against the wall.

While he yet spake, they came from the ruler of the synagogue's house and said, Thy daughter is dead: why troublest thou the Master any further?

Saartje rested her fingers on Francine's wrist. The gentleness of her touch. I knew what it meant, what she felt for.

She shook her head. 'I'm sorry.'

When the Monsieur heard this, his head went down on the bed. His shoulders shook as he wept.

I looked from Saartje to Francine. My darling girl.

'No . . . that can't be.'

I clutched her fingers, but I knew that the warmth in her hand was mine.

Saartje nudged forward her daughters, Margarieta, Isabella and Rachel, in turn. The youngest, Rachel, approached the bed first. She twisted her hands together, her steps faltering. Isabella was next. She was older – old enough to know that death can pull holes in the floor; that it steals as easily from the cot as from the aged in their beds. She glanced at Francine, then pressed her face into Saartje's sleeve, but Saartje pushed her forwards, her hands on her shoulders. Isabella's chin trembled as she prayed. Then it was the turn of the eldest, Margarieta. Her back was straight. She stared at Francine and did not blink as she placed a sprig of rosemary on the pillow.

I kissed Francine's hand, then each of her fingers. They tasted of my tears.

And he comest to the house of the ruler of the synagogue, and seeth the tumult, and them that wept and wailed greatly. Why make ye this ado, and weep? She is not dead, she sleepeth.

The scripture spun in my head and I closed my eyes so I did not see the truth before me. *She does not sleep.*

Saartje touched my shoulder.

'We have to wash and dress her. We will do this now. Monsieur . . .' She turned to him and bowed, a signal that he should leave.

I clenched my hands, digging my nails into my palms. I tipped my head back and as I rocked forwards again a sound pushed out from the deepest part of me. All that was, all that might have been: her birth, her life, her death – all of it, crushed together, and came from me in a long, low moan.

Saartje turned back the bedcovers. Taking away the pillows, she turned Francine on her side and smoothed the sheet under her. She unbuttoned the soiled nightdress, wrung out a cloth and washed her. She was accustomed to death and worked swiftly, but that did not make her careless.

'There,' she said and dabbed at Francine's cheek, at the rash that covered her, as if to soothe her.

I looked at the bruise on her knee from when she had tripped on the steps; a little bruise, no bigger than my thumb; a little grey bruise that would never heal. I had batted her away from me, I had shooed her off without a kiss.

Saartje shook out a linen dress and placed it next to Francine. It was not for a child and stretched out past her feet. I took the awful weight of her head, cupping it as I had when she was an infant. Her hair, still damp, fell between my fingers. Five years from birth was its length, dark, with a curl – not fair and straight like mine. *Francine*, daughter of France; his and mine; north and south combined in her. She might have been born in Deventer, but she would have lived in France. She would have lived in France and been educated. Paris, Châtellerault, Poitiers – he'd parted the curtains so we could see. She would not go. France would not know her. The curtains had been drawn and stitched closed.

Saartje and I each took a sleeve and drew them up Francine's arms. Her arms neither helped nor hindered.

She did not protest at being made to wear this strange, ill-fitting gown. I wanted her to struggle and scream, kick and bite and fight until this wretched garment was off her again. I slipped stockings over her feet, knotting the ribbons at each ankle. Saartje combed her hair and tucked the curls away under a cap.

When we were done, Saartje rested her on the bed so gently as if afraid to wake her. I crossed her hands and touched my finger to her lips. Her chatter, her songs, her laughter, her tantrums – all gone. All these silences where there should be sound.

Saartje placed the cloth in the basin, then passed it to Isabella.

'Here, and take Rachel with you.' She gestured towards her youngest daughter, standing back in the shadows. 'You can tell Monsieur Descartes we have finished.'

When the Monsieur came back in, she turned to him and bowed. 'I shall pray for her. For you all.'

Then she gathered up her prayer book and left us.

The Monsieur and I sat either side of the bed. He opened the Bible, but couldn't speak. I closed my eyes and started the prayer for him. The prayer passed between us like a thread, a thread that would weave earth towards heaven, misery towards hope, torment towards peace.

I wanted to believe this. But my darling child was dead. God had willed it.

Truth

WE BURIED HER that week. That night, I lay on her bed. I did not sleep.

'I have work I must finish, Helena, in Leiden,' said the Monsieur the next morning, his eyes red-rimmed. Sleep had kept from him too.

I stood there as he said it. No line between us, nor anything that would draw us close.

The world does not wait, I thought. *Not for me. Not for him.* It would move whether we wanted it to – with or without us. *It did not care.* It had no need for child nor woman nor man. And what was that, I thought, but a godless world? That needed not even God's guiding hand?

As he turned to go, I caught hold of his arm. It took me a moment to say what I had to, for the words had to swim up from a very great depth.

'Were you ashamed, Monsieur? Of me, of her?'

I had never seen such sadness in his eyes. He shook his head. 'Oh, Helena, no. Never.'

I looked down.

'Is that what you think?'

I stood there. I had neither yes or no in me.

'Helena, please . . .' He was shaking as he said it. He took hold of my shoulders, had hold of me too hard. 'Helena.'

'Will you be back?

'Yes. Yes, of course.'

I saw that he meant it. 'But why?'

'Why?'

'We had a child, Monsieur. Now we do not.'

I closed my eyes. My next words came from somewhere deeper.

'What is it you want, Monsieur?'

'*You*, Helena.'

I laughed – a small sound that would not be stopped from coming out.

'I cannot marry, you know I cannot.'

'*Marry?* I never asked you to. I never made you to. She's gone, Monsieur. Why should I ever want to marry you?'

And we stood there and looked at each other as though we had just met.

And I thought, *What now, Monsieur? What is left? Who are we, now she's no more? Did she make us more than we were, more than we could be? Had something of us gone with her too?* And I saw her loss as a hole no sea could fill; a hole the sea would forever pour into.

I took his hands from my shoulders and held mine up before me to stop him taking hold again. There were all kinds of goodbye in the world, I had learned. This was another.

'Go, Monsieur. Come back only when you are certain. Come back to me because you want to, because you have to, Monsieur. Because you know of no other way.'

After he had gone to his carriage, I went upstairs and lay on Francine's bed. I did not watch him go.

* * *

In the night, I went to the room that had been ours, to the dresser where the key to his trunk was kept.

The letters were arranged in bundles. The largest contained correspondence with Mersenne. I passed over these, and the letters for Huygens and Beeckman. Then I found the ones I was looking for. The letters I had written to him and his letters to me. I did not untie them. I locked the trunk again and went downstairs. The Delft tiles shone in the moonlight, their blue now paled to grey. All those cheerful little boats sailing and never arriving. Life was not like that – it pushed us, pushed us, whether we wanted it to or not.

The embers of the fire glowed as the paper smoked. I lifted the edges with the poker, so the flame would catch. My face glowed in the heat. I watched the flames die down and the paper become ashes, flaring red at the edges, then black.

All I had ever written. I could not bear the words to live when she did not.

Soot in the chimney.

And then, like her, they were gone.

EPILOGUE
EGMOND AAN DEN HOEF

Raindrop

I MARRIED. A widower, as Mother said I should.

Jan.

I do not know what of my story was told, but the Monsieur paid Jan a sum of money that fixed the roof of his house; there was money enough to buy a parcel of land, and more besides. I had a room, a table by the window where the light was best. Paper and ink, as needed. Jan never questioned the picture I kept on the wall of Francine and the Monsieur, nor ask that I take it down. He was not troubled that the Monsieur lived near by or that I spent my time drawing.

I had my own room.

I no longer counted the days.

Although I walked with a limp, I could make my way across the sand.

I found him where he said he would be, down by the shore, in among the dunes. These dunes: you needed to know your way. It was easy to get lost. It was easy to hide and not be found.

The last few steps, I ran to him. Though the sand dragged at my feet, it could not stop me.

'Monsieur!' I cried, and he turned and his mouth was on mine, kissing my face and neck.

I went to my knees and unfastened his breeches. Then he was on his knees and pulling at the fastening to my bodice. We lay together as if we had been felled.

I had his love and, at the end of that year, a son. My beautiful boy. My darling child. His hair curled at his ear, his eyes as dark as his hair.

FIVE YEARS LATER

I watched the carriage approach from the distance and, as it came closer, the past hurried towards me with it.

The man who stepped down was older, an old man now; what hair he had left, thistledown white. The hand that gripped the walking stick had swollen at the knuckles. When he looked up, his eyes were wet, as they were sometimes at that age. But this man had been crying. He folded a handkerchief into his pocket, then bowed stiffly.

'Mrs van Wel,' he said, as he straightened up.

'*Limousin*,' I scolded gently, 'there's no need.'

We did not shake hands nor embrace. Perhaps the peculiar family we had once been made that unnecessary. I led him inside, taking his cloak. He kept hold of his stick and chose a chair nearest the fire. He sat down and eased out his knee.

'I'm not so much falling apart as tightening up.'

'Justinus, bring wine for our guest, please.'

Limousin took the glass Justinus offered. 'Here,' he said and gripped Justinus by the elbow, 'come into the light, where I can see you.' He squinted and coughed. 'Oh, I see now, yes.'

He closed his eyes and his eyelids flickered as something long forgotten stirred there.

'I knew the Monsieur when he was a boy. Older than Justinus, but young enough, young enough . . .' A smile played across his lips. He let go of Justinus's elbow. 'You are just as handsome. Are you good for your mother?'

Justinus nodded so vigorously, a little wine sloshed out of the jug.

'Good!' said Limousin. 'And how old are you now?'

'Five!'

'The same age as me!' When he saw how wide Justinus's eyes had opened, he fell back in his chair and laughed.

'Off with you now! Go play.'

We watched Justinus run off.

'And the Monsieur? He knew the boy?'

'Yes. He did.'

'*But your husband?*' He looked about him and shifted in his seat.

I heard the surprise in his voice; the embarrassment his own question had caused him. I thought of the questions I'd been asked, the men who'd asked them. What were his to me now?

'We had an arrangement. One last one. Jan knew.'

He took a sip of wine, his breathing becoming laboured.

'The Monsieur told me little. And after he left for Sweden, I had nothing at all from him.'

We sat a while with our thoughts.

Limousin crossed himself. '*May his soul rest in peace, through God's infinite mercy.*'

'*Amen.*' I brought my hands together as I said it. I blinked hard, else I would have cried. How could a small word hurt so?

'Who told you?'

'Mrs Anholts. The Monsieur had left instructions for her.'

'Yes, I see. I would have come, if not. So that you knew.'

It was the closest he had come to admitting what had passed between the Monsieur and me.

'I was very fond of the little girl.'

I nodded. If he'd had his way, Francine would not have been. Perhaps he knew what I was thinking.

'Forgive me,' he said. His chin trembled. His eyes had lost their guard. I could see into him, into his soul.

I brought my hands together and straightened my back. 'I know you loved him, Limousin.'

'Sweden – what a place. Such cold. No Frenchman should be made to go there. He signed his own death sentence – but he never listened to me, you know that.'

'What will you do now?'

He gave a small laugh and shrugged. 'Who would want an old Limousin?'

'There are other masters – many still in Amsterdam. When she was here, Mrs Anholts talked fondly of you.'

He smiled gently at my teasing, but shook his head. 'Mrs

Anholts won't have me. No. I'll make my way back to France. Keep chickens, grow leeks.'

We laughed then. Chickens and leeks? We knew he never would. Now he had warmed through he looked about him, taking in the paintings over the mantel; the sketches on the table next to him; the small easel by the window.

'Your work?'

'Yes, Limousin,' I said. 'Everyone wants something these days. It pays.'

I thought of Mr Sergeant. Had he sold a book yet to everyone in Amsterdam? I liked to think of him living in a new house on Herengracht.

Limousin peered at an ink sketch I had made of flowers in a vase. I picked up a quill from the table, ran it between my fingers to smooth the feather, and turned it to centre it – a habit I could not let go.

'I like it,' he said, as he sat back. Then he seemed to remember why he had come. 'I have something for you.'

He opened his battered satchel, the same one he had in Amsterdam all those years ago.

'Here. One last letter.' He held it for a moment before passing it to me. 'And this,' he said, handing me a small object wrapped in white linen. A note had been bound to it with ribbon.

I watched the Limousin's carriage cross the fleet, and then he was gone – Limousin, the Monsieur's *conduit*, the manager of his affairs, valet no more.

He was wrong; it was not a letter, at least not what I had known from the Monsieur, what I knew his letters to be. Folded inside, several smaller pages – pages he'd titled: *Love,*

Passion, Desire. There were sketches too: Francine asleep in the garden at Santpoort; another of her I'd forgotten I'd drawn, with her arm wrapped around Monsieur Grat's neck; his own work too – the snowflakes in Amsterdam. In the centre, wrapped in a scrap of green velvet, his gold ring – used only to seal his letters.

I turned the small, oval object in my hand. The linen cloth it was wrapped in had come from one of the Monsieur's shirts. I knew what it was from its weight. The Monsieur's nocturlabe.

I slipped the note free. *For Justinus,* it read.

I looked up at the sound of rain on the window. I had felt it that morning in the air. I watched it run in crooked lines down the pane.

I reached for Justinus and drew him to me. 'Here, come and see.'

It was possible to see the world in a raindrop. All you had to do was look.

Monsieur. Mijn liefde. Of that I am certain.

Historical Note

HELENA JANS ONCE stood in front of 6 Westermarkt, Amsterdam, and wondered what lay inside and what her employer would be like. The house still stands and a plaque marks its most celebrated occupant: René Descartes, who lodged there in 1634. But Descartes did not live there alone. The house belonged to an English bookseller, Thomas Sergeant, and Helena was his maid.

Histories of women deal necessarily with absence, with gaping holes in the archive. What do we know?

In July 1635, Helena gave birth to a daughter, Francine. We know Descartes was the father, as he left a note to this effect. We know Francine was baptised in Deventer on 28 July 1635. The baptism record, as simple as it is, includes the names of the parents – Reyner Jochems (Reyner is the Dutch variant of René; Jochems means literally 'of John', the name of Descartes' father) and Helena Jans – and that of the child, Fransintge (a Dutch variant of Francine).

The archive cannot tell us whether Helena was sent to Deventer by Descartes, but he knew the town and had lived there previously with his friend Reneri. It is likely Francine was born there, as baptism tended to follow quickly after birth. In 1635, we know that Descartes is in Utrecht. It is not impossible to imagine him travelling from there to Deventer from time to time.

Two further documents refer to Helena, both written by Leiden notaries. The first, dates from May 1644, is a notice of her marriage to Jan van Wel. For this, Descartes provided Helena with a substantial dowry, believed to be a thousand guilders. In June 1644 (after Helena marries), her name appears again, this time at the head of an inventory that lists jewels and other items belonging to her at Descartes' house.

Although Descartes tried to hide his paternity, Helena did not share the fate of many other pregnant, unmarried women, who were often cast out. We know that Helena and Descartes corresponded. In 1637, Descartes writes via a third party, inviting Helena to join him in a house near Santpoort *and to bring her daughter*. We do not know whether Helena accepted. However, an anecdote survives of Descartes in his Santpoort garden, clapping his hands to create an echo for a small child to chase. In 1640, he makes arrangements for his 'niece' to stay with his aunt, Madame du Tronchet, in France, where she will be educated. This little girl was Francine. But Francine never made it to France. She died suddenly of scarlet fever in September 1640, aged five. Descartes knew of 'no greater sorrow'.

None of the letters Descartes and Helena wrote to each other is known to have survived. It was extremely unusual for a woman of Helena's social standing to be able to write. I wondered, how did she learn to do so and why? This question became central to the novel, in creating Helena's backstory and character.

Helena knew Descartes for at least a decade and certainly at a pivotal time in his life, before he published his first work. He wrote about candles, snowflakes, swallows, eels, salt, ticklishness and many other things. In the novel, we see these things through Helena's eyes, as part of her daily life, as well as of her struggle towards literacy and a deeper understanding of the world.

This is a work of fiction. It is not known whether Justinus was Descartes' son. However, the fact that Descartes and Helena kept in touch by letter, and continued to live in close proximity for years after Francine's death, suggests a complex relationship that mattered to them both.

If fiction can help tell Helena's story, it also enables us to revisit Descartes. Perhaps, when we look at him through Helena's eyes, we see someone less familiar and more complex than we might have imagined. He is often thought of as a loner. I'm not so sure.

Suggestions for Further Reading

Erik-Jan Bos and Theo Verbeek, 'Conceiving the invisible: the role of observation and experiment in Descartes' correspondence, 1630–1650', in D. van Miert (ed.), *Communicating Observations in Early Modern Letters (1500–1675): Epistolography and Epistemology in the Age of the Scientific Revolution*, London/Savigliano: The Warburg Institute/Nino Aragno Editore, 2013, pp. 161–77.

Enny de Bruijn, 'Truth before peace: Jacobus Revius, 1586–1658', PhD thesis, 2012, University of Utrecht: Utrecht.

Robin Buning, 'Henricus Reneri (1593–1639): Descartes' quartermaster in Aristotelian territory', PhD thesis, 2013, University of Utrecht: Utrecht.

Desmond Clarke, *Descartes: A Biography*, 2007, Cambridge University Press: Cambridge.

John Cottingham, *Descartes*, 1997, Phoenix Paperbacks: London.

René Descartes, *Discourse on Method, Optics, Geometry, and Meteorology*, translated, with an Introduction, by Paul J. Olscamp, revised edition 2001, Hackett Publishing Company Ltd: Indianapolis.

The Philosophical Writings of Descartes, vol. III, *The Correspondence*, translated by John Cottingham et al., 1991, Cambridge University Press: Cambridge.

Stephen Gaukroger, *Descartes: An Intellectual Biography*, 1995, Oxford University Press: Oxford.

A. C. Grayling, *Descartes: The Life of René Descartes and its Place in His Times*, 2005, The Free Press, Simon & Schuster: London.

Genevieve Rodis-Lewis, *Descartes: His Life and Thought*, translated by Jane Marie Todd, 1998, Cornell University: Ithaca.

Simon Schama, *The Embarrassment of Riches*, 1987, William Collins & Sons: London.

Christine Petra Sellin, *Fractured Families and Rebel Maidservants: The Biblical Hagar in Seventeenth Century Dutch Art and Literature*, 2006, T. & T. Clark International: New York.

A. T. van Deursen, *Plain Lives in a Golden Age*, translated by Maarten Ultee, 1981, Cambridge University Press: Cambridge.

Jeroen van de Ven, 'Quelques données nouvelles sur Helena Jans', *Bulletin Cartésien* XXXII, publié par le Centre d'Études Cartésiennes (Paris IV – Sorbonne) et par le Centro di Studi su Descartes e il Seicento dell Università di Lecce, 2001.

Richard Watson, *Cogito, Ergo Sum: The Life of René Descartes*, 2002, David R. Godine Publishing: Jaffrey.

Paul Zumthor, *Daily Life in Rembrandt's Holland*, 1994, Stanford University Press: Stanford.

About the Author

Guinevere Glasfurd's short fiction has appeared in *Mslexia*, the *Scotsman* and in a collection from The National Galleries of Scotland.

The Words In My Hand, her first novel, was written with the support of a grant from Arts Council England. She also works collaboratively with artists in the UK and South Africa and her work has been funded under the Artists' International Development Fund, (Arts Council England and the British Council).

She manages the Words and Women Twitter feed, a voluntary organisation representing women writers in the East of England and can be be found online at guinevereglasfurd.com and @guingb.

She lives on the edge of the Fens, near Cambridge.

TWO
ROADS

Stories . . . voices . . . places . . . lives

We hope you enjoyed *The Words In My Hand*. If you'd
like to know more about this book or any other title on
our list, please go to www.tworoadsbooks.com

For news on forthcoming Two Roads titles, please sign
up for our newsletter.

enquiries@tworoadsbooks.com

TwoRoadsBooks